Payton Edgar's Spirit

By M.J.T.Seal

For Isabel

Brace yourself, dear loyal readers, for it is about time that I shared with you one of my most treasured secrets.

Are you ready?

The secret is this; Harvey's restaurant, nested discreetly in a nook just off of The Strand, is without a doubt the <u>very best restaurant in London town.</u>

There it is - I have finally said it! And with some careful underlining, too!

For too long your favourite restaurant critic has shied away from naming his number one eatery for fear of spoiling the atmosphere of exclusivity that identifies it. Yet I can contain myself no longer! Each and every visit is no less than a delight, and I would urge any discerning city diner to reserve a seat as soon as possible. Do it now! Put down your newspaper and make that reservation!

Very little is known of the proprietor Harvey Blake, except that the small number of establishments that carry the name have emerged in recent years to a quiet cheer. The Blake name guarantees a certain standard high above many other joints that one comes across in my line of duty.

And so, having issued this brave declaration, the reader will not be surprised to learn that it was with barely-suppressed joy that I attended the Strand establishment only last week for yet another delightfully delicious experience with my dining companion, dear Mr Spence, by my side.

The facade of the building is impressive enough - one is greeted by a vast mahogany door, book-ended by large circular plain-glass windows, as Harvey's is thoughtfully built into a carefully refurbished coach house. Inside, the designers have wisely maintained the efficient brickwork and sturdy iron fittings of the original building. On the far wall a number of comfortable booths now mark out where the horses once rested not so very long ago.

I have always preferred a booth to a table when eating (yet another revelation, dear readers!) as one can relax in relative privacy with one's dining companion. Harvey's seating plan offers privacy in spades. What impresses me most about this establishment, however, is the stark lack of pretension. As regular readers will know, although I appreciate the qualities of a properly starched and pressed tablecloth, I am not a fan of unnecessary pomp and circumstance when dining. Harvey's Restaurant offers just the right balance of respect for its customer's sensitivities while sensibly disregarding any superfluous fluff.

The beauty of Blake's premier establishment lies - naturally - in the cuisine; the sourcing of the very best produce is clearly his aim. This is then presented with great imagination and flair by head chef, Arnold Prosper, and his talented underlings. There is no fixed menu as such - instead one is presented with a large board upon which is chalked the options particular to that evening.

Each and every dish is special at Harvey's, and I will depart from my usual breakdown of one evening meal and instead - at the risk of sounding like a radio advertisement - offer a brief overview of the stand-out plates which we have revisited during my many happy visits.

Arnold Prosper sources the butchery for the establishment, and his game choices are second to none. I also have particularly fond memories of the tender veal steak, the rich braised kidneys with their serene and mellifluous red wine jus, and the delectable vanilla cream macaroons that accompany coffee after dessert - an addition so sinful that one almost sprouts horns upon tasting.

Mr Spence is usually persuaded by a thick and tasty pea soup and any dish on the special menu involving seasonal seafood, for the man loves his fish. Without fail, Prosper offers a small but delightful menu, even during weekdays.

And so, fearing that the Blake family may feel obliged to offer commission, I end my first (and quite possibly my last) glowing review of a restaurant. Next time, my dear followers, I promise the usual judgement, disfavour and poison!

Prologue
In which Payton Edgar tires of the city and longs for adventure

Christmas 1962; *a date for your diary!*
YOU ARE HEREBY INVITED TO ATTEND FALLOW
HOUSE
FOR FESTIVE CELEBRATIONS.
MONDAY 24TH - THURSDAY 27TH DECEMBER
A Christmas to remember!
Further details to follow…

I was tiring of London.

I was tiring of the drizzle and the darkness. Tiring of wet cobbled streets and chimneys streaming black clouds into a black sky. Tiring of rusty railings and smeared windows, and the reams of men in long coats with collars lifted to their ears, striding purposefully through the smog.

I am an urbane creature at heart, but there are times when even I have to get away from it all.

November turned out to be an unusually chilly and miserable month, and the harsh weather matched my mood. One afternoon I decided to take my mood and share it with a friend. Unfortunately, Irving was lost in a creative cloud and offered little in the way of support or understanding.

'Perhaps you should get away, Payton,' he declared idly while standing hunched over his easel, speaking with all the intonation of a weary General Practitioner to one of his most bothersome of patients.

I grumbled a little to myself, for I had glared at his paint-spattered overalls for far too long.

'Take that Cotswolds trip!' he had added chirpily.

The Cotswolds yet again! Irving was unfathomably preoccupied with the idea of my taking a break in what he fitfully referred to as *"Shakespeare Country"*. He probably pictured me dancing along the narrow pavements and then supping on a cream tea in a floral tea shop, revelling in the history of the place and marvelling at the thatched roofs and narrow sloping pavements. In his fevered imagination I would even perhaps be reciting sonnets to entertain strangers as I sipped at my brew.

But it was an abysmal idea. I absolutely detest chintz

and have no interest in the countryside, dull old Shakespeare twaddle nor the pointlessness of live theatre. While I have always been tolerant of Irving's creative distraction, I have to confess to being annoyed at the side of him that occasionally dictated what I should or shouldn't do.

He was, at times, something of a gentle bully.

A case in point related to the beautiful gold-embossed card I had received in the dying days of Summer that year, teasingly inviting me to what was an apparently high-class event, judging by the quality of the stationery and the careful choice of font. However, key details - notably the source of the invitation - had been omitted.

At the time, Irving had fingered the card with a frown.

'What sort of invitation misses out the important facts? Who's it from? Where's the party?'

'I believe it is called a diary note, Irving. Diary notes are the *in* thing in certain circles these days. As it says quite clearly, more details will follow.'

In truth, I had never received a diary note before - it was all quite confusing, but somehow *proper*. My friend blew a tired raspberry.

'Then what's the point of it?'

'It is a prestigious promise, Irving. A promise of great things to come.'

'What have I said to you about chasing prestige, Payton? All that glitters is not gold!'

'A rather exhausted and pithy aphorism, Mr Spence!' I had replied, before snatching the card back triumphantly. 'And I think you'll find that the holly leaves at each corner are most certainly embossed with real gold leaf, so your aphorism is not only pithy but also quite, quite inaccurate!'

The invitation had remained in pride of place atop my sculpted mantlepiece, and now that Christmas was fast approaching, it came to mind.

I sat back in my seat.

'Perhaps I shall hear more about that diary note, Irving. My Christmas invitation.'

Irving huffed and re-coloured his brush.

'Christmas is coming, Irving, whether you like it or not. What are your plans this year? Mmm?' I allowed myself a little chuckle. 'A boisterous party? A lavish feast? Carols and crackers?'

We both knew full well that he had no plans, and neither would he make any. Christmas was Irving's least favourite time of year - which was quite understandable. What would a man with no family to speak of and no imagination when it came to gift-giving care about festivities of any kind? He didn't even trouble his knocker with a wreath. I had long since given up purchasing fine gifts for the man (such as the smooth new leather wallet and the lucky dice cufflinks I had once wrapped and presented with glee) as one received nothing as recompense but a vague and empty *"thank you"*.

Irving grumbled something or other in reply, dismissing my question with distracted noises.

I bit my tongue and bade my friend farewell.

I was still stewing over Irving's idea of escape the following morning when, after skipping breakfast, I set out to do some light shopping. It was a satisfactory jaunt despite the rain, ending at Fleet Street and the offices of The London Clarion, where I handed over my latest restaurant review.

Thistle House was colder inside than out, with its sturdy stone walls giving the reception area the feel of an airy cathedral, rather than a bustling city business. I shared a few idle words with Cockney Guy on the front desk before handing over my crisp and tidy envelope in return for two bundles of letters. The first was the usual bulging collection of pleas for help to Dr. Margaret Blythe from the more desperate members of London society. The second was a disappointingly small bundle of correspondence addressed to Payton Edgar, tied with a frayed piece of dirty string.

Guy began to talk with unwanted candour about his wretched home life and so I made my excuses and hurried back out into the drizzle. I eased the letters to Margaret Blythe into my satchel and tucked the few letters to Payton Edgar into my jacket pocket. I then disposed of the horrible piece of string into the nearest dustbin I could find.

Although she received a sometimes overwhelming amount of correspondence in comparison to my own, I felt no resentment to Dr. Margaret Blythe - for I *was* Dr. Margaret Blythe.

Peggy's Postbag had been trundling on for some years before my stewardship, when I had been forced to save what was once a baggy, hackneyed example of journalism and create a voice for the modern woman. Had any of my readers known that forthright and educated agony aunt Dr Blythe was in fact a forthright and educated middle-aged gent, there would surely have been an uproar amongst the many who read the Clarion, from the recesses of Cobham Common to the centre of The City.

However, my secret had been kept as just that, and the weekly piece was more popular than ever before.

As I left Thistle House, a familiar face caught my eye - Beryl Baxter, queen of the society column. Engulfed in an impressive fur, she was steadying herself against a bench with a thunderous look on her face. I watched as she sat and buried her head in her hands.

Beryl was perhaps the only person at The Clarion that I might call a friend, and although her sunny disposition was sometimes bothersome, it was concerning to see her deflated. I couldn't leave without finding out what could possibly have dampened Beryl's bombastic ardor, and so I approached the bench.

'Beryl?' I uttered carefully.

She looked up. Thankfully, she wasn't crying. In fact, she had the fearsome look of a woman who had just had her handbag stolen. She softened when she saw it was only me.

'Oh, Payton!'

'Are you alright?' I asked quietly.

'Not even nearly. I'm drained. Simply drained!'

I checked my watch. It was a quarter to two.

'Just coming back from lunch?' I enquired gently. Beryls boozy lunches were the stuff of legend.

'A celebratory lunch, no less,' she replied, 'with some of the girls.' Her auburn wig was a little askew, but I didn't dare point it out. There was a glint her eye was told me to keep my distance.

'My divorce finally came through this morning,' she declared almost casually. It was, by my count, husband number three.

'Oh. I'm very sorry to hear that.'

'Well don't be! We have been celebrating! And putting men in their place!'

'Quite so.'

Beryl pulled out a silver cigarette case and thew one up to her lips. She then handed me a matching lighter and allowed me to light it.

'I shouldn't be glum. My new solicitor, Mr Pinkerton, has turned out to be a decent enough chap, and single too, so I have been canvassing for hubby number four. Takes time and effort, though, and although Pinkerton is loaded, he is also a bit of a wet fish. And just now, as I was heading back to the office, it hit me. The finality of it! And at this time of year, too, I will be Christmas-ing alone this year - for the first time ever, Payton! Poor Beryl Baxter, all on her own. I shall never survive alone!'

'It just just another day, my dear. It will come and go before you know it.'

'Oh, I understand why you don't bother much with it, but I am popular, dear-heart! I've always made a thing of it all, with soirees and dinners and dances. I love all the food and drink, and the presents… and the cocktails and mulled wine. And I have some really rather fabulous festive wigs!' She sniffed, but there were no tears in her eyes. 'Poor Beryl! No husband to buy me glittering trinkets this year!'

I rather think she was enjoying this particular little drama.

I sat with her and made the appropriate noises for a while, until she declared that it was time she got back to her desk. By the end of our chat she was laughing and smiling, and, predictably, invited me to her office for a snifter of whisky.

I politely declined, and we said our goodbyes.

The clouds overhead turned menacingly dark and I sought refuge from the rain in my favourite tea shop of it's type; Mario's café, tucked away just off Eccleston Street. What the place lost in refinement it made up for with a convenient unpopularity. One could always get a plum seat at Mario's.

I sat adjacent to the constantly steamy window, ordered a pot and then pulled out my post. I was well into my correspondences when my teapot finally arrived, and I was pleasantly surprised. After countless years of tolerating chipped, second-rate crockery, Mario had splashed out on some more fashionable items, and a small and rather pleasing hexagonal pot with matching teacup had appeared.

I moved on to the final letter. The last envelope was square, stiff and quite difficult to find a corner at which to tear open. I resorted to using the end of a teaspoon as a makeshift paper knife before pulling out the contents - one stiffly folded letter on headed paper.

It was from Harvey Blake, of Harvey's restaurant!

The gold embossed diary note I had received at the end of summer had been from one of the men I most admired, and it was clear that he returned this admiration. My spirits lifted as I fingered the paper. It was of an agreeably superior quality, and contained a small number of lines written in elegant, swirling handwriting. The swooping letters were surely penned by a female hand, and I immediately pictured Blake dictating to his secretary from behind a vast mahogany desk, thick cigar smoke swirling in the air above their heads.

Blake had appreciated my review of Harvey's Restaurant in the Summer and was keen to meet with me. I should not have been surprised. Perhaps the only surprise should have been that this hadn't happened sooner.

It was an invite for two - inviting us to celebrate Christmas at the Blake family home and to enjoy a few days of game hunting, horse riding and winter games. My eyes hovered cautiously over the words - a more distasteful trio of pursuits was difficult to imagine. Nevertheless, I re-read the missive in a cloud of bliss. Once again, I had been recognised! Once again, Payton Edgar was in demand! A prestigious invitation from the mysterious restaurateur Mr Harvey Blake! It was to be an adventure… and an escape. An escape from the dull grey stone of London. An escape from the monotony of Christmas with my Aunt Elizabeth. An escape from the tock-tock-tock of her grandfather clock and from the stench of lavender and carbolic soap.

There was no doubt that I would attend.

No doubt at all.

And my plus one? Irving would never allow himself to be prised away from his canvases, especially for Christmas celebrations with a bunch of strangers. I knew better than to even ask. But it would be nice not to go alone - and it was obvious who I could call on. A friend who was dreading her first Christmas alone. A friend who needed a little Christmas adventure.

Beryl Baxter.

Part One
December 23rd

Chapter I
In which Payton Edgar is attacked by a monster

Fallow House
5th December 1962
Christmas Celebrations!

Dear Mr Edgar,

You will have received our informal diary note earlier this year - and I am writing to put some meat on the bird, so to speak!

I would like to invite you, and a guest of your choice, to our Christmas gathering at Fallow House, Tetherton.
I was both charmed and humbled by your review of my establishment in the London Evening Clarion this summer. I am an avid follower of your column and would consider it an honour if you could attend. There will be opportunities for Partridge shooting, riding and even some winter games.
We have ample supplies of equipment for all equestrian and shooting pursuits. I would especially like for you to extend your stay to begin on 23rd December, to give ourselves time alone to discuss matters of business and food before the festivities begin.

I very much look forward to your company.

Yours sincerely,
Harvey Blake

Whenever bravely venturing outside of the comfort of London town, one is always hit by the sheer preposterousness of the country; the absurd and unmistakably eerie slowness and silence, and the apparent indifference to the needs of modern man.

Hills, valleys, mud, and water all conspire to make the countryside experience a thoroughly undesirable one - and that's without mention of the abundance of wild creatures and their vile emissions. Contrary to popular belief there is nothing pleasant about the feculent air of the countryside, nor pleasing about the inconvenience of being so far from everything a decent human being needs in order to live a civilised life.

I nursed my dislike of the countryside while sucking on a lemon sherbet as the blur of boggy greens and dirty browns passed by my shuddering carriage window. I had expected the journey by rail to be uncomfortable in the extreme, and was not to be disappointed. The carriage was aged and decrepit, and the view from my filthy window unremarkable. Sitting opposite, Beryl Baxter was flicking through a magazine idly.

Suddenly, I realised that she had been talking to me for some time.

'…and usually, if one knows where to look, you can find all the information you need. For heavens sake - I know everything about everybody! My contacts have contacts! But even they failed me this time. He is simply the most incredible recluse! I can't fathom why, with all his success.'

She looked at me for a response, and so I gave her a nod and a smile. Thankfully, it was enough.

'Well, one thing's for certain, we'll know much more about Harvey Blake after this. There is, however, one particularly welcome and rather delicious fact I have been able to unearth - that Mr Blake is divorced. My kind of man!'

'I thought you already had your sights on husband number four? That solicitor chap?'

'Well, yes, but Mr Blake won't know that, will he?' Beryl slapped shut her magazine. 'And Blake must be loaded. A girl has to keep her options open!'

I could not help but raise my eyebrows. A *girl*? Beryl was even older than I was! She shuffled a little in her seat and lowered her tone.

'Payton, you will try to be nice to people over Christmas, won't you?'

I selected my most indignant glare.

'I always *try* to be nice to people, Beryl. If I don't succeed, it is entirely the fault of the person in question.'

She sighed.

'Still, rather a tired cliche, all this.'

'A tired cliche?'

'Christmas in a country house, stuck with a bunch of landed gentry.'

'A tired cliche, Beryl, is a boozehound society-page queen in a designer dress with two dozen designer wigs and twice as many ex-husbands.'

'*A boozehound*? Is that what you think of me?' She

laughed. 'Mmm, that's why I like you, Payton dear-heart - you call a spade a spade. We'll have fun, my irascible friend!'

'Beryl, I have absolutely no intention of *having fun.*'

I folded my arms and looked out the window.

'I miss London.'

Beryl cackled. 'Well that didn't take long!'

We lapsed into a companionable silence as the carriage shook alarmingly. I began to paint pictures in my mind, images of stiff-lipped, starch-suited Harvey Blake and his residence at Fallow House. The appointment was a promising one, and I was primed and ready for luxury.

We soon arrived at Lewes Station, where we had been instructed to await collection.

It took some time to find the exit, for although the station was modest when compared to the sprawling terminals a Londoner is used to, there was a baffling omission of signposts. This could have been down to a restoration that was in progress, as lads in overalls were dotted about, slapping colour on the walls from various ladders. I made sure to remain at the very centre of the walkways in fear of smearing my suit with bottle-green or beige paint. I was carrying my own luggage, whereas Beryl had conned a youth in tatty overalls into lugging her two bulging cases.

It was disappointing to find no car present and awaiting our arrival, and we set down our cases on the frosty pavement. I paced a little to keep warm. Beryl didn't need to pace for she was quite comfortably enveloped in one of her massive fur coats. I eyed her luggage and scowled.

'*Two* suitcases and *two* hat boxes, Beryl? For a three day visit?'

'One hat box, and one wig box, Payton darling!' came the reply. 'I have some particularly spectacular festive hair-pieces this year, my dear! Besides, you have two cases as well!'

'Under normal circumstances, Beryl, I am a light traveller. For this particular sojourn, however, I have brought with me some writing equipment and a backlog of letters for the agony column that require reply. I hope to get a little work done in the peace of the countryside, whenever possible.'

She needn't know that I had also packed four suits, three pairs of shoes, a modest number of my favourite ties and cravats and a symphony of fine silk handkerchiefs.

'You're not going to be working all the time, I hope?' said Beryl with a frown. 'The peace of the countryside? Sounds damn dull! I'm looking forwards to some merriment!'

The roar of an engine was carried along by the wind, and a shining red convertible appeared over the bridge. I hoped to God that this was not for us; Payton Edgar is far more suited to black cabs or limousines, and certainly no fan of toy cars. Beryl squealed a little as the vehicle swerved to a gravel-lifting halt just a few feet from my royal blue wing tips. The driver, resembling an R.A.F pilot in laughably outdated goggles and cap, lifted himself in the seat.

'Hie! Mr. Edgar? Mr. Payton Edgar?'

I blinked out a reassessment. The driver was a young woman!

'That is correct, I am Payton Edgar,' I replied with growing apprehension. 'This is my guest, Miss Beryl Baxter.'

'Hi, Lady!' Beryl drawled unnecessarily. 'Love the wheels!'

'Jump in, then!'

I was not about to *"jump in"* as ordered. I stood rooted to the spot, eyeing the monstrosity on wheels.

'Is there not another way? I am less than enthusiastic about leisure cars.'

Beryl was already heaving her cases onto the rear seat.

'Just get your stuff in, Payton!' she bellowed cheerfully.

'Must I?'

The driver sucked in her cheeks. 'It is a car, Mr Edgar. You must have them where you come from? One must get in it, in order to go anywhere.'

'Do you not have another one?' I asked miserably. 'A limousine, for example?' Beryl had finished with her luggage and placed herself in the passenger seat at the front. She turned to the driver.

'Oh, yes a limousine! Do say you have a limousine!'

'Harvey has plenty of other cars, including a limousine, but this little beauty is my favourite!' Here she slapped the steering wheel playfully with a gloved hand. 'Perfect for these country lanes, it takes a corner like no other. Now get in!'

I hesitated.

'Unless you prefer to walk?' the driver continued, cooly. 'It is a bracing forty-five minute hike, on a dry day.'

Resigned to my fate, I took my time to shift my luggage. There was no mention of helping me with my two rather bulky cases, and after a struggle across the gravel followed by a hernia-inducing heave, both of my custom-made leather valises were resting securely in the back. I would perhaps have sent on a trunk had I known that I was to do all the lifting and carrying.

I eased myself into the rear seat, nudging up against the tower of cases. The upholstery of the passenger seat was alarmingly cold, and the seat set worryingly low.

The driver turned to us both and smiled.

'I'm Alison Moore. *Miss* Alison Moore-'

'Don't tell me,' I interjected sharply, lifting a finger, 'Harvey Blake's secretary?'

She gave a curt nod. It was the neat curl of her bobbed hair that swooped out from under her cap to circle her un-pierced earlobes, and the efficient clip of her diction that had tipped me off. That and the fact that she had dealt with a fussy city-dweller with a notable efficiency. Here was a person well-schooled and in command; a perfect secretary for a high-flying businessman.

'Yes, I am indeed Harvey Blake's secretary. Been with the family for years. Business secretary, social secretary, treasurer, counsellor, odd jobber and, of course, chauffeur.' She cranked up the engine with a choke. 'Harvey demanded that I come pick you up, and I said I would only come if I was allowed to take this little lovely'. She ran her hand over the upholstery, leather on leather. 'I thought that with you being stuck up in London, it'll be a nice change to have a jaunt with the top down, wouldn't you say?'

She didn't wait for a reply.

'Hang on to your corsets, ladies!'

The engine roared and we sped away. How the woman could think that driving with the top down in December was in any way a *"nice change"* was unfathomable. I placed my hat on my lap and gritted my teeth as we ploughed noisily through the winding roads of Sussex. Beryl had one hand on her wig and was whooping in a most unbecoming manner. We were skimming through country lanes only inches from the ground. My hand found a handle on the side door and I gripped it tightly, my stomach lurching with every turn.

One did not expect a female of the species to behave in this most boisterous of manners but, to give the woman her dues, she displayed an impressive level of control at the wheel and clearly knew the roads well. After some time I allowed myself to relax as best I could. At this point my guide shot me a brief be-goggled glance and launched into a curious monologue. With her voice raised high over the blare of the engine, it was impossible to comment, only to listen.

'Harvey tells me you are a critic, Mr Edgar? A restaurant critic? Nasty business to be in, isn't it, criticism? I suppose complaining must come naturally to you?' At this, Beryl shrieked with laughter. 'Mind you, I read that great piece you did on the Strand restaurant earlier in the year. What's your rag? The Clarion?'

We took a right turn with no indication whatsoever.

'You'll have to review the others - Harvey's got six restaurants now. Opened the last one in Croydon, of all places, only last month. Yes, despite what they all thought, against all the odds, Harvey went and did it.'

This was said with a detectable note of admiration. Here was a secretary dedicated to her employer.

'And, I tell you right now, Mr Payton Edgar of the London Clarion, if you ever do write a bad word against any of Harvey's places, I will personally see to it that you end your days in pain and suffering.'

A joke, surely? She went on.

'It'll be refreshing to have some new faces around for Christmas this year. I can only imagine that you're escaping miserable family Christmas's of your own? Well, out of the frying pan, and all that!'

She crunched down on the pedals.

Soon the village of Tetherton came into sight. From the car we couldn't see much of the it, only a church spire and a small number of thatched rooftops rising from the dense greenery ahead. Wisps of grey smoke arose from many of the chimneys. But my eyes did not linger on the distant village - I was entirely distracted by *the house*.

To our left, a vast gateway with swirling ironwork announced the private driveway of the Fallow Estate. There was a cottage set back from the driveway to the left, a gatehouse of sorts, and then the drive itself, which swept up to where the grand house stood, resplendent.

I cannot deny it, my heart leapt a little at the magnificence of our accommodation. It was the perfect picture of a large English country manor, with just the right amount of ostentatious features to announce it as a residence of stature - a grand stone staircase rising from the driveway, columns aside the doors and a number of conspicuous turrets reaching up top. The building was formed of a dusky red brick, giving it the look of a gaudy, grandiose sandcastle. The surrounding greenery mainly consisted of plush and healthy perennials that remained vigorous despite the frost.

Payton Edgar belongs here, I thought to myself with something of a warm glow.

But we did not turn through to the driveway.

Instead, Miss Moore drove us past the grand gates and continued on for a short while, before taking a sharp turn onto a lengthy dirt track. This bumpy lane led us through a corridor of looming poplars to some garages within. Small puddles now turned to ice were dotted about on the gravel, crunching under the tyres as we went. At this point our driver casually offered an explanation.

'I come this way because I can't tolerate negotiating the car though those damned chickens from the gatehouse. They strut about like they own the road. And I'd get into trouble if I mowed them all down, fun though it might be. No, we'll go in the back way.'

We parked with a jerk and Miss Moore was out and throwing off her driving hat and goggles with aplomb before my door was even open. She stood, pushing gloved fingers through her flattened hair. 'We'll send Mr Lloyd, our old butler, out to get your cases.'

'You have a butler?' said Beryl quickly. 'What is this, the 1920s?'

'Of course they have a butler, Beryl!' I snapped, and would have gone on when, suddenly, a creature scrambled from a far doorway - a huge blur of matted red hair and pointed teeth. I gave a short shriek.

I am not a fan of dogs.

If one was asked to make a list of what was pleasant about the creatures and what was less than pleasant, it would be uneven to say the very least. The only good thing one can imagine about owning a canine would be the loyalty received. Indeed, if I could change one thing about my fat puss Lucille, it would be her temperament. It must be pleasant to be greeted upon arriving home by an appreciative, eager face and a wagging tale, rather than a sour, thin-eyed glare.

But where to start with the negative? I could begin at one end of the beast, with the fetid breath and slavering jaws, and finish up at the the other end, noting the vile recurrent deposits that litter the streets. And that matted hair! I can imagine few chores less appealing than giving a dog a bath.

And then there is the sheer size of the beast. Anything larger than a standard domestic cat must surely be classed as wild and potentially dangerous. This particular creature that bounded in my direction was certainly wilder than most.

'Silas! Hello, Boy!' Miss Moore called to the mutt affectionately. It was, unfortunately, much more interested in the well-dressed stranger. Instinctively I stiffened and raised both hands - I was not about to have my fingers mistaken for sausages and nibbled by some monster. The thing was almost as big as a pony, with long swathes of auburn hair shimmering in the spotted sunlight.

'*What...is it?*' I stammered as the thing raised two great fist like-paws and pushed them at my chest. I felt faint and whimpered a little, despite myself. It took all my strength not to collapse backwards, the force was so strong. But I stood my ground, mortified.

'Down boy!' Miss Moore snapped. The thing released me, but continued to dodge and slather at my feet. 'Silas. He's an Irish Setter. A gun dog.'

'Horrifying!' I exclaimed through clenched teeth. The creature turned to Beryl, who ran her hands over the beast's head and growled in an unbecoming manner. I flicked the filth from my breast.

'Please tell me that... *thing*... is not allowed inside the house?'

'Not a dog lover, eh?' Miss Moore muttered, smiling dryly. She collected a punctured tennis ball and threw it some distance with a practiced hand. The monster chased after it and she threw me a wink.

'Quick, inside!'

We circled the looming building and entered a passageway between two outhouses, moving past a large, cold kitchen and its pantries to arrive at the foot of a staircase. From here I could see the beautiful wood-panelled hallway and large mahogany door that would have greeted me had I entered as a respected guest and not as something resembling a back-door delivery man.

Besides a lively poinsettia on a small round table in one corner, there was no sign that it was only a matter of days until Christmas.

'Well, folks I'll get Mr Lloyd to take your cases to your rooms. Mrs Baxter, you have the Spring Suite at the top of the stairs on the second floor. Mr Edgar, you are to take the Winter suite to the right on the first floor. Emblem of the snowflake on it. The largest suites are named after the seasons - a bit crass, I know. Now, I'll stick you in the library and let Harvey know that you are here. We like to have guests wait in the library - it is suitably imposing and gives you something to look at.'

The library was the first opening we came to when advancing into the magnificent hallway, its door ajar revealing a vast wall of superbly displayed spines.

I approved of the room immediately.

Heavy wooden shutters on the back windows were only partially drawn, allowing a thick bar of dust-spattered sunlight to line the centre of the space, which in turn cast dark shadows to either side of the room. The walls were lined high with books, and there were a number of free-standing shelves dotted about. I was thrilled to see an extending wheeled ladder propped against the high bookshelves on the right-hand wall.

The few bare spaces of wall left in the room had been filled by glass cases of stuffed birds in nests and other deceased wildlife. A hostile and flea-bitten weasel snarled out of one case with pointed yellowed teeth. Another such case contained row after row of delicate butterflies, each pinned through their hearts onto a board, the vibrant colours of their wings having faded to murky pastels over time.

Adjacent to this, an ancient sword was sheathed and displayed on copper hooks. Three old car horns were mounted side by side on another wall, and there were two deer heads mounted further along, one with proud antlers rising from its scalp, the other with cut antlers, staring down with sorrowful eyes.

Beneath the doe was a mounted plaque with a reading from Shakespeare, all about sequestered stags and hunters, and wretched animals groaning in the throes of death.

Gobbledegook!

I moved over to the far wall, where there was just enough room for a beautiful worn map of the world as it once was, seen through the eyes of cartographers who never left their rooms but pieced charts together akin to a global jigsaw puzzle. Beneath the map sat a delightfully well-crafted writing desk in glistening varnished teak.

This was *a gentleman*'s library.

I took in a deep, satisfied breath. Harvey Blake was my kind of man; learned, traditional, well-read and, above all, distinguished.

I belong here, I thought to myself with a quiet pleasure.

Chapter II
In which Payton Edgar meets his host

Dear Mr Blake,

> **Thank you very much for your kind invitation, which I am delighted to accept. I am indeed free to attend from Thursday the 23rd, however I shall need to bring some of my Clarion work with me so as not to fall behind on my deadlines over the Christmas period. I shall require a sturdy writing desk and padded chair with high arms, preferably adjacent to a window.**
> **You mention opportunities for game hunting, riding and festive games. I shall not be embarking on any equestrian or shooting pursuits as - if I may be honest - I cannot imagine anything less appealing to do with one's time. I will instead look forwards to engaging company, scintillating conversation and fine cuisine.**

> **Yours sincerely,**
> **Payton Edgar**

I was admiring the library in an appreciative silence as Beryl and Miss Moore chatted behind me.

'Joan runs an extremely tight ship,' the secretary ended with a tinge of sarcasm to her tone.

'Joan?'

'Turpin. Joan's the housekeeper,' said Miss Moore. 'Lives out in the gatehouse. Been here for eons they have, the Turpins. Her husband, Harry, will be at home as usual. Bit creepy, Harry. He never comes up to the house, though, just lurks around the gatehouse all the time. Joan spends more time with Drinkwater, the vicar, than she does her husband.'

'*Really?*'

Beryl had perked up at the suggestion of impropriety.

'Oh, no, nothing juicy there, Mrs Baxter! How I wish there was something to get get excited about. The housekeeper's relationship with the vicar is entirely benign, I assure you. Mind you, that won't stop Prosper having a dig, believe me.'

I joined the conversation.

'Prosper? *Arnold* Prosper?'

'Yes.'

'He is here?'

'Arriving tomorrow.'

I shouldn't have been surprised. It made sense for Harvey Blake to steal the restaurant's head chef for such an important date in the diary. In part this was excellent news - Arnold Prosper was a wizard in the kitchen, and without a doubt one of my favourite city chefs. That said, his extroverted ways - in particular his boisterous table-side manner - had long been the only fly in the soup at Harvey's premier establishment. I was not looking forwards to having his bulbous strawberry nose pushed in my direction.

In any restaurant, a chef belongs in the kitchen, and Arnold Prosper's tendency to take to the floor and flit from table to table in search of complements about his cuisine was not a welcome one. The man was an unsubtle drunk, and had almost ruined a number of perfect dining experiences by his mere inebriated presence alone. An entire Christmas of his bluster was almost too much to bear thinking about.

Beryl gave a chuckle. 'Arnold Prosper - that old soak! The number of times I've seen his moon-face in the weekend snapshots.'

She caught my questioning look.

'Every Monday we have the weekend pics to sift through, to see who's who, and who's with who, who's going where and who's wearing what. Arnold Prosper's had a catwalk full of young fillies on his arm these past few years. Something of a ladies man!'

I gritted my teeth. '*Ye-es.*'

Suddenly a girl appeared through a doorway at the rear of the room. She stood in silhouette, framed by the light coming from behind.

'H-Hello there!' I stammered cheerily, trying to paper over my surprise.

After a second of hesitation, the newcomer stepped forwards, clutching a tattered red book to her chest. She was a young lady, somewhere in her teenage years, and a curious looking one at that. Her hair was long, straight and black. The face underneath was anaemic and drawn. She wore a crimson, rather festive dress, toned down by the addition of a drab green cardigan which hung loosely from her shoulders. The expression on her face was a little blank and ever so slightly pained.

'Hello,' she replied, sharply and without the merest hint of a smile. There was something about the young thing that was strangely unsettling; a pallid, porcelain doll with rather weak features, framed by that lank black hair.

She stood still, awaiting introductions.

'I am Mr Edgar - Payton Edgar, and this is my friend and colleague Beryl Baxter.' Beryl gave a little wave. 'We are guests, here for... for the festivities. Mr Blake-'

'I'm Maeve Taylor.' The girl spoke her name slowly and perhaps a little sadly. She deposited the thin red book under one arm, took a step forwards and held out her hand. It was an unexpectedly business-like gesture that felt rather odd coming from a young woman, but I returned the gesture nevertheless, and shook her tiny hand carefully as if it were indeed made out of china.

Something induced me to reach into my jacket pocket and bring out my crumpled paper bag.

'Lemon sherbet, Miss Taylor?' I asked, to which I received a polite shake of the head.

'You never asked me if I wanted a sweetie!' barked Miss Moore dryly from the doorway behind. She leaned on the woodwork, cackled caustically and continued in a high tone.

'Shouldn't you be busy decorating the tree or icing gingerbreads, dear Maeve?'

'I did the tree yesterday, as well you know,' came the sullen reply. Miss Moore hummed.

'Maeve will look after you now, Mr Edgar. She looks after everyone.'

The girl sighed.

'I see no reason to be rude, *Miss Moore.*'

Alison Moore issued an elongated sigh. 'I can always look for a reason to be rude, Maeve my dear.'

'And I'm sure you will find one.'

'I have only just started, dear girl.'

The child looked up from under her brow. 'Nasty seed bears nasty fruit, *Miss Moore.*'

'Of course, what a delightful phrase. Very you. Very *simple.*'

There followed a moment of silence between the two, during which I realised I had been witnessing some sort of verbal jousting. And yet, despite their terse words, there was a slyness, even conspiracy, in their delivery. It was the secretary that spoke again.

'Well, Mr Edgar, Mrs Baxter, I shall leave you with dear Maeve and let Harvey know you are here We'll be back in two shakes of a whatsit's tail.'

With that she was gone. My instinct was to thaw the frosty atmosphere that had been created by the two women, and I spoke quickly.

'You have a delightful name.'

'Taylor?'

'No, Maeve,' I said, smiling. 'Is it of Scottish origin?'

'Irish.'

'And yet you don't sound Irish,' I replied, although the girl's words did perhaps have a northern hint.

'No.'

I was beginning to tire of her one-word responses. Nevertheless, I persevered.

'You were brought up elsewhere, then? Do I detect a hint of Lancashire?'

'Scunthorpe.'

I had never heard of Scunthorpe. Indeed, if the place were as unappealing as the name, I had no desire to know any more details. Beryl spoke up, cheerily.

'I have a second cousin lives in Scunthorpe. Do you know a family by the name of Eel? Stephen and Mary Eel?'

The girl shook her head and inspected her shoes.

'Lucky for you!' Beryl continued with a twinkle. 'They are crashingly dull! He's a golf bore who collects cuckoo clocks and she is a maniac knitter with a headful of geraniums.'

I moved the conversation on with a gentle observation.

'This room is really quite remarkable.'

'Yes. Yes it is.'

'Really quite breath-taking!'

'I know,' the girl replied, warming up just a little. It was only as she moved a little closer that I saw the dark rings around her eyes - a sharp contrast with the paleness of her skin. What was it my mother would have called it? *Eyes put in with a smutty finger.*

'I think this is probably my favourite room in the house.'

'I do love books,' I put in kindly.

'Me too. All so ancient, so full of history.'

'Old stories, old lives,' I mused accordingly, my gaze following row after row of volumes up to the ceiling. 'Ancient, forgotten lives.'

'Yes. So many stories and secrets, hidden away in print. It is the perfect place to hide… in peace and quiet,' she added.

'And are you family?' I asked, perhaps a little quickly. In my haste to show polite interest I sounded prudish and sharp, and not unlike my Aunt Elizabeth or one of her Sunday morning cronies.

'Oh, no,' came the reply. 'I am… well… ' she stopped and allowed another heavy sigh. The question was apparently an exhausting one. 'I'm not sure quite what I am really. A friend. *A family friend*. And you are the writer, is that right?'

It seemed that everybody had been prepared for my visit.

I mulled over the word for a while, itching to issue a correction to the title. A writer? Not quite. A journalist perhaps - or better still a wordsmith. A wordsmith and a restaurateur - most definitely - but never a mere two-a-penny *writer*. That said, there was something about the girl's warm innocence that caused me to pause before issuing a clarification, and so I merely nodded amicably.

'You look exactly how I imagined you would,' Maeve continued with a disarming simplicity. 'Just how you sound in your reviews. Perhaps you can review our supper tonight!'

As if this had never been said before!

I had grown evermore displeased that everywhere I went it seemed that people wanted me to criticise their meal like some performing circus animal, born to amuse and entertain. I felt a flutter of anger. Could this be what Harvey Blake had in mind? Had I been invited here only to be laughed at? To perform like some dancing bear or juggling dog?

It had happened before.

'No, my dear, I am not here in my capacity as critic. I do indeed have some pieces to work on, some deadlines to reach for, however my mission over the next few days is to relax and to enjoy.'

There followed a lengthy pause in which we each waited for the other to speak. It was Beryl who saved us from the silence.

'Well, they're certainly keeping us waiting. I can't wait to meet Mr Blake!'

'Really?' Maeve squeaked. 'But Mr Blake never comes out of his room. *Never*.'

This came as a surprise. Would our host remain elusive

for the entire festive period?

'But Miss Moore has gone to fetch Mr Blake, has she not?'

'Well-'

'Harvey Blake?'

'Yes. Oh! I see!' Maeve rolled her eyes and pulled her red book up to her chest again. 'I was talking about Mr Blake, the Brigadier - Harvey's father. This is his house, you see. He is a very, very old man now. Mrs Turpin sorts him out. His room is right at the top of the house, in the attic. Unless you pop up there, you won't see him.'

'And so this is his library,' I said, more to myself than anyone else. That explained the aged décor and the deathly mustiness of the taxidermy. Perhaps Harvey Blake would turn out to be far more contemporary in his tastes than his ageing father.

The creaking weight of the old wooden staircase outside announced the arrival of our host. As Miss Moore appeared in the doorway I turned to say something to the young girl, but she appeared to have vanished into thin air.

A tall lady followed Miss Moore into the room, adorned in a splendid green velvet trouser suit with a queer pink collar.

'Payton Edgar!'

The lady in the green suit spoke in a rich deep tone and extended a slender hand, her eyes studying me with the steely glare of a hawk. She held herself with an impressive confidence and poise. She had a wide smile revealing excellent dentistry with only the merest hint of creases leading from her eyes. Despite the femininity of her attire, the jaw was square and firm..

This remarkable woman was clearly born of gentry. Harvey Blake's wife, surely?

I took her hand and shook it, surprised at the firmness of her grasp.

'Good afternoon,' I said, my eyes unavoidably dancing past her to catch sight of the approaching husband.

There was a moment where nobody moved nor spoke. Miss Moore made no introduction.

'And you are?' I enquired politely.

'I'm sorry?' She dropped my hand. She had clearly missed my point.

'I didn't catch your name.'

There was a nasty pause.

'Ah!' she sighed wearily.

'You expected a man?' Miss Moore hissed over her shoulder with evident relish.

'Don't worry, this happens all the time,' said the woman in green. '*I* am Harvey Blake, Mr Edgar.' She looked over my shoulder and smiled at Beryl. 'And you must be Mrs Baxter! I'm so very glad that you could join me for Christmas.'

Chapter III
In which Payton Edgar enjoys a tipple

Dear Margaret,
I live in a lovely semi-detached Georgian house, and the family next door is making my life a misery. I have three dogs, all delightfully obedient and house-trained, and yet my neighbours constantly complain about the animals barking and running on their lawn. They have a new baby and the crying at night sometimes keeps me awake - how can I make them see that cohabiting requires compromise?
Dog lover, Wimbledon

Margaret replies; *I am with the family next door on this particular issue. Although crying babies are certainly an irritant, they are outranked by the repugnance of the family canine. I too would loudly complain if your mutt did it's business on my lawn. Have some consideration - muzzle your dogs and train them properly Or, if you insist on letting them roam free, move to a more suitable, entirely detached abode. I suggest that the Highlands of Scotland are more fitting for your needs than Wimbledon Common.*

Humiliation!
For a moment I was speechless.
For several years I had held an image of the mysterious Harvey Blake as a firm-suited businessman with trimmed moustache, tailored to the hilt. The respect that was felt in culinary circles for this shrewd and savvy businessman was well known, and yet here was the proprietor of Harvey's Restaurant; undeniably foxy and without a trimmed moustache in sight.
Why had nobody told me? I felt my cheeks flame as she came to my rescue.
'Well, my dears! You both look like you need a drink. Come on through to the drawing room.'
We followed her automatically. As we went, Beryl leaned in and whispered in my ear.
'Oh, bums!'
'I beg your pardon?'
'Rather knocks my dream of husband number four into a

cocked hat, damn it!'

Harvey spoke loudly over her shoulder as we followed.

'Alison, you can leave us now, thank you. Could you check on the kitchens? I think I saw the bakers van just a moment ago. Make sure they've bought two dozen mince pies and three extra loaves.'

Miss Moore turned and departed with an unmistakably petulant air.

The décor of the drawing room was as bounteous in fashionable comforts as the old man's library had been in dusty literature. The most striking feature was the impressive bay window which looked out over the gardens at the rear of the house. An expanse of frost-tinged green led down to meet the banks of a glistening river. Inside the room, the plump Chesterfield and accompanying armchairs were freshly upholstered in best leather. Pleasing nick-knacks were dotted here and there - there were a number of pieces that I was sure would be classed by those with discernible taste as works of art. A couple of paintings on the wall were vibrant and contemporary, although not to my tastes.

On the far wall, next to one such painting, lay a large car horn mounted on a wooden plaque, an eyesore which stood out amongst the art, and clearly belonged in the cluttered library rather than in this stylish area. But it was quirky and unusual, and perhaps that was the point.

Irving would adore this room, I thought to myself.

Apart from the lone poinsettia outside in the hallway, all evidence of Christmastime had been banished here, and even then it was only a single tree. But what a tree! The fresh fir stood towering in the far corner, dotted with tartan bows, ribbons and baubles. Reaching up at the top and nudging against the ceiling was a large glittery paper star, and, far beneath, a small number of wrapped gifts lay amongst freshly fallen needles.

I allowed myself to be ushered to a fine padded red leather chair, and then Harvey Blake made her way to a drinks cabinet and began to set out three glasses.

'Drink, Mrs Baxter?'

'Not half!'

'May I call you Beryl?'

'Of course.'

'And I am Harvey. And you, Mr Edgar, are certainly a *Mr Edgar*, rather than Payton. Am I right?'

I nodded in a nonchalant manner.

'Care for a drink, Mr Edgar?'

Instinctively I glanced at my watch.

'Well-'

'I have a number of fine whiskies you can sample, but this afternoon I'd like to start with a bang and go for my very best single malt.' She had already poured three generous measures into a few wide tumblers.

'Ice?'

'Yes please', Beryl and I chimed in unison. I made a quick addition.

'And a splash of water, if I may?'

Whisky should always come with a splash of water. Beryl leaned in to my ear.

'Fabulous, isn't she? Not many women can pull off an emerald trouser suit with pink shrimp piping.'

I examined my surroundings a little further. To my left sat a cold fireplace with two ironwork stags leaping at each corner. Two photo frames sat proudly on the occasional table to my left. The first was a tired sepia snap of what must surely have been Harvey Blake's father, stiff and unsmiling in full military garb. The second photograph, this time with odd dashes of colour about it, showed three young girls in bathing suits and caps, sprawled out and smiling on a picnic blanket besides a glistening river.

Beryl was chatting idly as we were handed our drinks.

'... and this is such a delightful room, Harvey. In a delightful house. Despite the history of the place, you have a canny, modern eye.'

'Thank you.'

Harvey Blake smiled a wide, genuine smile.

'It is a great pleasure to have you both here. When I invited Mr Edgar I had no idea he would invite Beryl Baxter, scourge of the gossip columns! Such a delight!' She then lifted a hand in my direction. 'And I am especially looking forward to sharing a dining table with our very own deipnosophist!'

She was peering at me, awaiting a response.

'I beg your pardon?'

'I am referring to you, Mr Edgar. *Deipnosophist* - one who relishes and excels at dining room conversation.'

'Oh, of course, yes indeed!' I cursed myself. Humiliation upon humiliation! How could I not know this? One could scarcely imagine a more fitting description of ones self! Our host, thankfully, was kind enough not to dwell on the inadequacies of my vocabulary.

'I read your reviews religiously, Mr Edgar, and was delighted when they went fortnightly. A monthly appearance was simply not enough. I have the Clarion sent down here, believe it or not, along with The Times, to keep abreast of changes in the City and all that. I always find time to peruse your piece too, Beryl.'

'Jolly good!'

'And naturally I have a special interest in your restaurant column, Mr Edgar. You have an honesty about your writing that is extremely refreshing.'

Coming from anyone else this may have sounded fanatical or unnecessarily fanciful, but from Harvey Blake it was merely a statement of fact.   'I did, however, think that you went a little easy on my place.' She sipped her drink with an eyebrow arched. 'When it comes to restaurants there can never be any such thing as perfection, surely?'

Her honesty invited honesty, and I found myself chatting easily.

'I confess, Mrs Blake, I did have an agenda.'

'Harvey, please! Mrs Blake was my mother!'

'Harvey. Don't get me wrong, I have been enjoying Harvey's Restaurant for a number of years. I particularly like the lack of flummery, or pretension, you might say. And the food is-'

'I know all this, Mr Edgar. I read your review.'

At this she reached aside and lifted a copy of the Clarion which sat on the side, as if to illustrate her point.

I cleared my throat.

'Well, two things led to that particular review. One was my superior's ridiculous notion that I should, on occasion, pen a complimentary piece. My readers don't want praiseful recommendations - where is the entertainment in that? They clamour for poison and disapproval! However, my superior won out. Naturally, if I simply *had* to pen a recommendation, then Harvey's was my first choice.'

'Balderdash!' Beryl piped up. 'You told me you'd reviewed the place because you'd heard it was in trouble!'

'*Trouble*?'

Harvey Blake's eyes widened in my direction. I huffed

lightly.

'As I was about to say, the second reason for choosing your place is, well, perhaps a little more sensitive - thank you, Beryl!'

I hesitated.

'Candour, Mr Edgar, please!'

'An insider, a friend of mine, heard word that there may be - oh, how can I put it? Closures on the horizon.'

'*Closures*?'

'I have no wish for Harvey's to become a victim of the times, and so rolled out the glowing review I have long been writing in my head. My hope was that my words might be of benefit to your business.'

Our host sat still in thought for a moment, and then replied somewhat sharply.

'Mr Edgar, I can assure you that there are no such plans for closure of any of my establishments. I really can't think where that particular piece of gossip originated from.' She was looking at Beryl, who widened her gaze.

'Not from me, I assure you!'

'My restaurants have never needed to rely on media to gain attention, much as I appreciate your intent. I'm sure that you are aware of the power of plain and simple word of mouth?' She ran her finger around the rim of her glass in thoughtful con- templation. 'It is true that times are hard, and I may have been a little daring in opening my latest establishment, and it's also true that I may have to make some changes, as one expects when jug- gling businesses. But closures? Never!'

'I am extremely glad to hear that.'

She cocked a well-plucked eyebrow and shot me a foxy glance.

'If we may return to your reviews again, you fair ripped apart poor Mr Ferrier's last venture. Rather a cheeky hatchet job - I almost felt sorry for the man.' She issued a considered cough. '*Almost.*'

'Yes. There are, of course, a modest number of great eateries in London town, but also a surprising number of bad apples. I see it as my job to, as it were, to root out the maggots.'

'Quite so!'

We drank for a moment in a cordial silence. The whisky warmed my throat with a pleasing glow.

'I feel like I should apologise, to both of you,' said Harvey eventually. 'I hope that I didn't cause you too much alarm, by my-' here she once again cocked a saucy eyebrow, '-being a woman.'

I set down my glass.

'Goodness no. Alarmed? No, no. Well... in all honesty I am mortified at my reaction.'

'Same here!' Beryl trilled, a little sheepishly. I went on.

'In truth, I had in my mind a picture of the stiff businessman,' I went on, 'a man dynamic in his pursuits but equally as tedious in conversation. I am pleased that I will not be relegated to endless discussions of golf and motor vehicles and such like. I can keep my end up over food, drink and certain avenues of politics or history, but when golf enters the equation I am quite, quite stumped. I apologise for our surprise. It's just that we have for so long heard about the illustrious Harvey Blake that I think we had both developed a rather different image in our minds.'

'You are not the first, and you won't be the last.'

'I can't quite believe that it is not commented on in your press-'

'I make certain to remain in the shadows as much as I can. My establishments must stand on their own merits, you see, Mr Edgar. Over the years I have found that in business I have two obstacles to get over in order to garner respect in my peers. The first is that most terrible crime of being a woman!'

Here she left me a gap to allow me to react or to show my interest.

'And the second?'

'To prove that I am worthy of my position - that I am not some lucky amateur who has stumbled upon prosperity through circumstance.'

'Surely not-'

I was sharply interrupted as Harvey growled and waved a dismissive hand. 'Now, Mr Edgar, dear! Let's not be coy! I'm sure Beryl will agree that we live in a man's world, and that a successful woman in that man's world is often considered to have gained her position, either by inheritance or in some alternate, more unpalatable way. Sex is often what it boils down to, you see.'

'Couldn't agree more!' said Beryl as Harvey continued.

'Many believe that a successful woman must have sold herself or cheated her way into it. And yet this is so very far from the truth. Yes, this is my father's estate, but it remains so. My father - Brigadier Alfred Blake, whom you may have heard of?'

'Of course.' I lied without hesitation, hiding a little behind my glass. I had never heard of the man in my life until that day.

Harvey set down her drink.

'Then what did he do, Mr Edgar?' The question was delivered sharply, albeit with kindly eyes.

'I'm sorry?'

I was flummoxed by the sudden challenge.

'What did my father do?'

I hesitated.

Harvey sighed. 'Mr Edgar, if we are to get along - and I sincerely hope that we will - you must be honest with me. You don't know my father from Adam! I'll accept no airs or graces here, do you understand?'

I nodded with a blush which she excused by issuing a biography.

'My grandfather, Edward Alfred Blake, was a widely respected and heavily decorated Brigadier, and my father followed in his footsteps. He was at the forefront in the Great War. You will find them both in a number of history books if you know where to look. However if, like I, you find military history about as interesting as watching concrete set, you may easily have overlooked his notoriety. Poor Father was lumbered with two daughters instead of the son he had wished and planned for; the son who would continue the military legacy of the Blake breed. First there was my sister, Petra, and then I was born in the throes of death. My mother died in childbirth, you see.'

'I'm sorry.'

'Please don't be, it was a long time ago, and by all accounts her death was something of a relief for Father. I have always had pressed upon me the image of a rather severe Victorian matriarch. However, even though I was not the son Father had hoped for, he named me Harvey as they had planned, nevertheless. And if it is not too odd a thing to say, I have often felt like a man in a woman's body, if you can imagine what I mean by that? Although I could by no means have entered into a military lifestyle, I am proud to possess the-' here she stopped and hummed a little. 'How shall I say it? The *ruthlessness* that is required in business today. I certainly didn't get to where I am on Father's back. I sent myself up to Scotland, of all places - we have roots there, you see, hence the endless stag motifs of Fallow House. And from the damp hills of Scotland I fled to the rocky outcrops of southern Spain. Don't ask how I ended up there! But it was in Spain that I learnt all I needed to know about food, business and, perhaps most important of all - the nature of men.'

The fuzziness that comes with a good whisky was creeping over me, and I raised a finger.

'Aha!' I said, 'The continental factor. I understand that only too well. My appreciation of good food grew from a similar situation.'

I proceeded to entertain the two ladies with tales of my travels around Spain and France and, in particular, my time spent in and around the châteaux of the Dordogne. As I spoke, our host stood and retrieved first Beryl's empty glass and took mine from my grasp without a word, and returned to the drinks cabinet. Once our glasses were refilled and I had reluctantly accepted my seconds, I finished a particularly amusing observation about French haute cuisine and looked down into my drink warily. It can only have been around one-thirty in the afternoon. Beryl, I knew, was quite at home with downing spirits during daylight hours, but I was not. I have always found drinking in the afternoon to be both pleasurable and regretful in equal measures.

We had moved back to the subject of names.

'Payton - is that your given name?' asked my host.

'Of course.'

'Quite a fancy name, isn't it? I wasn't sure if that were a *nom de plume,* as it were. A very charming, if unusual thing to name a child.'

Pot and kettle!

'Baxter is my first husbands name,' Beryl was telling nobody in particular, 'back when I first started out with our lady's supplement. It stuck, despite my subsequent marriages.'

Harvey Blake shrugged. 'For some time I was Mrs Harvey Carter. But Mrs Carter lasted only a small number of sunny years and twice the amount of miserable ones.'

I watched our host as she went on. I have to confess that like Beryl, I too was a little in awe of the woman. Or was it just the whisky? I nursed my drink as slowly as I could, as I sat contentedly listening. She gave no further details of her unsuccessful marriage, and instead threw herself into tales of her successes - in juggling shares, forming alliances and building her vision of what might be the perfect restaurant. It was a stirring speech, at the end of which I was surprised to see that I almost finished my second glass.

'A winning story indeed,' I found myself chucking alongside Beryl, like some bawdy heckler in a seedy cabaret.

'Oh, some you win, and all that!' Harvey replied dismissively and with a solemnity so sudden it felt like a cool wind.

'And don't let me fool you - I have made mistakes, many mistakes. Some that I have repeated. You will meet Mr Carter tomorrow, for he is back in my life once more.'

'Your ex-husband?'

Harvey nodded.

'My ex-husband. I only have few weaknesses, Payton, but one, it seems, is for handsome, devious, cosmopolitan men.'

'Hear hear!' cackled Beryl.

'But I do believe - don't you - that a person can change over time - to go from a bad to a good egg?'

I wasn't sure that I did believe that, and nearly said something about leopards and spots, but instead found myself interrupted by Beryl.

'Any kiddie-winkles?' she chimed.

'No,' Harvey was quick to reply. 'Not any more.'

Her gaze was on her knees. 'We lost our daughter...' she said quietly. I shifted forward a little in my seat - my curiosity well and truly poked.

'Our daughter... died.'

A silence lingered.

Suddenly the drawing room door swung open.

'Well! That's the pantry stocked for the next fifty years!' Alison Moore sang as she crashed into the moment. 'Still, I sent back one loaf that would only be useful as a house-brick. I've said it before and I'll say it again, Soames is going downhill rapidly. The mince pies are in. Bit heavy on the icing sugar, which is always suspicious - something of a cover-up, I suspect. Well? Anything else you need me for, Harvey? Only I thought I'd knock off soon and take a ride on Merry-legs. I'll be up for supper, but I'll need rest to get up early for Brighton tomorrow.'

Having been denied the opportunity to elaborate on the subject of her daughter's death, Harvey still replied with a delightful softness.

'Thank you, Alison, you've done enough today. And I

shan't need you tomorrow. I will take the blue Saloon, and Mr Edgar-' she stopped and turned with wide expectant eyes. 'Oh! Would you please escort me to Brighton tomorrow, Mr Edgar? I have to collect my sister and Gideon, you see, and it would be wonderful to have your company.'

Gideon?

'Of course,' I was bound to reply.

'And you, too, Beryl?'

Beryl was already shaking her head. 'Thanks, but no thanks. I've had enough travel for one holiday. You mentioned horse-riding? I should love to take a horse out.'

'*You and a horse,* Beryl?' I found myself snorting.

'Don't look so surprised, Payton. I was brought up on an estate not so very different to this one. I should like to have a crack at a little hunting too, if I get chance while we're here. Or at least, clay pigeons. I am a pretty keen shot, dear-heart.'

'Mmm, I bet you are.'

Harvey nodded. 'Well that's settled, Mr Edgar, it'll be just you and me. We'll make an adventure of it!'

Alison Moore didn't bother to hide her disappointment.

'Oh, well it seems you have made plans then. I just thought, as we usually go together… but no problem. I know when I am not needed. I'll wander into the village high street and chase cars.' This odd comment was followed with a casual flick of the hand before she disappeared out of the door as quickly as she had come.

'Unusual woman…' The utterance was out of my mouth before I could stop it, thanks to the whisky.

'Rude, I call it!' Beryl put in sharply.

'Mmm. Sometimes, perhaps. But Alison's one of those people who have loyalty and efficiency in their blood. She's extremely competent, and very devoted, in her way. You just have to know how to take her.' Harvey drained her glass and checked her slender wristwatch. 'And so we have a few hours until supper. Tomorrow we have Christmas Eve in Brighton, and then the fun really begins.'

'I shall look forward to meeting Mr Blake at supper.' I replied politely.

'Oh no, no, no,' said Harvey sternly, 'my father will not be joining us. He eats up in his room.'

'Then perhaps I should pop up and say hello?'

My host gave a gentle sigh.

'You are a true gentleman, Mr Edgar. However, there is no need. My father is not a well man, and over the last few years he has lost much of the verve and menace that made him my father. He barely even recognises me anymore. A visit from you, however good the intention, would be - at best - a muddled interlude for him and a complete waste of time for you. You have no reason to greet the man of the house. Not in this case.'

I nodded, somewhat relieved. Verve and menace were traits I would quite happily avoid.

'A little top-up?' Harvey asked, with a sparkle in her eye.

'Don't mind if I do!' said Beryl, extinguishing a cigarette. I politely refused and we agreed to meet at six for supper.

I was in the doorway when Harvey stopped me with a low growl.

'Oh - and Mr Edgar, one other thing about my being a woman. You said that you'd be relieved not to talk of cars and golf? Just so you know, I collect brass-era cars, and love nothing more than tinkering under the bonnet on occasion. I have also been known to talk golf from time to time. I have a pretty good average, despite being of the female persuasion. I shall, however, try and not bore you with any of this over christmas!'

That told me.

Chapter IV
In which Payton Edgar meets the locals

Dear Margaret,
I married my solicitor husband in the spring last year and had planned to move to the countryside where we would raise two children in a lovely little English village. However George refuses to leave his job in the city for a provincial post. Central London is no place to bring up little ones, but I am fed up with asking him about it. What can I do to persuade him?
Betty, Brixton

Margaret replies; *and just what is wrong with our beloved capital? I should say it is a perfect place for raising future generations, with opportunities on every corner. You should be celebrating the fact that you live in vibrant metropolis with promise in the air. As I write this I am imprisoned in an English country house, and can report that the only thing noticeable in the air here is the heady scent of rot and manure.*

I would have liked to make the most of the hours before supper by taking a nap after settling in my bedroom, however it was not to be, for I found myself overcome by a curious restlessness.

First, I unpacked my clothes.

I am a fastidious packer. I have never met anybody as deft at folding and packing clothing as I, not even during my wartime days. It almost seemed a shame to unpack the case! Of course, a number of items would require a flirt with a hot iron, and my best trousers would benefit from a good pressing, but nevertheless I had done another superb job with my valise.

Show me a man with a well-packed suitcase and I will show you a hero.

I lifted out a carefully wrapped present, fluffed up the ribbon a little and set it aside. Beryl and I had agreed not to exchange gifts, and so this was the only present I had purchased that year - a gift intended for the businessman Harvey Blake. It was a carefully selected box of cuban cigars, impressively priced and sealed with a lime green bow. Of course, I wouldn't give these to the foxy and feminine Harvey Blake, but instead would take them back home. They would do for Irving, who sneaked a smoke every now and then and thought I didn't know.

I moved my toiletries to the bathroom before setting aside my shoes and trying out the bed. It was soft - perhaps a little too soft - with a horrifyingly itchy blanket hidden under the candlewick eiderdown. Thankfully the sheets were of a superior quality and would hopefully not allow the fibres of the blanket to irritate. I lay back on the top of all these covers and tried to rest.

Unfortunately, the whisky had stoked my imagination and I found myself unable to switch off some rambling thoughts. I was soon at the desk where I spent an hour or so as Dr Margaret Blythe, righting wrongs as only she can. The liquor had loosened her acid tongue somewhat, and I wrote a number of pleasing responses to the wittering of the irritating commoners of London Town.

Then, after setting down my pen, I found myself pacing the room a little. The thought of the ancient, mindless Brigadier shuffling about in the rooms above was suddenly an uncomfortable one.   I examined the room. Surely the best guest room in the house, it was plush and expensively adorned, from the thick red carpet to the papered walls which displayed irises shining out from amongst wild grass. I opened and closed a number of drawers in idle curiosity. They were disappointingly empty, with only a spent matchbook and a few magazines in one, and a dog-eared bible in another.

From the window I had a glorious view of the vast, frost-covered lawn, the white sheen broken only by a huge old oak near its centre, standing alone. The lawn led down to the river which glistened and sparkled under the winter sun. Framing the picture beautifully were the sprawling and hazy South Downs in the distance.

A figure suddenly caught my eye; the girl Maeve.

She was sitting on a bench carved out of a large fallen oak, a tartan blanket draped over her shoulders. Her eyes were raised to the sky, and at her side lay the book she had been clutching in the library. The pillar-box red of her book and the lines on the blanket were bold strikes of colour in amongst the surrounding achromaticity. Her breath, like tiny clouds, floated from her mouth and drifted away towards the river. She appeared to be gazing up at the sky, deep in thought. A tiny spot of colour within the landscape, the young girl looked so alone and for a time I contemplated what would have brought her to this place.

A friend of the family, she had said.

A curious statement for one so young. I watched her and the clouds gathering on the horizon for some time. After a while she lifted the book, pulled a pen from somewhere and began to scribble in its pages. The book she had kept so close was a note-book or diary. I am something of a fair-weather diarist, but still I understood the girl a little more; she was a fellow *thinker*.

The clouds that dotted the skyline hadn't yet blocked out the sun. It was a pleasant winter afternoon, far too pleasant for mooching about indoors, and so I pulled on my country shoes and my overcoat and took myself out for a stroll.

I left the house by a small door that was tucked behind the main staircase. A stubborn frost had taken hold of the path-way, and the undergrowth crunched a little underfoot. As I moved on down a footpath towards some trees I caught sight of Miss Moore in riding trousers and a heavy tweed jacket, tearing along the waterside on a large brown horse which was snorting plumes of hot air from its nostrils. I could just hear the thunder of hooves as it vanished from view.

After following the dirt track through some towering oak and silver birch trees, I laid out a handkerchief - my faithful cor-dovan brown affair - and rested on a fallen birch, taking a mo-ment to listen to the silence around me. Never before have I felt so removed from London, worlds away from the humming and whistling and honking of my stomping ground. As a child I had been fascinated by wildlife; weasels, badgers, woodpeckers and the like. To a city boy they seemed as strange and mystical to me as the fat elephants and lofty giraffes of Africa.

Now that I was a grown man, however, I shuddered at the thought of a flea-ridden beast coming anywhere near, and diligently remained alert for scurrying vermin. That said, the small wood was pleasant enough, the air still and clear, and I embraced it.

Unfortunately, it was not peaceful for long.

A sharp thud into the leaves on the soft ground to my left pulled me away from my reverie. Peering over my shoulder, I anxiously searched for rodents. The foliage remained still, and yet I kept alert for fear that some hairy pest would appear in a flash.

Another rustle and thud in a bush to my right side made me jump, and I leapt up, preparing to flee. The leaves all around remained stagnant. But this noise hadn't come from within - something had plunged down into the foliage from the sky.

After searching fruitlessly above my head, I lowered my gaze to see a young man standing within a clump of bracken. His arms were folded and he was glaring in my direction.

'Not supposed to be here!' the stranger growled.

Before me was an unwashed and unkempt vision of hostility, a far more fearful apparition than any sharp-toothed weasel or badger might have been. His hair was wild and knotted. A patchy beard spotted a weak jaw. His eyes were wide and accusing, and perhaps I should have been scared. A fat thumb rubbed over a smooth stone in his grasp.

I matched his rudeness with indignation.

'Excuse me! Have you been *throwing stones* at me?' I snapped.

'Not supposed to be here!' he grunted sharply.

'I beg your pardon?'

My adversary moved forwards through the bracken, revealing mud spattered clothes and a protruding belly. He had the gait of an unruly child. And then, with a flick of the wrist, he tossed the stone aside into the foliage, confirming my fears – I had been under attack!

'Private property,' grumbled the stranger, and a pointed tongue ran over his lips. '*Private property*!' he repeated inanely, with the look of a simpleton.

One of the least appealing factors about living in a capital city is that one becomes used to tramps and vagabonds lumbering from the shadows and begging for this or that. Such characters can be easily aggravated, and so I kept my voice low and calm and was sure to keep a tight smile fixed on my face. I introduced myself, pretending to be entirely oblivious to his hostility.

'Good afternoon. My name is Payton Edgar and I am staying at the Blake residence. I am a guest, here for Christmas.'

'A guest?'

'Indeed. Here for the festivities. For Christmas.'

He mulled this information over for a moment.

'Mmm. Not private for you, then.'

'No, indeed.'

He watched me for an uncomfortably long time.

'And you are?' I asked, to fill a space.

Nothing.

'What is your name?' I persisted.

This he understood, switching from blank stupidity to inane gesticulating.   'Turpin. I live over there.' He pointed a finger to my left.

'Turpin,' I said slowly, thinking back to what young Maeve had said. *The Turpins at the gatehouse.* Was this the gardener? I tried to recall the name.

'Harry Turpin?'

The man squinted.

'S' my dad. I'm Raymond. Call me Spud. Everybody calls me Spud.'

I would certainly do no such thing.

'Do you fly kites, Mister?'

'Kites? I can't say that I do, Raymond.'

'Huh!' Raymond Turpin grunted in disappointment. Looking closer at the chap I could see specks of grey in his beard. He raised a grubby finger once more.

'We live there. Wanna see?'

His eyes were wide in appeal and I dared not refuse. We were soon striding out of the woods towards the main gates. As the gatehouse came into view Raymond stopped - a thought had struck him. He grasped my sleeve with some force.

'You staying up at the big house?'

'Naturally.'

'I said *you staying up at the big house*?'

'Yes. I am. Yes.'

I forced a smile and pulled back my hand.

'You seen the ghost yet?' he asked forcefully. I was lost for words, and could only shrug.

'*You... seen... the... ghost... yet?*' he repeated slowly as if I were the simpleton, forcing me to offer a confused reply.

'No, no - not yet.'

'Be careful, mister. There's a ghost up at the big house!'

The chap was clearly two strawberries short of a Wimbledon picnic, and the words he used nonsensical.

I have an opinion about this sort of thing. Wraiths, ghosts and unsettled spirits do not exist except in the minds of the gullible and the insane. Sightings of ghosts can - without fail - be put down to an over-burdened imagination, an inebriated condition, or to plain and simple idiocy on the part of the believer. The humdrum normality of the human existence can easily lead simpler minds towards fevered fantasies of spectral menace.

He was still talking.

'Scares me. They come back! The dead come back! The ghost-'

His attention was taken by something over my shoulder and I followed his gaze.

The house we were approaching was a squat cottage which shared some of the red brickwork but none of the splendour of the main house. Creeping ivy had engulfed much of the lower part of the building. The windows were dark and cold. A figure was moving around the side of the house as if inspecting the roses.

'Father's in the garden!' my companion exclaimed, leaping forwards. 'Come on!'

I followed dutifully.

A number of chickens clucked fussily and pecked at the ground around us, and as we neared the gatehouse the white haired old man in the garden looked over. He had a thick, untidy beard that covered much of his face, and a bush of white hair that hung about his crown like a fluffy cloud. He watched us approach for a second before quickly disappearing around the back of the building. His father's swift vanishing act did not deter Raymond's bounding approach in any way.

The chickens scattered.

As we neared the wooden gate the front door opened and a pale, plump lady framed the doorway. She wore a well-worn pinafore dress and sun-bleached headscarf. In her hand was a large bunch of mud-caked beetroot.

'Spuddy?' she hollered, squinting. 'What've you got there?'

I felt rather like a goldfish in a bag.

'Who is it, Spud?'

'Man from the house!' Raymond Turpin was shouting at the top of his voice even though we were within speaking distance of his mother. I forced yet another smile. My cheeks were beginning to ache.

'Mrs Turpin? I am Payton Edgar, a guest of Harvey Blake, here for Christmas-'

Her face set in a mask of horror.

'Raymond Ignatius Turpin! Leave this gentleman alone

at once! Get over here!' She pulled her son away by his elbow and turned back to face me. 'I am so sorry, Sir. My lad likes to make friends with everyone. He doesn't mean any harm.' She turned back and scalded him like a five year-old. 'Get inside and wash yourself, lad! I'll need you up at them kitchens in a half an hour.'

Raymond vanished into the darkness of the gatehouse with a snort.

'Sorry about that, sir. You mustn't mind my little Spud. You probably gathered he is a bit simple-like. Harmless, of course!' she added swiftly. I very much doubted this. For all his childishness he hadn't seemed harmless when he had thrown stones and barked at me in the woods.

'I am Joan Turpin, housekeeper. I just popped home for the beetroot.'
She had a pleasant face, although weather-beaten, and, unlike her son, she spoke well and was careful to sound her haitches.

'Pleased to meet you,' I said, grappling for an appropriate pleasantry. 'It should be a lovely few days.'

'Oh, yes!' she said quickly. 'A lovely Christmas. Snow is coming, they say, but if it can't snow at Christmas, when can it? A lovely Christmas, yes.' Joan Turpin's cheeks were mottled pink and the teeth, all too clearly her own, were in a painfully poor state. Her tiny eyes were beset by grey bags, however they twinkled with a certain sincerity.

'How nice. Well, are you heading back to the house?' she asked before continuing without pause for an answer. 'I'll walk you back, Sir.'

It transpired that Mrs Turpin was to be responsible for supper that evening, hence the freshly picked beetroot.

'Mr Turpin brings up some lovely ones in our back garden, but far more than the three of us can eat.' She spoke with a humble glowing pride of her lot, and I chose not to inform her of my dislike for beetroot. There are not many foodstuffs I avoid, but beetroot is quite simply the single most vile growth on the planet.

We set off on our walk back to the house.

'Yes, we are a comfortable little trio, us Turpins. Are you here with your wife?'

'No, I am here with a colleague and friend, a Mrs Baxter.'

'That's nice. But you *are* married, Mr-?'

'Edgar. Payton Edgar.'

'Mr Edgar. You are married?'

'Divorced.'

'Oh! Oh, well, never mind!'

'I live with my bedridden, elderly Aunt.'

'How lovely! I'm sure you dote on the poor dear.'

'On the contrary, I do my best to avoid her.'

'How lovely!'

'She can be rather trying-'

'That's nice!'

'She is a parasite' I continued, drily. 'The reason for her very existence appears to be to goad and torment me.'

'Oh, how delightful!'

The woman wasn't listening to a word I said, but continuing her own amiable little conversation. As we walked on she began to chatter in unnecessary detail about potato blight, and I found myself lost in a one-sided chat of very little interest or consequence. A potato must be prepared, cooked, seasoned and plated up in order to rouse my interest.

I searched for another avenue of conversation as we strolled along.

'Have you worked for Harvey Blake for very long?' I enquired.

'Ooh! Decades. Since just after Spuddy was born. Getting on for forty years now. They've had their problems, the Blakes, but they've always been good to us, Harry and me. Some folks let hardship get them down, others gain strength and prosper, and that's the Blakes all right. Harvey has always kept her chin up, no matter what, and her father was a tower of strength, until his illness took him. Lovely man he was, the Brigadier. Hard-edged and proud, but with a fine strong, dedicated heart. You simply don't get gentlemen like that anymore. That's why I don't mind doing what I do for him now. He never knows who I am, mind, but he can look after himself in the main - it's his mind that's gone not his body, see. He's just happy to sit there picking at his blankets. Rita Grant from the village comes up every weekday morning to do for the old man, and out of the goodness of her Christian heart too. She's a black, you know, but very nice really and the old man doesn't seem to mind her. Makes him think he's back in Rhodesia.'

'There must be so much to do, running an estate like this. How do you manage it all?' I enquired, attempting to add a tone of admiration into my voice.

'Oh, it's not all me, and the place looks after itself right enough. Arthur does what he can, but he's a fair age now, older than most of the furniture-'

'Arthur?'

'Arthur Lloyd, Mr Blake's butler. Don't say you haven't met him yet? Who's been doing your fetching and carrying? You've never had to do it all yourself?' She tutted rapidly. 'Well, Arthur's an age now, but he does troop on, bless 'im. He's not a bad butler all-in-all. You'll meet him soon enough - he still buttles over events like this, bless 'im. It's in his blood. Think he'll do it 'til his dying day, he will. Probably pop off right then and there over the sprouts and gravy during service one day!'

'So there's Arthur helping out, and then there's Miss Nicks from the thatch in the village. Miss Nicks is in most days to spit and polish, like. You won't see her over Christmas, she did doubles in the week and now she's off with her in-laws, which suits us.'

'Still,' I said with discreet praise, 'it sounds like you are indispensable.'

'Oh I wouldn't put it quite like that, Sir!'

This last was said without a trace of false modesty.

'And your husband sees to the gardens, is that right?'

'Oh, yes, has done for donkeys years now. Dad's married to these gardens. He knows every shoot and every bud, I tell you. He planted all those sycamores up by the Summerhouse, and done this lawn something proud. You must come back in the Summer and see his borders. I always say it's just me and the two lawns in this marriage, this lawn and the one at Chepstow. He loves his horses, does my husband. Do you gamble?

'No.'

'No? Well good for you! Fine husband you make, I'm sure.'

There was a moment of silence in which I felt compelled to speak.

'And Raymond? What does he do?'

This question, although not unwelcome, was answered with a wet harrumph.

'What does my Spuddy do? Not much really. I won't have him near the main house these days, not usually. Although he likes to help with the cooking every now and then. He did have a job some time ago, in the village under Mr Pepperwick.

Lasted a good three months, but he couldn't keep it on. Said it was the early mornings but I know better. He'll never be good with the dead, my boy.'

'I'm sorry?'

'Oh, Pepperwick's is the undertakers. Made some silly mistakes, did Spud.'

She tutted again and then paused, leaving me to ponder briefly what mistakes one might make at an undertakers.

'He has a bit of a thing about dead bodies, which I suppose is quite natural really. He's a sensitive boy.'

I seized my chance.

'He said something about a… ghost?'

Mrs Turpin gasped theatrically.

'He never did! And you a guest of Miss Blake's! I'm mortified! You mustn't mind him, Mr Edgar. He's talking about poor little Lotty, of course, but that girl is no ghost. All I can say is that I'm very sorry, what must you think of us?'

Lotty?

'Taken with a pinch of salt, I assure you,' I replied smoothly, privately a little embarrassed at having mentioned the word at all.

'Well, that's good.' She chuckled. 'Ghosts, honestly!' She slowed her pace. 'But she did come back from the dead, mind.'

This was said so quietly I almost missed it.

'I beg your pardon?'

The housekeeper spoke firmly and without a trace of humour.

'There are no ghosts here, Mr Edgar. But there is a spirit. Oh, yes! A restless spirit resurrected!'

Chapter V
In which Payton Edgar is taken to the beast in the cage

Dear Margaret,
I have a nosy neighbour who makes my life a misery. She is always peering through her net curtains to catch sight of my gentleman callers, and if she's not looking out at the front then she's out the back hovering over the garden fence. She has no friends or family, and so spends all her time watching over her neighbours. I daren't ask her outright to stop, but it is extremely distracting, not to mention awkward. What can I do?
Sylvia, Northwood

Margaret replies; *it sounds to me that with your "gentleman callers" that you have been giving her something to look at, Sylvia! Well, you have your sport, and she has hers. The woman has a curious nature, so you might as well give her something to peer at, you strumpet!*

'I beg your pardon? *Who* came back from the dead?'
The housekeeper let forth a sly cackle.
'Shall I tell you a story?'
'If you have the time.'
'It's not a very happy one.'
'My dear Mrs Turpin,' I replied with my warmest of tones, 'I fear that I am far too old for *happily every after!*'
She sniffed and drew in a deep breath. We were making good progress to the house but she slowed a little as she spoke, and we eventually came to a stop aside a dense holly bush.
'We're going back years now. It was a Summer not long after the war ended. Spuddy must have been coming up on eighteen, just a little younger than poor Charlotte Blake - little Lotty. Lotty was a naturally pretty girl. A chatter-box, but so fair in manner. Beautiful, long shining black hair, she had. Never teased our Spud like the others would. Well, it was a burning hot summer day, and we was having one of the Blake summer parties. It used to be something of a tradition, see, midsummer gatherings. Lovely day, it had been. My Jack and the Brigadier pulled the piano out onto the lawn and Lotty played it beautiful-

ly. We danced on the grass, oh - wonderful! All the girls went swimming in the river. Mr Turpin had set up a rope swing from one of the willows.

'Let's see - there was Lotty, Constance Frick and big Fran - what was that girl's name? Fran Timpson or Thompson, something like that. Big boned, spotty thing, she was. They were a threesome, those girls, called themselves *The Bathing Beauties*. Got together and sang songs like, in the Summer Holidays. Set out some dances too - and wore some very inappropriate flimsies if I remember rightly.'

Suddenly I recalled the framed photograph I had seen in the drawing room, of three girls smiling in bathing suits.

'Lotty Blake was the pretty one, no doubt about that, and she led them all in it. Connie and Fran were both, well, a bit plain, and Frannie was a big girl, poor love. They were both girls from the village. Goodness knows what happened to them. From what I remember the Frick family moved away up north years back, and I think Frannie went too not long after, but I can't for the life of me-'

We were losing thread a little and I gave a polite cough.

'Well, anyway, my Spud had been having a great time - they all had. But come suppertime that evening nobody could find little Lotty. They set out looking. I heard about all this last because I had been in the kitchen. Always the last to know, me. Well, my Spud had gone down the bottom of the green, collecting up some towels and bits and bobs that had been left by the side of the river, when he saw her. My poor boy, can you imagine, finding one of his best friends dead like that? He came running up to the house, sopping wet, hollering something rotten. Poor, poor lad.'

She stopped and shook her head. I waited patiently, and then we continued on along the gravel pathway. An unappealing barking announced the presence of the vile red dog as it bounded across the lawn in the distance. Thankfully, it was headed to the river.

Mrs Turpin appeared lost in her thoughts, and I could wait no longer.

'What had happened?' I asked, eagerly. 'How did she die?'

'Drowned she was. She loved the river, poor little Lotty. Just like my Spuddy did. Seems she had gone back down for one last swim, and the weeds had got her. My Spuddy's never forgotten what he saw - face down in the water like that, her long black hair streaming in the current. Like some drowned butterfly, he said. Or I said that. One of us said it, anyway. I remember he did say that when he tried to pull her out, weeds had tangled in her hair and around her neck, pulling her down like the river wouldn't let her go. And her face! He couldn't get her face from his mind, poor love. Said she looked like she was screaming. Screaming in death!'

She sighed loudly.

'And now, little Lotty Blake is back. Back from the grave. We've all seen it with our own eyes, there's no denying it - she's up there all right, stalking the grounds. Mmm. There's been far too much death at that house.' We both looked up at the manor house, which suddenly seemed to loom ominously over the grounds. 'So many deaths, over time, there's dark shadows cast over the place. You'll feel it, Mr Edgar, I'm sure. That cool feeling of someone just behind you, and when you look, nobody there. The cold, cold presence of death… and loss.'

The housekeeper took a deep breath in through her nostrils.

'Well I mustn't keep you any longer, must get back to my roast. I promise you a splendid spread tonight, Mr Edgar.'

With that she turned and waved me off.

'See you later, sir!'

As she trotted away I mulled over the story she had told. Nonsense, of course. But there was something to be said about an old house and its history of death. Despite my reservations, it was surprisingly easy to imagine a restless spirit stalking the grounds.

I headed indoors, and found myself lingering for a minute in the empty hallway, the words of the housekeeper running through my mind. *The cold, cold presence of death.*

The place certainly seemed cooler and greyer than before. I observed some details that I had, at first, overlooked - the wrinkled wallpaper, tearing ever so slightly at the edges of the hallway. The staircase dipping just a little, old and worn by uncountable feet that had passed through over the years. The radiators so cold and unwelcoming.

In my bedroom, I stood and looked over the room with fresh eyes. The plush red curtains were just a little grey at the edges; the carpet shrank away from the wall in the corners. Many of the irises on the wallpaper were faded with time. I frowned down at the bed, which had a tell-tale dip in the centre, despite the plump bedspread.

Many have died here, I thought to myself with a shiver.

We had an unpleasant surprise during dessert that evening, in the form of sweaty, inebriated Arnold Prosper.

He was expected to arrive on Christmas Eve, just in time to knock up some festive culinary delights. Harvey Blake should perhaps have known her head chef better, for everybody who had met the man knew that he was unpredictable and something of a live wire. When he appeared unexpectedly on the evening of the 23rd he was on his very worst behaviour, bursting in with an unwelcome recklessness and rather spoiling an otherwise sedate and not entirely unpleasant meal.

Dinner had started well.

The elusive Arthur Lloyd turned out to be a man of few words, as butlers are deigned to be. I had shaken his papery hand and been shown to my place at the table. Lloyd was the last of a rare breed of servants, his every movement considered, his timing impeccable. The man reeked of noble subservience and discretion.

His very manner was achingly Victorian.

I studied him carefully as he stood aside the door with his hands clasped behind his back and a professional blankness to his gaze. He had the waxy complexion of a man who had never dawdled in the sun, and the thin strands of white hair that remained on his scalp were smoothed back with lacquer. The eyes were deep-set and black, and his lips tight and pale. There was no hint of humour behind the servant's mask. Despite all this rigidity, he had a gentle air about him that one could only admire.

It's always good to see a person thoroughly dedicated to their vocation.

I had been thrilled to be seated at the head of the table. Opposite, Harvey Blake played the queen to my king, with Miss Moore to my right and Beryl to my left. There was no sign of the girl, Maeve, at first. The dining table itself was an agreeable undressed oak affair, large enough to seat at least a dozen, and I spent much of the evening running a finger idly through the rings of its surface.

Mr Lloyd oversaw the drinks and positioning of cutlery,

while Mrs Turpin served as cook and waitress with a glowing pride, throwing me a cheeky wink as she collected up our empty soup bowls. It had been a delicious ham and celery broth, drawing a well-deserved compliment from my lips. At this the housekeeper shocked me with the revelation that it had been conceived and prepared by her son, the errant Raymond.

I looked down at my empty bowl disapprovingly.

Had I known, I may not have devoured the dish quite as thoroughly. A wonderful cook, his mother declared proudly. I rather doubted that - picturing the drooling imbecile standing in the kitchen and looking for the instructions on a egg.

Mrs Turpin shot me another cheeky wink as she left the room.

I was bracing myself for the appearance of the beetroot. It did not come with the main course which was, as Turpin had promised, hearty fare indeed. Once a proper London chef was in residence in the kitchens we would surely get delicately considered cuisine, and this meal was the complete opposite. Rich slabs of beef dripping in a thick, meaty gravy were accompanied by crisp and bursting roast potatoes, and generous portions of suede, carrots and greens. I glared at my plate, feeling the need to loosen my belt at the mere sight of it all. Glancing around the table I could see that I had been given by far the most generous portion, accounting for the wink from Mrs Turpin over the soup bowls.

I ploughed on and did my best.

Mr Lloyd presided over our meal with an admirable efficiency. One was never without a drink or a fresh napkin. I dared myself to say a few words about the ghosts Mrs Turpin had alluded to earlier, but it felt impolite to raise such a unusual subject over dinner. From my seat I could see out into the hallway, and was surprised at one point to see young Maeve Taylor lingering outside the room. Her pale face was drawn and sad - there one minute and gone the next. There was something unsettling in her presence, and something telling in her absence from the dining table.

Conversation at the table remained minimal and yet comfortable, the bulk of the chatter coming from Beryl's corner. The woman knew how to tell a story, and she kept us chuckling as we ate. Miss Moore's expression was pinched and grim throughout the meal, and when she did speak it was in an off-hand manner that was ignored by my fellow diners. Clearly they were all used to the secretary's sharp edges.

Dessert was, as is traditional in English meals of hearty fare, a choice of hot pudding, cold sweet or cheese. I was relieved to see slices of the beetroot had been used only as a garnish for the cheese and helped myself to those which avoided the purple juice. A quiet moment passed, when suddenly, the door to the kitchens was kicked open with a crash and Arnold Prosper made his entrance, rosy red nose and all.

'Merry Christmas, everybody! Peace and goodwill, blah blah blah and all that gubbins!'

He looked sweaty and fatigued, as though having just run a marathon, with the shiny bald head and the cracked burgundy cheeks of one who is accustomed to hard liquor betraying his forty-odd years. He enjoyed wearing ridiculous thick rimmed spectacles that magnified his eyes and gave him a look of an angry owl. Despite this vociferous intrusion, old Lloyd remained impassive and took the man's battered hat and coat in silence.

Prosper set his eyes on me.

'Well! If it isn't old Mr Pink-Whistle!' he cheered. 'Wonderful to see you, old fruit. My most faithful disciple joining us for Christmas - top hole!'

I sat silent and entirely baffled.

'And the Queen bee herself, Beryl Baxter, as I live and breathe! I bet half of London heaved a sigh of relief to hear that you were out in the sticks!'

'Good evening, Mr Prosper,' Beryl replied dryly.

'Good evening indeed, you little Christmas cracker, you! Trussed up like a french prostitute as always!'

'How dare you?' Beryl boomed, not without humour. '*French*?'

Prosper went on to greet the others in his boisterous, unbecoming manner. He seemed to have a silly name for everyone. He went on to announce that he had been unable to resist the pull of the country while drinking with friends in Soho. He paced the room and went into some unnecessary detail about the bar in which he had been drinking and its clientele. As he blethered on, I returned my attention to my cheeses.

I am partial to a good cheeseboard, but have my strict rules and regulations. Cheeses should be stored at room temperature for a minimum of six hours prior to eating. There should be no fewer than four pieces, and no more than eight, and the selection must contain at least one soft, one hard and one blue, and should be tasted in this order without deviation. Accompanying crackers must snap and not bend, and toast should be dry and almost - though never actually - burnt. And, much as I appreciate fruit such as figs or pears, the very best boards will always have a quince jelly. Sadly, the range on offer that night broke many of these rules and was too far on the mild side for my tastes.

Cheese should make ones mouth sing, not mutter.

Unfortunately, any attempts I made to tune my thoughts away from the bellowing newcomer proved unsuccessful. Prosper declared loudly that he would be up and out shooting game first thing in the morning in order to deliver us the perfect meal tomorrow evening. I doubted to myself that *"first thing"* meant anything before midday.

'I might join you!' Beryl had added, much to Prosper's delight.

'Nothing sexier than a woman with a firearm! You'll need a keen eye, though, Queen Bee. Ever had the privilege of tasting robin? Terribly hard to shoot but absolutely worth the effort.'

'Robin?' I found myself echoing in disbelief.

'Lovely plump breast if cut correctly - a delicacy in some countries.'

'Drunk as a skunk!' said Mrs Turpin under her breath.

'And you drove here in that state?' asked Miss Moore with distaste. Prosper wagged a finger dangerously close to her face.

'Damn right I did. Had a fat wager with Chippy Beauchamp that I'd not be dead in a ditch, and here I am, all in one piece! Owes me two pints, Chippy. Why? Did you miss me, Miss Moorish?'

'Of course,' she snapped. 'Like a hole in the head.'
Prosper did not appear to hear her reply, and smacked his lips together loudly.

'Well, Prosper's back now, you beautiful thing, you! And talking of beauty, who was that youthful chit of a thing I passed in the hallway just now? Rather puts your mature splendour into perspective, Alison. Please tell me it was a Christmas pressie for dear Prosper? I'd better cut some mistletoe while out on our hunt tomorrow.'

Mrs Turpin was doing her best to appear immune to

Prosper's drunken bravado, but was betrayed by the wringing of hands and her pink flushing cheeks. She quietly offered him something to eat.

'Ah, dear Mrs Turnip – always at hand with a delicious home-baked, stodgy something-or-other! What's on the menu this evening? Is it a pudding, or a door-stop?'

After some unnecessary deliberation he plumped for a large bowl of her formidable-looking spotted dick. What was left of our desserts were abandoned as the man took his place at the table and noisily gulped down his pudding. After a number of spoonfuls Prosper arched an eyebrow and pushed his glasses up the bridge of his nose.

'Crikey, people! What does a man have to do to get a bloody drink around here?' he asked, cream dribbling down his chin.

We sat in a very English silence as he wolfed down his food and spoke without inhibition.

'And how's that rancid old creature? Still with us?' he asked inexplicably as he chewed loudly. Surely he didn't mean the old Brigadier? It was an extremely disrespectful manner of address if he did.

Miss Moore stiffened in her seat as he went on.

'The old General still clinging on to life?'

I watched the faces of my fellow diners, but where I was expecting to see outrage, there were only signs of a practiced tolerance. Proper went on.

'That thing wants plating up while it's still fresh and plump and ready for the plucking! Ha-ha-ha!'

He set down his spoon and we all began to leave the table. Miss Moore had allowed herself to be rattled by Prosper's nonsense, and with a dark expression had uttered something miserably under her breath.

'I'm off to feed the General.'

She caught my inquisitive glance and immediately brightened.

'You did present our guests to The General, didn't you, Harvey?'

Harvey Blake had raised her eyes to the ceiling, at which her secretary gave an amused shriek.

'Now, Mrs Baxter, Mr. Edgar - you must be brought forth to the man of house immediately! You can't say you are staying at Fallow House until you have reported to the General.'

'Sorry, do you mean Mr Blake, the old brigadier?'

'Oh no - there're two fine soldiers under this roof, Mr Edgar. I shall take them straight away, Harvey, if that's okay?'

'Of course,' our host replied and smiled down at us. 'There will be a couple of whiskies waiting for you in the drawing room. You may need it.'

Miss Moore took me rather harshly by the elbow and drove me back in the direction of the library, with Beryl following dutifully behind. As I was practically frog-marched down the hallway she explained a little more. 'The General has lived at Fallow far longer than any human inhabitant. They say he was a hundred and two at his last birthday, though you wouldn't believe it to look at him. It's a scandal that we haven't mentioned him to you before!'

This was all very mysterious, and I can't say that I liked it.

We found ourselves ushered all the way through the library and further on towards the rear of the house where it was both darker and much, much cooler. A large oak door stood open leading through to what looked like a small cloakroom. To the left, a number of furs, hats and macs hung on high iron hooks. Directly ahead, adjacent to a window sat a small corner sink.

Miss Moore halted in the doorway and gestured somewhat majestically, inviting us to enter the room first. If this tongue in cheek pantomime was for my benefit it was a complete waste of time. I shot her a look of cool suspicion and moved into the room.

I was immediately hit by a curious smell that was tricky to place. Sawdust, perhaps? Sawdust and something else. Old fish?

'Pooh!' exclaimed Beryl. 'Stinks like Billingsgate!'

The cloakroom extended out to the right a small way to form an L-shape, where two things immediately caught the eye. The first was a large arched window that reached from floor to ceiling, the upper third of which had a pleasant yellow and green stained pattern of interlocking circles. Through the window there was a clear view of the gardens sweeping down to the water in the near distance beyond. The second eye-catching article was the tall ironwork cage that stood before it, reaching from floor to ceiling, cemented into place and clearly very, very old.

A cage, and that smell. There was a creature in here.

I moved forth cautiously.

The little room was silent. As I approached the structure, the beast within became apparent. In the centre of the massive domed cage hung an empty swing. To the left a large animal was perched on the branch of a silver birch, and it took a good few seconds to realise that this was some kind of bird. A bird like I had never seen before.

It was fatter than the plumpest piglet, and sat hunched over the branch in such a way that it almost looked as if it were about to topple forwards. It's dense plumage was a rich moss green, and when it turned it's head just a little to watch our approach, I saw that it had the beak of a parrot and the large grey eyes of an owl.

It did not look pleased to see us.

'Good heavens!' I found myself muttering.

Beryl cleared her throat. 'What on Earth is it?'

Miss Moore had moved up behind us and her voice was soft and quiet for once.

'Beautiful, isn't he? He's a Kakapo, often known as *the owl-parrot*. But to us he is known as The General. He was originally named General Custer, but has lost the Custer over the years. Now he is simply The General. He's the most reliable friend I have ever known. The General has been in the family for a century now.'

'Where is it from?' I found myself asking.

'He was brought over from some old colony in New Zealand by Harvey's grandfather, and has been looking out over the grounds of Fallow House ever since.'

Beryl scoffed. 'A century ago? He can't possibly be that old! He doesn't look it! A bird, one hundred years old?'

She was quite wrong. One could see from the creature's watchful, knowing eyes that it was as old as the hills. I posed a question.

'Does he talk?'

'Funnily enough, yes, but not like a parrot would. A parrot squawks, the General grumbles. He used to talk much more, but nowadays his words are few and far between. I tell you both, he is far cleverer than any bird I've ever met. The way he watches you, you'd swear he knows all.'

It was not hard to see what she meant - the miserable thing was looking at me as if he didn't like what he saw. It was hard to imagine any living being of a hundred years, and yet the wisdom in his eyes and the denseness of the plumage told me that this creature was indeed created for lengthy duration.

'Can he fly?'

'He never has, to my knowledge. We let him out every now and then for a stretch, and he bumbles about a bit like an old man. He sleeps most of the day. But this past year or so he's slowed down a bit more - he doesn't even want to come out of his cage half the time. We all look after him in a way, but since I've been here he's been kind of my responsibility.

Something in her tone told me that this was one duty she did not mind attending to. She clearly liked the ugly thing.

A curious rumble emerged from the throat of the beast. Miss Moore clasped my arm lightly and we listened as the owl-parrot issued a noise.

'Gooooooooooooooooolllllllllllld' it said in a deep rumbling tone.

'Fascinating!'

'Gold,' said the secretary, nodding. 'He says that a lot. I like to think that he sailed with pirates in his youth. He also says *"come 'ere"* sometimes, and he makes this amazing, deep booming sound in the night. Well, General, Sir, this is Mr Edgar and Mrs Baxter, who will be staying with us for a few days, with your kind permission.'

The General blinked slowly and glared blankly in my direction. Then, haltingly and rather coldly, he shuffled his weight on his claws and turned his head back to the wall.

It seems we had been dismissed.

**Part Two
Christmas Eve**

Chapter I
In which Payton Edgar takes a stroll along the promenade

Dear Margaret,
**I suffered a heart attack in the spring of this year,
and ever since then my wife won't let me do anything I want
to do. I used to enjoy a game of squash, a stiff drink or a
good meal, but all these joys have been vetoed in respect of
my health. I feel like a dried up old cracker - I am fed up
and I miss my past life. Any advice?**
Mr F, Camden

Margaret replies; *I have recently learned that the Kakapo, a
bird indigenous to the South Pacific, can live for well over a century. But to what end? To live a life devoid of stimulation, simply sitting around, fat and feathered, stuck in a seemingly endless
pattern of ingestion and elimination. Live your life! Enjoy a
game of squash, reach for that decanter of scotch and savour a
good meal; it is not how long we are around for, but surely what
with do with our time that matters.*

'We really shouldn't have him, actually,' Harvey said
breezily as we ploughed down yet another winding country lane.
It was the morning of Christmas Eve and, where snow
had begun to fall over Fallow House, down towards the coast the
clouds had parted to reveal a beautiful clear blue winter sky.
'By all accounts the Kakapo are something of an endan-
gered species these days. Some years back a raggedy-trousered
conservationist had quite an upset with Father - wanted to fly the
bird back to his natural habitat. But Father wasn't having any of
it. The General has always been in the family, and he is quite,
quite happy. The journey would probably kill him now, even if
we tried to ship him back. Grandfather brought him home for
my father as a gift. He'd been in some skirmish out there.'
We turned onto a larger road and Harvey pressed hard on
the pedal.
'Apparently the General was livelier when he was much
younger, if you can imagine it, but as far back as I can remember
he has always been a fat and sluggish thing. We all love him,
though - Alison and Joan especially. He is a wise old dear.

Sometimes we go to him with our problems, and it does feel like he listens. You should try it.'

I would do no such thing. I would never stoop to talking to a dumb bird, no matter how dire my circumstances.

We were on our way to Brighton. In all honesty, I was fairly glad to escape Fallow House after the embarrassment of the previous evening. After our visit to The General, Beryl and I had joined Harvey Blake in the drawing room, only for Arnold Prosper to make himself known and to sour the atmosphere as only he can do. Beryl took it all in her stride, as she is used to entertaining notorious simpletons, but it was not long before I tired of his jeers and saucy puns, made my excuses and disappeared to bed.

After an early rise, I had spent a good hour-or-so at the desk in my room ruminating over correspondences to Margaret Blythe and handwriting replies with my favourite pen.

Breakfast that morning had been a quiet affair. Arnold Prosper was absent - surely sleeping off his head from the night before - and the fact that Beryl wasn't an early riser hardly came as a surprise. There was also no sign of young Maeve or the spiky Miss Moore either, and so Harvey Blake and I enjoyed a light breakfast of eggs, toast, jam and tea served by mute old Mr Lloyd before we drove the not unpleasant little drive down to the South Coast of England.

I have never been a fan of seaside towns.

I have vague memories from my toddling years of a beach near Exeter, a bitterly cold sea and the torment of sand in my ice cream. Brighton, however, was not just another seaside town. There was no tang of seaweed in the air nor any sandcastles on the beach. And yet it had the feel of a place to escape to, a place to forget the trudge of real life, such was its carefree and gay, knotted-hanky-on-the-head atmosphere. We parked the car by the seafront at Hove and, taking advantage of the sunshine, walked from pier to pier.

Strolling down the prom in all weathers is a steadfast pastime in British seaside towns, and in this I found that Brighton was no exception. A number of young ladies passed us by dressed in an entirely questionable manner for the time of year, their tops shrinking down to reveal skinny neck bones and their skirts rising up over stockless legs, quite ignoring the crisp-

ness of the air. Such brazen attire was worn to the great indifference of passers-by. The girls beamed out innocently as they
clutched the arms of happy young men.

As Harvey and I walked we talked freely about our re-
spective upbringings, commenting on how wildly different they
had been. There was no shadow of an overbearing Mother for
Harvey, only an entourage of colourful nannies followed, naturally, by an exclusive private education at boarding school. We
chatted about her work for the war effort and the dreams she had
of running an elite eatery of some kind, dreams which were
made real by a cruel twist of fate.

'My daughter passed on. I was grieving, and had to have
a focus, a new project.'

I took a moment to reply.

'Mrs Turpin told me about your loss. I was very sorry to
hear it.'

If Harvey were annoyed at her housekeeper's indiscretion she did not show it. She looked to the sky, but said nothing.

'I noticed a photograph in the drawing room. Three girls
at the riverside.'

At this, my companion beamed.

'Ahh! The Bathing Beauties,' she said warmly. 'That's
what they called themselves. My Charlotte's the pretty little one
in the centre, with Fran Thompson on one side and little Connie
Frick on the other. They were best of friends, had fun, set out
some dances and ballets... more *duck pond* than *Swan Lake* I'm
afraid to say, but they enjoyed themselves. That photograph was
taken on the last... the last day.'

I allowed her a moment of silence.

'It's true what they say, about light coming out of darkness. When I lost Charlotte it spurred me on to make the most of
my work. A part of me had died, and all I had left was my work.
In many ways, it was the start of something new for me.'

'What about your husband?' I asked with an uncharacter-
istic indiscretion, the words out my mouth before I could stop
them.

'Gideon? Gideon was, well, a bit of a live wire in those
days. Ours was a tempestuous relationship, to say the least.
Gideon's roots are in Spain, and he has that fiery Spanish way
about him. And when we lost Charlotte - well, that was that. He
eventually moved back to Spain, much to the approval of Father
and Petra.'

'Petra would be your sister?'

'That's right. She lives just along the coast from here, Worthing way. You have something in common, actually. She writes too.'

'She is an author?'

'Children's books. She pens the Sylvester the Fox stories.'

'I see.'

To be quite honest, I didn't see at all. Harvey hummed a little.

'I feel like I should warn you about Petra, Mr Edgar. She is a creative soul, a keen potter and charitable when she wants to be. She teaches at the local Sunday School. She can, however, be a bit... *flighty* at times, and perhaps a bit bossy. But she has a good heart deep down. Very down to earth when it comes to the opposite sex, is Petra. She always saw Gideon for what he was; a liar and a cheat. She saw the things it took me twenty years to see.'

I could not resist a query.

'And now he is back?'

'Now he is back.' replied Harvey with a sigh. 'And he is a different man. I have forgiven him everything, and we are engaged again. Sometimes, it's right to just forgive and forget, don't you think? Forgiveness is the attribute of the strong, isn't it? Who was it said that?'

I had no idea.

'Do you believe that people can change, Payton?'

She had asked this same question the day before in the drawing room, and I was left to wonder exactly what response she was hoping to receive. I mulled this over, and decided to remain impartial.

'In some cases, yes. In some cases, no.'

'Well, I have come to see that time and experience really can change people. Gideon is like a different man, now. There is a maturity about him that just wasn't there before. I care for him, and he cares for me too. I have given him a second chance.'

It felt rather like she were trying to convince herself as much as anyone else, but I remained tight lipped. We approached the second pier, at which I flatly refused to pay the extortionate toll fee. We lingered a little, and Harvey pointed to a sign with a smile. In wiggly writing that was surrounded by clawed hands and skeletons, it read; *"Laughs, thrills, shocks and shudders in The House Of Hades!"*

'Fancy that?' she asked wryly.

I needn't reply, a look was all that was needed.

And so we ambled in-land, where Harvey announced that she required my nose to choose an aftershave for her beau. I confessed to having a talent for connecting colognes to individuals and enquired as to the man's nature.

'Scents are as individual to a man as the hat on his head or the shoes he chooses to wear on his feet. One would not splash an outgoing adventurer with a scent meant for a taciturn librarian, for example.'

'He is neither an adventurer nor a librarian. I'm just after something to douse over the wretched stench of his pipe smoke!'

In light of this, we plumped for *Old Spice*.

Brighton's narrow streets were bustling with Christmas shoppers, and we found ourselves swept up in the current. As we neared the turrets of the Pavilion we were stopped in our tracks by the sight of a familiar face. Alison Moore was propping herself up against a wall, a finger to her lips, deep in thought. A burning cigarette protruded from the corner of her mouth.

'Alison!' Harvey exclaimed, at which the poor woman jumped. She gave a start and snatched the cigarette from her mouth, not unlike a youth discovered smoking behind the bike sheds at school.

'Alison! What are you doing here?' Harvey asked, with a good-natured smile.

Miss Moore did not return the smile, and instead she thinned her lips, outstretched an arm and shook her bag in our direction.

'Last minute Christmas bits and bobs! Why else would I be here?' She shook her head and took on a puzzled look, as if we had asked a ridiculous question, and then raised her voice with an unexpected authority. 'I can come down to Brighton too if I want to, you know. Now I'd better get on. See you tonight!'

With that she replaced the cigarette and stamped away. Harvey and I exchanged uncertain glances, and she read my look easily.

'She isn't always quite so... stuffy,' said Harvey, 'I couldn't wish for a more loyal and efficient secretary. There is nothing that she won't do for me.'

We crossed the road.

'She's just a little hard boiled. At times she can be just a little… odd - doing the most usual, day-to-day things one can imagine and yet shrouding it in secrecy. I think that she likes to appear, well, more interesting than she really is.'

I thought about this for a minute. It was not a very favourable appraisal of a companion, it must be said.

'Do you have a secretary, Mr Edgar?'

The thought had never crossed my mind. What, I asked myself, would Payton Edgar want with a secretary? It might be beneficial to have a right hand man, but I had neither the funds nor the space. As I said something along these lines, Harvey must have sensed my hesitancy.

'It pays to have a number two, Mr Edgar. Having some-one to type up your work, to keep you to deadlines and all that. Alison is worth her weight in gold, so far as my business is concerned.'

A secretary? I thought to myself. *Perhaps.*

'To my mind,' Harvey continued, 'every man should have an efficient secretary and a solid solicitor. You may not yet have the former, but you must have the latter, at the very least.'

'Oh, I do have a solicitor, of course,' I replied, with perhaps a little too much confidence. Mr Crack, of *Hammond, Hammond, Hammond and Crack Solicitors*, was far from solid. In fact, one would describe him as limp and ineffectual at best. But he was my solicitor all the same, and Harvey Blake needn't know that he was an imbecile.

We soon found a delightful tea hut within the Pavilion Gardens and seated ourselves on rusty iron chairs under the sun. Taking tea outside in Winter was a daring pursuit at the best of times, but Brighton seemed to think this was all perfectly normal. I gallantly fetched a pot of tea for two and we shared a small plate of warm mince pies. They were surprisingly good, and we sat for some time in a companionable silence.

I had been watching with disapproval as a sullen-faced little boy with scuffed knees rather viciously chased seagulls across the green when my companion suddenly leaned in and spoke with a fresh urgency.

'I must say something, Mr Edgar - and I need your thoughts. Something wonderful has happened! Something wonderful and, at the same time, something dreadful. I just don't know what to do about it!'

I have to confess to feeling a little uncomfortable. I am

not a man used to receiving confessions and declarations over tea, akin to a gossiping fishwife. Nevertheless, I asked the only question that could be asked.

'What has happened?'

I was happy to wait for her reply, and when it came it was delivered with a soft secrecy and the urge to be understood.

'You met young Maeve yesterday.'

It was a statement, not a question. I waited and rounded up some mince pie crumbs as Harvey gathered her thoughts.

'Six weeks ago I was at the florists down in the village, picking out some flowers for the hallway - and there she was. My little girl. My Charlotte, standing there, admiring the carnations. A young woman, just as Charlotte was, not a day older. Before I knew it, she approached and began to talk, asking directions for the Post Office or something, I can't remember exactly what. Well, I barely heard a word she said, I was in shock - the likeness was simply unbelievable! It was my little girl in the flesh, standing there in all innocence amongst the flowers. Charlotte had come back into my life!'

Harvey paused in thought and after a minute I spoke my mind.

'You don't strike me as a superstitious person, Harvey. And you are most certainly not stupid.' She looked at me enquiringly. 'You knew that this was not your daughter?'

She nodded keenly.

'Of course I knew that. But everything about the girl, from her smell to the way she spoke, was just so... *familiar*. She introduced herself as Maeve Taylor, and said that she was looking for work, any kind of work. As it was, Rita Grant from the village was away on a church retreat and unable to see to Father for a fortnight. I can't deny it - I was simply enchanted by the girl, and so I gave her an offer. My father is too ill to remember his only grandchild, but I thought it might be good for him to spend time with Maeve. And I was right - she is a tonic. Like many old men, he enjoys the presence of youth.'

She let out a sigh.

'And so, ever since that day in the village, we have spent our time talking and getting to know each other. I've encouraged her to stay on and, if I'm honest, Mr Edgar, I feel like I have my daughter back.'

I could not hide my desire to point out the obvious, to encourage an element of rationality back into the conversation.

'And what of her history? What of her own parents?'

'Maeve is an orphan, that is all I know. She doesn't like to talk about her upbringing. She is a very private person. All rather... *mysterious*.' This was said with a touch of wonder. I persevered.

'You have known the girl for six weeks? You must have seen some differences in her behaviour in that time? I mean, this girl is not your daughter. There must be differences?'

Harvey pondered on this, and nodded.

'Yes. I was relieved, actually, at the little things that were different. Her eating habits, for one thing. She enjoys fish, for example. My Charlotte would never touch fish. And she is much quieter, more thoughtful. My Charlotte could be a whirl-wind at times, she really could. She was a Daddy's Girl, you see. Whereas Maeve is far quieter, more aloof. But there are things that she does, the way she speaks, the way she poses a question, that make me feel like my Charlotte was there... somewhere. And her hair - when we met in the village she wore it pulled up in a bun, which my girl would never do. But now she has changed even her hair - she wears it long and loose, just like Charlotte would.'

'And have you told the girl why you find her so fascinat-ing? Have you told her about Charlotte?'

'Not in any detail. It just doesn't seem right. Yes, she knows I had a daughter who died, and she must have seen the odd photo. But, well, you see, there is - well...'

Harvey paused, and then nodded, as if deciding upon a disclosure. She fixed my gaze.

'I have other reasons for finding her presence so utterly bewitching.'

She stopped herself.

'I can talk to you, can't I, Mr Edgar?'

'Of course!'

'Well, firstly, there is her birthday. She let it slip a while back - the twelfth of November. That is my Charlotte's birthday. The *very day*!'

She wet her lips.

'And then, a week-or-so ago, I heard her at the piano. I was in the hallway when it started, slowly at first, a slow, simple, ambling tune that repeated the same notes again and again. Da-da-dum-da-da, da-da-dum-da-da, over and over. And then the final line da-di-dum-da-da-da. This was Charlotte's tune - she and the girls would sing it, and they sang it every Summer. It was their song - The Bathing Beauties. I can picture, clear as day, my Charlotte at the piano, and Connie and Fran dancing around. *"We are the Bathing Beauties, we are the girls of Summer, and we do what we want together!"* And here was Maeve playing that very song in *my* drawing room, on *my* piano!'

Harvey's eyes were open wide in my direction.

'I was livid. It was Charlottes's song! Where did she hear this? Where did she get it from? And do you know what Maeve said when I asked? She said *"it just came to me"*. It just came to me!'

I was having none of this.

'She must have seen it, the piano score, on a paper somewhere.'

'Mr Edgar! Little girls don't write down sheet music, they make it up as they go along. It had been years and years since it was heard in the house, lost in time. Years since I had even thought of it. *So how did she know*?'

There followed another lengthy pause.

'I have my faith, and asked the vicar about it.'

'And what did he say?'

'Our Vicar, Daniel Drinkwater, has been in Tetherton for eons, and he knew Charlotte. I invited him to lunch and he met Maeve. He was as awestruck as I was, but also a little fearful. He thinks her unnatural, rather like Joan does. Joan thinks that she is blessed with the gift of a clairvoyant and will not shut up about it - she insists that my daughter's spirit has returned, which doesn't help a jot. And Spud seems to be terrified of the girl. In fact, Miss Moore and I are the only ones who treat her like a human being, poor thing.'

She shrugged.

'Do you know something, Mr Edgar? Young Maeve was born not long after my Charlotte died. Just a matter of months. And on my girls birthday! I know how it sounds, but I feel as though my little girl has, in some way, come back to me. Just as she was.'

I like to think of myself as an open-minded gentleman, but events of a supernatural bent are difficult to stomach at the best of times. In front of me was a grieving mother finding just what she needed to find in a daughter figure, nothing more. Surely Harvey Blake, the *"businessman"* I had come to admire in such a short time, was above all this nonsense?

I held my tongue and waited. Reading my thoughts Harvey shrunk back in her seat and thinned her eyes.

'You don't believe me? You think I am wishing it to be true. You think I am talking nonsense.'

A rather accurate appraisal.

'Well, I, er-'

'Well good!' Harvey replied with gusto. 'I'm on the edge, Mr Edgar, and I need some common sense right now. This is exactly why I need you this Christmas. Payton Edgar - critic. A man of high standards, someone with a no-nonsense approach. I want you to keep me sane. I need you to keep me grounded, Payton.'

'Mmm. I will do my best,' I replied uneasily.

'And if you can find a rational answer to this spirit that has been sent to us, then all the better.'

Chapter II
In which Payton Edgar makes a new enemy over a bath bun

Dear Margaret,
My husband is a stickler for tradition. He insists on spending our Summer Holidays at Sutton-on-sea, just as his own parents and grandparents always have. I would simply love to see the continent, or even just to explore Cornwall. I have an Aunt in Exeter who has invited us for the holidays, but my husband refuses. Do I not have the right to a say?
Bored, Bromley

Margaret replies: *I sympathise with your predicament, Bored from Bromley, as I once spent a particularly wet and miserable weekend in Sutton on Sea myself. I imagine there are far more pleasing sea views to be found in a picture postcard shop in Bromley itself. As for Exeter, give this a wide berth too. The place is unappealing in the extreme. As a child I once stubbed my toe badly on a rogue paving stone on the seafront and it has never properly healed.*

We were close to finishing our tea when Harvey Blake moved on from matters of spirits raising from the dead to other matters of family.

We were in Brighton to collect her husband and sister, and I seized the opportunity to probe for more details on her family background. She told me a little more about her marriage to Gideon Carter, and I could not help but offer a comment.

'You have - either by accident or by design - painted a picture of a rather shadowy cad!'

'Oh, don't get me wrong, Mr Edgar, Gideon has a heart. He just finds it difficult to talk. You know how men can be.'

'And what does Mr Carter think of Maeve?' The man was Charlotte's father, surely he saw through the nonsense even if Harvey couldn't?

My host gave a sharp laugh.

'He was very quiet at first. Saw her as a cuckoo in the nest. He wouldn't stay in the room with the girl for the first few weeks, she discombobulated him so much. And now... now there is a strange kind of quiet distance between them. It's hardly her fault, but he won't have much to do with her.'

Harvey ran her finger around the rim of her empty teacup.

'While I've enjoyed having Maeve around, Gideon certainly hasn't, and I'm dreading what my sister will say. Despite her capricious ways, when it comes to family our Petra sees things in black-and white. I have to be honest, I have avoided the subject of Maeve all this time. Petra has-'

She interrupted herself, snapped up her arm and glared at her wristwatch.

'In fact, we best be going else she will wonder where we are.'

I was confused.

'And Gideon will be there too?'

'With Petra? Good gracious, no! They are hardly the best of friends, I'm afraid. He lives just out of town - the plan is to pick him up on the way home. It gives me time to warn her. I have a double whammy of difficult news for my poor sister. You see, she doesn't know that Gideon is back on the scene, nor would she approve. And she hasn't met Maeve yet. I'm not looking forward to telling her about either of them.'

She shrugged.

'I am making her sound like the most unattractive of sisters, I know. Petra can be rather a dragon at times, but she suffers with her nerves terribly, and she is nice enough... when she wants to be. Still, I'm glad I have you here to keep her from blowing her lid entirely.'

It was clear that I was expected to be useful to Harvey Blake in a number of ways. Not only was I expected to stop her going loopy over the return of her dead daughter, but I was to act as a buffer between her and the more difficult members of her family. I felt a twinge of regret for leaving the quiet and comfort of my life back in Pimlico.

'Why would Petra disapprove of Gideon?' I asked, with the no-nonsense approach that my host had asked for.

She gave a considered pause before her reply.

'Because - well - we are sisters; she cares for me, and Gideon can be a pig. At least, he was way back in the day. He drank too much and lost on the horses and all that, and at the time it really bothered Petra. And then his behaviour got much worse after we lost Charlotte. Much worse. But he has changed, Payton. People *can* change, and I need Petra to see that.'

Harvey leaned in closer.

'I'm so glad that you came for Christmas, Mr Edgar. I need you to help me put out the odd fire or two!'

So that was why I was here.

I had neither the desire nor the inclination to tackle fires of any kind. And yet as I rested back in my seat and watched as she gathered her things, I quickly arrived at a conclusion. What was it she had said? *Payton Edgar, a man of high standards. Someone with a no-nonsense approach.*

It was only natural that a person of Harvey Blake's stature might turn to Payton Edgar for help.

The only thing I could possibly do was to see to it that she wasn't disappointed.

It was a little after two-thirty when we arrived at our rendezvous.

Harvey had arranged to meet her sister in an over-crowded tea shop with buns stacked high behind a steamy window. We found Petra Blake alone at the back, frowning over an egg-stained menu.

She was a buxom thing, with ruddy cheeks and a full bosom that pushed against the table top. Her clothes lacked the bespoke sophistication of her sibling's attire; instead Miss Blake opted for tweeds, woollens and hand-knitted apparel. Here was the poster girl for *make-do-and-mend*.

She looked not unlike a farmer's wife.

On the table sat a small plate with two bath buns on top. We were greeted with a roar and the conversation continued at this pitch from that moment on. Harvey's sister had certainly inherited her father's military styling. She pretended to be mortified that we had eaten and that she would have to tackle the glistening bath buns alone, and then proceeded to wolf them down in record time as she nattered gaily with her sister over steaming hot tea.

I sat in polite silence for a while, before Petra Blake recalled my presence and abruptly enquired into my line of work.

'Mr Edgar is a fellow writer,' said Harvey Blake kindly. This was waved away with a limp wrist.

'Oh, my giddy aunt! Every Tom, Dick and Harry has a novel inside of them these days!'

'I most certainly do not!' I replied uncompromisingly. I went on, only to be silenced by a crashing interruption which came as I mentioned my work for the Clarion. Miss Blake mooed and bellowed loudly that she disapproved of newspapers and all who work for them.

'Hacks and sneaks, spouting untruths and recreating history with pitiful puff pieces! Scandal and tripe! Not worth the paper it's printed on these days!'

She had never heard of Payton Edgar, nor my restaurant column and made no apologies about it. She moved swiftly from her merciless condemnation of the press to loudly pan our dear capital and all who lived in it.

The woman had a rather Dickensian view of my home town.

'London is not for the likes of me - oh dear me, no! Money, money, money is all the place is about these days. Fat bankers with sticky fingers! And those that aren't fat bankers are criminal lowlifes. London is nothing but a bear pit of whores and thieves, lurking away in stinking dark alleyways! The filth of our pitiful capital! Oh! The thought of it all sends my heart pounding! I can't even bear to visit, so why anybody would wish to actually *dwell* in the place is quite beyond me.'

A podgy potter's finger was raised in the air.

'Now, slap me twice, I tell a fib! I did have one pleasant experience in London. It was some years back, for a writers' convention. I stayed in a very impressive hotel in Pall Mall.'

She pronounced this *"Paul Maul"*.

I looked on sourly.

'Of course, I didn't dare so much as leave the lobby, but it was a delightful establishment, very high class. No, in my opinion, there are only two good things to have come out of London.'

She allowed a pause in which I was clearly supposed to make a polite enquiry. I merely cocked a tired eyebrow.

'Charlie Dickens and Beefeater Gin!'

I leapt on a mistake, hungrily.

'I think you'll find that Mr Dickens hails from Portsmouth-'

'Oh, don't be ridiculous!'

The vile woman did not seem to think it was necessary to allow me any time to explain why I chose to live in our beloved capital. Instead, she went on to share an unbelievably dull account of her recent encounter at a local dog show, in which she had acted as judge. I sat in silence, unable to focus on anything else but the thunderous rumbling of her voice, her baritone barking vibrating through every cup and saucer and every gateau and bun in the place. I found myself glancing at our fellow diners apologetically. At my side, Harvey sat calmly listening and stirring her tea, clearly accustomed to her sister's abominable caterwauling.

She went on.

On… and on… and on.

'-and it was cropped and shaved to within an inch of its life, the poor hairless beast! I should have disqualified the wretched thing, not crowned it! Horrible day! Dog dirt all over the place, and there I was in open toed sandals. Anyhow, Summer is over - back to Christmas! I simply must leave by the twenty-seventh, Harvey. I have a coach trip setting off the next morning and I'll need to pack. I'll be seeing the New Year in at the Hilton in Torquay. Have you ever been to Torquay, Mr. Edgar?'

'No, I-'

'A tranquil repose if there ever was one. Very airy and calming. You should go, have a getaway from the grime of the city, get some fresh air. I venture to Torquay every year, and wouldn't miss it for the world.'

'I fear that I wouldn't survive the journey,' I put in with a very deliberate air of disapproval. 'The rabble you get on these coach trips-'

'Oh, it's worth enduring the sing-along on the coach to get there, Mr Edgar. We can't all travel by private black cab, you know!'

There was a pause as Miss Blake finally took a breath, and then she sent another thunderous question in my direction.

'Do you like pottery, Mr Edgar?'

I allowed myself the pleasure of a cool rebuff.

'Pottery? Not a jot.'

'Mmm. A pity.'

The woman refused to be perturbed by my tepid reception.

'Do you teach, Mr Edgar? I enjoy the craft and construction of the english language, and am kept extremely busy at our local Sunday School, and during summer holidays-'

'I fear that have better things to do with my weekends than to house-train rapscallions,' I put in smoothly.

At this, she lifted her chin.

'Quite so. One needs a commanding spirit for that line of work. Did my sister tell you that I am also a published author?'

'She did.' I replied darkly. 'Books for children, I believe? Hardly *Charlie Dickens* now, is it?'

She pretended not to hear this.

'Are you here with your wife, Mr Edgar?'

'I am no longer married,' I replied carefully.

'Do you have children, Mr Edgar?'

I replied in the negative.

'But still, you will have heard of my work, the *Sylvester The Fox* stories? No? You will have seen it, though. The Fox in the top hat? My dear friend Geoffrey Willoughby illustrates - you must have heard of him? No? He is an exquisite artist. Made his name with satirical sketches in The Messenger, but he illustrates beautifully, putting pictures to my words with a deft hand. They are very, very popular with the libraries. You *must* have come across them! *Sly Fox and the Brown Hen*? No? Oh, well. I suppose that you are hardly the demographic.'

She turned back to her sister.

'So, who are we this Christmas? The usual suspects?'

Harvey took her cue and went on to list our company. She paused before adding her ex-husband's name, and then did so with a detectable quiver in her tone. She was wise to be cautious. Petra Blake slammed down her teacup and glowered at her sister.

'Snakes alive! That cowering cretin? What the devil is he doing back in the picture?'

And so it began, a good ten minutes of huffing and puffing on Miss Blake's part with Harvey doing all she could to keep her cool, occasionally shooting me an apologetic sideward glance.

'Oh, my nerves! Have you completely lost your senses? That swarthy heartbreaker? That calculating cad? That parasitic worm? Why, Harvey? Why?'

I was relieved when Harvey suggested we make a move.

'I have half a mind to go on home!' grumbled Miss Blake as she got to her feet.

'Please, Pet. I need you - I want to get the family together, just for this-'

'Get the family together? *What family*?'

'Come along!' said Harvey after dropping some coins on

the table with a frown. Miss Blake opted to trade her loud tirade for the polar opposite, and hit us with an icy disapproving silence that was to last much of the journey to collect Harvey's beau.

Gideon Carter had been watching out for us, for no sooner had we pulled up outside a rather shabby looking block of flats, the front door opened and a man appeared, leather travel bag in hand.

Harvey's ex-husband had a bronzed tone to the skin that gave him the illusion of youth. I appraised him carefully. He had a rather cosmopolitan air, retaining a good head of dark wavy hair, as Mediterranean types do. He wore an impeccably well-tailored suit, but despite this the man was tieless and his top button undone, an intentionally casual manner of dress that only seemed to add to his appeal. His dark eyes sparkled as he acknowledged each of us through the glass, extending a particular gesture of controlled pleasure in Miss Blake's direction.

As he moved around the car to the rear passenger seat Harvey turned to her sister who was seated up front, her chest heaving in silent protest. She delivered a firm speech.

'Pet, I invited Gideon with good reason. Now please stay calm and try to be nice. What's past is past. If he can pretend to be pleased to see you, then the least you can do is return the effort.'

By this time, Carter was in the backseat beside me. Upon closer inspection I could see that his jaws hadn't seen a razor for some days, and noted a hip flask poking from his jacket pocket. He reeked of tobacco.

'Gideon! This is Mr Payton Edgar of the London Clarion - my very special guest.'

Petra Blake was sucking in her cheeks and glaring directly ahead as Carter engaged me in a tight, dry handshake. Harvey released the hand brake with a jolt and we moved on. Unsurprisingly, Miss Blake waited only a few minutes before she issued a curt enquiry, her dark tone dripping with disapproval.

'Does anyone mind if I open the window a crack? It *reeks* of foreigner in here.'

From the corner of my eye I saw Carter smirk at his reflection in the window.

And so we set off, as dark clouds gathered overhead.

Soon, delicate snowflakes began to tumble from the

clouds, and the closer we got to our destination, the thicker the snow became. The peaks of the South Downs were lost amongst the swirling white flakes, and I stared out over the scene from my place at the car window with something of a warm glow inside of me. It was Christmas Eve, and, even if I were to share it with strangers, it promised to be a Christmas of fine food and choice wine.

As I watched the snow fall, I considered the company I was to keep. My host was delightful, there was no doubt about that, but her coterie left something to be desired.

There was the swarthy ex-husband, the tweedy, clucking sister, the psychic housekeeper and her deranged son. There was also the queen of the society columns, the spiky and suspicious secretary, the boisterous idiot-chef and - last but most certainly not least - the daughter who had returned from the dead.

And here I was; the polished, debonair, and widely respected city restaurant critic.

I rested my head back in wonder.

Was I really to be the only *normal* person present?

Chapter III
In which Payton Edgar is a bastion of comfort to a troubled young girl

Dear Margaret,
I am terribly tired of my humdrum life. I have a dull job, a dull flat and a dull husband. I long to do something different. How can I put the sparkle back into my life?
Mrs Duke, Harrow

Margaret replies; *I have a few suggestions. Why not try to write a children's book? This laughably easy pastime can reap dividends for even the most unimaginative of souls. Or perhaps pottery? It is the simplest thing in the world to shape some clay into something and call it "Art". Or what about a coach trip to the coast? The type of people who do this may be uncomplicated folk, but at least it keeps simpletons off the street. A few good suggestions for you there, Mrs Duke.*

I found Arnold Prosper in the kitchen, up to his elbows in blood.

I had hesitated for only a few seconds outside the kitchen doors before knocking firmly and entering, unable to resist the temptation to discover what might be on our menu that evening.

The kitchen at Fallow House was pleasingly sterile and efficiently set, with a grand AGA and leaping stag figurines book-ending a cold, empty fireplace. Shining copper pots and utensils hung from two long rails on the far wall. In the centre of the room sat an island of cupboards with an impressive marble work surface on top, now covered in blood and discarded fur.

'Edgar.' Prosper grunted, pulling a strip of stringy flesh up in the air until it tore.

'Ah!' I said with a frisson of excitement, 'rabbit! Not robin, then?'

'Not rabbit either - hare. Like you've never tasted be-fore, I promise you. This one here danced in front of me like it just wanted to be eaten. Teasing, plump little thing.' He slammed the meat down on the counter, took up a cleaver and deftly took off a limb. 'Bagged a nice couple of partridge for tomorrow, too.'

'Delightful!'

'How were things in bonny Brighton?' he asked idly, cleaver in hand. I suspect that, by his tone, he wouldn't have cared if the place were ablaze and the streets littered with feral, bloodthirsty hounds.

'Very pleasant.' I replied, denying the truth somewhat. Harvey Blake's vile sister had rather soured the visit. 'The weather held.'

'Well I've had a bloody wonderful day. Your mate's a shooting star, in every sense of the word.'

'My *mate?*'

'Baxter - Queen Bee. Game old bird knows how to point a barrel. Nabbed the fattest of the partridge too, I'm ashamed to say. It was the perfect set up, lucky Prosper squeezed between two women.'

'*Two* women?'

'Had a bit of fun with that pretty young thing. Tried to teach her to shoot.'

It was not hard to guess to whom he referred. There was only one person present at Fallow House who could qualify for the title of *"young"*, let alone *"pretty"*. The image of Prosper moving in on poor pallid Maeve was an undesirable one. I pictured his arms around her shoulders as she reluctantly handled a rifle, itching to get away.

Prosper moved on to describe the rather more ferocious and unappealing aspects of game shooting. Within a minute I had stopped listening, my thoughts wandering to a plate of scones that sat under a mesh dome by the window. I stepped lightly over to them and danced the fingers of my left hand in the air.

'May I? There is some time until the dinner gong.'

Prosper shrugged abruptly.

'Take what you like, they're not mine. Made by old Mrs Turnip them lot, and tough as bricks probably. You really should save your sweet tooth for tonight, Edgar. Tonight we will have a real dessert.'

I swallowed my first mouthful of scone, which was indeed borderline-fresh and a tad leathery.

'Dessert? May I be permitted a clue?' There was a lengthy pause before I continued with caution. 'A fig or plum pudding, perhaps?'

'I have indeed created the worlds finest plum pudding, but that is for tomorrow, of course.'

'Brandy butter, custard or cream?'

'Brandy butter! What else!'

Mmm. Brandy butter!

'What then, for tonight? Chocolate would follow hare well, I imagine..?'

Prosper was having none of it. He was washing the blood from his hands at the sink and shaking his shiny head.

'You'll find out tonight, Edgar. Now get out my bloody kitchen!'

Before I could move I was arrested by the ominous sound of distant footsteps. Slow and shuffling, they came nearer, a noise lifted straight from the soundtrack to a Boris Karloff picture.

Tap, tap, tap.

The tinny beat echoed around the kitchen, there was a short pause and then it began again.

Tap, tap, tap

I was startled to see that what I had taken to be a wood panel upon the wall was in fact a sliding door. Arthur Lloyd appeared from the darkness within, clutching a sizeable pan of leafy, dirt-encrusted carrots. The old butler acknowledged my presence with a curt nod and the absence of a smile, and made his way to one of the work surfaces. I leaned in on the flapping panel and observed cold brick steps turning in a corkscrew fashion and leading down to darkness.

'Oh, a cellar!' I exclaimed to nobody in particular.

At that moment the kitchen door burst open and Harvey Blake leaned in, her tone abrupt with urgency.

'Quick! A glass of water now, Arthur! My sister is… unwell!'

I had been standing closest to the glasses and so I milked the tap and within a flash was spilling water onto my wrist and following my host out into the hallway.

Petra Blake was crumpled up on the telephone chair, huffing and puffing like a stuck horse. Beryl was, as usual, in the thick of the drama, crouched aside of the huffing horse with a concerned frown. Despite her breathlessness, Miss Blake fiercely waggled her arms, shooing away any suggestion of comfort.

'Do get back, don't crowd me so! Get back, woman!'

Beryl slunk back, her face a picture.

'You don't need to fuss! I am quite alright! I just-' Miss Blake drew in a deep breath and it was evident that she was not quite all right at all. Her cheeks were even more florid than usual. Harvey took the glass from my grasp and passed the water to her sister. It was received with little grace.

Behind us, Mr Lloyd disappeared back into the kitchen as if nothing were untoward. He was no doubt long since tired of drama from the eldest of the Blake sisters. She was waggling an accusatory finger up at her sister.

'You could have warned me - that g-girl!' she stammered before taking a sip. The glass was then thrust into the air. 'Urgh! What the devil is this? I don't want bloody water! I said gin!'

The glass was wavering in Beryl's direction. She took it brusquely and murmured something or other before making for the drawing room, shooting me a disapproving look as she passed by. Harvey's sister was making a lot of noise and fanning herself ineffectively with a limp hand, the other fist clutched tightly to her chest.

It was only then that I noticed young Maeve in the corner. She was cowering with her back against the wall, nestled in close to the coats by the grand doorway. She had the pallor of over-cooked pasta. But it was Miss Blake who demanded attention.

'Oh my nerves!' she wailed. 'I feel like a frayed piece of string!'

'I did warn you, Pet.' Harvey began uneasily. 'I tried to explain.' Her sister was glaring daggers at the poor young girl. She grasped an old red scarf and waved it in the air.

'Where did you get this, eh? This was Lottie's scarf!'

Maeve stammered, touching her neck where, apparently, the scarf had been ripped from. 'I just found it in the blanket box. I was cold...'

'It's not yours to wear!' Miss Blake snapped, turning to her sister. 'You are quite wrong, Harvey, she is nothing like her! Nothing like our Lotty! A superficial resemblance perhaps, but that sad specimen is far too vapid and scrawny. Unnatural! And evil, too! *Evil*, Harvey! I see spite in those smutty eyes! Goodness knows why you have her here. Get rid!'

Beryl reappeared with the gin and thrust it unceremoniously in Miss Blake's direction. She took it and downed a gulp, and we watched as she shifted to the edge of her seat, scowling at the poor young thing in amongst the coats.

'You are nothing like my niece, my girl! Merely a poor imitation!'

Maeve trembled in the corner, speechless, as the wailing woman went on.

'Why are you here? You aren't family! You aren't anybody at all! You are an abomination! An unnatural! Get out of this house, right now! You're not welcome here!'

'Petra! Please!' This appeal came from Harvey who stood firm, as cool and calm as she could.

'Is this what you meant about getting the family together?' Miss Blake turned and growled. 'First you bring that tobacco-stained rat back in to the fold, and now you make a stab at resurrecting your dead daughter? What are you thinking? That girl isn't family! You don't have a family anymore! Pull yourself together, and get rid of her. Immediately!'

It seemed to me that, somewhere in amongst the insults, Petra Blake did have a point. And then she undid any sympathy I may have felt by spitting poison in my direction.

'And you - bloodhound! Don't you think you can be writing any of this for your city rag! Why did you invite a hack, of all people, Harv?'

'Excuse me! I am not-'

But Miss Blake had downed her gin and was panting loudly for more. I drew myself up to my full height.

I can be a noble creature sometimes. Sometimes I even surprise myself - and I surprised myself a little again as I moved over to the girl and, with an unexpected stab of compassion, moved her away.

I could see Harvey's reasoning - there was something about Maeve that gave one the urge to take care of her, and I found myself doing just that.

'Come on, let's get away from this. Let's get some much needed fresh air,' I said with a gentle smile.

Outside the snow had eased but rolling grey clouds still filled the sky. A light dusting of white covered the ground, and we strolled down a crunchy gravel walkway, all too happy to get away from the commotion inside. The frosty air and the stillness of the gardens was a welcome change to the stuffiness of the big house.

'I'm alright, really' the girl lied. 'There's no need to look after me.'

'I know that, my dear. To be honest, I just wanted an excuse to get away from that ghastly woman. Besides, it's too delightfully wintery today to be bickering indoors. That offer of a sherbet lemon still stands.'

I pulled out the bag and we both took one.

'The lemon sherbet, the Rolls Royce of boiled sweets!' I announced. 'Tarter than a miserable pear drop, and more dignified than the tonsil ticklers and gobstoppers that are so unfathomably popular.'

'I like liquorice.'

'Oh, good heavens, no!'

We walked on along the garden path for a while, sucking our boiled sweets.

'I know that you didn't mean to upset Miss Blake,' I began, with something of a guess.

'No, I didn't,' the girl said eventually. Taking a deep breath I took on what I felt to be the appropriate stance.

'But, whatever your intention, you did cause upset. Do you understand why?'

She nodded, quickly following this with a weary shrug. We had stopped under the great oak which stood alone on the lawn, reaching upwards and outwards with a defiant grandeur. Maeve kicked gently at its gnarled roots and posed an unexpected question.

'Is it wrong to dislike a man of the cloth?'

'I'm sorry? Are you talking about the vicar?' What was the name Joan Turpin had used? *Drinkwater*?

'He is not a very nice man. But he's not the only one.'

She turned her eyes to mine.

'Do you hate anybody, Mr Edgar? I mean really, really *hate* somebody?'

Aunt Elizabeth immediately sprang to mind - but then I stopped myself. Did I really hate her? No. In fact, in all honesty, I had grown to rather admire the woman. She was headstrong and honest - qualities one could only admire. And then there was Rosemary, of course. Again, I promptly dismissed the thought. Time and distance had soothed the acrimonious feelings I had once had for my ex-wife. What was once a burning irritation had simmered to a mild distaste.

'Do I hate anybody? No. I really don't think I do. Not really. Hate is a very strong word. There are many *irritants* I could list, but none that I would say I truly hated. There is a particularly loathsome, waspish actor that comes to mind-'

'I think some people deserve to be hated,' said the girl, quietly childlike.

'Hate is a particularly destructive emotion, my dear. I really don't think a girl of your age should be hating anything!'

'Oh, I do. If a person has done terrible things, no matter how long ago. There is no going back.' Maeve stood at the foot of the tree, cuddling her elbows with pale hands. For the first time I noticed how ill-dressed she was for the biting air. I had been too keen to escape the melodrama of Petra Blake, and too distracted by my own thoughts to care.

And so I slipped off my jacket and put it around her shoulders. I would have to suffer the cold instead. My jacket looked huge on her tiny frame.

One would perhaps expect thanks, but none came.

'I will have to go soon,' the girl uttered weakly.

'Where to?'

No reply.

'Where will you go?'

'I don't know, but I will go as soon as Christmas is over. I shouldn't have come.'

My instincts told me this was probably for the best.

'Your parents must miss you,' I said all too quickly. The girl sniffled. Was she crying? I chided myself for my tactlessness - Harvey had said that the girl was an orphan.

Words did not come easy.

'Maeve, I am sorry if I have caused upset. Harvey told me that your parents-' I stopped myself. Why was it so hard to find the right words?

'My own mother died last year,' I said, simply.

She shot me a glance with clear watery eyes.

'My mother died too - at the end of the Summer.'

'Oh. That recently? I'm sorry to hear that.'

I allowed her some time to think.

'That's why I'm here,' she began tentatively. 'I came to, well-' Suddenly, she stopped, as if regretting her words. I gave my warmest smile. There was no doubt about it, I was getting somewhere - edging closer to the truth about Maeve Taylor. She sighed, and I waited for more. It didn't come.

But I wasn't about to give up.

'You are something of a mystery, Miss Taylor,' I said in my warmest tone. The girl blushed a little, and pushed the lemon sherbet into her cheek.

'Taylor isn't my real name. I picked it as the first thing that came into my head.'

'But why the need to lie?' I asked carefully. 'What is your real name? *Who are you?*'

This final question, simply put, was one that the entire household would be keen to know the answer to - and there I stood, asking it.

She bit her lip, and swallowed.

It was clear that she was about to tell me.

'Hie, Maeve! Mr Edgar!'

Harvey Blake came crunching down the pathway in our direction.

'I've bought your coat, Maeve!' she sang. She also had the red scarf that had once belonged to Charlotte Blake. 'You can have this too, never mind what Petra says.' My jacket was handed back and Harvey took over, clucking and preening over the young girl.

'Never mind Petra, she just likes to make a scene. She needs a little time alone, she'll come around. Come with me!'

Harvey took the girl away in the direction of the summerhouse. I watched them go and gave the roots of the oak a gentle kick myself. It was obvious that the girl held secrets, and I had just missed the perfect opportunity to discover them.

Turning back to the house I saw Beryl in a window, beckoning to me urgently. I trudged back up to the house.

'Blimey, Payton! This house is bonkers!'

Beryl and I had started chatting eagerly the minute my bedroom door was closed. She listened to the story of Charlotte Blake and my Brighton jaunt with rapt interest, shaking her head and chuckling at all the right moments. Beryl loved a drama.

'I agree with you about Harvey's frumpy sister, the vile Petra.'

'They couldn't be more different, could they? Strange how it works with siblings sometimes.'

Beryl tutted theatrically. 'It's not so unusual, Payton.

My sister and I are opposites in practically every respect.'

'You have *a sister,* Beryl?' I asked, quite shocked. She had never said.

'Yes, dear-heart! Old Bunty. Never bother to talk of her. She lives in a surprisingly luxurious converted piggery in Llandudno, and we are entirely different species. Like chalk and cheese!'

'Really?'

'And how! Bunty is a bossy madam if ever there was one. Outspoken, over confident. And the most atrocious man-hunter...'

'Like chalk and cheese.'

'Exactly. She's almost as bad as the vile Petra. Funny, I have seen a few of the *Sly Fox* books and thought them quite sweet. Well, not any more! That woman's a gasbag of the highest order. But never mind - where the is a minus, there will always be a plus.'

'Meaning?'

'The best Christmas present a girl could have - dear, dark Mr Gideon. Quite a dish! I have to start dressing for dinner immediately. I am dressing to impress!'

'May I remind you that he is engaged to be married, and to our host, no less?'

'Oh, Pooh! A minor detail,' Beryl replied dismissively. 'He is simply a dream. He smiled so sweetly at me when we met.'

'Even a rotting skull bears teeth, Beryl.'

'Not only that, he kissed my hand, Payton! *He kissed my hand*! I almost fainted on the spot!'

'Mmm,' I grizzled. 'Well, be careful. There's something odd going on with this lot.'

'I don't disagree, darling. The spirit of Harvey Blake's deceased daughter stalks the grounds, raised from the dead. The girl makes my skin crawl, floating through the place with her smutty eyes and alabaster skin. We have a Christmas ghost story, Payton!'

I shook my head. 'I don't find it at all amusing, Beryl. In fact, it concerns me. She talked a lot about hate and hating. What would a person have done to warrant this from a child? I may flatter myself, but I am sure that the girl was about to tell me everything out there on the lawn. She appeared here for a reason, and if I could just find out why... well, then I might be able to help.'

I was quite right. If I had learned the horrible truth in time, then I may have been able to prevent the terrible, violent murders that were to come.

But it was not to be.

Not until it was far too late.

Chapter IV
In which Payton Edgar is visited by the spirits of the dead

Dear Margaret,
My daughter is growing up too fast, and I am concerned about her morals. I fear that she is heading down the wrong path - she is only just eighteen, and is always out on the town. Her boots are becoming longer and her skirts shorter, and she slaps on make-up like it was warpaint. What can I do to get back the quiet little girl I once had?
Sad Mother, Uxbridge

Margaret replies; *you will never get back the quiet little girl you once had and it would be unnatural to do so. Were you not young once? I suspect that the more you agonise over her style choices the more she will resist your wishes. Why not join her, arm in arm, along her chosen path? Perhaps complement her enthusiastically on her make up or her long boots. You could even purchase a pair for yourself! You may find that the best way to turn the child down a different pathway is for you to offer your parental approval.*

And so our Christmas Eve feast was revealed to be oxtail soup, followed by the hare, with a chocolate and raspberry baked Alaska and a cheese plate to finish.

I was horrified to find that the soup was unexpectedly pedestrian for someone of Prosper's talents - the dish was as good as any oxtail I have ever tried, but could only be described as competent. Our company had already been served a splendid soup only the night before, and it was a sobering thought that the housekeeper's boy had produced a broth superior to that of London's own Arnold Prosper.

However, all was not lost - the hare was herb stuffed and roasted to perfection. Petra Blake gruffly complained that it was *"far too chewy"*, surely for no other reason than to grumble, as the meat was as good as any I had ever tasted. I said something along these lines, sending her into a dark-faced silence.

'Whaddyathink of the stuffing then, Mr Pink-Whistle?' Prosper gabbled, and it took me a moment before I realised he was talking to me.

'I beg your pardon?'

'Whaddyathink of the stuffing?'

'Oh, delicious, of course, and beautifully seasoned,' I replied in some confusion. Who was this Pink-Whistle fellow?

Prospers piggy eyes and shiny cheeks glistened over his wine glass at my approval. Harvey Blake went on to say a few nice words about the meal, and Prosper batted them back to her with a drunken guffaw and a faux military address.

'Fine, true words well chosen, Mr Blake, Sir!'

Harvey ignored his nonsense effortlessly and dabbed the corner of her mouth with a napkin.

Somehow, Beryl had bagged a seat next to Gideon Carter. Her emerald dress was one of her De-Groot favourites, and the wig of the evening was a magnificent silver affair, which rose a good ten inches from her scalp. Not unlike a fat snowman, it had bumps and hoops all around, with large rings of hair resting around her forehead. She missed no opportunity to flirt, be it sending a giggle in the air or resting a gentle hand on Carter's forearm. Harvey Blake watched this display with the same cool indifference she had given to Prosper's words. She really was the calmest, most unruffled person one could imagine. And yet she thought that the white-faced young girl in the red dress sitting opposite was somehow her daughter's spirit, arisen.

Sanity and fantasy. A curious mix.

In conversation over dinner, Gideon Carter turned out to be quite the charmer. He chatted openly about his experiences travelling around Europe and the more pleasurable experiences he had had during the war with the lads in his regiment.

His approach to the cuckoo in the nest, young Maeve Taylor, was just as Harvey had said; a blank disinterest. It was as if she wasn't there.

Over dinner the conversation had hovered chiefly between Carter, Harvey, Beryl and myself. Naturally, crumbly old Lloyd served the meal with a professional stony muteness, and Arnold Prosper barely took his lips from a glass in order to engage in any kind of debate. As the meal went on, his bravado ebbed and his words slurred as he became more and more pickled by glass after glass of red wine.

Petra Blake was sullen in her silence and spent much of her time snapping thin eyed glances over the table at the girl in the red dress. The girl remained meek and withdrawn throughout the meal. Miss Moore appeared to be a little bemused by the gathering, and she was clearly determined not to let Harvey's sister dictate the mood. Every now and then she would cajole Maeve into speaking, canvassing her opinion over one thing or another. She behaved almost like an elder sister to the girl.

'I do think music is so much more exciting these days, don't you, Maeve?'

'I quite like the hare but I'm just as partial to a lemon curd sandwich, aren't you, Maeve?'

'Must we talk about history? Who cares about dead people? I couldn't abide history at school, could you, Maeve?'

At the tail end of our main course I found myself caught up in an unwelcome discussion about Chinese cuisine. Here, Miss Blake irritatingly found her tongue.

'Well! I can certainly understand the likes of Alison and Mrs Turpin never having tried a Chinese meal before, Mr Edgar - but *you*? A food *expert*? *A restaurant critic*?'

'I make use of a Chinese laundromat, that is more than enough for me,' I replied dryly.

'But still - you are *supposed* to be a professional. And to miss out an entire cuisine!'

'Payton Edgar-' I replied firmly, '-does not eat with sticks.'

The baked Alaska arrived just in time. It was good enough - but no more than that. After dessert came the cheeses, which turned out to be the same disappointing selection as the previous evening, and I gave them a miss.

Prosper excused himself immediately after dessert. He loomed over the table, swaying.

'Another tremendous spread by yours truly - no need for the three cheers, party people. Tinkety-tonk and goodnight, all!'

And then he was gone, lumbering with heavy feet as he went. Throughout the meal I had pondered on the absence of Mrs Turpin, for we had been promised *"a turn"* that evening. What could it be? Cabaret?

I sincerely hoped not.

As I drained my coffee my curiosity was sated when Raymond Turpin entered the room and announced that *"Madame Turpin"* was ready for us.

The first response was from a blotchy-necked Miss Blake as she issued an elongated groan.

'Oh, no, no, no! Not Little Tommy Black again! That tired old routine? Do we have to?'

Harvey was the first to move, and she stood with a loud scraping of her chair.

'Yes you do, now come along, everybody follow Spud.' Harvey pulled her sister up by the wrist. 'You know how much Turpin adores this, and it's always good for a smile. I have guests to entertain! And besides-' she added through gritted teeth, '-you could do with a little light relief, Petra.'

To say that I was reluctant about all this would be an understatement. Parlour games are most certainly not my style, and I was thinking how I might excuse myself without offence when Gideon Carter spoke my thoughts out loud with a grunt.

'You know this isn't really my bag, Harvey. I think I'll stop here with the paper and finish this.' He waggled his pipe in the air, but Harvey was having none of it.

'No you won't, Giddy! Come along now! You know the drill - this is a family tradition! And you too, Mr Lloyd. Pip pip!'

The butler gave no resistance and merely drifted from the room with a sombre shuffle. Beryl and I found ourselves herded from the table and we followed our enthusiastic hostess out of the dining room in quiet resignation.

The drawing room was candlelit and smoky with a heady, almost unbearable scent of patchouli in the air.

Someone had pulled a round kitchen table through into the centre of the room and covered it with a voluptuous purple velvet tablecloth. Blobs of dried wax dotted the fabric. Around us, countless candles and several incense sticks were positioned about the room. At the head of the table sat Joan Turpin, barely recognisable in a winding green turban and huge glistening hoop earrings. She looked ridiculous, but her pale and pasty face was set in stone.

'Be seated.' she boomed, and I struggled to resist the desire to chuckle. Thankfully, Miss Moore followed my lead.

'Oh, Joan. You look like a maharaja's plaything!'

'Alison, shh!' spat Harvey with a mock outrage. She turned to face me, and spoke with pride. 'You are one of the privileged few to witness this spectacle. Joan has been doing this for so many years now, she's practically a legend.'

'A party trick?' I whispered.

'It's much more than a party trick. Joan has *a gift.*'

Maeve Taylor spoke up, rather seriously. 'Madam Turpin has read my tarot, Mr Edgar. She does certainly have a gift.'

Harvey patted a chair playfully. 'Sit by me!'

If Joan Turpin had any connection to the spirit world it was surely that of a tot of mother's ruin, than of the supernatural variety. Her wrinkled fingers shook a little as she spread them wide on the table and took in a long, loud, deep breath. Behind her I caught sight of Raymond's pale round face in the darkness of the corner, his expression every bit as serious as his mother's. He moved forward out of the shadows, placed a pack of cards before her and then sat in the empty chair to her right.

The candlelit faces around the table watched on with a notable lack of anticipation, apart from Harvey who was faithful to her role as host, beaming and exclaiming when necessary. Glancing over my shoulder I noted Gideon Carter had managed to sit outside of our circle and was lounging back in an armchair, his smoking pipe in his hand.

'We will now form a circle. Link pinks!' Joan Turpin bellowed, and I found myself joining in as we all linked our little fingers. Harvey cast me a sly smile as she hooked her painted digit in mine. To my right, Miss Moore somewhat reluctantly did the same. I felt a very British pang of discomfort at this unnecessary contact. Across the table, Beryl giggled a little, caught herself and cleared her throat.

Mrs Turpin took up a chant.

'Spirit world, we are open to you. Spirit world we beckon you. To your lost souls… those that cry and yearn for peace. Spirit world we are open to you. Spirit world speak through me… *for truth… for love… for peace*!'

There was almost a full minute of silence. I could hear Carter shuffling in his stiff chair behind us.

'Hands flat on table now, please.' Joan Turpin instructed. Sixteen hands unlinked and rested around the table top. Mr Lloyd cleared his throat. Maeve Taylor's eyes were set on the table top. She had an unusually dark expression on her face, and was concentrating hard. From the corner of my eye I saw Petra Blake take a large swig of her drink surreptitiously in the darkness. Across the table, Mrs Turpin's mouth twitched a little.

She spoke softly and with an unwavering urgency.

'Tommy, are you there? Are you there, Tommy? Tommy, are you there? Come to me, Tommy. *Tommy?*'

The candles fizzled in the darkness, spitting wildly for a second. Mrs Turpin made a declaration.

'Yes! There you are. Tommy Black is with us once again. Hello Tommy! Poor little Tommy... my faithful guide. Tommy was just a boy when he passed, weren't you, Tommy?'

Miss Blake issued forth an indignant grunt. Undeterred, Turpin continued.

'Yes, Tommy, we know you fell down the coal mine. We know. So dark, the coal mine... so dark. You poor little thing, your time ended too soon!'

At these words, a curious thing happened - the unmistakable stench of coal filled the air. The dirty, smoky scent wafted throughout the room, and in spite of everything, I stiffened in my seat.

The old fireplace contained only smouldering logs.

'Now, Tommy, who have you got for us tonight? Spirits come forth to Little Tommy Black! Come forth!' Madame Turpin had raised her voice to a hollering crescendo, and then she softened once more.

'A woman has stepped forth. An *older* woman! Come forwards, my dear - come closer!' The housekeeper breathed deeply in and out of pinched nostrils. 'This poor soul has not long passed over. Barely a year! She has a message for one of us. A message for... for our guest, *Mr Edgar*!'

There was a sporting gasp from the circle and I felt all eyes turn in my direction. I merely pursed my lips. The charade was already beyond ridiculous, even if that inexplicable potent scent of coal had been a little unnerving.

'Who might this be, Mr Edgar?' Turpin sang over the table. 'Was there a woman in your life who has not long passed?'

I set my hands more firmly on the table top.

'No.'

'Mmm. No woman in your life?'

'No.'

A woman from your past? A family member?'

'Only my ex-wife, and she is - for better or worse - very much alive.' I was pleased to hear snorts and guffaws from Carter and Beryl, but felt Harvey straighten with reproach beside me. Turpin persisted.

'She knows you very well, Mr Edgar, this older woman. The bond is strong.'

'Sorry,' I said sternly with a growing obstinacy that was quite enjoyable. I would not budge on this one. 'No clue. Move on?'

The ridiculous woman was no more a clairvoyant than I was a bus conductor. Had Harvey not piped up at this point I would have escaped the limelight, and with relish.

'Why, Payton, didn't you tell me in Brighton that your Mother passed on, only last year?'

I sucked in my cheeks as Turpin leapt on this revelation. I had also told Maeve this fact just that afternoon, and so there was plenty of opportunity for Turpin to have learned this and used it to her advantage.

'A mother! Of course, why didn't I see it? Yes, a mother, here for her son. The bond is indeed strong.'

I said nothing. Our bond had been no stronger than a soggy cardboard box.

'She is crying, your mother. She weeps for you.'

The woman never wept for me when alive, and so I was sure that she would never bother in death. I remained mute.

'She wants you to know that she loves you. She is sorry for the dreadful secret she took to her grave.'

I waited.

'She is sorry for her lies, Mr Edgar. And one, great lie burdens her in particular. Does that mean anything to you?'

'No,' I replied coldly.

'A terrible family secret! One day, you will know. And there is more… she is worried, Mr Edgar. You have lost something!'

Yes. My respect for each and every person around this table.

'I am seeing an object… what is it? An umbrella? No, an umbrella stand! She asks you to look in the umbrella stand. *Fortune lies in the umbrella stand!* Do you have an umbrella stand?

'Of course I do!' I replied with a snap.

'Well, you must look! When you get home, you must look in the umbrella stand.'

Fortune lies in the umbrella stand? Preposterous tosh!

'Look in your umbrella stand. You must!'

I sensed Harvey's commanding presence beside me. She did not need to speak.

'I will.' I croaked, exchanging looks with Petra Blake.

She was enjoying watching me squirm. Thankfully, Joan Turpin moved on.

'Oh, spirit world, slow down! One at a time! Oh dear me! There is a great unrest tonight! A great unrest indeed! Come forth! Come forth!'

As the candles flickered wildly, Turpin wet her lips and leaned forward, her eyes closed.

'There is a dark, dark spirit present.' she said gravely.

Rather appropriately at this point, each candle in the room fizzled and spat as if a window had just been opened sending a breeze about the room. As the candles fizzed Miss Moore gasped and clutched her fist to her neck. It was hard to tell if she was joking, or genuinely moved.

As she returned her hand to the table, the candles settled and Mrs Turpin continued.

'The dark spirit is sad. So sad. He wishes us to know this. He knows one of us very well, and wants us to know that he is sad. He misses his brother. His strong, handsome, older brother. He wants you to know this... *Mr Carter.*'

Almost before she spoke his name Carter was up on his feet and grunting in anger, clearly aware of what was coming. He turned to make for the door, but did not take any steps. Joan Turpin raised her chest and her voice to the room.

'He is happy for you, Mr Carter. Happy for you, but so sad too. He needs you to know that. He wants you to live your dream, Mr Carter. To do what he didn't get the chance to do.'

'Utter pap, Turpin!' spat Carter.

I caught a flicker of hurt cast over the housekeeper's face before she set her jaw and spoke again.

'Do not be afraid, he is telling me. Do not be afraid, it will all be alright.'

Exactly what *it* was, and whether it really would be alright or not we were never to find out as Maeve Taylor suddenly and violently let out a loud, throaty scream.

We all jumped in our seats.

Maeve slammed her hands down with a thud, sending a glass spinning off of the table. As the glass shattered with a crash at our feet, the girl stared blankly ahead, her eyes wide.

Around us, the candles fizzled and danced.

The candlelight gave the girl's hollow cheeks a gauntness of skeletal proportions. Her hair had fallen from her shoulders to hang long and limp down the sides of her head, and a low, drawn-out wail came from her mouth; a noise like I have never heard before. The guttural moan drowned out any cries of shock that arose from the assembly. It seemed like the girl should surely need to stop and breathe, the noise was long, loud and low.

Her pupils had disappeared under her eyelids, and her nails clawed at the velvet tablecloth.

When the girl did take a breath in it was just as loud and just as long, a deep gasp as if the poor thing were unable to fill her lungs quickly enough. As this died away I heard sobs from Joan Turpin across the table. She had raised a wrinkled hand up to her cheek, her heavily mascaraed eyes now wide open and fixed on the girl. The look on her face was one of naked horror.

'*Please! Help me!*' Maeve, cried out in a high strangled tone.

Nobody moved.

'Mummy! It's me! Charlotte! Mother! Can you help me?'

Charlotte.

All hands had been pulled back from the table, and a wave of panic shook the room, with sharp gasps and the scraping of chair legs. Raymond Turpin was clutching his mothers arm, his chest heaving. Beside me, Harvey Blake gave an odd choke, struggling to speak.

'Mummy, it's me! Charlotte!'

'Charlotte?' whispered Harvey.

The name hung in the tense darkness.

Charlotte.

'It's so cold, Mummy. So cold.'

'Charlotte?'

'I can't breathe, Mummy. It's so cold, and dark. I can't breathe!'

'Charlotte?'

My heart was pounding as Harvey reached out hopelessly to the young girl who sat rigid, clawing at the table top, tears patterning her cheeks.

'Charlotte!'

'He's got me, Mummy. My head! I can't move my head! I can't breathe! I can't breathe! Why is he doing this? His hands are so tight on my head, holding me down in the water, I-' the girl began to choke in one great lungful after another of strangled air.

Harvey cried out wildly.

Across the table, Raymond Turpin let go of his mother and ran from the room. Petra Blake stood, pale faced, and moved from her place at the table back into the shadows. Beryl had lifted her hands to cover her mouth. Mrs Turpin appeared to gather herself, and drew a deep breath as she moved tentatively over to the young girl. She placed her hands carefully on the girl's shoulders.

'I can't breathe, Mummy. The water's… so cold. Daddy's hands on my head… Daddy's hands… so heavy. I can't… I can't…'

Maeve was weakening, her shoulders slumped and she lowered her head to the table. Mrs Turpin leaned in and clasped the girl to her bosom. Maeve's eyes were closed, her erratic sobbing slowly easing.

Harvey had her eyes set on the girl in disbelief.

Suddenly the lights were snapped on.

We all blinked, illuminated.

At the light switch stood Gideon Carter, an unyielding look of fury on his dark face. I noticed another empty chair at the table and looked up to see Mr Lloyd standing aside the drinks cabinet, retreating to his servants position as an act of solace. His expression was, as usual, unreadable.

Maeve's shoulders had fallen, her palms upwards, her lank black hair almost covering her face.

'What - what happened?' she stammered.

As if a performance had ended, Petra Blake swept across the room and passed out of the door without a word. Miss Moore remained in her place at the table, a baffled look on her pointed face. Nobody spoke for a minute. Harvey had crumpled beside me.

It clearly fell to an outsider to take charge.

'Mrs Turpin, I - I think you should help Miss Taylor to bed,' I said uneasily. Joan Turpin nodded curtly before pulling up the girl and ushering her from the room.

Gideon Carter had stepped out of the way to let them pass, his thin, angry eyes following Maeve all the way. After the door had closed he stepped over and laid his hand on Harvey Blake's shoulder. This was shrugged off with a violence that caught us all by surprise.

'Get off me, Gideon!' Harvey wailed, shaking off his touch. It was her turn to leap up and storm from the room.

Carter lingered in place with a simmering anger. For a moment I thought he would say something, but instead he turned and followed out the door with a defiant steadiness to his step. Suddenly the room felt still and calm, like a storm had just blown away in an instant. At the table, Miss Moore avoided my eye, her gaze fixed on the tablecloth. Beryl was picking at her wig mindlessly. Mr Lloyd began to clear glasses away, slowly but methodically as if it were the end of any usual evening of entertainment.

A cloud of smoke crept across the table from where Carter's pipe sat in the ashtray, burning down silently. I followed the movement of the smoke and gave a start. We were being watched!

Outside in the darkness of the night, a white face peered in through the window - an unfamiliar face. My heart jumped. The white, bony mask was that of an older gentleman with pin-prick eyes and a long frown. Long strands of grey hair swept from his crown to his neck. The stranger looked down in contemplation, before vanishing backwards into the darkness.

'Beryl - at the window!' I breathed. I lifted a pointed finger, but by the time she took my meaning, the face had gone.

'What is it?'

'A face at the window.'

She got up and and went to the window in her no-nonsense way, craning her neck to look left and then right.

'Nobody there. Just snow. Lots of snow.'

'There was… someone,' I said firmly.

'Another restless spirit?' said Beryl with the merest hint of amusement.

I was lost for words.

Chapter V
In which Payton Edgar receives a night visitor

Dear Margaret,
My mother is haunting our guest room. She died
from lung problems, and although neither I nor my husband
smoke, we can often smell tobacco coming from the room
where she died. On top of that, some of her old ornaments
move about the room, or disappear altogether. My husband
wants to move out, but I love our house. What can I do?
Annabel, Ealing Common

Margaret replies; *what nonsense! I'm sure if ghosts did exist*
(and they don't) then they would have better things to do than
smoke ghost cigarettes and move nicknacks around a room. The
obvious fact is that your husband chooses to have a crafty puff
and blame this on your dead mother. I suspect that he is also
guilty of getting rid of the more unattractive of her ornaments,
and moving trinkets about in the hope that you will be spooked
into buying a better property - somewhere less drab and dreary
than Ealing Common, no doubt.

The night before Christmas had been a restless one.
It was a half-past one in the morning and I was wide
awake, mulling over Maeve Taylor's strange performance at the
seance. It wasn't so much the fact that she had pretended to be
consumed by the spirit of Harvey Blake's dead daughter that disturbed, but what her words had *implied*.
Murder.
I had found myself giving in to my restlessness and
plunging into some Margaret Blythe correspondence. I was just
signing off on a letter when there was a sharp knock at my door.
I jumped and began to pull my papers together.
'Just a minute!'
The door opened and Harvey Blake entered the room in
a shiny blue silk dressing gown tied hurriedly at the waist.
'Hang on!' I grumbled, hastily shoving my papers into a
file.
'Oh, I thought you said come in!'
'I said hang on!' I replied, turning my back to my host
and pushing files into my briefcase. It would do no good for

anyone to learn that I was Margaret Blythe, especially not my fabulous host. I turned to face her and forced a smile.

'Mr Edgar, I am so sorry to disturb you at this hour,' she began uneasily, 'I saw the light on under your door. I simply couldn't sleep...'

'Neither could I,' I interjected, intending to ease some of her concern. My words, however, did not have had the desired effect.

'That is what I was afraid of. I came to say that I'm sorry. We all made silly fools of ourselves after dinner, and I wanted to apologise - to you in particular.'

'A-apologise to me?' I stammered.

'For what happened tonight - all so unnecessary. A silly trick that just got out of hand. I didn't invite you here to witness this kind of behaviour, Mr Edgar. It is not our usual way and I promise you that there will be no more drama.'

'Well, it was indeed an unsettling thing. And quite unnecessary, I agree.'

'I know. Ridiculous, really. Mrs Turpin always wheels out Tommy Black, every year - rubbing charcoal a centimetre down each incense stick to give us the smell of the coal mines, and injecting water into certain points of the candles so they fizzle...'

So *that's* how it was done!

'It's the same each year. But normally it's just a bit of fun, with silly predictions like finding a fortune in your umbrella stand. It has always been a bit of entertainment, no matter how seriously Joan might take it.' She sighed. 'It stopped being fun tonight. What Maeve said...' Her words trailed away.

What Maeve had said! She had said that strong hands held Charlotte Blake under the water all those years ago. She had said, in no uncertain terms, that Charlotte Blake's death was murder, and she had pointed the finger at her father. I didn't need to repeat this out loud, we both knew it.

Harvey was looking at me with an urgency in her eyes.

'What Miss Taylor said and did was just as much rubbish as what came from Joan, and I want you to ignore it. I will deal with her. I know what she was implying, but my daughter drowned in a terrible accident. *An accident.* We have always known that. Whatever was said tonight doesn't change that.'

'But why would she-?'

'I don't know, Mr. Edgar, I really don't. But I will find

out. And that is my business. I just wanted to say that I am sorry you had to witness it, and we will have no more silliness from now on.'

She made for the door, but stopped at the dressing table where I had placed the gift of cigars for businessman Harvey Blake. She reached out and touched the paper.

'Of course, we mustn't forget that it's Christmas.' She fingered the bow and tag. 'Oh - a gift for me! You really shouldn't have. I shall pop it under the tree with the others. Thank you, Payton.'

With that, and a rather forced smile, she left the room before I could protest.

I switched on my bedside lamp, turned off the main light, and stood in the gloom of the room for a little. I found myself guided to the light coming through a crack in my curtains. It was snowing very heavily outside. I watched the flakes twist and tumble hauntingly from the black sky. Suddenly, something caught my eye, as torchlight cut through the shadows down to my right.

Someone was moving through the darkness outside.

The torchlight guided its bearer along the uneven pathway and up to the house. The light was extinguished as the bearer approached the house, but I managed to catch a brief glimpse of the lacquered hair and pale face of Arthur Lloyd before he vanished into the building. Yet another prowler in the gardens. What was going on in this crazy place - with restless spirits, accusations of murder and shadowy men stalking the grounds?

Where had the butler been at this hour?

This fresh mystery did little to ease me to my slumber. Nevertheless, I put myself to bed, and stared at the ceiling for some time. As a young boy, Christmas Eve had always felt magical, full of anticipation and a kind of muted joy - no matter how disappointing my Christmas Days had always turned out to be.

But now, all grown up, and after the strangeness of the day, I felt no joyful anticipation whatsoever. I simply felt uneasy and concerned for what was to come.

It felt as if a storm were brewing.

And I was right.

By breakfast we had a dead body on our hands.

Part Three
Christmas Day

Chapter I
In which Payton Edgar meets an old adversary

Dear Margaret,
Two years ago I was cursed by a gypsy and have been ridiculously accident-prone ever since. Last year I spent much of my time in hospital after being knocked from my bike by passing cars on three separate occasions. Everything I touch seems to break and my arms are covered with cuts and bruises. My wife is tired of patching me up, and calls me accident prone, but I know that it's more than that. What can I do to break this curse?
Kenneth, Ealing

Margaret replies; what on earth did you do wrong to receive a gypsy curse? What utter nonsense! You are nothing more than a clumsy and blundering fool, and searching for excuses for your incompetence helps no one. It sounds to me as though you are a liability on a bicycle and so you should keep off of the roads entirely. Your wife is quite right, and if she has any sense she will be hoping that the next inevitable accident you have proves fatal so that she can get some peace and quiet away from you and your idiotic misadventures.

Christmas Day.
After a fitful sleep I left the warmth of my sheets and pulled on my dressing gown before opening the heavy curtains. The early morning light outside was a surprise to tired eyes; the sky was bleached white and the ground matched it. A good many inches of snow had fallen. The stillness of the scene was arresting, and I watched over this picture-postcard winter wonderland for some time.

I then attended to my toilet in something of a dream. I had already selected my best shirt and silver holly leaf cufflinks, and pondered for a moment over my suits - should it be the duck-egg tweed or the cobalt blue? Eventually I plumped for the cobalt, and then found myself at the mirror where I ran a comb through my remaining hairs distractedly.

My head was full of questions.
The performance at the seance by young Maeve was

troubling - it had been so odd. Very strange indeed.

What had the girl been playing at?

However convincing the production had been, I was in no doubt that there was no such thing as a spirit world, and certainly not one that would channel an impressionable child and force her to spout accusations of murder. The unpleasant scene had ruined the evening, and I felt a curious flicker of anger towards the girl.

It had been an odd night all round. I recalled the men I had seen stalking the gardens. I had witnessed the butler moving by torchlight in the dead of the night, and before that the strange white face at the window after dinner. Who was that man? It was the face of an older gent, but surely too young to be the ancient Brigadier, who reportedly never left his attic room. So who was it?

I rubbed at my eyes, hoping to revive my thoughts.

It was a little after eight o'clock when I descended the staircase, only to find each room downstairs devoid of life except - much to my distaste - for the long haired mutt. The dog danced around me playfully as I pulled my hands up close to my chest. I did what I could to shake it off, but without success.

In the drawing room, the table stood where it had been placed for the ridiculous seance the night before, but somebody, most probably Mr Lloyd, had seen fit to remove the tablecloth and candles and place a spotty pot with an erupting poinsettia in the centre, as if to exorcise unwanted dark spirits.

The dog followed with excitement as I moved on to the kitchen. The idea of a hairy, flea-ridden creature around clean kitchen surfaces was unappealing to say the least. It followed me in eagerly, nevertheless.

I was vexed to find no help available. Nobody had seen fit to rise early and prepare what was needed for Christmas Day morning. I should have been greeted by hot tea and cereal followed by fried eggs, tomatoes, sausage, bacon, baked beans, fried bread and perhaps black pudding, kedgeree or bubble and squeak, all rounded off with buttered toast and marmalade and a final swig of tea. To my extreme disappointment, there was no food in sight and I was forced to help myself to a glass of cold milk from the fridge.

Eventually, the dog lost interest and padded away after finally taking the hint that I wasn't about to attend to it in any way.

I took my drink over to the cool Aga, where I mindlessly examined the ironworks. Brass ivy adorned the rather simple fireplace. Atop the old mantle on the near side stood yet another brass figurine of a single leaping stag. These figurines were present throughout the house, bookending every fireplace. This stag's antlers were dark and it had not been polished for some time. In the opposite position there was a noticeable space – the creature was missing a mate on the far left.

There was a plop as the kitchen door swung shut and I turned to see Alison Moore standing hesitantly in a silk quilted housecoat. She pulled up a tight, forced smile.

'Merry Christmas, Mr Edgar.'

'Merry Christmas,' I replied.

Looking back to the window I heard the chink of glasses and the pull of the refrigerator as she helped herself to a drink. There was a moment in which we probably mulled over similar things - whether to exchange banal festive pleasantries or whether to acknowledge the events of the night before with caution. In the end it seemed that neither of us wanted to speak, and Miss Moore would probably have slipped out of the room had Prosper not burst through the doors in his usual clumsy way.

'Good morning, Mr Pink-Whistle!' he sang.

Just who was this Pink-Whistle chap?

Without awaiting a reply he greeted the woman at the fridge by placing a hairy hand against her hip with a rub and a growl. Miss Moore stepped quickly away, her nostrils flaring.

'You can stop that straight away, Prosper,' she snorted. 'If you want to keep that hand.'

I adopted my most disapproving glare, but the man simply laughed and matched my glare with a defiant nod.

'What's wrong with you? Fancy it for yourself, did you? So... what time did you lot get to bed last night?' He asked this with little interest as he filled a glass with water.

'Later than you,' Miss Moore said sharply.

'Aha!' the man boomed proudly, 'Not so! Had a quick kip, then I picked myself up, got out and went and had some fun!'

'Fun?' Miss Moore echoed, as if it were a dirty word.

What sort of fun was there to be had in the middle of the night around Fallow House?

'So how was the after dinner entertainment, then, Miss Moorish? Did the old bag get her turban on again? Restless spirits aligning under the sign of capricorn, yet again?'

Prosper failed to notice that our silence was a difficult one, and coughed up a throaty chuckle. 'Ah, reckon I got out at just the right time.'

'Yes, I think you did.' Miss Moore mewed, and we exchanged glances with an air of conspiracy. She turned back to the chef. 'Where is the food, Prosper? Not a hot sausage in sight!'

Prosper grunted. 'I don't do breakfast! You should know that.'

It was at that moment that the back door of the kitchen burst open with a crash and Raymond Turpin entered with a feral cry.

His usual gormless expression had been replaced by one of horror, his mouth open wide as he gasped for breath. Water gathered in drips on the lino at his feet. The fear in his eyes was chilling.

We had all started a little at this soggy interruption.

'Good God, Spud!' Miss Moore exclaimed. "What's up?'

'It's happened again!' he cried, 'Murder! Murder in the river!' He panted a little, and gathered his breath.

'It's happened again!'

The girl was face down in the water, her arms outstretched.

She wore a thick housecoat over a pale cream nightgown, which billowed and folded gently over itself in the pull of the river. As the icy water flowed around her, the back of her head broke the surface like a crimson island in the current. The exposed crown was matted with dark blood. Her long black hair was pulled by the current, the red scarf reaching from her neck and flowing along with it. Beneath the nightgown two thin, pale legs disappeared into the murky black water. Thick strands of green weed reached up from the riverbed to twist around her ankles.

Maeve Taylor floated just an arms length from the edge of the deep river.

I was one of the first on the scene, and had lingered as others came and went. Raymond Turpin had been dragged away to the gate house by his mother. I have never before seen a human being quite so distraught, the poor man had been shaking violently from the freezing cold and the shock of it all.

Shortly after that, Miss Moore had persuaded a stunned and silent Harvey Blake to return to the house. Gideon Carter was conspicuous in his absence, although I saw a shadow in an upper window of Fallow House that I took to be him.

Beryl eventually joined me at the riverside and, after looking down on the girl in a respectful silence for a while, I could contain myself no longer.

'Finally dragged yourself out of your pit, Beryl?'

'Meaning?'

'It is almost mid-morning and I can still see the pillow marks on your face!'

'A girl is dead and you want to tell me off for over-sleeping?'

'Yes, I do. I could have done with you earlier.'

'I don't see the point of early rising, dear-heart.'

'The early bird catches the worm, Beryl.'

'Exactly. Who wants *worms*?'

We fell silent for a moment, and then she leaned in closer and whispered urgently.

'Oh, Payton, I feel like tinsel in a bag of string!'

'I beg your pardon?'

She opened her fox-fur coat with a frown. She had made quite an effort for Christmas; her dress was a very red affair, with a large, firm green sparkling collar and glistening holly leaf broach. Her wig was a chestnut bob with matching holly leaf clips.

'A murder scene is hardly the place for Coco Chanel and a cheeky wig, is it? Do you think I should change?'

'Perhaps,' I replied diplomatically.

And off she went.

I considered my attire for a moment, and concluded that I had made the right decision with the cobalt blue - the lighter duck egg tweed could have been seen as frivolous, given the circumstances.

When the police finally arrived, I was standing in the snow between Arnold Prosper and Mr Lloyd, each of us frowning down at the corpse as if we were workmen inspecting some dissatisfactory piece of shoddy plastering.

First, two officers came down to the river where, after glaring down at the corpse for a moment, one fumbled clumsily

with some photographic equipment and the other, a stout little
man, ploughed through the snow along the sides of the river. As
we watched, we failed to see a third officer approach our little
group.

'Out of the way please, gentlemen!'

A short, solid man with a violent moustache and long,
bushy sideburns limped past. He wore a drab mackintosh and
leaned heavily a stick. As he peered back at us with an air of
official suspicion my heart gave a sharp jump of surprise - which
was swiftly followed by acute irritation.

I had met the man before.

'Inspector!' I exclaimed before I could stop myself. The
inspector appraised me with small wary eyes. His uncultivated
eyebrows raised high in what I took to be bemused disbelief.

'Good grief! It's you - *Mr*-?'

He knew my name only too well!

'Edgar. Payton Edgar,' I pushed out a smile, before returning his mischief with one of my own.

'And you are Inspector-? *What was it*?'

'I'll have to move you along, Gents, please!' he went on,
pointedly ignoring my question. I peered unhappily at the man.
Inspector Albert Standing was an imbecile - a truly terrible ad-
vert for the British constabulary. If he was to be in charge of this
particularly blood-soaked murder then I feared for the outcome.

The portly uniformed constable approached Standing,
panting like a whippet at the races.

'Bad news, I'm afraid, Sir. Mr Hermann definitely can't
make it today.'

'Damn! We're on our own then. This is the worst -
simply *the worst* day for this kind of thing!'

'Hermann?' I enquired idly.

'Nathaniel Hermann, our pathologist,' replied the inspector wearily. 'We really are a skeleton crew. Blasted Christmas!'

'What on Earth do you need a pathologist for?' I asked.
The inspector huffed.

'To verify time of death, cause of death...'

I went on, only too happy to interrupt.

'Well, given that the girl was sitting up with us in the
drawing room until late last night and her body discovered first
thing this morning, I can pretty much tell you when she died.
And that bloody mess our killer's made of her head rather gives
away how she died-'

'Yes, thank you, Mr Edgar. There is rather more to it, you know. More than a lay person such as yourself would understand.' Standing turned to the constable. 'Tell me you found something on your search, Whitby!'

His subordinate sighed.

'Looks like there's nothing near the water on this side, Sir. My bet is it was tossed into the river. Something must have sunk deep. Don't know what did it. Bashed in good, she is.'

'Yes, thank you, Whitby. We'll have to scout the far bank, then. But not until we fish her out. Tell Jacobs that when he's finally finished messing about with the camera he'll have to get on the rubbers. He'll need you to help him, and then after that, get yourself over to the far bank.' The inspector shooed the young officer away, but he only took a few steps away and loitered with a look of curiosity. Standing stepped closer to our little gathering with a frown.   'I'll have to move you along now, Gents, please. This is a crime scene. Are you all staying up at the house? In that case, have to take your names, we'll have a little chat in a minute or two.' A pencil and pad appeared and Standing pointed the pencil at the closest man.

'Arthur Lloyd, butler. I have been in service for the Blake household for-'

Standing grunted with a wave of a hand. 'As I have just said, and quite clearly, names only, please. Details later!' His brusqueness must have irritated the old butler although - inevitably - it did not show on his face. I, on the other hand, was only too happy to issue a critical glare. The man's approach was irksome in the extreme. How on earth did he get any results in his investigations? His manner only encouraged one to clam up with disfavour.

'Prosper. Arnold Prosper.'

The chef was waved aside, and the pencil pointed in my direction. I allowed a telling pause, as Standing looked at me with those glistening, piggy eyes.

'Need I repeat myself? *Payton Edgar*. I cannot recall your name, Inspector-?' I gave the man my coolest stare. He replied in a clipped, unquestioning manner with more than a hint of boredom in his tone.

'Inspector Albert Standing.'

'From Scotland Yard!' Whitby put in enthusiastically and with a twinkle in his eye.

'Yes, thank you, Whitby!' said Standing with an impatient grunt. 'If you can help Jacobs with his rubbers and then get over to the far bank, now please. There has to be something somewhere, despite all this snow.'

Constable Whitby trotted away.

'So you work on Christmas Day, Inspector?' I asked pointedly.

'Regrettably so,' he grumbled. 'Crime cares not what day it is.'

'And you are down in the countryside now?' I went on. 'Out in the sticks!'

If my words irritated he did not show it.

'For a time, yes. After sustaining my rather nasty injury in the line of duty I have re-allocated. As you know full well, Mr Edgar, I was shot and badly wounded.' He brandished his stick with something that may even have been pride.

'I will never forget,' I replied stiffly.

'I bet you won't. And neither will I.' At this, the inspector leaned in ominously. 'I certainly will never forget that you had a heavy hand in that particular affair, Edgar.'

I adopted my most innocent tone.

'I rather think you chose to step in front of a bullet, Inspector. You cannot hold me accountable for your own actions.'

'Mmm. Well the idea was for a bit of peaceful recuperation in the calm of the countryside. And now this!'

The insufferable twerp was looking at me as if it were all my doing. He really was an irritant of the highest order - and it was obvious that his pathetic injury had only made him more so. How did he expect to tease out information from his suspects with the approach of a grunting bull?

He was blethering on about responsibility when he stopped himself. 'Look, I can't be standing here explaining myself to the likes of you! Just move along please, gents. It's Christmas Day and we all have homes to go to.' He cleared his throat noisily.

'I fully expect to get this matter cleared up by teatime.'

Chapter II
In which Payton Edgar demonstrates his skills of detection (and rather impresses himself)

Dear Margaret,
My husband insists on cultivating a huge moustache, which I loathe and detest. He spends a lot of time shaping and perfecting it, and thinks it makes him look distinguished, when in fact it makes him look like a poor Albert Einstein impersonator. I dread kissing him, and wish he would shave. How can I possibly broach this with him?
Jackie, Elephant and Castle

Margaret replies; *bushy moustaches are indeed a vile appurtenance. While your husband may take great care to cultivate it, it will always remain an unnecessary and ugly adornment. How can you broach this with him? Demand that he shave immediately and, if he refuses, withdraw all kisses. If that fails, perhaps grow a moustache of your own and see how me likes it when the boot is on the other foot.*

Pick any one of the absurdly popular and ever-spawning detective novels that hit our bookshelves and they will tell you that the amateur investigator - be it an innocent old lady or a plucky young couple - always manage to slip easily in alongside the investigating forces to smoothly and succinctly solve the murder.

Reality, however, is an entirely different kettle of fish.

Had the fool inspector cottoned on to the benefits of my gift for a deft observation, then I dare say the investigation itself would be over far sooner and with much less fuss than under Standing's watch. The man had bared witness to my skills in the past, so why he chose to ignore the fact that I could be a boon to his investigation remained a mystery.

The signs were there, for it was not a minute after our tepid reunion on the lawn at Fallow House that I was to demonstrate my skills of detection once again. I dare say I surprised him, and Beryl too.

In fact, I even surprised and impressed myself.

I was reluctantly plodding through the crisp snow back up to house after being dismissed by the inspector, when I stopped suddenly at the old oak tree. Something in the snow had caught my eye - something odd. A dark patch of liquid had eaten through the snow and stained the lawn. Oil? It was a considerable distance from the driveway and the garages. Why was it here? How did it get here? And was it important?

It was only as I stepped back into the kitchen that it dawned on me that perhaps it had not been *oil* at all.

And then there was something else - something in the kitchen caught my eye. Or rather, something *missing* from the kitchen had caught my eye.

I was staring down at the fireplace when Beryl appeared. She had replaced one rather outlandish dress for another, this being a brown pinafore with orange lace at the neck and cuffs. She had also removed the Christmas clutter from her chestnut wig.

'Blimey, Payton - puts rather a damper on things, doesn't it?' She fingered her collar. 'D'you think this is alright? It feels wrong to dress festive now, but I haven't bought anything black! Why would I? The closest I have is my navy blue trouser suit, and even that has glittery silver cuffs! And I was saving that for dinner.'

I raised a hand.

'One minute, Beryl.'

'What is it? What are you looking at?'

'The murder weapon,' I replied. 'Or lack thereof!' I turned to my friend. 'Wait here.'

I pulled my coat tighter, went back outside and stamped down to the slow-moving trio of officers near the river, quite without a care for the damage this outdoor trudging in sludge might be doing to my shoe leather. The short, plump young constable called Whitby was fiddling with a wetsuit and chatting with the other officer as I approached. He stood firm, blocking my path.

'Officer, I must speak with the inspector immediately!' I declared bravely. The squat young man had clearly spent too much time in Standing's presence, as he had adopted his senior officer's frustrating aloofness. He issued a flick of the hand in my direction, as if I were a hovering insect.

'Please go back up and wait in the house, Sir.'

'I must speak to the inspector!'

I was speaking slowly and clearly. I was not about to cause a scene.

'We will be interviewing in the dining room, one at a time. You must-'

'But I have information. *Vital information*!'

'All in good time!' said the young man with a slithering tone that only served to fuel my fire. The inspector was milling around only a short distance away, and I was overcome by a hot flash of fury.

'Hey! Standing!' I called out with all the gravity I could muster. 'Get over here immediately! I have important information. I know what happened, where the girl was killed and what with. I can show you!'

I had spoken out with an assurance I did not necessarily feel, but there it was; my cards were on the table. The terse young officer gave a low growl and lifted an outstretched palm. Before he could speak, however, Standing had approached and leaned in over his shoulder.

'Alright, Whitby, stand down. You have information, Edgar?' The inspector asked his question curtly and without the merest hint of interest. There was, I observed, more than a smidgen of disbelief in his tone. Naturally, I matched his brusqueness with my own.

'I believe I know exactly what happened to the girl. Come with me.'

Although I turned back towards the house, they did not follow.

'If you have something to say, Mr Edgar, please explain it here.'

I wasn't about to be deterred, and looked back without a smile.

'I can explain far better with reconstruction. Follow me, please.'

As I stamped back across the vast lawn it was hard not to suppress the smirk of a man who has the upper hand. I tried hard not to care what the inspector thought of my officiousness, but still it was heartening to see that they were indeed following, albeit some way behind. Standing obviously liked to make a meal of his injury.

After kicking the snow from my shoes and entering the kitchen I waited for them besides the Aga.

'What's going on, Payton?' Beryl asked with excitement

in her eyes.

'I am drawing a few conclusions, Beryl. You will see.'

Standing and the dwarfish constable followed into the kitchen with an air of disapproval. I struggled to quash a well of uncertainty somewhere in my stomach, and began my speech with as much confidence as I could muster.

'My theory is based on a number of deft observations I have made this morning. I believe that young Maeve Taylor was killed much closer to the house and not at the river, where she was found. She was attacked just about there...' I squinted down my arm and pointed to a spot on the lawn. 'Just past the tall oak, about a halfway between the house and the river itself. And she was killed with this!'

Swinging around I reached up and grasped the leaping stag figurine from the right side of the mantle. It was cold in my grasp, and heavy too.

A perfect murder weapon.

'Or, indeed, the twin of this. As you can see by the bare patch in the dust on the far left of the mantelpiece, until very recently there was a second stag book-ending the shelf. There are a duo of stags in each of the fireplaces in this house. Only yesterday I observed the two stags here in the kitchen - and now one is missing!'

Standing was frowning. Behind him I could see that the plump young constable was scribbling in a pad. His attention gave my words a welcome authorisation.

'And where exactly is this second, missing stag?' Standing enquired with a trace of insolence that was not easy to ignore.

I lifted a finger.

'I will come to that.'

I clutched the stag to my chest rather like an Oscar winner does his trophy, and took in a deep breath before continuing. This was my moment, and I would cherish it. And this time the inspector would listen to me.

'I suggest that our killer had either planned to meet young Maeve in the gardens, or saw her out there by chance. My guess would be a rendezvous, as the old oak out there is a perfect landmark, and it was hardly the time nor the weather for a young girl to be out for a simple, pleasant stroll. She had thrown on that heavy coat and gone to meet her killer. Any clandestine meeting on the far side would be well sheltered from the windows of the house, and any foul play would not be spotted. Come with me please, gents!'

I replaced the heavy brass figurine in its place by the Aga, and took up a lighter trinket, a silver serving spoon.

'What we need to find is the second stag, missing from it's place here on the left.'

'Why the spoon?' Standing grizzled.

'For the purpose of demonstration. You will see!'

I stepped triumphantly through the back porch and out into the garden. The policemen followed. Behind them, Beryl pulled on her fox fur and trotted after us. The snow had began to fall again, albeit lightly, and we were soon at the old oak which stood alone at the centre of the lawn. When we were a few strides past, I stopped our small party and pointed upwards.

'The perfect meeting place and, if we stand just around here, we are sheltered from prying eyes up at the house by this bounteous oak.'

Standing had allowed himself to dance to my beat, craning his hairy neck either way to test my theory. It was true that from this secluded spot any meeting could take place in relative privacy.

'You think she was killed here?' asked Standing with some disbelief.

'Not quite.' I strode three steps away to where the dark oily patch stained the grass. 'She was killed... exactly *here*. You'll see that someone has attempted to kick snow over the area, but the liquid has stained the grass beneath it and eaten into the snow somewhat.'

I allowed the gentlemen time to peruse this spot. Standing tapped his third finger gently to the ground and inspected the tip, nodding slowly.

'Blood?' said Beryl, eagerly.

Standing nodded.

'So our murderer took up his weapon...'

I raised the serving spoon ominously above my head to cosh the inspector. He gave a start and moved swiftly aside as if I might have indeed brought it down on his skull. I thwacked it down in the air over the puddle of blood.

'Whack! She was hit here, perhaps a number of times.'

'And the body dragged to the river.' said Standing.

Our eyes followed, and from where we stood it was just possible to see the trace of a channel in the snow leading down to the river.

'Yes, the body was dragged to the river. Although fresh snow has covered the tracks fairly well.'

The inspector grunted. 'But why drag her down there at all? Why not leave the body here, well sheltered?'

I had already thought about this.

'*Poetry*,' I replied.

'Poet-? I beg your pardon?'

It was all too easy to fox Standing, and I continued with confidence.

'If you do your homework, Inspector, you will find that eighteen years ago a young girl drowned in that river. A young girl of Maeve's age and make up, and-'

'Thank you, Mr Edgar. I think we can talk to the family about the history of the house,' Standing cut in with a sigh. 'Now you have painted us a picture of the crime scene, perhaps we will be allowed to get on with our job?'

'But that's not all, Inspector!' I waggled the spoon. 'We have the question of the whereabouts of our murder weapon, the twin stag missing from the Aga. And I think that I know where it might possibly be!'

Standing didn't even bother to respond.

'After the deed was done, the body can't have been dragged away immediately. The leaping stag ornaments are considerably weighty, hence my using a spoon for the purpose of demonstration. It would be difficult for our murderer to drag the girl, however delicate she may have been, with the heavy stag figurine still in his hand.'

I raised the spoon.

'Our murderer would need to dispose of the murder weapon first - thus!'

And with this I swung my arm, flinging the article aside into the snow-covered bracken which reached out across the lawn from the left side. The spoon fell out of sight, but landed with an unexpected sound - a heavy clunk of metal against metal!

We all gasped.

Before the others could move Beryl had shot away in the direction of the noise. I followed her into the foliage, stepping carefully as I could. Heaven knows what the soggy bracken was doing to my trouser legs. After a moment, Beryl lifted not only the spoon, but also a brass figurine from within.

'Payton!'

'She passed me the leaping stag figurine, and I held it aloft in silent triumph.

Standing was hobbling towards us.

'Put that down immediately! It is a murder weapon!' he cried.

I would have liked to say that I saw a new found respect in the inspector's eyes following my dramatic revelations, but this was not the case.

I had impressed him, of that I was sure. I had certainly made some pretty accurate deductions. However, one would think I had merely pointed out that the sky was blue or that the sea was wet, for he accepted my information as his own from the very minute that I had discovered the murder weapon.

He ordered me to rest the leaping stag aground before calling over to his portly aide, who retrieved it in gloved hands and whisked it away in a brown bag. Standing placed a firm hand on my shoulder and, with what I hoped was a degree of admiration, softly asked me to return to the house. He would catch up with me there.

Beryl and I made our way back to the house, nattering in excitement. The building loomed large as we approached, the windows dark and unrevealing.

'And you said you wouldn't have any fun!' Beryl said as we stopped at the porch door to kick the snow from our shoes before returning to the kitchen. I had been sharing some details about Inspector Standing and his stark lack of competency as we went, and failed to notice Beryl stop by the Aga. It was only as I held open the kitchen door that I saw she was loitering at the fire place.

'Payton! Come back! Look at this!'

I joined her.

'What is it?'

She pointed down. 'Don't you see?'

At first I didn't see anything remarkable.

'No…?'

'*Look!*'

And then I saw it. I blinked twice in disbelief.

In the fireplace there now sat a leaping stag figurine *on either side* of the mantle. *Two* leaping stags! The empty space where the murder weapon had once sat had now been filled - and only in the short time in which we had all been outside on the lawn!

A replacement - replaced by a murderer!

Chapter III
In which Payton Edgar mingles

Dear Margaret,
My fiancé is fanatical about going to the pictures. He sees a film two or three times a week, and often cancels our dates if there is something he has particularly enjoyed in order to see it again before it closes. He especially likes musical films, and knows all the songs and the dances. I dress up smartly for him, cook for him and try my best at conversation, but it is never enough. How can I win his attention?
Ethel, Battersea

Margaret replies; *you must be insufferably dull to fail to compete with the false glitter of Hollywood, my dear. And musicals are positively the worse genre of film that there is. I should leave him at the box office and find yourself a normal young man who is partial to the odd war film on a wet Sunday afternoon, and nothing more.*

And so, in the short time in which I had demonstrated to the police my astounding skills of detection on the lawn, our murderer had surreptitiously replaced the stag figurine in the kitchen in the hope that we wouldn't notice.

But *nothing* escapes Payton Edgar.

Admittedly, it was Beryl who had noticed the replaced figurine, but I wasn't about to let on to the idiot inspector. I had solved the mystery of the murder weapon and managed to get both myself and Beryl off the suspect list in the process. I was quick to point out to the officers that we had been in their company all the time and could not possibly have replaced the figurine.

This development also ruled out the idea of a passing stranger being responsible for the death of Maeve Taylor, as only someone from *inside* the house could have replaced the figurine. Inspector Standing should have been delighted that I had made his job easier, now that the list of suspects had been dramatically narrowed down, yet he continued with something of a storm cloud over his head. He had grumbled and grizzled as I quickly made a sensible suggestion.

'Inspector, each fireplace in the building contains matching ironwork. There are many twin sets of leaping stags all around the house. This replacement must have come from somewhere. Do you not think that it would be pertinent to seek out it's origin?'

'Of course, Payton! That's the thing to do!' said Beryl at my side.

Standing ignored Beryl's enthusiasm, and addressed us sombrely.

'We are setting up an enquiry room in the dining hall. Please wait in the drawing room until called.'

'Perhaps I could be of help-'

'The drawing room, please, Mr Edgar! I won't tell you again.'

And so I beat an angry retreat to the hubbub of the drawing room where everyone in the house was gathering.

'I know that face!'

I uttered these words in disbelief the minute I stepped foot in the drawing room.

The face in question was the pale face I had seen peering in at the window following the seance. The face belonged to the local vicar, the Reverend Drinkwater. Beryl had already met the man, and furnished me with a few details.

Quite what a man of the cloth had been doing stalking the grounds at night and peering in windows was a mystery.

A mystery I intended to solve.

The gathering in the drawing room resembled a Christmas cocktail party, were it not for the grim faces and shifty looks. The atmosphere in the room was somewhat charged - any trace of festivity that one might expect on Christmas Day had been irradiated by the presence of a sudden and violent death.

The Reverend Drinkwater was a tall skeleton of man with a rather shocking face. It gave one the impression of a long, drawn ram's skull, with a pointed chin reaching down to his dog collar and a high forehead reaching up to a sweep of grey hair that was pulled back over his scalp. He was a dusty old thing. His pallor was grey, and the only thing he was missing from the ram's skull were two great curling horns.

I told Beryl what little I knew - that the dead girl had expressed her dislike of the man, and that I had seen him peering in from the garden on Christmas Eve.

'Young girls never like old vicars,' she replied casually.

'Is that a fact, Beryl?'

'It is, actually.'

'But what would he be doing loitering in the gardens at night?'

'Perhaps he was miffed not to have been invited to dinner.'

'Mmm. There is something sinister in his bearing. He doesn't look like a village vicar to me...'

'*Really*? Sunken cheeks? Piercing eyes? The look of dogged serenity? Looks exactly like a vicar to me.'

'Perhaps I should say something about what we know. He looks on edge... *shifty*.'

'Payton, dear-heart, everybody looks shifty and on edge - a girl has been murdered! You can hardly run to the inspector with half-baked ideas about murderous vicars tearing through the night!'

'That imbecilic inspector!'

'Hmm. I rather like him.'

'No, you don't, Beryl! I know you! You're just being provocative!'

Mr Lloyd approached us with a faint smile to take our order for drinks.

Beryl requested a large gin and tonic and I ordered a tomato juice. The butler returned to his post at the drinks cabinet by the piano, where Arnold Prosper was helping himself to a particularly generous whisky with much banging and clinking of bottles and glasses. I watched as Lloyd waited patiently for the chef to move on before preparing our drinks with a practiced hand.

'He's very good, isn't he, Mr Lloyd?'

Beryl huffed. 'Is he? I hadn't noticed.'

'*Precisely my point.*'

'Well, I'd like him to be a little quicker, myself,' said Beryl. 'Now if *I* had a butler I wouldn't have some starchy antediluvian with cobwebs around his ears. No, I'd have a young buck... suave and debonair. And quick with his hands, too.'

'Then thank goodness you don't. I'd fear for the poor thing.'

My thoughts drifted back to the night before, when I had seen the butler in the gardens with a torch. I said a few words about it to Beryl.

'What is it with old men stealing through the gardens in the darkness? What goes on here at night? I love to know.'

My friend huffed. 'I'm starting to wish I was back at home. It's all a bit grim, isn't it? I miss Christmas.'

'You can hardly expect cracker pulling and endless rounds of *The Minister's Cat* after what's happened, can you?' I shuffled impatiently. 'This is so frustrating - I'd dearly love to be a fly on the wall in the dining room, to hear what everyone has to say...'

'Really? I should have thought it far more interesting out here,' said Beryl casually. 'In front of the plods all you'd get are guarded replies and practised responses.'

I looked squarely at my friend.

'You might have a point there. Yes... out here, we can mingle with the suspects in their natural habitat, as it were! We could learn much, much more, Beryl!'

'Perhaps. But you have to be careful, dear-heart.'

'Oh, I'm always careful. Always.'

She peered up at me, suspiciously.

'You're *enjoying* all this, aren't you? Mystery and nonsense! Happy as a duck in a puddle!'

'Oh, be quiet.'

I was saved from having to comment any further by Mr Lloyd, who had returned and was holding up a little silver tray with our drinks on top. Something about the butler's taciturn calm enticed me to say a word to him about what I had seen from my bedroom window. I took my drink and leaned in a little closer.

'I do hope you don't think I'm prying, Mr Lloyd. I saw you out and about in the early hours, around one-ish this morning. I just wondered what a butler would be doing out in the gardens with a torch in the dead of night?'

If I had hoped for a reaction of any kind, guilty or otherwise, I was to be disappointed. He looked at Beryl then back at me, and blinked. From across the room, Petra Blake bellowed an order for orange juice as she sat heavily on the Chesterfield. Without a word of explanation, as if I hadn't said a thing, Mr Lloyd pushed the tray under his arm, turned on his heel and headed back towards the drinks cabinet. There was something, perhaps even menace, in his silence.

Beryl nudged me and nodded in Petra Blake's direction.

'Look at that sour-faced old prune, giving Arnold the evil eye!'

She was indeed scowling up at the chef.

'Quite.' I mulled over my options. 'Beryl, I think it's time to mingle.'

'Mingle?'

'And to observe. I'm going to pop over to Miss Blake and have a word.'

'And what about me?'

'How about you sidle up to Prosper, see if you can find out what he was doing last night? Make yourself useful and snoop a little.'

'Snoop, Payton? That's not my style.'

I couldn't believe my ears.

'Beryl, may I remind you that you are a gossip column queen. Your very job description is to be a nosy snoop.'

Looking displeased, she nodded, nevertheless. 'Alright, if I have to. But we'll meet back here in five minutes, tops.'

'Good. But keep your wits about you, Beryl.'

'Always do, dear-heart!'

And so we went our separate ways. I stepped over to Mr Lloyd, who was just about to leave his station, an orange juice on his little silver tray. I reached over and took it.

'For Petra Blake? Allow me.'

Harvey Blake's sister barely looked up as I offered her the drink, and took it without as much as a word of thanks. Positioning myself carefully on the sofa - far enough away to be comfortable but near enough to talk - I made the appropriate noises. *A dreadful business. Quite, quite shocking. And how awful for poor Harvey.*

I received only a small nod and a shrug.

I persevered.

'And absolutely terrible for you, of course-'

As if a switch were flicked, she sprang to life.

'Shocking! My head's been spinning like a jenny! And at Christmas, too!' She went on to wail her woes, telling me how terribly wretched she felt and how her nerves were jangled like never before. As she drew breath I enquired politely after her sister.

'Dr Lorimer from the village came up,' she muttered.

'Gave her a sleeping draught in the end. I could do with one my-self!' Her face was certainly very pale. 'Hang on, I do have lit-tle something-' She trust her glass into my hand, ploughed through her handbag and pulled out a small pink pillbox, from which she retrieved two round yellow pills. She dropped the tablets onto her tongue, took a sip of the juice and threw back her head.

'My poor, poor nerves!' she breathed by way of explana-tion. I was careful to nod with understanding. We looked out on the room.

Beryl was chatting with Arnold Prosper, and was joined by Miss Moore. They appeared, rather inappropriately, to be sharing a joke. At any rate, Prosper was chuckling gaily. The far door opened gently and Gideon Carter appeared. He wore many layers - a neatly pressed linen suit, then a free-flowing open-necked shirt with a buttoned undershirt beneath. He looked the very picture of a debonair Mediterranean gentleman. He had a newspaper and pipe within his grasp.

Miss Blake's expression darkened, and she watched as he reclined in the leather armchair beside the bay window, eyes out to the gardens. I wasn't surprised to watch as Beryl broke away from Prosper and Miss Moore and headed straight for Carter.

Suddenly Miss Blake moved herself a little closer on the sofa and lowered her voice.

'I simply can't understand it! Just what was that silly girl up to? Playing everybody up like that? It could only end badly. There was nothing coarse or false about our Lotty. She was a dear child. But that Maeve? A cuckoo in the nest if there ever was one!' She drew breath. 'I know that one shouldn't speak ill of the dead, but what on earth was she thinking? That Harvey would take her on as a surrogate? Well, it nearly worked - my sister is behaving as though she has lost a child all over again! What was the girl *thinking*?'

She sniffed.

'Still, lies and deceit catch up with us all in the end. A girl so young - and to do what she did! And at Christmas, too. It just doesn't feel right, her ending things like that. Such a silly, selfish thing to do.'

'I'm sorry... *what did you say?*'

'I knew the girl was an oddity from the minute I clapped eyes on her, and I have been proved right. But still, one never suspects that a girl so young could be capable of taking her own life. It is baffling.'

'Miss Blake,' I began tentatively. 'Maeve did *not* take her own life.'

Petra Blake spluttered out a wet laugh.

'Well of course she did. She drowned herself, we all saw her! What else could possibly have happened?'

This was a question I did not wish to answer, but the facts spoke for themselves.

'Miss Blake, she was... bludgeoned... to death. *Murdered.*'

There was perhaps a kinder way to put it, but I didn't have the energy to search for it. Besides, these were the facts. My confidant was peering at me, goggle-eyed.

'But she was found in the river. Surely she drowned?'

I shook my head, and then watched her face as she processed this news, taking a sip of her drink distractedly. Slowly, incomprehension was replaced by a cold glare.

'*Murdered.* Of course, that makes much more sense. I should have realised.'

It was a curious reaction. The woman had found the idea that Maeve had taken her own life indigestible, whereas if it were murder - well! That was apparently so much more palatable.

'Of course, of course, of course,' she chanted to herself over and over. Finally, she slapped her knee.

'Well, the police will clear it up pretty sharpish, then.'

'I very much doubt it. I have dealt with Inspector Standing before, and I promise you the investigation will be carried out with a staggering amount of unnecessary deviations and falsehoods.'

'Well, why aren't they getting on with it? Why herd us up like this?'

'We are to be fleeced for information, one by one,' I said, not without relish.

Miss Blake gaped at me. 'Well, I can save them a lot of bother! I have one or two things to say about the matter!' She stopped for a moment in silent calculation, and when she spoke it was in a whisper, and to herself rather than to the gentleman at her side.

'The girl was trying to tell us something last night, wasn't she? All that nonsense about the river... it was all about

Lotty. A murder, not a suicide. There's only one answer to it all.'

I did not need to reply. Suddenly, she straightened and, with a grim expression, fixed her eyes on Carter across the room.

'It's no coincidence!' she hissed. 'The truth will out, *the sly fox*!' A puffy hand fluttered up to her wrinkled neck nervously. She was motionless for a moment, and then cast me a surprised look as if recalling my presence.

'Excuse me! I have to-'

Whatever it was that she had to do was left unsaid as she pulled herself to her feet and hurried out of the room.

Carter knew full well that he was being talked about, and watched her go with a wary look on his face. Beryl was chatting away at his side, but his attention was elsewhere. Suddenly, he caught my eye and gave me a mischievous wink. At the same time, Prosper broke away from Miss Moore and stepped across the room in an overly casual manner. He put a hand on the arm of Carter's chair and leaned in.

Carter's face dropped. He gave a snarl. The chef whispered something. Whatever he had said, his words were unwelcome.

Suddenly, it was rather like watching two ill-bred dogs thrown together. Carter stood and squared up to Prosper, raising himself on his heels, but the chef stood his ground and raised his chin with an air of challenge. Beryl had her hand to her heart and was watching with excitement. From my seat I would see Carter's eyes, and they were full of fury. The rest of the company appeared unaware of this stand-off until the first punch was thrown.

As brawls go, it was a rather pitiful display. Prosper swung drunkenly, missing his mark. In response, Carter pressed closed fists up against his opponent's chest and gave him a sharp push. Prosper fell back, took a breath and then retaliated, again rather clumsily. There was a brief scuffle, ending with Prosper hitting his back hard against the wall, where a painting came crashing to the floor. The tussle ended as abruptly as it had started, and Carter turned with a lurch and made for the drinks cabinet.

Mr Lloyd received him with a blank look.

Arnold Prosper, his face even more florid than ever, took a minute to straighten his shirt before staggering out of the door. Quite what he had done to deserve Carter's wrath was unclear.

Beryl was now sitting alone, and she beckoned me over cheekily. I raised a finger carefully. *In a minute.* A direct path had cleared across the room to the vicar and Mrs Turpin. I simply had to know what a man of the cloth was doing loitering in the gardens at night, and so I leapt upon the opportunity. On the way I paused, not wanting to appear too eager or purposeful in my mission. I feigned interest over one of the absurd mounted car horns that had pride of place beside it.

The vicar was standing aside the housekeeper who, after the distraction of the fleeting brawl, had continued her conversation near the vicar's ear. I moved in closer.

'-and at Christmas, too. I said to my Harry, I've never known anything like it. If only you'd been here, yesterday, Vicar. But then-' She saw me lingering and stopped mid-sentence, and then made her introductions with a plummy tongue. Mrs Turpin was the sort of woman who feel it necessary to adopt airs and graces in the presence of the clergy.

Reverend Drinkwater issued an anaemic smile and shook my hand. I was struck by his icy blue eyes, which drained all colour from his face. The stringy grey hair that was swept over his crown came to rest at his shoulders in a most unappealing manner. At the front, loose strands had been tucked behind large ears.

'Good morning, vicar,' I began, sensibly.

'If only it were. If only it were,' he replied dryly. 'Such a shame for you, Mr Edgar, having come all this way, as an honoured guest. And then for this to happen. And yet, Christmastime is a time for finding light from the darkness. We must all look towards the light for reassurance, the light of our Lord. Thy word is a lamp unto my feet and a light unto my path.'

Joan Turpin was nodding, entranced. He went on, his voice so painfully monotone and his approach so crashingly dull that I soon found myself without words. Before I knew it, the three of us had fallen into a cloud of awkward wordlessness. The man gave no clue as to having seen me through the drawing room window on the previous night, and I was wondering how I could work into conversation his habit of skulking in the dark when he suddenly appeared to perk up, and spoke with a squeak.

'You were admiring the old man's horn!'

'Admiring the- *sorry?*'

He pointed to the instrument mounted on the wall.

'The car horn. The old brigadier collected them, they're

dotted all over the house. That one's from the Brigadier's very first jalopy, quite an antique these days. It's a wonder the rubber hasn't perished. Miss Blake had it mounted for her sister's birthday, I believe.'

'Really?' I replied, struggling to conceal my indifference. I stepped things up a little by pretending to search my memory.

'I'm sure that I have seen your face before, I believe, Vicar. Did I not see you loitering just outside of that very window over there sometime after dinner last night?'

Both the vicar and Mrs Turpin first looked to the window and then stared back at me with bewildered eyes.

'It wouldn't have been the vicar, Mr Edgar!' Joan Turpin said with bewilderment.

'Indeed it wouldn't. What time was that? I would surely have been setting things up for midnight mass at that point.' He issued an unconvincing chuckle. 'What on earth would I be doing peering through windows on Christmas Eve?'

'*What indeed*?' I replied pointedly. Joan Turpin gave a little, embarrassed laugh.

'Reverend Drinkwater wasn't invited to dinner last night, were you vicar? I was just saying what a shame that was… first time, too. You are normally there, every year, aren't you? But Harvey wouldn't have you, for some silly reason or other.' The housekeeper waved a limp hand in my direction. 'Daniel is a pillar of the community, aren't you, dear? We all turn to him for a comforting ear. I can't think what Harvey was thinking, not inviting you-'

'Never mind, Joan. Never mind,' the vicar sang, 'I am here now, and just in time. This is indeed a dark, dark day. I fear that folk need my comfort and help to drive out the darkness. I can but try to cleanse the place of sin. Do excuse me.'

One could be forgiven for thinking that he was keen to get away, for within the blink of an eye he was across the room, cupping Miss Moore's hands with his and uttering soothing nothings in her direction. Joan Turpin moved in rather too close for my liking and peered up at me, searchingly.

'So you saw a vision in the darkness last night, did you, Mr Edgar? It was indeed a very unsettled evening, and unsettled spirits make themselves seen, you know. The spirits were out in force, were they not?'

'No,' I replied without a quiver of doubt, 'it was no vision or wandering spirit that I saw, Mrs Turpin. It was certainly the vicar, peering in furtively at that very window.'

He had been out there in the darkness. And he had lied about it. *Why?*

A thought occurred to me.

'Did you go to midnight mass, Mrs Turpin?'

'Of course! I always do. Me and Spud always go. Harry won't ever bother-'

'And was the Reverend Drinkwater there?'

'Yes. I'm sure he was about there somewhere.'

'But did you see him? Actually see him?'

Mrs Turpin bit her lip.

'Well, now you come to mention it, no. Johnny Smith, his underling, took mass, and it was lovely!' She did not pause for a minute to consider this information. 'But he'll have been around somewhere. I was quite shaken after all that commotion last night, and so it soothed me nicely. Yes, Mass by candlelight is always something to behold. Quite an atmosphere. Beautiful.'

Mrs Turpin began babbling something more about unsettled presences, but I was tiring of her nonsense and so waved her away with a polite hand, a smile and an excuse.

I made my way back to Beryl.

'Well, I've mingled and observed, Payton,' she whispered with a smile as I sat at her side.

'And?'

'And….' she took in a deep breath. 'I can pretty much sum them all up in one word. Miss Moore - thorny. Drinkwater - creepy. Turpin - batty. Petra - bossy. Prosper - idiot!'

'And that's your in-depth summary, is it?'

'It is indeed.'

'And what are your thoughts on Gideon Carter?' I put in quickly.

'Ooh, how could I forget Mr Carter! *Dreamy*!'

'What was it he said to Prosper? What was that fight all about?'

'Oh, I didn't hear anything. I was too busy admiring the cute little dimples that appear in his cheeks when he snarls!'

'And that's it? You were sitting right in the middle of it! You didn't hear a thing?'

Beryl shrugged with an infuriating indifference. Suddenly I was taken over by impatience and set my barely touched tomato juice down on the side.

'That's it! You can sit around here drinking and getting nowhere. I'm off to report to the inspector. At least one of us has gained some information that would help the investigation!'

Beryl happily ignored my scolding, and I left her nursing her drink and dreaming of Gideon Carter's cute little dimples.

Chapter IV
In which Payton Edgar is accused of being a gentleman

Dear Margaret,
I am so very shy, and because of my shyness I find it hard to do normal things that most other people find easy. I can't keep down a job as my bosses always tire of my nervousness. I am so jumpy around new people that I find it hard to make friends, and have never courted a boy properly as I am frightened of the very idea. What can I do?
Shy Patty, Enfield Town

Margaret replies; *shyness is an unattractive feature, and you must conquer it immediately! From your overlong letter it is easy to see exactly what sort of person you are; your inadequate vocabulary and baggy syntax denotes a sorry specimen indeed - a rather willowy and pathetic figure. I suggest you buy yourself some block soles, straighten up your back, look everyone directly in the eye during conversation and buck up your ideas. Failing that, a generous nip of brandy before you try anything that makes you nervous should do the trick.*

The meeting with Inspector Standing didn't quite go as I might have planned.

Had I been expecting some shift in their approach towards me following what was a thrillingly insightful demonstration of detection at the crime scene, I would have been disappointed. Standing and Constable Whitby sat across the table like a particularly inept and stuffy interview panel. Whitby's inexperience was all too apparent as he licked his lips and scribbled something with his pencil after every little thing that was said. Even though Standing also had a pad and pencil on the table top, he didn't bother to make notes. The man had the irritating way of watching with a cold expressionlessness as I revealed salient fact after salient fact.

'You seem to know an awful lot about the goings on here, Mr Edgar,' he began.

I was careful to smile pleasantly.

'I have two eyes and a keen brain. I observe, Inspector Standing. That is all.'

'Well then let's get the inevitable over with then. Go on - share some of these observations with us.'

'I'd be delighted.' I leaned in to the table, casually. 'May I have a drink?'

'No, you may not.'

The inspector matched my movements at his side of the table, glaring dispassionately. I felt a familiar fire in my chest but did my best to conquer it. I was determined to keep my cool.

'So? Did you search for the missing iron stag?' I enquired stiffly. The inspector conceded, as he surely owed me at least this little bit of information.

'We did, and we found that a stag figurine was indeed missing from one of the guest rooms.'

'I thought as much. May I ask whose?'

'Mr Carter's room, if you must know. But, of course, that alone is not conclusive evidence of guilt. '

I cut in.

'I quite agree! But interesting, nevertheless. Everything seems to point to-'

'Let's just crack on shall we, Edgar? Tell us what you think of our suspects. Why not start with Carter?'

I hesitated. Was the man truly interested in my opinion, or was I merely being humoured - or worse, toyed with?

I set my doubts aside.

'Gideon Carter brings an air of cosmopolitan intrigue to the place, but despite his shady past and dubious nature my instincts tell me that he is a fair man and not the cad nor the gold digger some have suggested he may be.'

'You are aware of a shady past?' said Standing with the merest tang of interest.

'Of course. I am aware of the gambling issues which led him to flee his marriage some years back.'

'I see.' Standing lit up a cigarette, but made no efforts to share information. 'And could Carter be the murderer?'

It was very satisfying to be asked such a direct question. Perhaps the inspector really did hold my opinion in some regard, despite the nonchalance of his approach.

'I would like to think not, but it is a possibility.' I replied with some compunction.

Standing bumped a fist onto the tabletop, at which poor constable Whitby gave a start and almost dropped his pencil.

'Alright then - quick fire! On to Harvey Blake. Tell me

your *observations.*'

I disliked the way he put a sneer into this final word, but battled on regardless.

'Harvey Blake is, in my opinion, something of a genius in business and culinary circles. I have known her only a matter of days, but during this short period she has shown herself to be an extremely gracious and considerate host.'

A pause. Standing winced through whirls of smoke.

'Is that it? No more details? I was hoping that you could give me a gripping account about each of our suspects lives, their strengths, their foibles and desires.'

'What exactly do you want, Inspector? Harvey Blake is every inch the businessman; considerate, impartial, hawk-eyed and responsible to a fault. Her favourite colour is bottle green, and she enjoys golf, clay pigeon shooting and collecting classic cars. She also appreciates good food, drink and company. She carries some guilt over the death of her daughter many years ago, and has recently resumed relations with the father of the girl. She has a strong sense of family and a keen eye for art.'

I did not mention her confusion about the appearance of Maeve Taylor and her uncanny resemblance to the dead daughter. I would leave that for Harvey to tell.

'And could Harvey Blake be the murderer?' asked Standing without preamble. At his side, Whitby was scribbling eagerly onto his pad.

For a moment I mulled this over, before lifting a finger.

'I pause only to give your question the credit it is due. No, Inspector, I do not believe she is.'

'And her sister?'

I cleared my throat.

'Petra Blake is a singularly unattractive creature. She has a rather high-handed nature, yet despite this she appears to suffer with a fragile persona, or what she would call "*nerves*". I suspect that she relies on this to excuse bad behaviour in certain situations. She has never married and shows no interest in ever doing so. She likes dogs and is a keen potter. She teaches at a Sunday school and I believe she has scribbled out a couple of children's books.'

This was the nicest of descriptions I could give for the woman.

'And could Miss Petra be the murderer?'

'Inspector, I-'

'I merely wish to hear your opinions, Mr Edgar. Could Petra Blake be the murderer?'

I swallowed as Standing blew two plumes of smoke through his nostrils.

'She was, until just now, under the impression that the girl had died by her own hand. I had to put her right.'

'Murderers can be the very best of actors, Mr Edgar. With that in mind, could she be our man?'

'I think not.'

'Tell me about the cook.'

This came quickly, and I was momentarily wrong footed.

'Do you mean Prosper?'

The inspector swung his note pad around on the table. It had been upside down. He read.

'Mr... Arnold Prosper.'

'I have been acquainted with Prosper for some time, through the restaurant adjacent to The Strand, where he holds the position of Head Chef. He is an exceedingly unsophisticated and boorish gentleman, yet his menu is consistently excellent. Prosper is especially gifted at preparing fish and game. We were looking forward to partridge for Christmas dinner. The man certainly has talent. That said, his manner leaves much to be desired. He is a drinker, a womaniser and an idiot. I met him for the first time back in London when we dined at-'

'Could Prosper be the murderer?' the inspector cut in.

Swallowing some irritation, I allowed a pause. Prosper was prone to passionate outbursts and at times appeared to be quite out of control even on his own restaurant floor.

'It is a possibility.'

Standing blew a few smoke rings idly.

'And the secretary?'

'Alison Moore? Miss Moore is a bit of a queer fish, and yet she appears to be an attentive and efficient secretary. She clearly dotes on her employer and can hold her own against the likes of Arnold Prosper. She has never married, to the best of my knowledge, and enjoys horse riding in her spare time. And before you ask - no, I do not think she could be the murderer. She seems to be far too preoccupied in her role to deviate to criminal activities. And her affection for the Blake family is evident in everything she does. I hardly think she would wish to cause the family distress or scandal in this way.'

'Tell me about the butler.'

I paused, daring myself to request a beverage once again. This interrogation was drying out my mouth somewhat.

Perseverance, Payton! Perseverance!

'Arthur Lloyd has been in service for the Blake family for the entirety of his lengthy professional life. He is an accomplished butler, and is very loyal to the Blake family, and also to the Turpins. I do not believe he has ever married. He says very little, as is his want.'

'Not much flesh on those bones, Edgar. Is that all?' asked Standing.

'Yes,' I replied.

'Could Mr Lloyd be our murderer?'

The image of him sweeping though the darkness by torchlight, that grim expression on his pale face, haunted my thoughts.

'It is possible.'

'You mention the Turpin family. Tell me about them. Mrs Joan Turpin?'

'Again, a dutiful servant to the Blake family, Mrs Turpin is a homely and motherly woman. She appears to be happily married, enjoys her work and considers herself a medium of the spirit world.'

'And could she-'

'-be the murderer? No. I think not.'

'And what about her imbecile son?'

'Inspector, I am not sure that Raymond Turpin is an imbecile, as such. He has some degree of, well, difficulty with, well…' I was having some trouble finding the right words. 'I believe he has difficulty in grasping certain concepts. Certainly a bit slower than your average man on the street. However, I would say that it appears he has been a decent son to his Mother, and was a good friend of Harvey Blake's little girl back in the day. Raymond, who is also known as Spud for some unfathomable and entirely unnecessary reason, likes the undeniably infantile pursuits of swimming in the river and kite flying. He is also a surprisingly good cook. His soup-'

'Could he be the murderer?'

To my shame, I did not need to hesitate. The mans brutish welcome in the woods was fresh in my memory. He had thrown stones at me!

'Yes, quite possibly. He discovered Charlotte Blake's body all those years ago, and again this morning, he was the one-

'And what of his father?'

'I know very little of his father, having only waved to him from afar. He is an elderly, shy gardener who has had little impact on my visit thus far, and I feel that he has little impact on this case.'

'I see.'

'Rather like old Mr Blake, the brigadier, whom I have not had the privilege of meeting. The man in the attic suffers with a softening of the brain, by all accounts, and is so decrepit that he cannot descend the stairs, putting a murder in the snow quite out of the question.'

'Quite so.' said the inspector.

There followed a curious silence, until a bemused look spread across Standing's whiskered face. The arrogant sneer alone was enough to deter anyone from helping the police in any way ever again. He nodded to his subordinate.

'Constable Whitby, you have been taking notes during our interview? Would you mind giving me the page you have been writing on?'

'Give you the-?'

'Rip out the page, man!' Standing bellowed. Whitby carefully tore out the last page of his notebook, the tip of his tongue protruding a little. He passed the paper to the inspector, who pretended to read for a moment.

'Your observations, Mr Edgar…'

'Yes?' I replied, carefully.

That stony glare was again fixed in my direction. The inspector screwed the page up into a small ball in his palm, lifted the ball of paper pointedly, and then threw it at the far wall. There was no dustbin for it to fall into, but the gesture was there. With tight fists under the table, I calculated my hatred for the man. He went on.

'I have some observations of my own, Mr Edgar. One can't help but notice the lack of forensics in your analysis-'

'Forensics?'

'Forensics.'

'Well, why should there be forensics? I am a restaurant critic, not a policeman. I'd have thought that forensics would be your responsibility, wouldn't you?'

A grunt.

'Nevertheless, you give a very skewed appraisal, Mr

Edgar. Tell me, has anyone ever told you that you are indeed a gentleman when it comes to the fairer sex?'

'I beg your pardon?' I coughed as the inspector extinguished his cigarette into an ugly ceramic ashtray that may have been one of Petra Blake's pieces. He pressed his stomach even further in to the table and waggled a finger in my direction. Whitby was now resting back in his seat with a similar air of smugness.

'It is no coincidence that for each of the females discussed you have denied the possibility of murder, however for practically all of the males under this roof you have *condemned* them to this very possibility! Women are capable of murder too you know, Mr Edgar.' He allowed a pause, grinning pointedly. 'A soft touch for feminine wiles will lead you nowhere in this game, isn't that right, Whitby?'

'Quite right, Sir.'

I bit my lip. He continued.

'I would say that the only male suspect that you hesitated to condemn was Gideon Carter. True?'

I did not reply.

'Interesting that you should discount him as suspect. You have been misinformed when it comes to our foreign friend. You mentioned a shady past? Would it surprise you to learn that Carter did not flee his family over some petty gambling issue as you claim, but that he has recently been released from service at Her Majesty's pleasure? I have no doubt that the Blake family have been keen to keep this fact a bit hush-hush, to save face and all. But the fact is that this violent man was put away for the best part of a decade! And for what offence, you might ask?'

I didn't ask.

'Assault and battery!' Whitby squeaked. Standing cast a look over his shoulder.

'Yes, thank you, Constable! Well, now that particular cat is out of the bag, I might as well tell you that he was incarcerated for battering a man to near death over a gambling debt owed, no less. Assault and battery indeed. So, are you still convinced of his innocence, Mr Edgar?'

I remained mute.

'And in your so-very-well-observed account there is no reference to motive. It appears you have no consideration for motive or opportunity. You-'

'You asked for observations, Inspector. I gave you my

observations.'

'Indeed. I rather think *trite* would be the word to describe them.'

Trite!

'I do my best!' I huffed. 'I am not a police officer-'

'Indeed!'

'And there is one suspect you have not allowed me to mention! There is the Vicar,' I continued with a whisper, 'Reverend Daniel Drinkwater.'

The whispery eyebrows sank lower.

'The village vicar? Really?'

'I've just met with Drinkwater out in the drawing room, and yet I had witnessed the man skulking around outside of that very room during our séance last night...'

'Séance?' the inspector was quick to deliver a judgmental, wide-eyed glare.

Whitby followed suit with a little snort.

'Oh, yes, Inspector! *The séance.* There is something else you have neglected to consider, Inspector Standing. There is a supernatural element to this case. A supernatural element that-'

'What rot!' Standing spat. 'I am interested in facts and facts only, Mr Edgar. Not hocus-pocus!'

'Then I shall let the others tell you about it, if you'll allow them to,' I replied firmly. I then lifted my chin and allowed a gentle sigh. 'I am nothing but an innocent guest, merely a spectator to the circus. However, I did witness the vicar out in the gardens, peering through the window on the night of the murder. And when I asked him - just a few minutes ago - why he was out there in the dead of night, he flatly denied it. I also saw the butler out skulking in the garden late last night. I cannot doubt the evidence of my own two eyes, Inspector! The vicar was fibbing, the butler is suspicious, and I suggest that you find out why.'

At that moment there was a knock at the door, a sharp, urgent knock that could not be ignored.

'Enter!' Standing hollered. The door opened and the third officer of their motley trio entered with a suitcase. He was red in the face, as if from running.

'Searched the girl's room, Sir. Nothing much there, save for clothing.'

'Yes, thank you, Jacobs-'

'Usual girly stuff, I'd say. Something important, though

- seems she was off, Sir. Case was packed, ready to go. Here it is!' He lugged the suitcase onto the table top without a care for the polished surface, and rested a roll of paper on its top. 'Just this case, one or two toiletries and that poster on the wall by her bed. No books or letters or nothing. Not much in the case either, 'cept some clothes, soap and a hairbrush.'

While Constable Jacobs spoke, Whitby stood and moved over to the window. Something had appeared to catch his eye. Standing shooed Jacobs out of the room, lifted the flimsy poster up, unrolled it and peered closely at it with a frown. I could see it had been pulled from a magazine by two small staple holes in its centre and I examined the outline of a woman's face as Standing held it up to the light.

I am no follower of Hollywood and the films produced therein, but I recognised this particular face by the thick dark hair and carefully placed beauty spot.

'Hey-up! Someone else is on the off, Sir!' Whitby spoke up from his position at the window. 'That tomato-faced chef's doing a bunk!'

We could hear the rev of an engine in the distance.

'Go out and get him immediately, Whitby! Fetch him back and take his keys. In fact, take the keys from each and every one of them while you are at it. Nobody is permitted to leave! Nobody!'

Whitby raced out with the air of an attack dog. Alone with the inspector, I drummed my fingers idly on the table.

'May I have a look at that poster?'

I had anticipated the reply.

'Certainly not!'

'It is evidence? I see...' I hummed with some rancour.

'It is irrelevant, that is why! A poster from a girl's bedroom, that's all. Some Hollywood bint! Now, let's see what is in this case.' He unclipped each clasp with a snap.

'You may go now, Edgar. Back to the drawing room. Go on - scat!'

I stood, but purposely hesitated at the door.

'I am not sure that the poster is altogether irrelevant, Inspector. In fact, I think you may be in need of one of my *trite* observations.'

'What?'

'It is a photograph from a picture magazine, is it not? A photograph of young Maeve's mother, I believe.'

He laughed freely. 'Wrong!'

'Oh, I don't think so, Inspector. It is Elizabeth Taylor, the actress, is it not?'

The inspector blinked, looked to the poster on the table and then back in my direction, his eyes thinning.

'You're not telling me that... that she is the daughter of...' He trailed off, aware of the absurdity of his question, and then continued to rummage through the suitcase, muttering. 'You are more deluded than I imagined, Edgar!'

'No, Maeve was not the daughter of Elizabeth Taylor, but she would have liked it to be true. I know a girl back in London, Inspector, who took the name of a film star out of some similar romantic notion. All young girls like moving pictures, do they not? And a girl looking for a new name looks to her hero, I imagine. Clearly *Taylor* was not young Maeve's real name, Inspector.'

The girl had insinuated as much in one of our chats. I pulled open the door dramatically, dismissing myself. The image of the healthy young lady sat on the lawn scribbling in her book was set in my mind as I paused in the threshold, and then asked a question.

'Inspector, there doesn't happen to be a red journal in amongst the girl's things?'

The inspector shook his head impatiently.

'Should there be?'

'Perhaps,' I replied enigmatically.

'So then, what was it, Edgar? You seem to know it all!' Standing raised his voice as he issued his challenge. 'What was her real name?'

I shot him a smile.

'That I don't know – yet. But I think that if you found out her real name, you might have some answers to what's been going on. Oh, and Inspector, there is something else that you seem to have failed to elicit from your questioning. Concerning *spirits.*'

'Spirits?'

'There is something of a ghost story to all this. It seems to be at the centre of whole sorry situation. I suggest you focus on the séance in your questioning of the others-'

'The séance?'

'Yes, Inspector, the séance! Whether you like it or not, if you are looking for the truth you should look into that, and not the suitcase. I am certain that you will not find any truths in that bundle of flannels and underpants! Good bye.'

I closed the door behind of me and walked away with my head held high.

Trite, indeed!

Chapter V
In which Payton Edgar lets something slip

Dear Margaret,
Every few days I drop into our local sweetshop for a quarter of something-or-other, and now I fear that I am falling in love with the proprietor. He is a friendly, mature gentleman who lost his wife in an accident six months ago. I am happily married with no children, but I cannot get this other man out of my mind. How can I avoid falling in love?
Anonymous, Islington

Margaret replies; *"happily married"? I think not. And what are all these sweets doing to your waistline? I foresee nothing but misery and elasticated skirts for you, Anonymous of Islington. I suggest that you buck your ideas up, give up on a love lost and go on a diet before you lose the chance to appeal to any man, including your poor ignorant husband.*

After my incompetent interrogation at the hands of Inspector Standing I was loathed to be herded up like a brainless sheep and return as instructed to the drawing room.

Instead I found myself loitering in the hallway. It would be a sweet victory over the inspector to unearth the truth behind Maeve Taylor's real name - but without the girl to tell me more, who would know her secrets?

I ambled along in something of a dream, only to collide with Prosper and a sweating constable Whitby, coming in from the cold. Prosper was protesting loudly, uttering rubbish about going down to the village for provisions. I watched with amusement as the plump young officer struggled to get the man to give over his keys. Whitby was probably doing the man a favour by running him aground - he had already helped himself to the drinks cabinet and downed enough to make a carthorse giddy. Had he hit the roads he would surely have come a cropper. Prosper, however, didn't see it this way, and gave quite a fight before the keys were safely in Whitby's grasp.

He was then bundled into the interrogation room.

I shuffled towards the library, guided by my feet and not my head.

The room was welcoming in an airless, somber way. Stepping into it felt rather like stepping back into another time; a quieter time, a time of peace and contemplation. It was easy to see why young Maeve had taken to hiding out in there, and here I was doing exactly the same.

I sat for a while in one of the beautifully preserved stiff leather armchairs, ignoring the dozens of fixed beady eyes that stared out at me from their wall-mounted glass cases. After a while I found myself thoughtfully perusing the bookshelves, resisting the draw of the wheeled ladder. Each tome I pulled out was weighty and musty with age. This was an old man's library indeed.

There were numerous encyclopaedias, what must have been the complete works of Shakespeare and far too many volumes of poetry for my liking.

One bookcase caught the eye, in the far left-hand corner of the room, just below eye level. It had only four or five narrow shelves, but all were stuffed with colourful spines. It was a child's bookcase, full of picture books and the like. Some were a little dog-eared, and many of the colours on the spines had faded with time.

A name on one spine caught my eye, and I quickly pulled out the book and read the title. *"Mr Pink-Whistle Comes To Play."*

This solved the mystery of Prosper's ridiculous name calling. The cover showed this Mr Pink-Whistle as a short, fat, pig of a man with rosy nose and pointed ears. He appeared to be dancing with a squirrel in a bow tie. He was an unattractive imp with a suspicious face, and I immediately saw Prosper's insult for what it was.

I returned the book to its slot.

The top shelf was lined with a collection of books in far better condition than the others, with ruby red jackets and thick cream wording on the spines.

I picked one out.

Sly Fox and the Brown Hen, by Petra Blake. Illustrations by Geoffrey Willoughby.

On the front cover, a fat chicken in a red bonnet pecked innocently at the ground, while in the foreground a fox stood absurdly on it's hind legs sporting a top hat and monocle. This peculiar protagonist looked more like the bloodthirsty slasher of Victorian back-alleys than a farmyard animal. One could easily picture blood slathered on his jaws.

It was with idle curiosity that I flicked through the book. The story was short, poorly told and its moral message unclear. It appeared to be saying that if you leave your hat lying around, people will assume you have been eaten.

Hardly a pertinent message for the youth of today.

I picked out a second volume; *The Sly Fox and the Farmer's Wife, by Petra Blake.*

For the finale of this story The Sly Fox donned a curly wig and a nightgown for some duplicitous reason, and again I set the book down, unimpressed.

A deep growl gave me a start and I glanced around hastily. The room was empty and still. I returned to the book, slotting it back into place.

Then came the noise again - this time a low staccato groan. I stood motionless for a moment in alarm, and then rested my shoulders as I recalled the beast in the cage around the corner.

The General didn't greet me as I turned the into the cold cloakroom and peered into his stinking cage. The vile thing, still hunched over a branch, blinked once slowly and then raised its beak, appraising his visitor. It then omitting a low clicking sound, as if it didn't like what it saw.

'You're not so special yourself,' I found myself uttering to the bird. 'Over a hundred years old, and what have you got to show for it? Caged and forgotten. Like a old book in an old library.'

We stared at each other for a while.

'You're a funny looking thing, aren't you?'

'Goooooooooooooooolllllllllld' it grumbled in that ugly, rumbling tone.

I turned my back to the beast and stepped over to the window. Even though it was caged, the bird had a good view of the grounds, a view that might have given it the illusion of freedom. The snow-covered oak tree under which the girl had been coshed stood tall, now a symbol of violent death rather than one of nature's beauty.

The clopping of hooves on stone announced Miss Moore on horseback. She appeared to be taking herself out for a ride.

She handled the horse well, with the stern control I was coming to expect of her. Suddenly she turned her head and then stopped the beast as Whitby appeared, waving hands and shaking his head. I chuckled a little as he received the sharp end of the secretary's wit. They exchanged words and then, to my surprise, she conceded, dismounted and led the horse back towards the stables.

I continued to watch out over the wintery scene in peaceful contemplation long after they had disappeared from view.

My stomach rumbled. Despite all the drama, the thought of a sumptuous festive spread was a pleasing one. Perhaps. I told myself, we could pull off a fairly normal, delicious Christmas dinner if we all put our minds to it.

Behind me, the thing in the cage tutted deeply.

'What do you want?' I asked under my breath. It blinked twice. Perhaps it wasn't tutting disapprovingly at me. Perhaps the bird was hungry.

A small chalky white cuttlefish bone sat on the corner of the windowsill and, in a moment of softening, I took it and posted it through the bars. It plopped to the floor of the cage, much to the indifference of the Kakapo.

'No? Don't want it? Fine,' I snarled. 'Be like that - mangy beast!'

I did not want to smell fishy residue on my fingers and hastily rinsed my hands in the corner sink, berating the lack of soap. There wasn't even a hand towel.

I flicked the water from my fingers and left the ungrateful creature grumbling to itself.

Suddenly there was a shrill cry from out in the hallway. I cantered through the library, out into the hallway and to the foot of the staircase.

At the very top of the stairs, Miss Moore, clad in riding jacket and jodhpurs, was clutching Harvey Blake in what looked like a desperate bid to stop her from throwing herself down the staircase. My host looked a fright, adorned in a hastily tied silk robe, her hair wild and uncombed, her face innocent of make-up. Miss Moore's hands were planted on her boss's shoulders.

'Please, Alison! I have to do something!'

The secretary held her employer firmly, chanting that hysterics would not help the situation and urging her to keep her cool. Her voice then slipped to a calm quietness.

'Harvey, you have had a shock, and then those sedatives. You should be resting, not flying down the stairs! If you won't try and sleep then you can at least calm down and rest. You have to remember who you are, Harvey Blake! As you have said to me many, many times - decorum and poise. *Decorum and poise.*'

Her words appeared to work. Harvey stood mute for a second, and then suddenly twisted her neck around to face me with open eyes, as if seeing me for the first time.

I watched as the facade of a genteel host settled over her.

'I am so sorry, Mr Edgar,' she said. 'What must you think of me?'

I was careful to smile gently.

'Merely that you have suffered a dreadful shock, and are understandably upset.'

'Yes. Of course.' Harvey studied the carpet for a moment and then turned her wide eyes to mine. 'May I speak with you, Mr Edgar? In my room?'

I began to move up the staircase.

'Harvey, you need to rest!' said Miss Moore.

'And I will, but first I'd like a word alone with Mr Edgar!' She smiled in my direction. 'If you don't mind?'

'I should get changed,' said Miss Moore with a sigh, before directing an order disguised as a request in my direction. 'Can you help her back to her room please, Mr Edgar? And don't excite her!'

As if I would!

And so I found myself in Harvey Blake' plush bedroom, straightening covers and plumping up bed sheets as effortlessly as any well-practiced nursemaid.

The plaque on the door announced *The Summer Suite*, and with this moniker one would perhaps expect bright floral wallpaper and matching curtains, yet this was not the case. The room was wood-panelled and efficiently sparse, and with its dark green soft furnishings it gave the visitor the impression of a dense forrest glade. There were few clues that this was the bedroom of the lady of the house. Even the dressing table was devoid of the usual cosmetics, paints and brushes one might expect to find.

There was, however, a very clean, feminine scent in the air.

Harvey insisted that I pull the chair from her dressing

table over to sit by her bed akin to a hospital visitor, and I did as I was told.

'Mr Edgar, I am so, so sorry about all this-' she began. I cut her off.

'Nonsense, Mrs... *Harvey*. You couldn't save foreseen what would happen. Nobody could.'

'But what *did* happen?' replied the woman in the bed. 'It makes no sense. Why did Maeve die? Why did she say those things last night? It was awful. She talked about hands pushing her down, as if –' She stopped herself and shut her eyes for a moment. 'Eighteen years ago, my Charlotte drowned in an accident. *An accident.* There was never any question that it was anything more than that, not at the time. There were no strong hands holding her-'

I had to stop her there.

'And there still is no question. What the girl said last night was a barrage of claptrap, and you mustn't think otherwise. There is no spirit world where ghosts can channel themselves through the minds of impressionable young girls! And therefore what she did can only have been an act that she *chose* to play out. Whether someone put her up to it, or she did it out of her own mind, we may never know.'

'It was frightening,' replied Harvey.

'Only if you choose to let it frighten you. Perhaps that was exactly what was supposed to happen. Try not to let it worry you.'

My host could not suppress a warm smile, and I saw that I had restored her confidence, if only just a little.

'You are quite right, of course. I don't know what I'm doing, letting myself get all upset over a silly seance. The girl is dead, and I should be mourning her, not getting all het up over Mrs Turpin and her spirits. Silly really.'

'Exactly!' I replied with stern command. 'Silly is just the word for it. And anyone who believes any of it is just as silly.'

At that there was the briefest of knocks on the door and, right on cue, Petra Blake entered the bedroom. If she wondered what I was doing at her sister's bedside she gave no indication, and instead launched into a wailing lament, somewhat in the manner of a Greek soothsayer. It was as if I - a guest in the house - were not present in the room at all.

'Harvey dear, get out of bed immediately, I need you! I

warned you! I have always warned you! The truth is clear to me now, and we can't let him get away with it! We must act, and act immediately!'

I watched as the ease on Harvey's face slipped away. Her sister continued.

'It all makes sense now, now that girl is dead. I knew it was murder! Lotty didn't drown all those years ago, I've always thought it, and now we have proof. Look at the way he is acting.'

'You have always thought... w-*what*?' stammered Harvey, her words barely audible. Miss Blake stepped up to the bed with raised eyebrows. She was hovering over my shoulder.

'I'm sorry, I know how upsetting this is, but we have to face the truth now. A terrible injustice was done here eighteen years ago, and now it has happened again. I know you think that I disapprove of Gideon for no good reason, but it is much more serious than that. Much more serious! He cannot get away with it!'

'What are you saying, Petra?' Harvey asked quietly. I wondered if I should interject, for she appeared to be taking her sister at her word.

'I think you know what I'm saying. I'm sorry, Harvey, but that foul man murdered your little girl. I never thought he was really capable of it before, always a doubt in my mind. But after this - well!' She drew in a deep breath. 'He murdered Charlotte all those years back, and now when he felt threatened with exposure by that silly girl last night, he kills her in cold blood too!'

'Now really!' I had to protest, 'You have no evidence of that. You cannot-'

'Such a hateful man,' Miss Blake went on, entirely indifferent to my presence. 'And such a hateful murder. It has Gideon Carter stamped all over it!'

I sat back and examined her face. Her expression was one of naked repulsion.

'This has his sly ways all over it. I've always said you couldn't trust him, all those elicit affairs with beautiful women. Other women were only a game to him, Harvey - a distraction from the truth of it all. Cowardly - that's what it was, to cosh a girl over the head with one of our best brass ornaments! I've been speaking with the inspector, and it has to be him. That business with the stag figurine is something only a foreigner would think of-'

'Excuse me, Miss Blake!' I interjected, raising my voice to match her feverishness. I could take no more of her accusatory guesswork. 'You have no real evidence of Cater's guilt. We only know one fact; that the stag figurine came from Mr Carter's bedroom. That alone does not make him the murderer. It could be a careful set up, or-'

'I beg your pardon?' Miss Blake asked breathlessly. Suddenly she saw me. Harvey was shuffling in the bed.

'What is all this about a stag figurine?' she asked blankly.

Her sister pulled herself up to her full height and glared down like I were a doggy deposit on a picnic blanket.

'Well!' she trilled, 'the inspector informed me that the girl was coshed with one of the brass figurines from the fireplaces. However, it appears that Mr Edgar knows something more. So the figurine came from *his own bedroom*, did it?'

Whoops!

It seemed that I had let something slip.

'So then, now we have it! Evidence! What the devil are those moronic police officers doing? They must arrest the man immediately! Heaven knows he has form! He can't keep his fists to himself!'

Poor Harvey was blinking, struggling to digest all this new information.

'You said-' she stammered, ' you said that you've always believed that Charlotte was murdered?' She blinked up at her sister. 'Did you *really*?'

'Now this is nonsense,' I declared, determined to bring some semblance of rationality to the conversation. 'Petra, you cannot stand there and accuse the man of cold blooded murder-'

'He already stands accused!'

This deep and booming declaration came from behind - a voice in the doorway. Joan Turpin stood against the frame with her arms folded over her pinafore and a grim look on her face.

'It is true,' she continued. 'The victim herself accused him only last night. You are quite right, Miss Blake. He has been exposed as a murderer. We channelled some terrified and vengeful spirits here yesterday. I have never felt anything like it. Those who suffer an untimely death will always seek vengeance, and now we have all witnessed it for ourselves.'

Harvey was sitting up in bed, speechless. Her sister

nodded firmly as Mrs Turpin took a step into the room.

'What Mr Edgar says only serves as proof of what we should have seen. This news about the weapon from Mr Gideon's own room tells us all we need to know. The man is a killer. Your poor girl told us that she was taken at the hands of another, Harvey. And now we're all culpable, for we have let him do it again. He must be stopped.'

'We have to tell the police!' Miss Blake spat in a conspiring whisper.

'They may not listen,' Mrs Turpin put in, gliding over to join her at the bedside. I felt myself shrinking into the chair a little. There was a chill in the air.

'Then we will make them listen,' replied Miss Blake quietly.

'Or we confront him ourselves?' said Mrs Turpin.

'He would only lie to our faces! He has had decades of practice.'

'Nevertheless, when cornered a killer's true colours may be revealed!'

Poor Harvey Blake was looking up at the conspiring women with a furrowed brow.

'What's going on?' said a voice at the door, and Miss Moore joined the party. She had exchanged her jodhpurs for a brown tweed jacket and trousers.

Miss Blake turned.

'Gideon Carter murdered the girl,' she said simply. 'Mr Edgar tells us that the murder weapon came from his own bedroom.'

Miss Moore glanced at me sternly. 'What did I say about not exciting her?'

'He murdered Charlotte too, all those year back,' Mrs Turpin put in, with a twist of delight in her high voice. 'We have seen the proof. We must seek justice! '

'The swine!' Petra Blake added forcefully.

Miss Moore had the good sense to look doubtful.

'Hold on, ladies. I don't see quite how-'

'It's true, Alison,' Harvey broke in. Her tone was clear and serious, and yet fragile, as if she could break at any minute.

'There can be no other answer.'

Harvey stood, retrieved her robe from the side, tied it hastily around her waist and went to slip on her mules.

'I trusted him, again and again. You tried to tell me, Pet,

and I didn't listen. Again and again. And yet I suppose that knew… there was always something, well, not right.'

'He is a *killer*, Miss Blake,' said the housekeeper with menace.

'And he must be punished for it!' Miss Blake added.

With tears in her eyes, Harvey drew herself up to full height.

'Let's go,' she said, grimly.

Chapter VI
In which Payton Edgar is caught up in a witch hunt

Dear Margaret,
My husband is absolutely terrible at buying me Christmas presents. I drop gentle hints throughout the year about a new radio, a particularly pleasant writing set or even a bicycle, but all I ever get are cake tins, saucepans and rolling pins. What can I do to get the message through to him?
Audrey, Lisson Grove

Margaret replies; *I fear gentle hints are not enough in this instance. You need to drum the message into him with a clear list of desirables, in order of price or preference. If he continues to buy you kitchen durables then it may be that you need to find another, perhaps more violent use for the saucepans and rolling pins, if that is the only way to hit your message home!*

Hysteria!
I tried to follow after the gaggle of women as they stormed down the staircase with Harvey Blake in the lead, but my composed words of peace were only drowned out by their senseless jabbering. I fear that I only added to what had quickly become a furious mob.
Scruffy Raymond Turpin was shuffling about in the hallway. The approaching gang gave him a start and he danced aside as his mother, Harvey and Miss Blake pushed past, with Miss Moore and I hot on their heels.
To my alarm the women did not proceed to the investigation room to report to the police. I had imagined an interesting confrontation with Standing, but instead they veered off to the drawing room. They were following the scent of pipe smoke, and as soon as I saw Carter's dark expression as we entered the drawing room I could see that there would be trouble. Beryl was at his side chatting, and the look in her face as she was interrupted by the mob was priceless.
'Gideon! We have to talk! We must have the truth!'
Harvey shrieked, all decorum and poise flying out of the window and over the hills.

'We *know* the truth!' Miss Blake hollered over her sister's shoulder. 'Murderer!'

Mrs Turpin followed suit, and the scene descended into a frenzy of high-pitched accusations and growls of anger. During all of this, Gideon Carter remained mute with his pipe suspended in the air at his side. His eyes did not move from Harvey, and he said nothing. With high eye-brows and sucked-in cheeks, Beryl had stood and slowly edged aside, out of the line of fire.

It was easy to see the hurt on Carter's face as he stared up at Harvey, and one couldn't blame him for remaining silent. What else could he have done? Had he wanted to defend himself, it would have been fruitless against the torrent of anger that was bearing down on him. The others went on, but Harvey had stopped.

In a momentary lull, as his accusers finally took breath, Carter attempted to stand only to be pushed harshly back in his chair by an hysterical Petra Blake.

'You're not going anywhere! You will stay until you confess to the truth. You murdered our Lotty and now you've done it again! We want you gone - out of our lives forever!'

I could take no more. I hurried to the hallway, intending to summon the inspector and his officers to sort out the mess. I needn't have bothered, as they had heard the commotion and were already heading in our direction.

'What's going on?' Standing grunted.

'A witch-hunt, Inspector!' was all I could say as the officers bundled past.

Last out of the dining room was the vicar, who had evidently been under interrogation when the riot broke out. Again I was struck by Drinkwater's cold blue eyes. Now he was on the move I could see how alarmingly tall the man was.

'Is something happening?' he enquired with what sounded suspiciously like delight. He craned his neck to get a better look. I suspect he had been glad of the interruption. 'What's all that shouting about?'

'A witch hunt,' I repeated. The phrase was worth repeating for it was the best description of the frenzy in the drawing room. 'The female contingent has decided that Mr Carter is the devil incarnate.'

'Oh dear.'

'Quite.'

'Oh dear, oh dear!' the vicar said again. 'Perhaps I

should step in… to calm the waters?'

It was a question, dripping with reluctance.

'I think it may be in our best interests to keep out of the way. It's all turning pretty ugly and I don't think any amount of common sense can douse the fire. Best to leave the inspector to it. I'm sure he is more than capable.'

I was sure of no such thing, but quite happy to leave the man to sweat it out.

'Yes, you're right, of course.' There was relief in the vicar's voice.

After a minute of heated exchanges, the noise in the drawing room softened somewhat and then suddenly the police were back in the hallway, with Gideon Carter marching aside of Inspector Standing, a grim look on his tanned face.

Carter stopped by the vicar and spoke through gritted teeth.

'I'm sorry, Daniel,' he said with a sigh. 'I've no choice. I'm telling them everything.'

The vicar paled to the point of transparency and watched as Carter was led away by the law and the dining room door closed behind them. He began wringing his hands nervously and I could not help arching an eyebrow in his direction.

'Are you alright, Vicar?'

He was breathing rapidly, a grimace on his face.

'Oh dear! Now everyone will know!'

He spoke these words to himself, but got quite a shock as he turned.

The four ladies were lined up in the hallway. Miss Moore was smiling uneasily, and Harvey's expression was blank. Both Petra Blake and Mrs Turpin were red faced, struggling to compose themselves after the fight.

Mrs Turpin cocked her head to one side. 'Everyone will know what, Vicar?' she asked in a small voice. She had probably shouted herself dry.

The vicar wrung his hands together in discomfort.

'Nothing!' he squeaked, weakly.

'Everyone will know what?' Mrs Turpin repeated.

'Daniel?' said Harvey, quietly. Drinkwater sighed.

'We were… that is, a number of us were, well…' He wet his lips. 'We were in the summerhouse late last night.'

'*The summerhouse*?' Joan Turpin exclaimed. 'At night?'

'Of course! '

I could see from the tilt of her chin that Harvey had worked out what this meant.

'Who was in the summerhouse?' asked Miss Moore sharply. The clergyman continued sheepishly.

'There were six of us. No harm was done. But I am ashamed to say, I was a part of it.'

'A part of what?' asked Petra Blake.

'*Gambling*,' Harvey croaked. The vicar was quick to respond.

'Only cards, just a little wager. Very little money changed hands - well, on my part at least.'

'You were… *gambling*, Vicar?' Mrs Turpin shrieked. The vicar stood firm. The man was quick to rat on his fellow players.

'Your Harry was there too, Joan. And Mr Carter, Mr Lloyd and Mr Prosper. I was barely involved, and sat out after a few rounds.'

The weak-willed clergyman was singing like a canary. There was a pause as we digested the news, and then I broke the silence.

'You said there were six of you,' I began, tellingly. 'I count five, so far.'

Much as I deplore card games, I was just a little put out at not having been invited along to this gentlemen's gathering. Of course, I would never have dreamed of attending, but it would have been nice to have been asked.

The vicar smiled feebly.

'Mrs Baxter also played a few hands.'

Beryl! I set my eyes on my friend.

'Who invited you?'

'I rather invited myself,' Beryl shrugged. 'It was fun.'

'Well! I would have thought you'd invite me!' I spluttered.

'Invite you?' Beryl parroted, daring a laugh. 'Payton, darling, you'd have a coronary over a game of Snap!'

We exchanged looks.

The vicar continued.

'I really didn't do so well and gave my hand in early. I am not a heavy gambler, please believe me, Joan. I did it… to pass the time.' He turned and addressed Harvey. 'But Mr Prosper and your Mr Carter were on something of a mission, the stakes got a bit - how shall I put it - unrealistic. There were tensions, undesirable consequences-'

Harvey was nodding.

'And Gideon lost the lot.'

This explained everything. It explained what the vicar and Lloyd had been doing nosing around the gardens that night, not to mention Prosper's bravado and the scuffle between the men at breakfast. At my side, Drinkwater stood deflated, his secret out. Mrs Turpin continued to glare at him with disappointment. Behind her, Miss Moore was grinning with bemusement.

Drinkwater swallowed. 'Murder was far from our minds. And I would include Mr Carter in that count.'

I had to say something.

'This hardly takes you off the suspect list - any of you. With all five of you lurking in the grounds late at night, any one of you could have met with the girl.'

There followed something of a pregnant pause. The witch-hunting women looked subdued, and Harvey Blake looked positively drained of life.

Suddenly there was a crash from behind as Raymond Turpin pelted into the hallway and collided with the sideboard. He stomped towards us, running his hands over his head in an extremely unsettling manner. His bloodshot eyes were wide with terror.

'Heavens to Betsy, Spuddy!' Mrs Turpin spluttered.

'It's happened again!' he cried, gasping for breath. 'Come quick! M-m-murder! Murder!'

I believe the term for the feeling I had at that particular moment is *deja-vu*.

Chapter VII
In which Payton Edgar hides his guilt

Dear Margaret,
I simply cannot find a good man. I am approaching my 40th birthday, and have had dalliances in the past, but every man I meet is never good enough. My mother says that I am far too picky, but I cannot tolerate unusual foibles. My last boyfriend was far too keen on outdoor pursuits, my previous one forever distracted by his stamp collection. What should I do?
Miss Lonelyhearts, Snaresbrook

Margaret replies; *I shall do my very best to refrain from rolling out the hoary old adage "beggars cannot be choosers" for I suspect that your mother has used this time and time again to no avail. However, it is hard to ignore the fact that men prefer tedious stamp collecting or the masochistic pursuit of cross-country rambling to your company, and so there is only one thing that can possibly be said on the matter. Beggars can't be choosers, my dear.*

To say that Raymond Turpin was in quite a state would have been an understatement.

He grasped his mothers wrist and pulled her along, and we all followed on behind. The inspector and Whitby appeared and watched as we paraded down the hallway. We followed on through the library and into the cloakroom.

'Look!'

Raymond stood pointing a shaking finger down at the ground.

A heaped bundle of ruffled feathers lay in a clump in the sawdust. The beast in the cage lay motionless.

'Oh no! The General!' one of the women exclaimed. Harvey deftly slid a catch and dragged open the huge iron door, which screeched reluctantly. For a moment we all stood looking down at the dead thing, and then Inspector Standing pushed through. He stepped gingerly into the cage and, rather disrespectfully, gave the pile of feathers a sharp nudge with the toe of his boot.

The bird rolled over a little, exposing a frothy neck, a

wide open beak and staring black eyes. From its beak leaked a stream of curiously foamy white spittle.

'What the devil is that, Sir?' Constable Whitby breathed, and the inspector leaned in closer as if he were Holmes with a magnifying glass. He dabbed the foam and then sniffed the tip of his finger.

'Soap, or some such product.' He stated grimly. 'This bird has been poisoned.'

There was a shocked silence, and then it was Miss Moore's turn to push through, shoving the inspector aside with a satisfying ferocity. Without a care for the dirty sawdust scattered about, she knelt in the cage and held a shaking hand out to the dead creature, helplessly. And then, much to my surprise, she gave a sharp sob.

'Who would do such a thing?' she cried in distress.

Behind us, Petra Blake also issued an exclamation, much to the indifference of everybody in the room.

'Oh, my heart! Oh, the horror! I can barely breath!'

'Mmm. But why soap?' Standing grunted, caressing the handle of his stick.

'Why soap?' echoed Whitby.

'Inspector!' Mrs Turpin piped up from besides the window. 'We keep a bar of soap here on the window sill, and it is gone!'

A bar of soap on the windowsill?

'Murder!' the housekeeper gasped.

A bar of soap? Not a shard of cuttlefish bone?

'But why would someone do this?' Miss Moore wailed, clearly the most troubled by the demise of the rancid thing. 'An innocent bird!'

I bit on my lip.

A bar of soap! Not a shard of cuttlefish bone!

Harvey Blake lay a hand on her secretary's shoulder.

'There is a clear view to the garden. Perhaps-' Mrs Turpin declared loudly, extending a finger to point out of the window. 'Perhaps he saw something!'

We all looked over to the window.

'Are you saying..?' began the inspector, only to be interrupted by his podgy deputy.

'A witness, Inspector!'

An odd stillness descended on the room. Outside, the snow had picked up to something of a blizzard, with snowflakes swirling and dancing around the oak tree that stood innocently in its spot. And then officer Whitby spoke again, slowly and grimly.

'The bird knew too much. It had to die!'

It was hard not to roll ones eyes at the absurdity of it all. Soap. Not cuttlefish.

'There is a clear view out to the tree and down to the riverside,' continued Mrs Turpin. 'The General must have bared witness - and had to be silenced!'

'You think the bird would have talked?' asked the inspector.

Before anyone could reply, Arnold Prosper pushed Beryl out of the doorway and bundled into the room. He took in the scene and, much to my surprise, gave a wicked laugh.

'Ay-up! Kakapo for supper tonight, then?'

Miss Moore shot him a look of undisguised hate.

'Arnold!' Harvey scolded the chef with a glare.

Joan Turpin folded her arms. 'You're a devil, Arnold Prosper!'

'It is a well-known fact,' Constable Whitby declared proudly, 'that soap is poisonous to some birds.'

'It is really?' I found myself asking aloud in disbelief.

'I had heard that somewhere, too,' Mrs Turpin put in. 'Oh the poor, poor General. Your eldest relative!'

These last few words were said to the Blake sisters without a hint of mockery. Miss Blake was huffing and puffing, but Harvey stood mute, her face set as if she had spent all her emotions and had nothing left to express. She looked exhausted, and I wondered how the mix of murder, sedation and group hysteria had affected her mind. There was certainly scant evidence of the cool confidence I had seen in her at the start of my visit.

She was the first to turn and move out of the room, and she did so in a grim silence. She was followed out by her sister, Prosper, Raymond Turpin and then his mother. Miss Moore sat by the feathered corpse, fixed in a state of grief at the side of the cage.

Whitby looked up to his superior.

'It's going to be hard to establish a time of death, Sir,' he added sternly.

Chapter VIII
In which Dr. Margaret Blythe receives some food for thought

Dear Margaret,
I am a bright young woman in her early twenties. I am keen to study hard to become a surgeon, however my father refuses to allow it. He is a traditionalist and believes that I should be working towards finding a husband and raising a family. What can I do to change his mind?
Ambitious, Clapham

Margaret replies; *I shouldn't bother if I were you. Why would any self respecting young lady wish to be a surgeon? The idea of slicing up diseased bodies day-in, day-out is an unspeakably nasty one and surely not an option for a sensible young thing such as yourself. The smell of surgical spirit is repugnant, and even more repugnant are the true odours which the spirits are used to cover up. This is no job for a lady. Parenthood will be a much easier and far more appropriate option.*

I was not about to tell anyone that I had accidentally murdered a one hundred year-old parrot with a bar of soap.

Instead I retreated to my room and polished up a couple of Margaret Blythe's letters. The snow had eased, but only a little, and the sky remained as white as the ground below. With every snowflake that fell it became increasingly probable that we would be stranded at Fallow House for some time. I tried not to be distracted by the wintery scene outside, and looked to my letters.

Within the bundle of correspondence I discovered a telling missive from a regular, and read it with some amusement. I had a small number of regular correspondents, all taking the time to put pen to paper and berate Margaret Blythe for either encouraging sin and depravity and the ills of society, or inferring that her letters were in some way critical of the female of the species.

They were quite, quite wrong. naturally. Dr Margaret's replies offer healthy advice from a woman who is quite obviously an exemplar of women's rights - a paragon, no less. Who could complain about that?

I perused this particular letter with a contumacious air before crumpling and disposing of it in the waste paper bin under the desk. I was hunched over my papers, dealing with a trifling matter of poor personal hygiene, when there was a firm knock at the door.

'Just a minute!'

I scrambled to gather my papers together and thrust them into my briefcase, and went to the door.

Harvey Blake stood outside, with a curious look in her eyes.

'This is the second time I've interrupted you in your room, Mr Edgar. I do apologise. May I come in?' I stepped aside and allowed her in.

She had washed and dressed and now carried herself with a confidence that had been sorely lacking earlier that after-noon. She had painted her face, although not heavily, and pulled her hair back with a brown band. She looked refreshed and con-fident, and yet there was the tell-tale hint of dark rings around her eyes, if one looked closely.

In her hands she held two presents, one that I had wrapped for businessman Harvey Blake, and another, smaller gift. She perched on the bottom of my bed and set these aside.

'Well,' she said, 'I have learned that sedatives sometimes do more harm than good. However, I've enjoyed a short nap and a long bath, and feel much more myself. I was hoping that you'd join me for a drink downstairs, if you're agreeable?'

I accepted gracefully. The poor woman was obviously in need of some calm, sensible, intelligent company.

'I have also come to apologise, for my actions and all the ridiculousness you really shouldn't have witnessed. I invited you for a comfortable family Christmas, and, so far, it has been anything but. We have all behaved in a very unbecoming man-ner, and I'm sorry.'

She spoke as if she alone had whipped up the hysteria that caused the witch hunt against poor Carter.

'Your sister had more than a hand in it,' I reminded her.

'But it wouldn't have happened like that if I hadn't been there. It shouldn't have happened like that. I let myself be talked into a lie.'

'You think him innocent?' I found myself asking openly.

'I do. I really do. When I saw Gideon's expression - the hurt on his face - I realised that what we were doing was wrong.

Silly, ridiculous behaviour. It was grief, I suppose, on my part. That and the medication. Petra and the others are still convinced of his guilt, but I know that look on his face.'

I could not find words to say, and so said nothing. Harvey was fingering the ribbon of her present.

'And then, when The General was murdered, I knew for certain that he was innocent. Gideon loved that bird as much as we did. He would never do anything to harm it. Gideon is many things, but he is certainly no murderer.' She sighed. 'I don't want any more drama. I just want a quiet evening, even to enjoy a traditional Christmas dinner, if we can.'

This was good to hear, and I forced a smile as best I could. Harvey read something into this.

'Oh, don't get me wrong, I certainly don't want us to pretend that nothing has happened. I am desperate to know the truth and to understand what's been going on. But, at the same time, I think we should raise a glass to stoicism. And, I'm sure you agree, it would be a shame to waste Arnold's talents and let the food spoil.'

'True. Very true!'

Shaking off a bad thought, Harvey gathered herself and picked up the gifts.

'We must not forget that it is still Christmas Day, Mr Edgar, and in spite of all that has happened I would like us to exchange our presents.'

I had arranged purchase of the present in her left hand with the businessman Mr Harvey Blake in mind, and went to object, only to be silenced with a firm shake of the head as my little package was held out in my direction. It was about the size of a small baked potato, but flatter, and the berries on the glittery holly leaf print sparkled pleasingly.

Harvey began to pull at the paper in her lap. I felt I must say something, and quickly.

'Miss Blake - Harvey - I must tell you that I made that purchase before I knew-' I hesitated. 'Well, when I thought you were a *man* of business, instead of-'

The paper was off, and the box of cigars sat in my host's palms. She peered down at them for some time, and then a look of pleasure spread over her face. That eyebrow was arched once more.

'Gran Corona, am I right?'

I bit my lip, for I had no idea. Grace had made the selection and kindly wrapped it too. Harvey inspected the box.

'Thank you so much, Mr Edgar. I simply adore a fine cigar after a good meal, and these are just wonderful! A perfect choice. I have a darling little guillotine in the shape of a rutting stag, something of a family heirloom, and I shall look forward to cutting one of these after dinner tonight. I trust you'll join me?'

I did not reply. Cigar smoke is simply the most unappealing stench known to man, and I would do what I could to avoid going near the things. By way of distraction I turned my attention to the small gift in my hands. It had been firmly taped, and I struggled a little, but eventually had it open. Inside the paper was more wrapping, a wrinkled lavender tissue paper, and inside that, a key.

The key was large, old fashioned and ornate, and would surely would only fit a large, old fashioned and ornate type of cabinet or bureau.

'It is a symbolic gift,' said Harvey, as if I should understand. I turned the key over in my hands. It was certainly an elegant key - but just a key, nevertheless.

'Allow me to explain. You noticed in your review that Harvey's restaurant is set in amongst a number of covered stables. Many cover the restaurant floor, and a number cover the kitchens. Beyond that are a small number of office spaces, the first used by my administration staff. The next two spaces are vacant. I am giving you the key to an office, Payton. An office away from the noises of Fleet Street. A place where you can hone your craft in peace, adjacent to one of the best restaurants in London.

'You will-' she added, '-also be granted a substantial discount on your bill, should you choose the restaurant for any business meetings you require.'

I looked down at the key in delight, and then back to my host. I was lost for words. It was too good to be true!

'That is... *perfect*. And so very thoughtful, Harvey. For how long?'

'For as long as you require it. The offices are small but clean and functional. Yours is laid out with a cosy reception area and then a short corridor leading to a back office. I suggest you start looking for that secretary you so badly need!'

I could have cried. Was this the nicest, most thoughtful gift I had ever received? Quite possibly.

'I just don't know what to say.'

'Say "*thank you*"!'

'Thank you!'

She could not have failed to detect the appreciation in my eyes.

Suddenly, and with some aplomb, she stood and clapped her hands rather like a school mistress.

'Come along! Let's head downstairs and do our best to add a little sparkle to the day!'

Harvey and I had not long settled in the plump armchairs of the drawing room, whiskies in hand, when her sister crashed into the room, immediately staining the atmosphere with yet more of her melodramatic idiocy.

'Harvey! There you are! That silly secretary of yours is burying the General in the grounds like it were a state funeral!'

She shook her head with contempt. Neither of us replied.

'The police have had Gideon in again, no doubt peeling away his lies and putting the whole jigsaw puzzle together. It'll not be long before they take him away and we can all relax again.'

I looked from sister to sister. How could it be that they were so very different; one a thoughtful, elegant sophisticate and the other a hysterical, irritating harpy. Were they really born of the same stock?

Thankfully, elegant sophisticate Harvey Blake wasn't about to get caught up in her sibling's hysteria again.

'Petra, please! No more talk about what's happened. I have been thinking, and we were wrong – very wrong. We had no right to attack Gideon in that way-'

'But surely-'

'If you insist on joining us, Petra dear, please sit and amuse yourself quietly. No more talk of murders and murderers. I want the rest of the day to be quiet and calm, despite what's happened. Mr Edgar and I are enjoying a peaceful Christmas tipple.'

'Did someone say Christmas tipple?'

How Beryl manages to detect the opening of a decanter from fifty paces escapes me, but there she was in the doorway, grinning. She too had changed, into a brown and cream affair, with a square lace neck and red trim at the hem. Her wig was a conservative and unusually straight brunette affair. She caught me looking.

'I hope this is alright, it's the nearest I come to a mourning suit.'

Harvey was at the drink cabinet.

'No need for mourning dress, Beryl. It is still Christmas Day.'

Beryl plonked into an armchair. 'It's actually a Van Deursen and - terrible confession between friends - not this season. But I adore it.'

'You look delightful,' said Harvey, holding out a whisky. 'To Christmas.'

We raised our glasses, slightly guiltily. I noted the absence of a "*merry*" in the toast.

'To Christmas.'

Petra Blake held her glass in her lap.

'Well I can't wait until it's all over. I'm simply longing for the clear, gentle air of Torquay. They'll be no blood and violence there.'

Harvey Blake tossed her sister a copy of the Clarion that had been lying on the side.

'Why don't you have a quiet read of Mr. Edgar's column?'

Miss Blake received the paper with little enthusiasm, but opened it nevertheless.

'Page twelve!' I was quick to point out, a helpful direction that was only returned with a flicker of a scowl. Harvey and I returned to our current topic, Soho verses Bloomsbury for up-and-coming eateries. I had barely noticed when Lloyd shuffled in to the room and began to tidying around the cabinet. The man was a shadow.

After a while, Harvey turned to her sister.

'Well? Did you enjoy Mr. Edgar's review?'

Miss Blake grunted.

'Skimmed over it,' she replied casually, without further comment on the matter. I watched her with distaste as she continued to flick over the pages. 'I'm just looking to see if that other column's still in it, the problem page thingy!'

Beryl's eyes met mine.

'Another great Clarion piece,' she said, grinning.

'Good lord, woman, nobody enjoys that drivel!' Miss Blake scoffed. 'What is it? Winifred's Letterbox or something?'

She found the page she was looking for. '"*Dear Margaret.*"
Ugh! A foul woman offering the worst advice possible! Dreadful approach. She sends women back to the dark ages!'

Beryl looked me in the eye shrewdly and tried to calm
the waters.

'Well, I'm sorry, Petra, but I quite disagree. Margaret is
a wonderful character.'

Harvey nodded. 'Well, I do have to agree with my sister
on this a little I'm afraid. The woman does have an alarmingly
pre-suffragette stance on women's issues. She does nothing for
our cause, and even rather damages it, unfortunately.'

My heart sank

'It is just a bit of fun,' said Beryl carefully.

'Fun can be damaging, Mrs Baxter,' replied Miss Blake
without compromise.

Harvey made an attempt to lighten the debate. 'Well, I
do have to confess that despite all that, I have been guilty of enjoying that page every now and then.'

Her sister gave an animated whinny.

'*Enjoy it*? Are you out of your mind, Harv? Dear me!
I've never read anything so ridiculous in my life! She really is
the most frightful bore! I am quite appalled by her attitude. She
has no concept of sisterhood! Silly woman.'

I went to speak, but could not get a word in.

'The woman simply doesn't have a clue! I'd bet my bottom dollar that miserable Margaret's some chain-smoking, ad-
dlepated old bag who puts together the horse racing sections,
with no qualifications or life experience to speak of.'

I grumbled a little, and found Miss Blake glowering in
my direction.

'You work with her, don't you, Mr Edgar? Have you
met her? Am I right? What is she like?'

The women were all looking at me, Beryl with a mischievous twinkle, Harvey with some concern, and her sister
clearly awaiting some slanderous anecdotes about the apparently
ghastly Margaret Blythe.

I sat for a moment or two in a silent rage. The heat in
my chest had risen, and I tried desperately to compose myself.
As I spoke, addressing Miss Blake alone, it was hard not to
stumble upon my words.

'Dr Margret Blythe is a remarkable woman, in actual
fact... with a true intellectual mind and vast life experience An

exceedingly respectable lady. She is certainly no "*old bag*" as you put it. Her advice, although perhaps controversial, is always given with the correspondence's best interests at heart.'

'Here here!' sang Beryl.

Miss Blake had the temerity to laugh doubtfully. Harvey leaned over and gently touched my arm.

'And she is clearly a good friend of yours, Mr Edgar. I am sorry if I or my sister have caused offence.'

'A really most remarkable woman!' I repeated, before throwing back the remains of my drink, jumping to my feet and making a move to the door. I could stand Petra Blake no longer. As I approached the door I could feel her cunning eyes on my back.

'Please excuse me, ladies. I need some fresh air.'

I went straight up to my room with something of a cloud over my head. It wasn't what her sister had gabbled on about that upset me so, but what Harvey Blake had said. Dr Blythe had an alarmingly pre-suffragette approach to women? *Really*?

I took out some of my correspondences. The evidence was there, if I looked for it. On the whole, Dr Margaret's advice was sound - but perhaps, at times, she was indeed a little old-fashioned, putting women in their place in a way that a man might.

For first time in my life, I sat and pondered over my approach to women. I considered the events of the past few days. I had disapproved of Miss Moore's reception and driving. Would I have felt the same it she were a man? The inspector had pointed out that I favoured females when weighing up the possibility of violent murder. Did I really have a skewed view of the fairer sex? Should I even be calling them 'the fairer sex?"

I felt a bit giddy.

And then, of course, I had been so shocked when businessman Harvey Blake had turned out to be a woman.

Pulling myself together, I fished out the small batch of letters awaiting reply. One or two letters in particular presented a perfect opportunity for me to reset the balance - if I was brave enough.

I picked up my very best pen and set to it.

Chapter IX
In which Payton Edgar searches in a haystack and finds a needle

Dear Margaret,
My husband wants me to get a job. I am a dutiful housewife; I cook and clean and do what needs to be done, but he is a modern man who believes that if one is fit to work, one should - male or female. I have tried to tell him that I am happy with my place, but he won't listen. What can I do to make him see sense?
Angie, Earls Court

Margaret replies; *an acquaintance recently pointed out to me that, at times, my attitude towards the rights of women over men could be seen as questionable. It takes a brave and canny mind to consider their conduct and admit their mistakes, and after much soul-searching I acknowledge whole-heartedly that I could do more to champion the independence of women. To that end, I agree with your husband on this issue. The only advice I can give you, Angie, is to follow the lead of many strong, independent women around the country and get to work with your head held high. You might even enjoy it.*

The smell of cooking vegetables wafted along from the kitchens and pulled me downstairs.

In the hallway, Constable Whitby was crouched over the telephone, booking a number of rooms for the night at an inn called the Blue Boar. He was nodding like a puppy as I passed by.

'I do appreciate that, thank you. It's for the local force. We're stuck up at Fallow House and there's no chance of us getting to the station in this snow.' He listened for a minute. 'Just the one? Well, I suppose that'll have to do. Any chance of any hot grub?'

Smiling at the thought of the three officers crammed into one grotty guest room, I took a moment to contemplate my next move. I thought of Maeve, and pictured her sitting outside wrapped in blankets under the pale winter sun, bent over, writing in her red book.

The missing journal. *Where could it be?*

It hadn't been in the suitcase of things retrieved from her

bedroom, but I was certain from the way she held it that it was too valuable to have ever be left lying around for anyone to find.

So where was it?

I passed through the hallway and was distracted by some hurried, urgent voices coming from the rear of the house. Prosper and Carter were exchanging words in the porch at the rear. The back door was ajar allowing icy air to flow in - but neither seemed to notice or care.

The chef was swaying as he stood and braying like a donkey, apparently taking yet another opportunity to goad Carter into a fight.

'Man or mouse, eh, Carter? Man or mouse? Fancy a re-match tonight? Up the stakes, what?'

'Shut your fat yap, just for once, Arn.'

Prosper issued a rasping chuckle.

'Moth-eaten wallet, eh? I'm sure you could put a little something else on the table, eh? To keep the peace-'

Carter squared up to the chef. I was careful to remain out of sight.

'Don't push me, Prosper. You don't have anything-'

'Not even the girl?' Prosper pressed with a chuckle. Carter stepped closer.

'Not even the girl,' he said with a glint in his eye. 'So get off my back.'

Prosper gave an exaggerated shrug. There was something rather vaudevillian about his actions.

'Then there must be something you have of value? What about a car? No? What about one of m'lady's bloody cars? She's got enough, wouldn't notice if one drove away and never came back-'

'Watch it!'

'Come on, Carter! Finish on a high, for God's sake. Scared? Where's your fight?' Prosper was nose to nose with his adversary, and Carter took the opportunity to grasp his opponents lapels.

'I'll give you fight, if you want it, Arn!' He pushed, not sharply, but the chef was tiddly enough to stagger back and career into the wall as though hit with some force. After a dazed second, he let out a loud, bawdy laugh.

Carter left the chef cowering and headed in my direction.

As quickly as I could, I ducked into a recess and watched him go. I heard the click of the back door as Prosper went out into the cold. Alone again, I took in a deep breath and made my way back out into the hallway. Carter disappeared into the drawing room, and I found Beryl following in his wake. She peered at me curiously.

'What are you up to, Payton? You have that look!'

'What look?'

'Befuddlement, I suppose. You look confused, dear-heart. Can I help?'

I pictured the red journal.

'I am looking for something, and don't know where to begin.'

'Perhaps I can help?'

I tried to let her down gently. 'I hardly think so, Beryl. It is a big house, and I just don't know where to start.'

'Well, perhaps if you tell me what you're looking for?' Beryl persevered. 'I am not a complete idiot, you know.'

I huffed lightly.

'A book, Beryl. Where might I find a book?'

She cocked her head to one side.

'Why, in the library, of course.'

Her eyes twinkled innocently.

'That, Beryl, is the most obvious-'

I stopped myself.

The library.

What was it the girl Maeve had said, only the day before? That the library was her favourite room in the house.

And then what else was it she had added?

'It is the perfect place to hide.'

A place to hide, I thought to myself.

'Beryl, you are a genius!'

'I know. Now, if you'll excuse me!'

She tottered after Carter, and I made my way to the library with a renewed vigour.

I paused at the threshold. A well-worn expression sprung to mind; *like a needle in a haystack.* Where better to hide a book – than amongst a huge collection of books?

I set to searching straight away.

It is a bore to be so terribly correct all the time. It took me quite a while to find the little red book, but find it I did. It was tucked between two larger red volumes at a child-friendly height on a shelf which faced away from any casual observers. Fingerprints in the dust were revealed upon close inspection.

Maeve had kept the book in this slot, away from prying eyes. Strange that the girl hadn't kept it in the safety of her own bedroom. But what, apart from the diary itself, had she been hiding?

I pulled out a heavy chair, set it at the desk and dived into the book. The journal may have once been private, but now the writer was dead and someone had to discover her secrets. It was only natural that it should be me.

The writing was surprisingly well schooled, and one could not deny that the girl had a way with words. Almost every entry was heartfelt and somewhat revealing. I only interrupted myself once, for the sun was setting quickly and casting shadows across the room. I found some matches and continued to read by candlelight. I was there for some time, occasionally issuing a gasp or sigh as secrets and sadness were revealed.

And by the end - which came all too abruptly - I knew who the girl was. Not only that, I knew why she had come to the Blake house, and why she had done what she had done. And - quite possibly - why she was murdered.

I also knew what I had to do.

I had to call a house meeting.

Chapter X
In which Payton Edgar tells of a deathbed confession

Dear Margaret,
My daughter is a tom-boy. I wish that she would wear pretty dresses and have beautiful long, shiny hair like any girl should. However, she prefers to wear trouser suits and flat shoes, and has short, cropped hair just like a boy. She has landed herself a good job, but she is almost twenty, and I fear for her finding a husband if she carries on this way. What can I do?
Dorothy, Chiswick

Margaret replies; *your daughter sounds like a sensible, modern, strong-minded young woman. I'm sure that - if she wants to - she will find herself a husband who is attracted to sensible, modern, strong-minded women. Would she be happier if you forced her to grow her hair and wear a dress? I very much doubt it. Men and women come in all shapes and sizes, and this is a fact that we should applaud, not condemn.*

I am not an impetuous soul.

I had carefully considered what to do with the information gleaned from the pages of Maeve Taylor's diary, and identified three possible options. I swiftly discounted two.

The first was the idea of confronting those implicated of wrong-doing alone and face to face. It was an idea fraught with potential danger. I wasn't about to put myself in the firing line of any bloodthirsty murderer. The second option was to hand the information over to Standing - this being equally undesirable, for the obvious reasons. I wasn't about to show my hand early, or to allow him to claim my deductions as his own.

And so, there was only one sensible action to take. I would demand a house meeting and reveal all in the safety of company.

To do this I would, of course, have to gain the consent of the plods, and for that reason I knocked harshly on the dining room door and entered without command.

Having finished an afternoon of interviews they were obviously none the wiser as to what was going on, as was evident by their irritated expressions as I entered. The room was hot, and stuffy, their faces red with frustration. I lifted my chest and my chin and briefly announced my intention. As expected, Standing wasn't about to let me get my way. He probed wearily for details, but I am proud to say that I kept my cards close to my chest and merely insisted that I would need the household gathered in order to reveal some truths.

'Truths?' the inspector had grumbled.

'*Truths,*' I replied with confidence.

In the end, in the face of defeat and much to my delight, Standing agreed that I could gather the house in the dining room.

I sent Beryl upstairs with the message, and then made my way about the ground floor ordering people to congregate in the dining room immediately. I found Harvey Blake rinsing glasses in the kitchen and told her about the meeting, adding some carefully chosen words.

'I am afraid that a number of secrets will come to light. It may not be what you want to hear.'

Her response was firm.

'As I said before, Payton, I just want to know the truth, and get it all over with.'

She would not be disappointed.

Beryl was soon back from her errand and, as we went to the dining room together, she goaded me cheekily for information. I delighted a little in keeping her hanging.

'Not until everyone is here, Beryl dear!'

Slowly, the others arrived and gathered around the large table. After politely asking Mr Lloyd to open a small window and let some cold fresh air settle the room, I stood at the head of the table, the little red book clamped under my right arm.

At first, Inspector Standing refused to come any further into the room than the doorway, where he held the swinging door and leaned heavily on his stick.

'Right then, Edgar. This had better be worth it!'

'It will be, I assure you.'

'And none of your flim-flam. Just tell us who did it!'

Flim-flam!

'Oh, I am not about to do that, Inspector,' I replied quickly, and with an effortless control.

He pulled one of his faces.

'Then what the devil have you gathered us all here for?'

'Inspector, we are not two-penny characters in some cheap crime novella! I am merely here to share some knowledge that will be of help to your investigation. To drop a little oil into the water and watch it spread.'

'Oil in the-?' Standing began, before swallowing it with a growl.

'You may not like me, Inspector, but the truth must come out one way or another.' I spoke loudly, smoothly and with confidence. All the faces around the table turned in his direction.

'*Like*? Like doesn't come into it, Edgar. Do my best not to *like* anyone.' He nudged a finger into his moustache. 'Doesn't do. Not in this game.'

That, I suspect, was exactly where the man went wrong, but I wasn't about to point that out to the whole room. Instead I began my speech, slowly and carefully.

'Now then... it has been a terrible day, I'm sure you all agree. But we can make some sense of it.' Here, I raised my voice. 'I have gathered you all here to reveal some truths.'

No one spoke, and for a moment I enjoyed the silence

There was quite an audience before me. Beryl was to my left, Harvey Blake to my right. Behind her Miss Moore leaned against the wall, still in mourning over the dead bird, and then Petra Blake sat to her right, grim faced and resolute. At the chair in the corner, Gideon Carter bit down on his stinking pipe. His expression gave away nothing. Arthur Lloyd stood firm in his place by the cabinet, and propped against it was Prosper, drinking. Joan Turpin and the vicar shared the chaise-lounge at the far wall. I hadn't bothered to invite the housekeeper's anomalous son, and had left him outside on the lawn, frolicking in the snow with the massive red dog.

Inspector Standing allowed the door to slam and moved to a place at the far end of the dining table, where he sat and glared over his wild moustache. The nasty thing curled over his lip like a hairy croissant. Whitby was beside him, pad and pen in hand as always.

I would be lying if I said that all this grandstanding didn't give me a fizzle of pleasure. I cut straight to the chase.

'Young Maeve told me, in confidence, that she hated a member of this household. One has to ask - why should an innocent young thing harbour such a malignant emotion? This book may shed some light on that.'

I held out the red book and let it drop to the table.

Silence.

I studied the faces around the room. Surely some of them recognised the book. Our murderer had perhaps even been searching for it in vain.

'What is that?' asked the inspector, obviously determined in his petty-minded way to remain stubbornly unenthused by anything I had to declare.

'A diary,' I replied simply. 'Maeve Taylor's diary.'

'Where did you get it?' Whitby asked with a squeak. 'We cleared her room!' I merely raised my eyebrows. That would remain my secret.

Standing clicked his fingers twice and held out his hand.

'Let's have it here, then!' he ordered, obstinately.

I raised an open palm with the air of a traffic warden.

'There is no need, Inspector. I have taken the time to read the entire journal. The are a number of details within that shed some light upon recent events. It is, in actual fact, an extremely revealing document, from which we can draw a number of conclusions - revelations even - about a number of the people in this room today.'

I knew that I wouldn't be making any friends with these words, and yet I was still little perturbed by the palpable change in my audience. The questioning looks had given way to suspicion, even animosity. Even Harvey was studying me suspiciously. Beryl was smiling, but it was a noticeably uncomfortable smile.

And yet I soldiered on.

'When the girl appeared six weeks ago, she caused quite a stir with her resemblance to tragic Charlotte Blake-'

Joan Turpin gave an involuntary snort. 'Resemblance! It was more than a resemblance! Downright unnatural!'

I jabbed a finger in the direction of the housekeeper.

'Indeed. And the girl was treated as nothing more than an anomaly, even an aberration, by certain members of the household. You, Mrs Turpin, were one of the worst. Young Maeve has much to say about how you treated her, and it was not favourable. She was a guest in the house-'

'Phhh! Pah!' This trumpeting came from Petra Blake.

'A ghost in the house, more like!' Joan Turpin put in wildly.

'That kind of comment is exactly what hurt her so much! You made her feel unwelcome and unwanted, Mrs Turpin.' I knocked on the book. 'It's all in here. You rather frightened the poor girl.'

'Nonsense!' This was from Prosper. 'Old Turnip couldn't scare a boozy goose!''

The housekeeper frowned.

'I quite agree! What rubbish! I was nice enough to the girl. I read her the tarot-'

'Indeed you did, and it put the fear of God into her. You predicted nothing but misery ahead, identified her as an outcast and claimed that the cards suggested that she should leave as soon as possible-'

'Tarot is an extremely serious business, Mr Edgar!' the housekeeper snapped with surprising brutality. 'It is hardly all ponies and play-tents! Even for a young girl-'

'A young girl indeed. A young, *frightened* girl.'

Joan Turpin looked like she had been slapped. She hitched up her bosom with crossed arms. 'Well, I certainly never meant-!'

I moved on.

'But there was worse for poor Maeve. She may not have been the most comely girl in the world, but she had youth on her side, and this led to some… unwanted advances, as you might imagine.'

Clearly keen to move the spotlight elsewhere, Joan Turpin glowered at Prosper.

'Mmm! And we know exactly where they came from, don't we!'

Dare I say it?

'Actually, Mrs Turpin, you would do better looking to your *right*. Although the girl did bat away Prosper's wandering hands yesterday, she took all of that in her stride. Prosper may be a lecherous imbecile, but lecherous imbeciles can be easily handled.'

'Well, thank you very much indeed, old fruit!' Prosper coughed. I continued, undeterred.

'Maeve's unwanted advances came from another, altogether more unexpected quarter.'

Joan Turpin turned her head. To her right sat the vicar, and then Arthur Lloyd. Neither said a word, but their expressions spoke volumes. Arthur Lloyd's face remained impassive and stony as ever. The vicar, however, was rapidly reddening. I continued bravely.

'The diary tells us that Daniel Drinkwater has been making overtures to the girl for some time, and even quite forcedly of late. You rather scared the poor young thing. This, Reverend, is why you were not invited for Christmas this year.'

This particularly ugly cat was out of the bag, and I encouraged it to spit and claw a little.

"Poppycock!' said the vicar, weakly.

'Father Drinkwater?' Joan Turpin whispered. She was inspecting his face, and clearly didn't like what she saw. Suddenly, she lifted up her handbag, stood abruptly and stamped from the room. Drinkwater watched sadly as she went.

'Poppycock!' he said again. 'Whatever the child has written - just fiction, all of it! Lies... nonsense...' The clergyman's words were hollow, his dampening brow and raging skin telling another story entirely. Harvey Blake was nodding, just a little. She knew the truth.

'Are you saying,' Inspector Standing ploughed on, 'that the vicar killed the girl?'

I was quick to jump in.

'I am saying no such thing! Although one cannot overlook the possibility, with this information in mind.'

Daniel Drinkwater, red faced and wide eyed, made some unhappy noises and then took up his coat and went out after the housekeeper. Beryl leaned in and whispered in my ear.

'You're doing great, Payton, just great. Keep this up and in ten minutes you'll have cleared the room.'

I shot her a look.

And then Alison Moore joined the conversation.

'Okay then, Mr Edgar, let's get the rest out of the way quick as we can. What did she have to say about me? What did I do to upset the poor, innocent child?' Her words were laced with sarcasm, and I was pleased to be able to look surprised.

'Actually, Miss Moore, you barely feature at all in the journal. She scribbles a little about your frankness, and I rather think she appreciated your honesty. You might pretend to dislike her, but in truth, when alone, you shared confidences. Perhaps she told you a thing or two that might help this investigation?'

'I wish she had,' she replied regretfully.

'Well, that is all there is concerning you, Miss Moore. As far as the diary goes, you are hardly important. You and Harvey here were the only two people the girl had anything nice to say about.'

'Can we stop talking about what's *not* important, and talk about what *is*?' the inspector said with unnecessary urgency.

It was time to get to the heart of the matter.

'Young Maeve Taylor was more than just a stranger here, Inspector. She was much more than just a girl who dropped into the village by chance. She came here quite deliberately. Her visit to Tetherton was something of a pilgrimage. She came to where she might belong. You see, Maeve Taylor was *family.*'

Here my eyes met Harvey's.

Her expression was unreadable, and I steeled my heart. I had no intention of hurting my host, but the truth had to come out sooner or later. And she herself had insisted that she wanted the truth.

'I have suggested to the inspector that Taylor was not the girl's real surname. And if not, then what was it?'

I allowed a tasty pause.

'This photograph can provide us with the answer!'

I pulled out the photo frame I had retrieved from the drawing room and turned it out to face my audience. For a moment I examined their faces, their enquiring eyes, knowing that to at least one of them, an examination of this photo would be unwelcome in the extreme.

'Three young girls, in the height of summer, relaxing by the riverside eighteen years ago. The bathing beauties; Charlotte - or *Lotty* - Blake in the centre, Fran Thompson on the right, and here, Constance Frick to the left.'

Here I left another beautifully dramatic pause, which was swiftly ruined by the inspector.

'So what of it?'

Determined to hold court, I purposefully hesitated before continuing.

'An eighteen year-old girl, Constance Frick. *Maeve Taylor's mother.*'

I was expecting to witness surprise, perhaps even shock, in my audience. However, I got very little by way of a response. Carter remained mute and puffed on his pipe. Harvey had set her chin firm, lips pursed. The others just looked confused.

I continued with confidence.

'In the diary, young Maeve Taylor, or Maeve *Frick* as she was christened, writes in detail about the recent death of her mother, way up in Yorkshire. She inherited little, for there was little to inherit. But what she did receive was a deathbed confession. In her last hours, her mother informed her that she was conceived at Fallow House, eighteen years ago, when her mother was only a child herself. She was the result of an illicit affair with her best friend's father - Gideon Carter.

'That deathbed confession sent Maeve down to Tetherton, on a quest to find her father.'

And now I had some rumbles of interest from the officers in front of me. Standing turned on Carter.

'She would be Charlotte's half-sister, hence the likeness. Well, is this true?' he boomed.

Carter's eyes were fixed on Harvey.

'It was a long time ago,' he said, his words barely audible. And then the pipe was down and his head lowered. Unable to help myself, I took a moment to gaze at Standing with a glow of self-satisfaction.

Petra Blake had been uncharacteristically quiet during all this, but now she spoke up, her words dripping with poison.

'I knew it! Nothing but a cheating snake!'

'I'm glad that it's out in the open, actually,' declared Carter with some vigour, lifting his head. 'It needed to come out, I just didn't know how. Harvey, when you bought the girl home in November she told me pretty much straight away who she was. I hadn't even known Connie had gotten pregnant. It was a stupid mistake. *Another* stupid mistake. And I know it was wrong.

'They moved up north that Autumn, and pretty sharpish - do you remember? And now we know why. Connie told me nothing of this – never heard from her again after they went. And then, this Autumn, there was this girl, claiming to be my daughter. And looking just like our Charlotte. But not like our Charlotte, really. This girl was hard, cunning even.'

'An innocent child!' Inspector Standing corrected him with a roar.

'Hardly, Inspector. I'll admit I didn't welcome the news, not at first. I gave her a pretty short thrift, and yes, I'm sure that it upset her. But I'd needed time to sort it all out in my head. It just didn't make sense - why she came to Fallow House and, well, bewitched you in that way, Harvey. Just to get to me.

'By the time I felt ready to admit the truth, Maeve was dead set against me. I tried, I really did. I tried to talk her, even to get to know her. I tried to work out how we could tell you who she was, Harvey. But she was flat against it. Wouldn't talk to me, wouldn't even look at me. As far as she was concerned, I had already ruined any relationship we could have had. You mentioned hatred, Mr Edgar - these last few weeks, she's hated me. *Really* hated me. What do you think that performance at the séance was about? She practically accused me of murdering my own daughter!'

Harvey, to my surprise, was nodded at his words. What that sympathy in her eyes?

Carter saw this.

'I didn't mean to hurt you, Harvey. I really didn't. It was all so long ago. When we reunited, we agreed to leave the past behind - to bury any past mistakes. Didn't we? *Didn't we?*'

Harvey nodded and even smiled, and I surely wasn't the only person in the room to acknowledge this with a start. Was the woman going to forgive him all this?

'I don't think she hated you, Giddy. Not really.' Harvey was speaking softly and surprisingly warmly. 'Sometimes it's simply easier to hate than to love. But there is a very fine line between love and hate.'

Tears formed in the foreigner's eyes, and I was awaiting his response with bated breath when Inspector Standing crashed in.

'You do realise, Carter, that this gives you a big fat motive for murder?'

Gideon Carter flushed a dangerous red and then stood, stepped up and slammed a fist onto the table.

'I didn't kill the girl, Inspector, for the last time! What would I have to gain from that?'

'To silence her, perhaps?' Standing continued. 'I severely doubt that you were really thinking of telling everyone the truth, to shout her illegitimacy from the rooftops! Was she about to reveal her identity, against your wishes? What would that do to your chances of re-marriage into the Blake family?'

The inspector was chewing this over with an ignorant confidence.

'Harvey would forgive me,' Carter stated without hesitation. 'We have an agreement on the past.' He looked to his fiancee, appealingly.

'It's true, Inspector,' said Harvey, gently.

'Then what about the death of Charlotte Blake eighteen years ago? The girl appeared to know some truth about that. Another part of the deathbed confession?'

Gideon raised his voice and cut off the inspector sharply.

'I did not kill my daughter, Inspector! *Either* of my daughters!' His voice cracked. 'Charlotte drowned all those years ago. It was an accident. An accident!'

'And yet Maeve Taylor's death was far from an accident!' said the inspector with relish.

At this, Harvey was up and at Carter's side. She placed a hand on his shoulder and a tanned, hirsute hand reached up to grasp it.

To my surprise, the inspector was now staring directly in my direction.

'Well?' He asked, impatiently and with a whiff of help-lessness, 'What now?'

I looked to the floor. I had nothing else to say.

After a while, Standing smacked his lips together and came to a decision.

'Due to the snow, we are staying down at the Blue Boar in the village tonight. Perhaps, Mr Carter, it would be best if you joined us down there, in light of this-'

'Absolutely not, Inspector,' Harvey piped up. 'Is he un-der arrest? Do you have any evidence against Gideon?'

'Evidence?' The inspector chuckled. 'The murder of his illegitimate daughter, coshed by a statue from his own bedroom? I should say that's a pretty good start!'

'You know that's not enough, Inspector!' Harvey replied sternly.

'Do not force my hand, Miss Blake.'

'If he is not under arrest then Gideon will stay with me tonight,' Harvey stated, holding out a hand. 'Come along.'

'Harvey, no! The *scoundrel*!' Petra Blake shouted, but to their backs. One could almost see the storm clouds gathering above her head.

I watched as Carter slid his arm around Harvey Blake's shoulders and they led each other out of the room. Whatever I had imagined might happen in light of the diary's revelations, it was not this.

Suddenly, Standing completely forgot about his injury and leapt to his feet. Before they could reach the door, he blocked their way.

'You are forcing my hand. Gideon Carter, I am arresting you for the murder of Maeve Taylor.'

'Frick!' I put in quickly.

'For the murder of Maeve Frick.'

'No!' Harvey wailed. Carter stood still, helpless.

After the inspector had finished and the cuffs were on, he turned to Whitby.

'Call ahead to the Blue Boar, have them find a lockable room for Carter tonight, even if it's the bloody broom closet. We'll move on to the station first thing tomorrow, if the damed weather's better.'

And so Gideon Carter was arrested and led away, leaving Harvey Blake alone. Her face was a picture of frustration and something else - fear.

I moved to her side.

'I'm so sorry-' I began, but was cut short. With a shake of the head, she pushed me aside and fled from the room.

Behind me, Beryl gave a little cough.

'Well! That was fun!' she droned sardonically.

Chapter XI
In which Payton Edgar confesses his guilt

Dear Margaret,
I fear I may have been too hasty in calling off my wedding. My fiancé is dreadfully clumsy and inconsiderate, and just two months before our wedding day he fell asleep while smoking and set alight to my grandmother's gooseberry-print eiderdown. I am devastated by the damage to what was a cherished family heirloom. Although he has never liked it, I know that it was an accident, and he has done everything he can to apologise to me since. Should I take him back?
Jackie, High Barnet

Margaret replies; *my dear Jackie, there is no such thing as an accident. You say yourself that the man didn't like the eiderdown, and so I doubt he feels any remorse over his actions. It sounds to me that you loved the eiderdown more than you loved him. You are probably better off without him. Next time it perhaps won't only be a rancid, musty old eiderdown that he burns to a crisp.*

There was no roast partridge nor a grand gathering for Christmas dinner that evening, despite what Harvey Blake had said. In fact, she was notable by her absence. True, my declarations in the dining room had perhaps soured things a little bit, but it was a shame to miss out on a roast bird and all the trimmings. I wondered if I would still be granted those wonderful offices adjacent to Harvey's Restaurant, fingering the key in my pocket thoughtfully and contemplating a knock on her door.

I decided against it.

The inspector and his gang had retired to the Blue Boar, no doubt enjoying the hearty cooking and home-brewed ale on offer, the bill settled by the taxpayer's pocket. It was a painful fact that Gideon Carter, despite being under arrest for murder, would eat a better Christmas dinner than any of us up at Fallow House.

Prosper turned out a surprisingly disappointing cold buffet for those who felt like joining the table to eat. It is well known that I am no fan of a buffet, and the sight of one for

Christmas dinner was heartbreaking. The salad garnishes had been competently prepared, but with little flair, and the meats were absent-mindedly selected and cut. The mediocre spread wasn't helped by the unsettling presence of an unusual carrot puree in a silver dish. I observed the buffet mournfully, and resigned myself to the fact that there would be no sign of the promised plum pudding with brandy butter.

A sorry state of affairs indeed.

At first there was only Prosper and I at the table. He stared at me with amused, mocking eyes, but thankfully kept his mouth so stuffed with food that he barely said a thing. I watched as he feasted greedily, as though nothing untoward had occurred, slathering his bread with almost half the butter in the dish and taking large gulps of wine in between mouthfuls. My appetite had dwindled, but I did my best. I had helped myself chiefly to the crackers, pickles and cheese, with only a spattering of salad leaves, and found myself pushing a fork lazily across my plate.

Every now and then Arthur Lloyd appeared with something or other to add to the buffet table. Soon Prosper was nodding off over his empty plate and drooling unappealingly.

And then suddenly, as I lay down my fork in defeat, the room began to fill. Beryl came first, selecting only one or two items for her plate. She was one of those people who coyly make small selections from a buffet, only to return umpteen times, the total sum of these small selections being a gargantuan portion. We exchanged some comments about the spread, but quietly so as not to disturb Prosper from his slumber.

Next, Alison Moore appeared, sending us a tight lipped and courteous smile before turning to the buffet. Beryl went back for seconds.

'I should avoid the carrot puree,' I said, in an unintentionally ominous tone. Prosper, awake and befuddled, shot me a dark glare. Miss Moore poked her fork at a plate.

'What's this grey meat?' she enquired suspiciously. 'Turkey?'

'What do you think it is?' Prosper piped up. 'Wasn't about to let 100 year old meat go to waste, was I? Despite his vintage, old General Custard certainly had some meat on his bones! Ha-ha-ha!' The man couldn't resist pulling her leg, even though we all knew she had respectfully buried the dead bird earlier. He knew how much the secretary had loved The General, and appeared to find its demise amusing.

'It's partridge, and certainly tastier than it looks,' I said quickly, and we all looked disparagingly at Prosper.

Miss Moore was gathering up a choice selection of the meat when Miss Blake entered the room. She acted as if the rest of us were merely furniture and headed straight for the secretary.

'Well, Alison? Did you know?'

The secretary spooned some egg onto her plate and sighed.

'Did I know *what*, Petra?'

'About the girl and where she came from? You seem to know every little thing that goes on in this house, and you two were thick as thieves, apparently. You should've told Harvey.'

'It was as big a surprise to me as it was to you, I assure you,' replied Miss Moore, although with little conviction in her tone. She sounded bored.

'I knew about it!' Prosper spoke up from his place at the table. He was so well-oiled that his voice was high and cheery. Both ladies glared at his red-cheeked grin. 'Well, it was obvious. She had some moxie about her that's missing from the Blake line. She could only have been Gideon's girl!'

'Shut up, chef!'

This came from Petra Blake, who headed for the door and, for a moment, looked as if she was leaving. Then she turned on her heel.

'Who told you?' she demanded, bypassing Miss Moore and directing her focus onto the chef. He was nibbling on a large wedge of cheese, holding it aloft on the end of a long knife.

'Nobody told me.'

'Of course they did! Is that why you and Carter are forever at loggerheads?'

'I simply worked it out, my dear Petri-dish. Did it really come as a surprise? Two girls who look alike - it's not hard to work out that identical blooms stem from the same seed now, is it?'

Having made this surprisingly astute point, he went on, slurring his words as he spoke.

'It seems that it is the time for secrets to be uncovered, what? Skeletons to come rattling out of your closets? Long discarded bodies to come bobbing to the surface...'

'I don't know what you mean!'

'Oh, I think you do!' he chimed. Miss Blake's expression darkened.

'If you think I had anything to do with that girl's death, you are sorely mistaken!'

'Oh, I quite agree!' Prosper cackled. 'I was talking about another little secret, dear Petri-dish. No, as far as the murder is concerned, if you ask me that potato-headed retard from the gatehouse did her in!'

'Arnold Prosper!'

Joan Turpin stood in the doorway in heavy boots and a long macintosh. She looked tired and slumped a little, but there was detectable fire in her eyes. 'To whom are you referring?' she asked heavily.

'You know full well!' Prosper replied lazily, nibbling on his cheese. He let out a proud belch. The housekeeper lifted her chin and addressed the secretary.

'Alison, I'm off home now. It's still quite the blizzard out there. I'll try and get Harry out on the drive with the salt and grit first thing, once I can prize him out of his pit.'

Nobody responded, but she wasn't ready to go yet. She cleared her throat loudly.

'Well, I'll be back up first thing, get the laundry going. I for one shall sleep soundly in my bed tonight knowing that Mr Carter's out of the way.'

Still nobody reacted, even Petra. Miss Moore was digging about the beetroot with a slotted spoon. Prosper had set down his cheese and was circling the rim of his glass with his fingers. Beryl was back at the table getting her thirds.

I gave the housekeeper a forced smile, which took some effort. To my surprise, she returned this with a scowl.

Suddenly there was a fierce rapping on the window pane, and we all jumped. Outside in the gloom stood Inspector Standing surrounded by falling snowflakes and looking for all the world like a furious snowman. His collar was up around his neck, his eyes wide and angry, and he looked more like a wolf at The Three Pig's door than a man of the law. He gesticulated in the direction of the door, then vanished. Mrs Turpin went to let him in, and we could hear exclamations from the hallway.

Pulled by curiosity, we all followed.

'Well? Where is he?' the inspector was shouting.

He was greeted by a chorus of *"beg pardons?"* and *"whats?"*.

'Carter's done a runner! Gave Whitby the slip and pelted off into the snow. He won't have gone far, and I'll bet my gold tooth he's come back here. Whitby! Search the house immediately! Make a beeline for Harvey Blake's room!'

Whitby tossed his coat aside and bounded up the staircase like a hound on a hunt. The inspector stomped upon the welcome mat, snow falling from his coat and shoes. He kept glaring in my direction, Heaven knows why.

Behind us, Arnold Prosper chuckled.

'What was that you said about sleeping soundly tonight, dear Mrs Turnip? Seems there's a murderer on the loose!'

The search for Carter proved fruitless.

They were still looking when Beryl and I sneaked off to the drawing room. She fixed herself a disproportionate gin and tonic, and a tomato juice for myself.

'Hadn't you better slow down a bit, Beryl?' I dared to suggest. 'You have been drinking, well, perhaps to excess…' I faltered. 'Just a little…'

'Christmas is all about excess, Payton dear-heart!' she sang with aplomb. 'Gorging is what one does at this time of year, and don't you dare try and tell me otherwise.'

She caught my look and softened her tone.

'Despite the horrible things that have happened, I am just trying to inject a bit of normality into the day.' She raised her glass. 'And *this* for me is normal. Now be quiet and enjoy your vegetable juice.'

'The tomato is a fruit, Beryl.'

'Oh, pooh!'

Soon we were sitting and sharing gossip, speculating and ruminating like two old dears at a bus stop.

'Do you know, they've laid out the poor girl's body in one of the garages! Covered in old curtain!' said my confidant with a detectable element of fascination in her tone.

'Who told you that?'

'Who do you think? Our friend, Prosper. He knows everything.'

'You are far too cordial to that man, Beryl. He may be a wonder of a chef, but he is a prize idiot.'

'One gets ones thrills where one can, dear-heart. But it's not a nice thought, is it? Here we sit trying to enjoy Christmas and with that corpse laid out in the garage. Nowhere else to stick it and nobody to take it away, I suppose. Sad to think of her lying there, cold and alone. Creepy too.'

Our chatter eventually turned to the absent Mr Carter.

'Bah! Dear Gideon is no more a murderer than I am a tightrope walker!' said Beryl with feeling. 'He is far too handsome.'

'Handsome, perhaps, but the man has a shady past, Beryl.' I told her briefly about the man's stint in prison and, to my amazement, my friend merely shrugged with indifference.

'Can't say I'm surprised, darling. What would surprise me, however, would be if he had anything to do with the murder of Maeve Whatshername. Men like him might have a problem with gambling or keeping his fists to himself with other men, but to murder a young girl? No! Not him. Not his style.'

'You are too easily enticed by dangerous men, Beryl.'

Her eyes sparkled.

'I know. *Marvellous*, isn't it?'

There was a pause, and then she moved in closer.

'What I don't understand, Payton, is all this bird business. I can't really bring myself to believe that the violent assassin who so brutally butchered that girl would then bother to poison a fat old bird with soap! If I was them and I wanted it gone, well, I'd simply snap it's neck or... or bash it with a hammer or... or even just throw it out the window into the snow. That would've done the trick.'

I said nothing, and would have covered my silence with a drink but I had drained my glass. I glanced around the room. looking for a different topic of conversation. Beryl, unfortunately, knew me too well.

'Payton? What is it?'

Jolted, I lifted my shoulders. 'Nothing! What?'

'You have that look on your face. You *know* something.'

'I assure you there is nothing-'

'Don't you give me flannel, Mr Edgar! You're as shifty as my bookmaker! What is it? Tell Aunty Beryl!'

I was lost for words.

'We can't have secrets between us, Payton. Not you and I! I simply won't let you out of this room until you tell me!'

I swallowed, and considered my options. It would be good to share my guilt, to make a confession to a friend - so long as it would go no further. I made Beryl promise that she wouldn't breathe a word, and then told her slowly and carefully about how I had accidentally terminated the ancient family pet with a shoe of soap.

To my horror, she threw back her head and roared.

'Oh, Payton, darling! Only you!' she exclaimed in between guffaws. 'Wonderful! Only you could do that!'

She stood abruptly, shook herself down and moved over to the bar. She didn't even try to stifle her giggles as she unscrewed the cap of a bottle.

'Only you! Oh dear! You do know what this makes you?'

'Quiet, Beryl, please!'

She was so engrossed in drink preparation that she failed to see the door open. Harvey Blake appeared, followed by her sister.

'This makes you a murderer, Payton!' Beryl continued with faux solemnity. 'A murderer! But don't fret, I will keep your sordid secret. You cold, calculating murderer, you!'

Harvey looked on with surprise. At her side, Petra Blake cleared her throat.

'I beg your pardon, Mrs Baxter?'

Beryl swung around.

'You appear to know something we don't!' Miss Blake continued sternly. 'Let's have it!'

Beryl swung back to face me, her eyes wide.

'Sorry!' she mouthed, and bit down on her lip.

'Well?' Miss Blake pushed in her irritating, shrill tone. 'Tell us! What have you done, Mr Edgar?'

Chapter XII

In which Payton Edgar contemplates events over a steaming cup of Horlicks

Dear Margaret,
I am a retired schoolmistress and I am very worried about the attitude of modern children today. I am often cheeked or jeered at in the street by youths who should be taught better. I take Sunday school at our church and am finding it increasingly difficult to keep the group in check. I have heard that you have a background in education and would very much appreciate your advice.
Mrs Swann, Epping

Margaret replies; *education is one of the few areas in which I have no academic grounding, so I fear you have been misled. Those who specialise in schooling are, more often than not, oppressive dictators with a view that they - and they alone - can change the world. You sound no different. Perhaps if you can no longer rule your class you should consider full retirement and let the youth of today grow up in today's world, and not yesterday's.*

Petra Blake closed the drawing room door firmly, and then pushed past her sister. She descended upon me with a suspicious glare.

'Well then!' she barked. 'What's the beef?'

Harvey Blake was looking at me questioningly. I was quick to speak.

'I assure you, Miss Blake, I am entirely innocent of any wrong doing. Isn't that so, Beryl?'

'Then why is Mrs Baxter calling you a murderer? And what is this *sordid secret*? Eh? Come on!'

I appealed silently to Beryl. My friend was a quick thinking soul, and an expert liar - surely she could come up with something! To my horror, it was Harvey Blake who spoke up.

'I have twice caught Mr Edgar up to something in his room, hurriedly hiding documents of some sort as I entered.'

It was a shock to see how quickly Harvey could turn the finger of suspicion in my direction, and yet she was looking at me with sad, almost apologetic eyes. It can only be because she wanted to protect her jailbird ex-husband. I tried not to look too affronted.

As if coming to a conclusion, Beryl straightened and moved to my side. I thoroughly expected a clever lie - anything to get me out of the sticky situation.

'I think you'd better come clean, Payton,' she said grimly.

Oh dear.

'Come clean?'

'About who you really are.'

Baffled, I squirmed a little in my seat.

'I am Payton Edgar!' I bellowed, truthfully.

'I think, Payton, that you should tell them about *Margaret Blythe.*' Beryl said this slowly and carefully, pronouncing every syllable. 'And how you plan to terminate her.'

Miss Blake took the bait. 'What about the Margaret Blythe woman?'

Beryl perched on the edge of the armchair and weaved her fingers together. 'Payton was talking about terminating the piece, ending the agony column. Effectively murdering the poor woman. I am quite, quite against it...'

I ground my teeth together. I didn't like where this was all heading one bit.

'And the sordid secret?' Miss Blake asked sharply.

Beryl nodded with resignation.

'Payton *is* Margaret Blythe. Payton writes the agony column.' She revealed my greatest secret in a matter-of-fact tone and pressed her hand onto mine. 'And he mustn't kill it off - it is a popular staple of our daily newspaper. Almost as popular as my society page!'

'Is that all it is?' said Harvey. She looked, perhaps, a little relieved. 'You, Payton, are Margaret Blythe?'

'*Doctor* Margaret Blythe!' I put in, unable to stop myself, before giving Beryl the evil eye. I would, perhaps, had preferred that they knew I'd offed the ancient bird rather than share this particular little secret. Petra Blake was just beginning to chuckle when Arthur Lloyd made his entrance, noiseless as ever. I took this as a cue.

'Now that we have cleared that up, I should like to retire elsewhere.'

'I bet you would!' Miss Blake boomed.

I made my way across the room, my head high, and turned casually to the butler.

'I'll take a Horlicks in the library, if I may, Mr Lloyd? Four heaped teaspoons mixed to a smooth paste with a dash of cold milk, then topped with hot, rested two minutes off the boil. Thank you.'

The butler gave a hint of a bow and departed. I followed and, as I closed the door behind me, glanced back at the Blake sisters. Harvey simply looked surprised, but her sister's face had widened with the smuggest impression on her loathsome face.

As I left the room, her chuckle rose into a guffaw.

The butler prepared a near-perfect steaming mug of Horlicks, and I sat for a while in the cool, dark library, feeling like something of an unwanted house guest. I found myself missing Pimlico, the cat, Irving, my slippers, Grace and even Aunt Elizabeth. Christmas may been a bit of a miserable experience at home, but at least it *was* Christmas. Sitting in this library on Christmas day, it felt as far away from Christmas as one could imagine. No carols were playing, and the room felt dead. I eyed up the wheeled ladder against the far wall, resisting the urge to play a little.

I should have stayed at home, I thought to myself. As intolerable as Aunt Elizabeth can be around this time of year, at least I could have enjoyed escaping to Irving's house for a tipple or two, and a good old moan.

Why was I here?

I had been invited.

And what for?

A sojourn of parlour games and socialising? It had turned out to be the oddest gathering I had ever been to. If it weren't for Beryl, I would have felt entirely alone, and even she was now in my bad books after that scene in the drawing room. Fancy telling Harvey and Petra Blake - of all people - about Margaret Blythe!

I looked around the library, the stale air so still and lifeless.

After a while I plodded over to the wireless. Once it was switched on I did not need to turn the dial, for the pleasant, soothing sound of *"In the Bleak Midwinter"* wafted through the air. I returned to my seat and listened for some time.

A scraping noise shook me from my thoughts and, to my

horror, the huge red dog ploughed through the doorway. It padded heavily in my direction, and I pulled my drink away before it could stick it's long wet nose anywhere near. It stopped and looked at me, it's rasher-like tongue hanging unappealingly from it's jaws. I lifted myself up to my full height and fixed the beast with my most uncompromising glare.

'Shoo! Go on! Get out!'

After blinking its big black eyes a few times, it turned and padded slowly out of the room. Now that I was on my feet, I could resist the urge no longer, and found myself with one foot on the first step of the wheeled ladder. I gave a push with the other foot, and was delighted as the ladder slid easily along the wall. A second push sent me gliding again from corner to corner, and with a third push I was flying back when a cough from behind gave me a start.

'Enjoying yourself?'

Petra Blake hovered in the doorway, smirking. I stepped off the ladder and prepared myself for a fight.

It didn't come. Instead, she glanced down at the wireless.

'This is nice. *Snow on snow, snow on snow* indeed. I had almost forgotten it was Christmas.'

She stepped into the room. I returned to my seat.

'I came for a book.'

'Any news on Carter?' I enquired.

'Nowhere to be found!' She replied, idly fingering the spines on the second shelf. 'At least we know for sure now.'

'Know what?'

'Must I point out the obvious? Let's just say that while an innocent man might use words, the guilty use their feet. He'll be on his way to France or Scotland by now.'

I sipped on my Horlicks as the carollers sang.

'Why do you loathe the man so much?' I found myself asking. The question, once asked, felt like a very pertinent one. Ever since meeting the woman, she had never missed an opportunity to castigate her brother-in-law. Yes, he had treated her sister badly in the past, and yes, he was a criminal. But if Harvey had found it in her heart to forgive, why couldn't Petra?

She was frowning. My question had apparently been very unwelcome.

'I could count on my fingers and toes the reasons, Mr Edgar, but I would run out of digits. You only met the man yesterday, and can't possibly know how much pain and hurt he has caused over the years.'

'Mmm,' I hummed.

She looked up, and shocked me with a little smile.

'I quite admire you, actually, Mr Edgar,' she said, answering a question I had not asked.

'I beg your pardon?'

'Taking on the role of problem-solving fishwife with the agony column. From a creative point of view, it has some merit. You found a voice, and constructed quite a character, albeit a rather vile one. Perhaps you have do a novelist inside of you after all.'

Stunned, I sat still and speechless.

Miss Blake was smiling in my direction, almost sweetly.

Suddenly, the carol ended. At this, she moved to a bookcase, selected an apparently random tome, issued a curt 'good night', and was out the door with admirable speed.

Everyone's least favourite carol, *"Away in a Manger"* began.

Miss Blake had been almost civil - a Christmas miracle. A fittingly strange end to a strange day, I thought to myself.

Perhaps it was time for bed.

Part Four
Boxing Day

Chapter I
In which Payton Edgar happens upon a corpse

Dear Margaret,
I am often laughed at about my weight. I find it hard
to find clothes that fit, and I have tried to trim myself down
but nothing has worked. I am a good person, I try hard to do
well in life and yet I struggle to make and to keep friends.
People see me as slovenly and lazy and it makes me dreadful-
ly unhappy. I am fed up with feeling outcast, and being seen
as somebody I am not. What can I do?
Gert, Hornchurch

Margaret replies; I am very sure, Gert, that you are a delightful
person. All girls cannot be catalogue models - jolly, rotund people have just as much a place in our society as other, more perfect people. I am surprised that you struggle to make friends as,
in my experience, large people are often the life-and-soul of a
party, and good for a few chuckles. Perhaps you simply have to
learn to relax and to laugh at yourself, before others laugh at you.

Hot buttered crumpets!
I awoke violently, with an overwhelming hankering for
toasted bread-stuffs. It took me a moment to realise exactly
where I was, and then the irritating twittering of some country
bird, a flighty, repetitive chirping, reminded me. I pulled my
sheets up close to my chin and grizzled. What is the *point* of
birds? Why do they exist, I asked myself, if only to chirrup and
to annoy and to drop their dirt?
After the misadventures with the now-departed General,
I had rather gone off all things feathery.
I was up, washed and dressed before seven-thirty.
Outside, the snow may have ceased, but not before covering every inch of ground and every branch of every tree. The
scene from my bedroom window was so white and still, almost
alien in its serenity, and I watched it for a while. It would be
nice, I decided, to step gingerly through the deep, crisp snow.
After a hot cup of coffee and those warm buttery crumpets, perhaps.
I took up my winter coat, my divine smooth leather

gloves and my stick and left the room.

It felt as though I was the only person in the house as I padded along the hallway and down the beautiful staircase towards the kitchens. There was a notable absence of the enchanting smell of coffee or the welcoming aroma of toasted bread that should have been wafting through the building on Boxing Day morning. The place was cold and still.

I felt a sudden pang for Grace's perfectly timed boiled eggs and generously spread and uniformly cut buttered soldiers.

The kitchen was in disarray. I saw this immediately as I entered. A silver tray lay upturned on the floor with shattered cups and saucers littered around it. I huffed in disapproval and poked at the broken crockery with the end of my stick. Not only was there no breakfast to greet a hungry guest – somebody had made a mess and not bothered to tidy up either.

The kitchen was cold. *Ice cold.* I noticed with displeasure that the far door stood wide open.

What I failed to notice was the blood-stained corpse slumped over the counter in the far right-hand corner of the room. The crockery on the floor and an upturned stool in the centre of the room should have given me fair warning that all was not well, but - in my defence - I was sleepy and hungry, and not in the best of moods.

I was crossing the room to close the back door against the cold when I came across the corpse, and the image before me took some time to sink in. The bright red puddle of blood across the counter put me in mind of the rabbits Arnold Prosper had been tearing apart at that very spot a few nights ago.

But he would butcher rabbits no more, for the man was dead.

His left arm stretched out over the kitchen counter. His face was buried in the table, and a small sharp knife sat innocently to one side. A dark pool of blood spread tellingly from his neck.

I have to confess that, after surprise, the second thing I felt was sadness - a deep, enveloping grief. Grief for myself and for the savvy diners of central London. Never again would we enjoy one of Arnold Prosper's wonderfully prepared dishes. His talents with meats and sauces had been a joy.

What a dreadful, dreadful loss.

Chapter II
In which Payton Edgar is accused of tampering

Dear Margaret,
I have to keep an impeccably clean house, and drive myself to distraction over it. I scrub my floors daily and wash all surfaces and corners several times a day. I am so afraid of bugs and bacteria that I have to wash my hands a hundred times a day, at least. I have never wed, for I fear what filth a husband and children would bring into my house. Most days I don't go outside for I am too busy cleaning, and I loathe the dirt and smog of the city. Is this normal?
Trudy, Holloway

Margaret replies; *oh, the joys of an impeccably clean house! I salute your fastidiousness when it comes to hygiene, for I too cannot tolerate a filthy abode. It is perfectly normal to desire cleanliness in everything around you, and your spick-and-span house sounds like a true haven. Good for you!*

The telephone number for the Blue Boar was scribbled on a pad by the hallway telephone, and the inspector and plump little Constable Whitby were at the house within fifteen minutes of my call. They were both rosy cheeked and out of breath after a hurried trudge through the thick snow, and I greeted them at the door.

Standing had the cheek to eye me with suspicion as I showed him through to the grisly scene while giving him a quick account of how I had come across the body.

'Who was first on the scene? Who found him?'

'I did, Inspector.'

'And why were you in the kitchen?'

An interrogation already? I set my hands on my hips.

'Inspector, would it surprise you to know that a man who enters a kitchen first thing in the morning would be seeking breakfast? I was led there by my stomach. Much to my chagrin, no coffee or hot buttered crumpet greeted me-'

'Anyone else involved?'

'I think I am the only one up and out of bed as yet, Inspector.'

'And is the kitchen exactly as you found it? It is a crime scene now.'

I took his insolent enquiry for what it was.

'Of course the kitchen is as I found it! What do you take me for? I am well aware that it is a crime scene! Why should I wish to interfere? I have done my very best to leave things exactly as I found them.'

'You're quite certain that you haven't touched anything?' the inspector growled after we had passed through the kitchen door. He was questioning me with a doubtful tone, as if this latest mortality were entirely of my own doing.

'Quite certain, thank you!'

I moved over to the counter and took up my drink.

'Then what, Mr Edgar, is that?'

He issued this query with a grim look on his face. Completely ignoring the blood-stained corpse, he was pointing at the half-filled glass in my hand.

'Inspector, any idiot can see that it's a glass of water. I had to have a glass of water,' I replied. 'I was in shock!'

The inspector continued, remorselessly.

'And to whom does this coat belong?'

He was pointing to my navy tweed winter coat that I had mindlessly plonked on the back of a chair. He knew full well that it was mine. I had intended on stepping just a few feet outside to see the snow and breathe in the cold morning air, and before I could, I had made the grisly discovery. What else should I do with my coat? I said as much.

'And those tatty old gloves on the top?'

I sighed impatiently.

'Mine, Inspector. And I'll have you know that they are calf hide with a delightful knitted lining.'

Standing grumbled something through his whiskers and cast his eyes over the room. Whitby was at his side, emulating his senior's movements. They were both looking deadly serious, so much so that it was almost comical. Whitby stepped across the floor and tried the back door.

'Door's locked, Sir. From the inside.'

'Oh, I locked it! It was wide open when I found it-' the words were out my mouth before I could stop myself.

'You closed and locked the door, Edgar?' The inspector grunted.

'It was cold!' I protested. 'What else would one do with an open door in late December but close it?'

Whitby had moved on to the corpse. He bit down on his pencil.

'Throat slit, Sir. Odd looking knife, certainly not a kitchen knife. Not seen one like that before.'

'Mmm,' replied the inspector thoughtfully, 'I have... *somewhere.*'

Whitby went on.

'Probably got from behind, didn't know what hit him. Must've been quick, no signs of a struggle. Kitchen's pretty neat.'

Inspector Standing frowned and stepped over to the counter, where three stools sat lined up in formation. His eyes moved to the fourth stool over near the back door.

'There is a stool out of place. How did that stool get over there?' he asked to nobody in particular. I bit my lip. I wasn't about to give him the pleasure of ticking me off again. Of course I had righted the upturned stool. I am fastidiously tidy. Standing was scanning the kitchen like lasers were firing from his eyes. All of a sudden he stomped over to the far wall, dropped to a crouch and retrieved something from the corner.

'What's that, Sir? What have you got?' Whitby breathed, not unlike a child in wonder.

'Crockery, officer Whitby. *Broken Crockery*. A cup handle here, and what could be a splinter from a saucer or plate just there. There may have been a struggle, but over in this corner and not where the man was killed. Odd, though - there's only a few tell-tale signs. Someone has tried to clear up the-'

Suddenly his eyes were on mine.

I balled my fists at my side, my shoulders tensing. Standing's glare was uncompromising, and I was compelled to speak.

'Well,' I explained, 'what could I do? There was a terrible mess, and I couldn't just leave it. There were broken cups and saucers all over the floor! Somebody could have hurt themselves. That giant dog could've cut its paws or... or something.'

They were both staring at me with unwelcome judgement.

'Well, I shall leave you to it then.' I turned on my heel and left the kitchen, slowly and with the confidence of a responsible citizen.

In the hallway I was greeted by Joan Turpin, laden with folded sheets, and Petra Blake, buttoned to the hilt in her Sunday best. She was pulling on a heavy overcoat with a fur collar.

'Has anybody seen Mr Lloyd this morning?' croaked the housekeeper, 'He's not turned out yet. Most unlike Arthur. Bolt to the side door was still shut over this morning - I had to come in the front way.'

Petra Blake snorted.

'I'd like to know where the bloody man is too. I had requested a hot pot of tea first thing, but it didn't show. And now I'll miss it before church and be parched by ten thirty. Excuse me!'

She pushed by, but I was quick to stop her with a harsh word.

'Please stop, Miss Blake. There is something I have to tell you - some bad news. You too, Mrs Turpin.' I swallowed dramatically.

'Arnold Prosper is dead.'

'*Dead*?' They chimed together.

'Murdered,' I added darkly. 'His throat cut. In the kitchen.'

'Good lord!'

This high-pitched exclamation came from behind, where Harvey Blake was leaning over the bannister. She made her way down the stairs. She too was in her Sunday best; a rather fetching black suit with sky-blue trim, and a blue patterned tie-neck blouse underneath.

'Arnold? *Murdered*?' She whispered, a little dreamily. She reached the final few steps. Miss Blake hummed a low, gravelly hum.

'Where is he, Harvey?' she asked.

Her sister blinked. We all knew who she was talking about.

'I haven't seen Gideon, if that's what you mean.'

'Pffh!' Miss Blake huffed. 'Surely no coincidence, the man missing and now another terrible murder!'

'But why hurt Mr Prosper?' said Joan Turpin. 'None of this makes sense!'

And there the four of us stood like plums for what felt like an eternity, nobody knowing quite what to say. Eventually it was Petra Blake who broke the silence with a loud sigh.

'Well! I shouldn't have bothered to have this blouse ironed. We shall never get to church now!'

Joan Turpin had a strange look on her face, her eyes squinting in thought, lips pursed. She raised a finger to her chin. Her trance invited my attention.

'Mrs Turpin?' I said as gently as I could. 'What is it?'

I had hoped for a sensible reply, perhaps even an idea as to the reason for Prosper's untimely downfall. I should have known better.

'The rule of three,' she said quietly. 'We can be sure of one thing, Mr Edgar. There will be no more death. The rule of three.'

'The rule of *what*?'

'Death goes in threes.' She spoke solemnly, as if issuing a statement of fact.

'Threes?' I parroted.

'Indeed. Death follows in threes, it is well known. And Mr Prosper makes three.'

I couldn't let this pass.

'I think you may have miscounted, Mrs Turpin. I count two - the girl and now the chef.'

'You forget the General?'

I had indeed forgotten the bird, and quite happily, too.

'Surely that doesn't count,' I began.

'Oh, it counts!' replied the housekeeper. 'First, young Maeve, then The General, and now Mr Prosper. *Three.* There will be no more death.'

Suddenly, the kitchen door banged loudly. I'm sure the inspector had done this on purpose to gain our maximum attention - and it worked, for we all jumped and turned.

'Three indeed, Mrs Turpin. It is lucky - if you can call it that - with this weather our killer will be as trapped as we are. And we will find him! Interviews will re-commence in the dining room shortly. I have to know everybody's account of the last twelve hours, any more night-time shenanigans - everything! Nobody is permitted to leave the house. Please assemble in the drawing room. And the kitchen is out of bounds to all!'

This last addition was aimed in my direction.

'But I am in desperate need of a cup of tea!' exclaimed Petra Blake desperately. 'My poor shredded nerves!'

'Oh yes,' said Mrs Turpin. 'We have had a dreadful

shock, Inspector. We will certainly need tea.'

'You shall be restricted to the drawing room drinks cabinet for the time being I'm afraid, Miss Blake. I'm sure that the old servant will oblige.'

'He isn't here!' Miss Blake was quick to reply.

'He has vanished!' Mrs Turpin put in, her voice quivering. 'He hasn't attend to his duties at all this morning!'

'Really?' The inspector opened his eyes wide, clearly jumping to a conclusion.

'It would appear so,' I said, feeling it was time I that said something. I turned to Harvey. 'Perhaps it would be prudent to check on him. If you would direct me, I shall pop to his room and-'

I could have predicted the interruption from Standing.

'No need, Mr Edgar! We shall do the checking, thank you very much. I want everyone to proceed to the drawing room at once!' The inspector turned and bellowed back into the kitchen. 'Whitby! We have a second person to add to our missing person's list! Butler's gone AWOL! Put out a search for the old man immediately!'

Chapter III
In which Paytum Medgarm sees something in an old family photo

Dear Margaret,
My mother drives me around the bend. She adores my two children and they adore her. In fact, I often feel left out and resentful of their close relationship. They have even started using their own in-jokes and secret games that are making me feel even more excluded. Mother is kind to me, and she is wonderful with the children, but it is making me terribly unhappy. What should I say to her?
Housewife, Islington

Margaret replies; *of course your mother and your children have a special relationship; they have a common enemy - you! I advise a discreet plan; start a new game and create a whole special new language between you and your offspring, one that she isn't privy to. Also, ration out treats strategically. Suggest she take the children on that long dull ramble in the country and then make sure that you take them to the circus the next day. Ask your mother to accompany the children to the dentist, and then you take them to the seaside at the weekend. How will they feel about her then?*

The old butler, it turned out, was nowhere to be found in the house.

We had no reason to think that he was in danger or had become a victim of our Christmas assassin. All points indicated a swift exit. I could tell by the inspector's thin eyes that Arthur Lloyd had suddenly become the number two suspect, just pipped at the post by the absent Gideon Carter and his history of violence.

We gathered, as instructed, in the drawing room.

There were noticeably less of us to round up this time. There was Beryl, looking just a little hungover, Harvey Blake and her sister, and finally Joan Turpin, who's face had darkened at the absence of tea. Her son was absent, a fact that nobody appeared to notice. Miss Moore had been taken in for interrogation, and Officer Whitby was stationed in the doorway like an over-eager, stout guard dog.

Harvey touched my elbow and pulled me to a corner gently. I listened as she made vague excuses for ever having doubted my innocence. She went on to apologise for her coolness, her grief and her absence. I accepted her apology yet again, as gracefully as I could.

I can be a forgiving creature, sometimes.

Harvey then took herself over to the Chesterfield and joined the room in conversation. 'It seems strange without Mr Lloyd here,' she commented, and we all agreed.

Her sister scoffed.

'He's not the man they want, mark my words. Arthur's never done anything wrong! Simply not got it in him!' She fiddled in her handbag. 'The old man can barely mix a competent martini, let alone mastermind a series of murders!' She pulled out a handkerchief with one hand and waggled a podgy finger in the direction of whey-faced Officer Whitby with the other. 'We all know who is responsible for all this! Do we need more proof? This has the brutal paw prints of my ex-brother-in-law! Oh! My mouth is as dry as an old carpet!'

I found myself watching her thoughtfully. Her relentless persecution of the man was a curious thing. I watched as she lay back like a fish out of water, huffing and puffing and waiting for someone to bring her a drink. Of course, without dusty old Lloyd, she was left wanting. I certainly wasn't about to offer the woman a beverage. In my opinion I ranked far higher on the list of guests than she did - and as the sister of our host in her childhood abode, she should have been making *me* a drink.

I mulled things over in my head, and came to a decision.

What if I could find old Lloyd before the inspector? It would be yet another sweet victory. But the house had been searched, top to bottom.

Or had it?

An idea sprang forth. There was one place that they might forgo. I turned to Beryl and leaned in to whisper.

'I have an idea.'

My friend chuckled. 'You're hungry for it, aren't you?'

This took me by surprise somewhat.

'Hungry?' I asked, a question that was received with a knowing smile.

'For the truth.'

I shook my head.

'The only thing I am hungry for, Beryl is a hot buttered crumpet. But as that, sadly, is a pipe dream, I must distract my-self with some… investigation. To do this, I've got to discreetly slip out of the room, though. Can you assist?'

Beryl glanced over at Whitby, grinned and nodded. I watched as she made her way to the bay window, and waited a few seconds before squealing loudly.

'Oh! I think I see him!' she trilled. "Officer Whitby - is that Mr Lloyd out there near those bushes?'

'Out the way!' said Whitby as he pushed past. I stepped gingerly to the door. All heads had turned to the window. As I sneaked out, I heard Beryl tut loudly.

'No, perhaps not. Must have been a fox or a badger or something.'

Once out of the room, I made up the stairs with the air of a man on a mission. I headed on upwards to the attic, and to Al-fred Blake, the old Brigadier.

This is one place the officers might not bother to check – one witness they might discount. What could a senile old man locked in his room have to say about the whole affair? Quite a lot, perhaps? If there were any skeletons in the Blake family closet, it could be that he knew more than anyone could have guessed.

I knocked upon the door that led up to the attic. There was no reply, and so I eased it open to reveal a worn stone stair-case. The air inside was cool, and I shivered a little before mak-ing my way upwards. There was no door atop the stairway, only an unusual wooden swing gate such as one might find outside a country cottage. It was more than a little odd to find a tatty old gate on the uppermost floor of a manor house. I knocked polite-ly on a wooden panel, flicked the latch and passed through, being careful to close it behind me.

The attic room was spacious and dark, with only a nar-row dirty window at the far wall and a few panels of filthy glass in the old roofing. At the far end of the room was an armchair. It was facing the window, as if it revealed a beautiful landscape and not the watermarks and bird dirt that were all that could be seen.

In the armchair sat the old Brigadier, staring at his knees.

There was a sweet smell in the room, an acrid stench that at first I couldn't place - and then, when I did place it, I wished that I hadn't. I resolved to keep my arms at my side and not to touch a thing during my visit.

I coughed and muttered *excuse me* a few times but the Brigadier made no response until I was at his side, and then he merely looked up, blankly. The man had the bushy white moustache of a military general, not to mention impressively hairy chops - truly the bountiful whiskers reminiscent of a bygone age. He may have had the fuzzes of a military man, but that was all that remained. The eyes were weak and sunken, his mouth bereft of teeth. A fat tongue rolled around the inside his cheeks.

I gave my introductions.

'I do apologise for interrupting you, Brigadier. I am Payton Edgar, Sir. A guest of your daughter, here for Christmas.'

The Brigadier gave an impish smile, but thankfully did not proffer a handshake.

'Your name, mmm?' he croaked.

'Mr Payton Edgar,' I repeated patiently.

'Good evening, Mr Medgarm. A pleasure indeed, mmm!'

Good evening? It was a little after nine o'clock in the morning. I watched as the tongue rolled around and around, seemingly without control.

'It is Edgar. Mr Payton Edgar.'

'Mr Paytum Medgarm. Please, do take a seat, mmm.'

There was no chair on which to do so, and in the ensuing silence I found myself searching the room for a conversation piece. A single, well made bed stretched along one wall with a sagging chest of drawers at its side. On the opposite side of the room, large brown maps were open, strewn across a long table and fixed in place by numerous ornamental paperweights. It seems that the Brigadier had been assembling his troops for battle.

I had been mistaken in thinking that I could uncover any family skeletons this way. Sitting in the armchair was just a simple old man, a body trapped in the final years of life, the mind swimming around somewhere far back in time. He was looking up at me with heart-breaking, innocent eyes. On his lap sat a photograph album.

'Are they your photographs, Brigadier? May I have a look?'

The well-worn book was passed up to me without complaint, and it was only as I took it that I recalled my intention of keeping my hands to myself. The book was sticky to touch and my stomach lurched. Hesitantly, I opened the first page, and as I did so a bony finger wavered in my direction.

'That is me,' declared the old man, 'on my wedding day, mmm. Good old days. A Wednesday, it was… the luckiest day. A Wednesday, yes. Dear, dear Ada, mmm.'

This was a blatant untruth. There were no pictures of him in his youth. The first batch showed Harvey Blake marrying Mr Carter, the grainy black and white prints making her look mature and matronly and he more handsome than ever. Her smile was radiant, and Gideon Carter cut a dashing figure at her side. They were the very picture of a happy couple. To the right of the bride stood Petra Blake, clutching a small bouquet. It was somewhat startling to see her as a young bridesmaid. She was a bonny young woman, pretty even, with an unusual expression cast on her smooth face. It was not disapproval, however, but something far more subtle.

I had seen that look somewhere before.

I moved on. The pages were stiff and cracked as they turned. I moved through more wedding pictures and some dull snaps of a steam train to a number of bleak holiday snaps that looked to be Dartmoor or some similar dreary location. And then we came to a Christening. The baby Charlotte was wrapped in a fine lace blanket, and looked just like a frowning turnip. Harvey was holding her close in the foreground and forcing a tired smile.

In the background, Gideon Carter exchanged a word with an unknown girl, and both were laughing, clearly unaware of the camera aimed in their direction.

And then I gave a start. The girl was Petra, her face un-recognisable in an expression of joy. Her chin was lifted up to Mr Carter with that same expression - an unmistakable expression of affection. All of a sudden it was clear why the woman professed hatred to her brother-in-law at every available opportunity.

Love.

What was it Harvey herself had said, quite innocently? *There is a fine line between love and hate.*

I should have seen it. What had Petra called him, over and over? *A sly fox.* And what had she written about all these years? A sly fox. It was surely no coincidence. Petra Blake had hidden these feelings for years, perhaps even from herself. She didn't detest Carter, she had been in love with the man all along.

It was all there in the photograph.

But could this detail have anything to do with the murders?

I closed the book and returned it to the old man with thanks. He took it and made like he had never seen it before, placing it carefully on his lap and cooing with glee as he began to turn the pages. As I discreetly wiped my hands over my handkerchief, a movement in the sunlight outside caught my eye and I leaned in to the dirty window.

Far below I could just make out Raymond Turpin strutting around in the snow, raising his arms to his head in what looked like a crazy dance. It was a while before I realised that he was in distress, slapping his palms forcefully against his temples repeatedly. *Was everybody in the place a raving lunatic?*

He disappeared from view.

'Good old days, mmm,' the Brigadier muttered sadly.

Suddenly there was a flush of a toilet coming from behind a small door over beyond the bed. The door was set within the panelled wall and almost invisible when closed. The door opened, and Gideon Carter stepped out, wringing his hands.

'Bloody Hell!' he exclaimed, startled.

'Carter!' I greeted him with a squeak, and was suddenly on my guard. I had unearthed a fugitive, possibly a maniacal murderer! For a moment I tensed like a coiled spring, but when Carter didn't attack I allowed myself to relax.

Like Beryl, I simply didn't believe he was a murderer. Yes, he was, by all accounts, a cad when it came to ladies and he may have been keen with his fists in the past, but even during his heated scuffles with Prosper he hadn't thrown a punch. I quickly mulled over my options.

'Mr Edgar,' he said quietly. 'So I've been found.'

'Does Harvey know that you're up here?' I asked.

He shrugged.

'I'll take that as a "yes". I suspect it was her idea.'

His face gave nothing away.

'The police are after you,' I said, a little too obviously. And then, examining his features carefully, I decided to test him.

'And there has been another murder!'

'Another… *what*? Really?'

'Arnold Prosper was found dead in the kitchen this morning.'

'Prosper?' Carter rasped. 'Dead?' I nodded solemnly.

His reaction, one of shock, certainly looked genuine enough.

'Prosper?' he said again, pulling his bottom lip. '*Why Prosper?*'

This I could not answer.

'And they think that I killed him?'

He looked frightened. He paced a little, digesting this news, and then turned and made an appeal.

'Please, please don't reveal my whereabouts, Mr Edgar. I need to keep out of the picture, until the real killer is found.'

I hesitated.

'They will pin this one on me, too. I fought with Prosper over the card game, they all saw it. I won't have a leg to stand on. That inspector has it in for me. He doesn't listen - he is a buffoon.'

Never had truer words been said. Carter's feelings about the inspector had me on side, and I found myself agreeing to keep mum.

'I cannot lie to the police, however,' I added sternly. 'If they ask me directly if I know where you are, I will have to speak the truth.'

'I understand,' Carter replied reservedly. 'Thank you.'

I excused myself, and it was only as I was passing through the gateway that the Brigadier spoke again, to himself.

'Good old days, mmm,' he repeated sadly.

Chapter IV
In which Payton Edgar finds red snow

Dear Margaret,
I am terrified of death. I am just coming up on my
fiftieth birthday, and cannot stop obsessing over illness.
Every lump or bump is a cancer, every twitch a stroke. My
doctor refuses to see me now, I have visited so often. Both
my parents perished in their early fifties, and I fear I am to
follow. How can I stop these feelings?
Jim, Golders Green

Margaret replies; *why should one fear death? One is "dead"*
for eons before birth, and so some would say that to end as natu-
rally as one began should perhaps be a calming thought. I dare
say that fretting as you do will only bring forward the inevitable.
Take a walk in a cemetery on a sunny day - perhaps if you can
appreciate that death is an inevitable natural event, you might
have a better life because of it. In short - cheer up and enjoy
today, you old misery!

I might have found it tricky to keep the secret of the
fugitive in the attic above had there not been another ripe melodrama occurring in the rooms below. I found myself immersed
in the drama as it was dwindling, and as it involved Raymond
Turpin behaving oddly I was glad to have missed it.
'Get a grip of yourself, Turpin! Stand still!'
Inspector Standing had got a hold of Raymond's sleeve
and was pulling him through from the kitchen. Lumps of snow
fell to their feet.
'Stand still, man!'
But the inspector had quite the wrong approach. This
was no man, this was just a boy, and a very frightened boy at
that. He had stopped hitting himself about the head, but tore free
of the policeman's grasp and began to circle the hallway like a
cat chasing its tail. He was sobbing and uttering gibberish.
'Blood! Blood! Red, red snow!'
'He's flipped his lid!' Petra Blake exclaimed unhelpfully
from the drawing room doorway. Beryl was at her side, watching things unfold..
Alison Moore came up behind me.

'What's going on?'

'Something's upset the lad,' I replied, rather obviously.

The question was repeated by Joan Turpin as she appeared from the dining room. Seeing her son's distress, she jumped to a conclusion.

'Spud! I know that look! You've been in the kitchen, haven't you? And after I told you not to! You're like a magnet to a corpse, young man!'

The inspector tried to calm the waters. 'Come though to the drawing room, lad. I'll let your Mother get you a nice hot cup of tea.'

'Don't like tea!' Raymond Turpin replied loudly.

The housekeeper did her best to calm her son, but he was having none of it. She held him by the shoulders. There were tears in his eyes.

And then he started to mutter again. 'Blood! So much blood! Red snow!'

Suddenly free of his mother's grip, he bounded out of the front door. She ran after him, but nobody else bothered to move.

'Red snow?' I uttered to Miss Moore. 'That doesn't sound like our corpse in the kitchen.'

Something about all this wasn't quite right.

Harvey Blake joined the party.

'What's all the commotion?' she asked. Her sister tutted.

'That inbred cretin's going off on one of his backward rants again,' she groaned. Her pasty face was a picture of disgust. 'If all this wasn't hard enough, we have gibbering imbeciles to contend with!'

'Alright, if you can all move on through to the drawing room now!' said the inspector, trying to gain an ounce of control. Everybody began to shuffle along.

Constable Whitby caught my arm as I passed.

'Mr Edgar, may I have a quick word?'

We moved aside.

'Something you said to me yesterday has been preying on my mind, and I wondered what you meant by it.'

'Oh, yes?'

The inspector may not care a jot for what I said, but his young protege was apparently more keen minded. He was whispering furtively.

'You said we should be looking at the supernatural element of the murder of Maeve Frick. That someone added a supernatural element with purpose. What did you mean by that? What did you have in mind?'

Not long ago I would have seized this opportunity to speculate quite happily, but after my discoveries in the attic I was finding the whole affair quite baffling. I replied with shrug and a dismissive wave of the hand. He went on.

'You see, I think you had something there, Mr Edgar. And I think that, well, it can only be that someone put the girl up to it, that supernatural nonsense about Charlotte Blake and the drowning, and perhaps it was all done to point a finger at Mr Carter.'

'I have said that all along, constable, but nobody listens a word I say.'

'Well, I think you have something. See, I've been thinking about it - it's all about who put her up to it-'

He stopped and straightened, for his whisper had become a bark and we were getting looks. He turned to Standing.

'Sir, may I have your permission to do a quick search of the bedrooms? I have an idea. It can only have been one of the two of them, you see-'

'Yes, yes, Whitby, if you have to!' Standing replied. 'But be ready in the dining room in five minutes! Everyone in the drawing room as soon as possible! Miss Petra, we'll have you first - in the dining room in five minutes sharp.'

I watched Whitby pelt up the stairs and then it was Harvey Blake's turn to demand my attention. We went to the drawing room where she patted the cushion of the chesterfield. I sat dutifully. Before she could say a word, however, I leaned in closer and surprised her with a declaration.

'I know where Carter is hiding!' I whispered. Her face fell.

'No! Please-'

'Don't fret, my dear! I won't say a word. I firmly believe that he is entirely innocent.'

She set her chin high.

'You really won't say anything?'

'No.'

'Well... that means a lot to me. Thank you. They must never know.' She touched a warm hand to mine. 'Gideon is indeed entirely innocent. But who is doing this, Mr Edgar? And where is Arthur? That man's as loyal as the day is long. He wouldn't have anything to do with this. He just wouldn't!'

I looked over to the bar, where the old butler might have stood. In my mind I heard his feet tap tapping up the cellar stairs into the kitchen, and remembered his pale face rising from the darkness.

The kitchen cellar!

The police would certainly have searched the place, but then something else came to mind. The broken crockery! It had been scattered on the kitchen floor just besides that first step down to the cellar. Who in the house would carry a tray of crockery but the butler?

And what would cause a dedicated butler to drop a tray? *A corpse*? And yet, if old Mr Lloyd had discovered the corpse, what then? Why run? Lloyd was too methodical and dutiful to do anything else but report the crime. What had stopped him?

What else! What if he had not only stumbled upon a corpse, but a murderer too? Had Lloyd stepped up out of the cellar and caught our killer quite literally red-handed? He would surely drop the tray! But what would have happened then?

He would have fled. The open door! I had closed and locked it, but when I first entered the kitchen, it had been wide open.

Before I knew it, I was uttering distracted *excuse-mes* to my host and was on my feet. I beckoned Beryl over. 'I have just had a thought, Beryl. Quick - come with me!'

She followed obediently, asking questions that I chose to ignore. We were able to duck into the kitchen without question. We both started, for although the blood had been cleaned from the marble surface, Prosper's corpse was there on the floor. It had been helped to the ground and covered by a large pale green blanket. As we looked down at it, I gathered all my strength and spoke urgently.

'Red snow, Beryl! It can't be Prosper Turpin junior's been crying about - he was eliminated rather efficiently here in the kitchen. Raymond, so fond of playing outdoors, must have seen another corpse altogether.'

'My goodness!'

'And so we need to find Mr Lloyd. We've all said it - the man is quiet as a ghost. And the broken crockery was right here,' I tapped a toe at the ground, and stood where the butler must have stood. 'With a little imagination, we can re-enact Mr Lloyd's movements. Quietly, coming up from the cellar, he sees our killer fresh from dispatching Prosper. He drops the tray - crash! - then runs. He surely wouldn't double back down to the cellar, and trap himself. There is the door to the hallway, and the door outside, which is much nearer. The sensible escape would be to throw open the back door, and flee.'

I opened the back door.

I was only in my shirt and jacket, and yet had no thought for the freezing cold air. Beryl and I stepped out into the snow and looked both ways. To the right was a thick smooth covering of snow, but to our left - tracks!

'He went that way!' said Beryl near my ear. I went to move, but she caught my arm.

'Hang on, Payton. Shouldn't we say something to the others?'

'And say what? We are acting on guesswork, and there is nothing the inspector likes less. He'll need evidence - and we have to find some.'

'I'm just, well, a bit anxious about what we might find.'

'Squeamish, Beryl?'

'Absolutely not! Just cold. And my winklepickers weren't made for artic conditions.'

'Oh, come along!'

As I tracked the footsteps in the snow, Beryl followed with some hesitation behind. I could understand her reluctance, and I gathered my nerves in anticipation of what we might find. As we stepped around the building, those words Raymond Turpin had said before ran over and over in my mind.

Red, red snow.

And then we both saw it, in the ditch at the side of the walkway; a foot protruded awkwardly from within some wet nettles.

I took a deep breath, and a step forwards. The white ball-like face of Arthur Lloyd was just visible amongst the snow covered foliage. A dark red puddle created something of a bathing cap effect at his scalp. A few feet away sat a blood-encrusted house brick.

Beryl issued a cry.

The snow was indeed red.

Chapter V

In which Payton Edgar suffers a poorly made cup of tea and exposes an affair of the heart

Dear Margaret,
My husband is a know-it-all. He always thinks his opinion is the correct one, and is constantly spouting trivia about anything and everything. If I offer him a cup of tea, for example, I have to sit through endless facts about the varieties of tea, their histories and the ideal brewing technique. It is very hard to have a proper conversation with someone who thinks they know everything about everything, and I am getting fed up with his bravado. Any advice?
Mrs B, Brompton

Margaret replies; *either you are married to a polymath - a man who deserves everyone's ears and whose opinions demand respect - or a tireless bore who deserves nothing more than a slap in the chops. I rather favour the latter. You have done the right thing by writing to a rare example of the former. My advice is to silence him with the concept of annulment. You won't need to go into detail about your decree nisi, as he will undoubtedly know all the facts. Indeed, if he truly does know-it-all, he should have foreseen this inevitable development.*

After my latest grisly discovery, I found myself reclining in a chair with a slab of shortbread and a disappointingly weak cup of tea.

As I looked down with sadness at the pale brew I made myself a promise - I would sit tight and hold my tongue. No more investigations, no more canny observations, no more revelations. Members of the household were being violently offed, one by one, and I had no intention whatsoever of being the next cadaver.

I had not expected any thanks for directing Inspector Standing to poor Mr Lloyd, the latest corpse, and I did not receive any. Even so, I didn't envy the man in his job one bit. It all seemed such a mess. We now had three dead bodies laid out in the garage; young Miss Taylor, boisterous Arnold Prosper and now the virtuous butler.

Following the shock of our discovery, Beryl and I allowed the others to fuss about us a bit. As Mr Lloyd was permanently indisposed, Alison Moore begrudgingly adopted the role of help. She was buoyed on by Harvey Blake, who seemed to find strength from somewhere, busying about with a contagious alacrity.

'It's horrible! Simply horrible!' the secretary said, her spiky edges smoothing. 'There's a fox in this hen house! Who will be next?'

'Nobody will be next, Alison. This will stop, now. It'll be only a matter of time before the police get the clue they need to sort all this out.' Harvey said this with a warmth and conviction that was delightfully soothing. She followed it with a smile.

'Let's all have some tea.'

There was something of the Dunkirk spirit in her actions, and she had goaded the inspector enough for him to provide sufficient access to the kitchens for emergency hot beverage-making purposes. It was heartening to see our host back on form, and so I held my tongue and chose not to gripe about the poor quality of the brew.

I was, however, pleasantly surprised by the buttery wonder of the shortbread, and could not let this go without comment. Harvey nodded in agreement.

'Raymond Turpin's handiwork, would you believe?' she replied. 'Between you and me, I think the batches Spud puts out surpass his mother's attempts.'

'The boy has hidden talents,' I uttered politely as I discreetly laid the shortbread aside.

The news of the latest death had quickly spread to the village, and Daniel Drinkwater made a somewhat brave reappearance following his morning service. He was sitting beside Petra Blake with an irritatingly sympathetic smile plastered on his serene face. He had no cup of tea, and instead his long, bony fingers formed a triangle in his lap. I suppose he thought that his mere presence in the house was in some way reassuring. Nobody had mentioned the accusations from the dead girl's diary, and I dare say the clergyman hoped that it had all been forgotten.

I, however, would never forget, and I made sure to give him short shrift.

While the vicar did his best to look thoughtful and caring, Petra Blake invested no energy in her expression whatsoever, and she scowled openly across her steaming teacup.

'So-' began Harvey from her place at the drinks cabinet, '-we just have to stick together and wait it out. Everything will be alright.'

I very much doubted this. It had been a disaster of a Christmas for all concerned (particularly for those who had ended up rather more dead than they would have liked). Nevertheless, I gave a charitable smile. An uncomfortable silence soon descended upon the room.

The vicar coughed.

Miss Blake glowered at the floor.

Beryl stirred an inexcusable amount of sugar into her teacup.

I shifted in my seat.

And then Joan Turpin entered the room, having disposed of her son at home. Why she had returned to the house was unfathomable. If I had a cottage to hide away from all this death and danger then I certainly would have used it. We soon found out why she lingered, however, for she had a twinkle in her eyes.

'Perhaps I shouldn't say, Harvey, but I overheard the inspector talking outside.' She spoke carefully, but loudly enough for us all to hear. 'It's about Mr Carter...'

'Tell me they've found him!' Petra Blake boomed. The housekeeper shook her head.

'No, not yet. They were talking about some evidence. It seems that Mr Prosper was... well... *offed* with a particular knife, not a kitchen knife. A cutting knife, they said. The knife Mr Carter uses to cut his pipe cleaners.'

We let this new information sink in, and I watched Petra Blake, expecting a barbed response. She remained mute however, and Joan Turpin continued.

'I'm sure there's nothing meant by it, Harvey, but I thought you should know.'

Harvey Blake's blank expression gave nothing away.

'Vicar, may I have a word?' asked Mrs Turpin meekly. 'I wondered if you could come down to the gatehouse to see my Spuddy. I've tucked him in with a hot toddy, but he's in quite a state, as you can imagine.'

Thrilled to be in any way required, Drinkwater stood and followed after Mrs Turpin, who had apparently forgiven his indiscretions. As they went, I saw something pass between them. A shady look? Or had I imagined it?

At my side, Beryl spoke up in a questioning tone.

'Dearie me! Just like with the girl, everything is pointing to Mr Carter.'

'Indeed,' I said thoughtfully. 'A pattern, so to speak. Rather begins to tell a tale-'

'Giddy is innocent,' Harvey put in with an uncompromising firmness.

'Pah! Come on! You still believe that?' said her sister from her chair. Her disapproving glare became something altogether darker. '*Why* is everything pointing to Gideon? The most obvious explanation is often the correct one, Harv.'

Harvey stood.

'I must go and speak with the inspector.'

Alison Moore slammed down her cup and followed on after her employer without a word. After a minute, Beryl also returned her cup to the saucer and stood.

'Well, I'm going to pop to my room, power my nose. Payton - don't let anything happen without me!'

And so I was left alone with Petra Blake.

For a moment nothing was said, and then she launched into a speedy monologue dripping with hate, all about Carter and his machiavellian ways. She appeared to think of me as a confidante, having said a few nice things about my writing the night before. But it would take more than a few icy compliments to get me on side. In fact, my simmering dislike of the woman threatened to approach a boil.

I hadn't planned to challenge her over the Carter affair, but suddenly, at that moment and with the two of us alone, it felt like the right thing to do. She was looking at me as if she had an unpleasant taste in her mouth before I even said a thing, and so I drew in a deep breath, ripe for a confrontation.

'It may be in your interests, Miss Blake, to display a little more tact when revealing your feelings towards your brother-in-law. '

'I'm sorry?'

'One cannot fail to register your disapproval of Mr Cater, and thusly, one cannot help but wonder why-'

'Is that any business of yours?'

'With your quick accusations and angry outbursts, I think you make it everyone's business. But you must be careful, Miss Blake - your *actions* may give the wrong impression. Or perhaps, the correct impression.'

'What are you gabbling on about?'

'A quote comes to mind. *"The lady doth protest too much."* Some say that there is a fine line between love and hate. You have been dancing on that line for many years, haven't you? Your feelings towards your brother-in-law are all too obvious. Loving someone you can never have, and for so long, must have been very difficult. But if you are not careful, one day your sister will come to question the true source of your dislike for the man.'

There - I had said it!

'I... I don't know what you mean!' The accused pushed her cup and saucer aside with a rattle and a crash. Her left hand reached up to her neck and her fingers began picking mindlessly at the folds of skin. I watched as her cheeks flushed an impressive crimson. Suddenly she stood, and made a beeline for the door.

I raised my voice just a little.

'I saw photographs of you with Carter from twenty-odd years ago. Your family may not see it, but it was all too apparent, if one looks for it. You were in love with the man-'

'Nonsense!'

'-and I think that, perhaps, you still are.'

And at this Miss Blake swung around and glared down at me in my seat rather like a hungry cat to a cornered mouse.

'I think you'd better keep your preposterous observations to yourself, Mr Edgar!'

'And I will, Miss Blake, indeed I will. I merely wanted to warn you, in private, that if you continue to attack the man so publicly then it will only be a matter of time before someone asks why. Even your devoted sister may come to see it. Think about it.'

I retrieved my cup and sipped at the tea with the satisfaction of a point well made. The drink was tepid and unappealing, but I was careful not to let it show on my face. I found that I had more to add.

'You put yourself in the frame, too,' I went on. 'Our killer clearly has it in for Carter. It can't be long before even the ineffectual officers in the other room make that connection. You harbour an apparent hatred for the man, and now he stands accused.'

There was surely nothing for her to do then but to storm from the room, and yet she stood still, looking down at me. She shook a little, her eyes grew wet, and then, much to my horror, she closed the door firmly, bounded across the room and fell on to the chesterfield, sobbing. The air of tension that had pulled the room tight popped like a balloon. She wiped tears from her cheeks with quivering fingers.

I sat rooted to my seat, dumbstruck. There were no tissues to hand, and nobody else to come to her aid.

I waited.

When she didn't stop crying, I found myself lifting my pocket handkerchief and passing it over. It was taken without thanks, and as she snivelled all over it I said goodbye to one of my better silk accessories - puce with black stitching, from Ahlers at Saville Row - with a sad heart.

Eventually, the sobbing woman spoke, this time softy and with some feeling.

'You seem to understand something about love, Mr Edgar. For me, it's just something that happens to other people. I've never found true love, nor a happiness of my own. Not really. Harvey's always been the lucky one. The only love I've ever known was... never mine. Do you understand, Mr Edgar?'

She held two balled fists to her mouth, broken. I could find no words to say. What did she expect? Shared confidences? I had nothing to share with the woman! Should I utter soothing words? Perhaps this would only set her off again, and all I really wanted was for her tears to dry up. Eventually, she went on.

'I try to stop myself, I really do. I say to myself *"leave it, Pet! Don't let the man upset you so much!"* But he does, he really does. I thought I was over it all, that he was gone. And now this Christmas, to find him back in our lives... it was all too much. All those old, buried, turbulent feelings come flooding back. They consume me, and I hurt so terribly badly. A wretched feeling. Oh, the pain!'

She looked at me with red eyes.

'You have quite the wrong way of going at it, Mr Edgar, but what you say is right. I can see that you understand unrequited love. *Secret love.* Am I right?'

I remained mute - in truth I was quite, quite baffled at what she might mean.

'You needn't say anything... I understand. Thank you for listening, Mr Edgar. I hope that we can keep this to ourselves?'

'Indeed,' I replied, only too happy to do just that.

Miss Blake sat for a moment and gathered herself, before emitting one last burst of a sob as she fled from the room.

I allowed myself to rest. Now that the truth had been spoken out loud, perhaps we would hear less clucking and fussing about Carter's guilt.

After a minute, and with my top pocket now empty, I set off to fetch a replacement handkerchief.

I came across Inspector Standing huffing and puffing in the hallway with Officer Jacobs. Jacobs took off in the direction of the kitchen, and I would have passed by without comment had the inspector not surprised me with a question.

'Edgar, have you seen Constable Whitby? Just had to dispatch old Prosper in the garages without him, and damn near busted my leg again. Was he in the drawing room with you?'

I replied in the negative.

'The last time I saw the man was when he requested your permission to search the bedrooms.'

'So he did!'

And then, with as little hobbling as he could, Standing and his gammy leg were mounting the stairs. I waited for a moment, and then followed on after him. As he turned the corner of the stairwell he clocked my approach.

'I don't need you to join the search, Edgar!' he grunted.

'I am heading for my bedroom,' I replied, entirely truthfully. 'I wish to collect a fresh handkerchief.'

Once on the first floor, I watched with some amusement as the inspector limped from room to room, calling out Whitby's name. The entire floor felt still and empty. Finally, he limped in my direction.

'And this one!' he said with his usual lack of compromise. I stood firm in the doorway, blocking his entry.

'I hardly think Constable Whitby would be hiding out in my bedroom, Inspector.'

'Let me through!'

I pushed the door open with my rear. 'By all means!'

We both moved into the bedroom. I was glad that I had made my bed so neatly and folded my pyjamas under the plump pillow. Standing brushed a finger over my desk and allowed them to dance a little over my paperwork.

'Still enjoy playing the old lady, Edgar?' he asked in his horribly goading tone. I had quite forgotten that he had found out about Margaret Blythe earlier that year. 'A very worthwhile endeavour, I'm sure, listening to women's moans and groans about poor downtrodden husbands, and sorting out petty disputes from within knitting circles-'

'Hardly, Inspector. I have never written about knitting circles!'

'Surely only a matter of time!' came the reply.

I did not respond, for I was given no chance. The inspector let out an involuntary shriek as he rounded the room.

'Good Lord!' He dived down behind the bed. There, on the floor between the bed and the iris wallpaper, lay young Whitby. He was on his side, his head thrown back, his eyes fixed wide open. The inspector was fumbling for signs of life, but it was all too clear that the man was dead.

Standing lifted a leaping bronze stag, dark red blood glistening on it's antlers.

'Again!' the inspector gasped.

I felt a little dizzy. A corpse in my bedroom! Suddenly, and with a very real sense of terror, I feared for my safety. Someone in this house was proving to be very adept at swift terminations, dispatching members of the household with impressive skill.

It seemed that not even the police were safe. I caught my breath. The killer under our roof suddenly seemed very dangerous indeed.

A sharp noise brought me back to my senses - a click of the lock! I raced to the door and grasped the knob tightly. The sturdy oak door didn't budge an inch. It had been locked from the outside.

'Inspector-' I exclaimed helplessly, 'we have been locked in!'

I lay my hand on the woodwork, realising with a heavy heart that the killer under our roof was right there, on the other side.

Chapter VI
In which Payton Edgar THINKS

Dear Margaret,
A newcomer is threatening to disband our knitting circle. I have been the chair for ten years, but a vivacious new member constantly undermines my authority. She has made herself treasurer, and yet treats everything like it were a joke, gleefully breaking all the rules of our set and encouraging others to do the same. I am quite timid, whereas she is a Pearly Queen, and such a boisterous person - how can I keep her in check?
Supreme Knitter, Lambeth

Margaret replies; *your newcomer sounds like a irritant of the highest order. Any farsighted leader knows that house rules are the linchpin of any successful organisation. If you are unable to reason with the woman (which is highly likely with a person who chooses to dress like a glitzy chicken) it may be necessary to resort to dirty tricks. You say that she has made herself treasurer? It would be wicked to suggest tarnishing the woman's name with an allegation of sticky fingers, but your circle will be all the better without her. Sometimes one has to match deviousness with deviousness, when it is for the greater good.*

And so I found myself trapped in the bedroom with only Inspector Standing and a corpse for company. An undesirable state of affairs to say the very least.

Standing was infuriated by the locked door, and spent some time unnecessarily stamping about and cursing. He attacked the door until the knob was almost out of its holding, and then flung open the window. For a moment I thought he might leap out, but the drop was a perilous one, despite the soft snow on the ground below. There were no tree branches or drainpipes nearby that one could shimmy down, not that I would be inclined to do anything of the sort. Surely the best thing to do was to wait it out. We would be missed eventually.

I said as much.

'Pppfff! Time is of the essence, Edgar. I can't sit about in here while a murderer runs amok outside before making a getaway!'

'In this weather, Inspector, I don't think anyone is about to flee. Much as they might like to.'

This truth was greeted with a grunt. I sat on the bed, as far from Whitby's body as I could. A sudden thought popped into my mind - was Beryl safe out there? She was made of tough stuff, but even so... there was a killer on the loose. Suddenly, I was disturbed by a tugging at the candlewick eiderdown.

'Move your rump, Edgar!' Standing grumbled. I got to my feet in time for him to whip off the top cover. My annoyance was quelled, however, when he used the eiderdown to carefully, respectfully, cover the officer's body. I cursed myself for not having thought of this. Standing laid the eiderdown with great care and then stood over it for some time.

I sat back down on the bed.

'We could make use this time, you know, to think-'

'To *think*? To *think*?' Standing began pacing again. 'Yes, of course! Let's all sit around and think while everybody dies around us! To think!'

'Yes, to think, Inspector. Capital letters - THINK! It may be useful for you to know, Inspector, that thinking is often the method that solves the crime. I suggest you try it.'

He huffed and puffed like a cornered steer.

'Thinking won't get handcuffs on our missing man Carter, Mr Edgar!'

'Inspector, if you approach everything akin to a hammer, all you will find are nails!'

That had him! He was grinding his teeth and pacing as I continued.

'So, let us *think*. *Why Whitby*? Why did Whitby have to die?'

The inspector plonked himself into the chair at the desk. Of all the things he could have said, he took the most irrelevant and infuriating avenue of enquiry.

'The question should perhaps be *why did he die in your bedroom*, Mr Edgar?'

In spite of the unwelcome tangent, I mulled the question over.

'I can only imagine that our murderer chose this space as the best place to hide the body.'

'Hardly hidden, Edgar!'

'True, but there are no better places on this floor, are there? You have all the bedrooms and bathrooms, all frequently used. The killer would swerve using their own room, naturally, to avoid suspicion. Bundling Whitby just out of sight here may have bought him time. Either that, or your constable simply ran in here to escape, unsuccessfully. So - the question remains, why did Whitby have to die? What was our killer thinking?'

The Inspector sighed.

'Police work is hardly about reading minds, Edgar.'

Really! How this oaf had risen through the ranks of the police force was a mystery, so limited was his mind-set. That said, the inspector's ineptitude only sharpened my mind to the question at hand.

'Whitby was a conscientious officer, wasn't he?' The question was rhetorical, and yet it was answered.

'He was indeed. He was thorough, insightful... an all round good egg.' Standing was looking so mournful it was almost touching. 'I've only worked with him for a short while, but he was a boundlessly enthusiastic officer, and I had high hopes for him. Never told him that. I wish I had, now. Heaven knows what I'll tell his wife, Pru. A nice lady. They've just had their first born, a boy.'

There was no time for sentiment. I pictured Whitby with his keen eyes, lapping up my every word in the dining room, and a thought sprang to mind.

'Inspector, Whitby had only been here a matter of days. He would hardly be a part of our killer's master plan. One can only conclude that, in his investigations, Whitby was on to something. Did he say anything of note to you?'

Standing laughed.

'Gather the evidence, Whitby, I always used to say. The man had theories galore, but often his evidence to back up his fanciful ideas was left wanting.'

'Mmm. I suspect that he went after evidence today, and his actions got him killed.'

Standing stiffened.

'Are you saying, Edgar, that his death was somehow my fault?'

'By no means. All I am saying is that, in his quest for the burning truth, young Whitby may have fluttered his wings a little too close to the flame.'

'Speak English, man!'

I sighed. Being trapped in a room with the inspector was proving to be a trying experience, and it was hard to resist poking his soft spots.

And so I didn't resist.

'There is one thing about Whitby you are overlooking, Inspector. You said that he was a thorough officer. Indeed, I have not seen him these past few days without his pad and pencil in hand. Might I suggest those pages of his notebook may hold a clue?'

The inspector quite forgot to be annoyed at my superior tone, for the suggestion was a good one. He was soon down on all fours, his fingers in Whitby's pockets. It was a fruitless search.

'He carried that pad everywhere with him.'

'So, now we have an idea why he was murdered. He was perhaps on to something. Why else steal the pad?' I scratched my head. 'Inspector, what did he say to you downstairs, when he asked to check out the rooms?'

'I don't recall.'

'No? Well it's a good job that I do. He said something about the supernatural nonsense, and then I rather think that you interrupted him. He was about to say something - what were his words, exactly? Something about the two of them? The two of what? Yes, he said - *it has to be one of the two.*'

'The two of what?'

'That is what we must deduce, Inspector.'

'I wish we had that bloody notebook!' Standing growled. He hobbled over to the door, rattled the knob uselessly once more and called out a few times. Nobody came to our rescue. I sat quietly, trying not to be distracted by the noise, mulling everything over.

The two of them.

'Inspector, I think it's important for us to focus on the real murder!'

'Beg pardon?'

'When I say the real murder, I mean the first murder, the murder of Maeve Frick. It seems to me that any subsequent deaths appear to be hurried, perhaps reactionary affairs. But Maeve's death feels far more calculated. Maeve herself laid the groundwork for her demise, making up stories about the murder of Charlotte Blake and the body in the lake. If the theory is correct, to uncover the truth, we must think carefully about that first murder.

'I believe that Maeve was put up to it. I think someone

persuaded the girl to act out the charade during the seance, the outcome of which was to point the finger at Gideon Carter.'

'You think that Carter killed his daughter all those years ago?'

'No, Inspector, not at all. If I may stick my neck out a little, I believe that Carter is entirely innocent. I always have. I also believe that Charlotte Blake died from drowning, as was thought at the time. There was nothing sinister about it - just a tragic accident. But Carter is right at the heart of what's been going on here and now, isn't he? That's why you arrested the man, as you were supposed to. He was accused of murder during the seance, and then his accuser was murdered. The stag figurine was missing from his room. His knife was used to kill Arnold Prosper. Someone has been working hard to make it look like Carter was behind it all, and you fell for it.'

'If you ask me, Edgar, you have just listed the reasons why it is so very obvious that Carter is our killer. And I might remind you that he slipped away and is still at large.'

'Too obvious, Inspector! Besides, the man would have to be a very witless criminal to use the stag figurine from his room and his own knife as murder weapons.'

Standing laughed a throaty, phlegm-filled laugh.

'Well I say this is a violent man's murder - and that Carter's the only viable suspect. But I will humour you. So, with the very-guilty-looking Carter entirely innocent, which tree would you bark up, eh?'

I was not about to be deterred by his witless sarcasm.

'I think that the pertinent question would be *"why Carter?"* Yes, it could be that our killer just needed someone to pin the murder on, and Carter would certainly fit the bill nicely. But this feels much more... *personal*, than that. Perhaps it was a simple matter of hatred for the man - hatred or revenge for behaviours past. If this is the case, those with the strongest motives would be the two sisters, however unlikely that seems. Or perhaps our killer's intention was simply to get Carter out of the way. Perhaps somebody wanted nothing more than to send him back to prison. But why? To get to Harvey Blake?'

I was going round in circles and getting nowhere. It all seemed very muddled. Those words of Whitby's kept coming to mind - the two *what*?

I emitted a gasp, quite unintentionally, as I completed the sentence. I had just said it!

The two... *sisters*?

One of the two of them.

I swallowed as the inspector spoke.

'Perhaps it's not all about Carter, Mr Edgar. Perhaps someone just wanted to bump the girl off.'

I took a moment to think this over before returning to the conversation.

'Maybe. But it seems to me that they have gone to almost ridiculous lengths to point the finger at Carter. However, taking that into account, we have two questions to be considered before we find our murderer. Who had reason to harm the girl, and who would have wanted Carter out the picture? There are only couple of people who fit this bill, if I may play devil's advocate for a moment?'

'We have Petra Blake, who has allowed her strong feelings towards her brother-in-law to fester - did she see an opportunity to get him out of the way once and for all? She was certainly angered by Maeve's appearance. And then we have Harvey Blake, who has forged a relationship with the girl only to find out that she is the illegitimate fruit of her husbands loins-'

'You coin a phrase beautifully, Edgar.'

'Here we have a woman who has just got around to forgiving her husband for his past when it is strongly suggested that he had a hand in their first-born's untimely death. You could say that Harvey Blake has every reason to hate the man.'

I was warming up quite nicely now.

'Could this really be what Whitby had seized on? One of the two sisters?'

'You seem to be discounting a lot there!'

'Namely?'

'Well, the oddball Turpin lad for starters! Forever present in the unveiling of a fresh corpse...'

'Raymond Turpin, though two strings short of a tennis racket, has no ill will against Carter as far as I know. Also, he had little or no relationship with the girl Maeve, and is hardly a calculating killer.'

'What about the vicar?' Standing put in, archly.

'Well, certainly there was ill will between him and the girl - Maeve said as much in her diary. But would that really lead to murder? And why would the vicar have it in for Carter?'

'He exposed their midnight gambling sessions,' said Standing.

'Inspector, that particular revelation came *after* Maeve's death. No, the vicar may have motives, but only extremely tenuous ones. Besides, he is too pathetic and willowy by far!'

'Joan Turpin?' Standing continued. 'Her and the vicar are thick as thieves, and I noticed that she was quick to forgive his gambling and ignore his advances towards the dead girl. He told me it was his job to drive out sin. Could that be his motive? And with Turpin in on it? One of the two of *them?*'

I mulled this over.

'Well, firstly, I see no reason why Joan Turpin would want to point the finger at Carter, do you?'

I paused for breath, but was quick to continue before the inspector could interrupt me further.

'And then we have Miss Moore, who certainly has the cool ardour and devious streak one might look for in a killer, yet she suffers from a lack of motive. She is no fan of Carter, but one cannot see why she would wish to hurt him or the girl.'

'In actual fact, Miss Moore was one of the few people the girl actually appeared to get on well with,' said Standing. 'They had a rather sisterly relationship by my reckoning.'

'That is true, Inspector.'

'And everyone else is dead!'

'Indeed,' I replied.

'Which leads me back to Petra Blake, who clearly hates her brother-in-law. You reckon she could be up to it?'

It was nice to be asked, and to hear the inspector lower his guard and speak freely for once.

'It is a possibility, however I can't help but think she is *too* passionate about the man to really want to hurt him. No, I don't believe that she would ever want Carter out the way. On the contrary, I think that she loves to hate his company. There is certainly a fine line between love and hate, in this case.'

'What? Unrequited love, you think?'

I was impressed that the inspector had listened attentively to my words.

'Without a doubt,' I said cooly. 'But *murder*? I'd need some convincing.'

'Mmm,' the inspector hummed. 'Can't see her as a cold-hearted killer.' He took in a deep breath. 'And so then we are left with Harvey Blake.'

Here, I took off my hat of impartiality.

'I have to say, Inspector, that I have a great deal of respect for Harvey Blake, and am inclined to discount her outright. Despite the circumstances, she has tried hard to keep things together, all in all. She makes a fine host, at her best.'

'A fine host can still make a fine murderer, Edgar.'

'I know, but I just can't see it. She cares so much for Carter, and-'

'And so she found out about his true relationship with the girl Maeve. That must hurt. Hands her a pretty weighty motive, I'd say.'

'Perhaps, but I'd like to give Harvey the benefit of the doubt. I don't believe she is our killer.'

'Or maybe you don't want to believe it!'

'Perhaps,' I said again. And there it was, the outcome of my summary. I was suddenly overcome with a heavy feeling of defeat. 'It seems, Inspector, that I don't believe that anybody is guilty! I have talked myself out of options. A waste of time, it seems.'

'Not so! Somewhere in your summary, there will be the answer. You have been mulling and chewing in a manner akin to the most prudent of detectives, Edgar.'

I took this as the compliment it was. Then it was the inspector's turn to pose a question.

'There's one thing that doesn't quite fit with your theory. If this was all to get at Carter, why bump off the girl at all? Why not simply kill Carter and have done with it?'

'Mmm. A pertinent question!' I replied.

'And what about the dead bird? Where does that come into it?'

A less than pertinent question.

Thankfully, we were interrupted by a shout from the other side of the door.

'Payton? Payton?' came the muffled cry. The door-handle wobbled. Standing leapt to his feet and limped to the door.

'Who is that? Jacobs?'

'No, it's me, Beryl!'

'We've been locked in, Mrs Baxter! Is there a key?'

'No key that I can see,' came the muffled response. She pulled on the doorknob from the outside. 'What're you doing in there?'

I stepped up.

'Beryl, get something to break down the door!'

'Righto!'

'Mrs Baxter! Fetch Jacobs!' Standing stepped up to the door, and I pulled him back. He began to protest.

'Let me deal with this, Edgar! She should get help-'

'Inspector, you don't know Beryl Baxter!' I said pointedly. Suddenly, the door crashed inwards and Beryl bundled into the room, wide eyed and victorious. I held out my hands to steady her, and she collapsed onto the bed, whopping and laughing. She caught a sight of the body on the floor and stopped abruptly.

'Oh, Lordy!'

'Let's get out of here!' grumbled the inspector.

Suddenly a thought sprang to mind and, before he could move, I caught his sleeve.

'Before we go, there is another question we haven't asked ourselves, Inspector. An important question. Why lock us in here?'

Standing shook off my hand.

'I should have thought that's obvious. To stop us finding the culprit!'

'Perhaps, but we were bound to be released before long. Our incarceration would only ever to be temporary, for we would be missed, wouldn't we? What did our killer need to do in these precious minutes?'

The inspector shrugged carelessly.

'I suggest, Inspector, that we keep our eyes open to any changes, anything that's happened in our absence. Eyes and ears, Inspector. That may direct us to the truth.'

Chapter VII
In which Payton Edgar observes something fishy

Dear Margaret,
My best friend has terrible problems with personal hygiene, and I cannot bring myself to raise this with her. She often has dreadful halitosis and also suffers from a perspiration problem, especially in the Summer months. We normally tell each other everything, but I cannot bear to hurt her feelings by raising this particular problem with her. What should I do?
Deborah, East Croydon

Margaret replies: *pass the posey! How on earth can you stomach being around someone who soils the air in this manner? I suggest some subtle actions - ask her to keep her jacket on when she visits, have a scented handkerchief at the ready and open the window pointedly. Failing that, tell her about the problem immediately, and then if she fails to eradicate her odours, stay well away. It is her problem - it needn't be yours.*

Constable Jacobs met us at the head of the stairs and issued a warning.

'Be careful, Sir,' he said slowly. 'There's something… fishy afoot.'

'Fishy?'

'I was out skirting the grounds as you instructed, Sir, looking for Whitby. No luck there, but when I got back inside there was, well, how can I put it? An atmosphere in the house.'

'An *atmosphere*?' This was me.

'Just something wrong. Can't quite put my finger on it. The secretary's her usual self, but the other two, the two sisters, well… they're behaving oddly.'

'The two… *sisters*?' the inspector repeated pointedly. He turned in my direction with a raised bushy eyebrow. Something had indeed happened in our absence. Our incarceration had surely not been without reason.

Soon Beryl, the inspector and I were on our way downstairs, leaving Jacobs frowning over poor Whitby's corpse. I fancy there was a new air between the inspector and I - a common goal, an understanding. I was almost warming to the man.

Almost.

In the drawing room, the three women were sitting still as if posing for portraiture. Harvey and her sister were on the chesterfield and Miss Moore was reclined in the armchair. All three had long, set faces. Harvey looked concerned, Miss Moore merely tired, and Miss Blake like she was about to have one of her turns. There was, indeed, an atmosphere.

Miss Moore, however, was certainly the odd one out. The two sisters were both red in the face, and turned away from each other.

The two sisters.

'Constable Whitby has been murdered!' the inspector announced frankly and with his usual lack of subtlety.

Had this news broken at any other time, the reaction would have been one of shock, concern and dismay. At that moment, each of the women barely reacted. It was extremely odd, as if they already knew, or as if there were concerns far greater than this at hand.

What on Earth had happened while we were locked in that blasted bedroom? Something certainly had.

Fishy indeed.

A tense silence followed. Standing was clearly wondering how to continue, when Harvey Blake broke the silence with a statement. A statement so unexpected, that had she sprouted wings and flown around the room I would have been less surprised.

'I know where Gideon is, Inspector. He is hiding in the attic in my father's room. There are a number of panelled, hidden rooms.' She looked up at us with a blank expression. 'You may go and arrest him now.'

A few hours ago, the inspector would have leapt on the opportunity. As it was, he took this information in with a slow nod, and leaned in to my ear.

'May I have a word, Mr Edgar?'

Never one to be left out of a drama, Beryl followed us out.

Once in the hallway, Standing shook his head.

'Something's certainly afoot! It's all wrong! Fishy doesn't quite cover it!'

Beryl and I nodded quickly.

'I quite agree. A few hours ago Harvey Blake would've done anything to keep Carter's whereabouts a secret. And here she is, giving him up so easily! What are you going to do?' I asked, perplexed. The inspector took in a breath.

'Nothing else I can do, but go upstairs and arrest Carter.'

'Really?'

'And while I do, I want you two back in that room with those three. Get them to talk, if you can. Split them up, get them talking. Something's going on, and I suspect that we won't get to the bottom it while they're together.'

I was actually a little touched. Standing was relying on me for help. I went to return to the room, and he stopped me with a hand on my arm.

'Be careful, both of you.'

'Eyes and ears, Inspector,' I replied. 'Eyes and ears.'

Chapter VIII
In which Payton Edgar is all eyes and ears

Christmas 1962; a date for your diary!
YOU ARE HERBY INVITED TO ATTEND Fallow House
FOR FESTIVE CELEBRATIONS.
MONDAY 24TH - THURSDAY 27TH DECEMBER
A Christmas to remember!

The three women hadn't moved an inch, and for a moment Beryl and I hovered at the threshold of the drawing room and observed the scene.

If there was indeed a murderer in this room, then they were well hidden. There was concern and tension in Harvey Blake's eyes. Miss Moore held a weak smile and was inspecting ceiling as if it held great truths. My eyes, however, were drawn to Petra Blake and that twitchy finger that was up at her neck, fiddling with the blotchy folds of skin.

'May I bring you ladies anything? A hot drink, perhaps?' I asked openly, to no response. That twitchy finger plucked anxiously.

'Miss Blake? You look like you could use another cup of tea?'

She snapped out of her reverie and something like relief spread over her face.

'Yes. Yes, of course, Mr Edgar. Tea would be nice.'

'Then come with me to the kitchen. We can brew a pot together.'

'That sounds lovely, Payton. Off you both pop!' said Beryl swiftly. She plonked herself down in a chair. 'I'm quite overcome by all this!'

It was a bold move, and it worked. Split them up, get them talking, the inspector had said. Petra Blake followed me out, like an obedient puppy.

The kitchen was cold and still, with the ghost of Arnold Prosper eerily present.

I found the kettle, filled it and set it on the gas. Miss Blake was with me, but entirely distracted, and as the kettle was warming she fidgeted about, circuiting the floor and plucking at her neck.

'It's a terrible time, isn't it?' I said gently, pulling over a teapot and removing an unappealing knitted cosy. 'There's no wonder your nerves are playing up.'

'My nerves,' she replied absently. 'Yes, my nerves.'

'I expect you will be glad that it's all over, now that Carter will be arrested.'

'Yes,' she replied, rather like an automaton. Despite her reply, she looked far less than pleased. All the fight and nervous energy, so hideously irritating before, appeared to have drained from the woman. Suddenly she snapped from her thoughts, fetched four cups and four saucers from a cupboard and set them on the countertop.

'Teabags! Teabags!' she sang as she danced around the kitchen.

I took in a breath, and ventured forth.

'Forget the teabags for a moment. There's something going on, isn't there?'

She froze.

'You can tell me. In confidence-'

I didn't need to press any further, for she turned and exhaled loudly.

'You are discreet, are you not, Mr Edgar? And I can tell that you care for my sister. It's terrible! So terrible!'

'What is?'

'It's all such a mess. But it's all coming to an end now. I pressed Harvey to give up Carter, and she has.'

'But why now? She's never listened to you before!'

'You don't understand. He has to pay! He's been in prison, it didn't ruin him. In fact, he came out of it seemingly better than when he went in. Prison would kill Harvey, though. So it must be him that goes away for it.'

I thinned my eyes at her.

'But you don't think he's guilty?'

Her look gave everything away.

'You think it was *Harvey*? You think that your sister murdered Maeve Frick!'

Miss Blake glanced around furtively, as if searching for eavesdroppers. She lowered her tone, and spoke with a quiet urgency.

'I don't think it - I know it. But you must never say, Mr

Edgar. She mustn't suffer for it. It's all his fault! It was his dirty past that turned up again and caused all this. Harvey's always been an impulsive person. She comes across as strong and businesslike to the likes of you, but a sister knows. She's led by her heart, when push comes to shove. And she would do anything for that man.'

I couldn't quite believe what I was hearing.

'And you really believe that Harvey killed Prosper, and Mr Lloyd?'

'Oh, I don't know what to think!' Miss Blake snapped impatiently. 'All I know is, at the heart of it, it's all down to that man, and he must pay. But if you say anything, I shall insist that Harvey had nothing to do with it. I'm sticking to that story. Carter did it all. The evidence is there, and that's that.'

A noise at the door turned our heads.

In the doorway, Alison Moore had a lazy hand held up to the frame as she smiled that weak smile again.

'I just thought I'd come and help you with the tea,' she said smoothly.

Split them up, get them talking.

'Perfect!' I replied, almost gaily. 'If you could help Petra find the teabags, I must have a word with my host!'

And so I was out of the kitchen and back in the drawing room as fast as I could shuffle. As I entered, Harvey Blake stuffed a handkerchief up her sleeve and sniffed. She had been crying. Beryl was at her side, frowning.

'I'm so sorry-' Harvey sniffed.

'You don't have to apologise!' said Beryl.

'Indeed you don't,' I replied. 'I think I understand what is happening.'

Harvey gave an involuntary chuckle, a laugh of tired resignation.

'Do you really?' She looked up at me with shrewd eyes. 'Do you know, Mr Edgar, I wouldn't be surprised if you did. You have a canny knack of getting to the heart of things.'

I nodded in agreement, but much to my surprise she went on to issue a clarification with an altogether darker tone.

'I feel that I should stress to you, Payton, that we now know who was responsible for these horrible crimes. Gideon will pay, and that is the end of it. I know that you have been enjoying flexing your investigative muscles, but it ends now. All facts point to Giddy, and that will be the end of it.'

'You don't really believe that he's guilty?' I scoffed, despite myself.

'I do, Mr Edgar,' she replied with a cool frankness. 'Petra had absolutely nothing to do with it, and that is that.'

Why was she so keen to damn Carter's name all of a sudden?

'You do realise that he might well hang for this?' I found myself saying with an uncompromising clarity. Harvey flinched, and I pressed the matter. 'You are truly certain that he murdered Maeve, and then Prosper and Mr Lloyd? And now poor officer Whitby?'

My words were unwelcome, and, just for a split second, I thought I had made her angry. Instead, she softened and issued a smile.

'Mr Edgar, I am asking you - as a friend - please stop. Just… *stop*. Giddy won't hang, I'll see to that. We have excellent lawyers who have been dedicated to our family for years. But he must be punished. He has tolerated prison walls before, and was all the better for it. It didn't break him. In fact, it made him… better somehow.'

These words mirrored her sisters, and set me thinking. Were they conspiring against the man? Was that what had happened during our incarceration in my bedroom? Had the sisters come to an agreement?

Hang on!

Go back, Payton! What had she just said? *Petra had absolutely nothing to do with it.*

She had been quick to add this point, so quick that I had nearly missed it. I hadn't implied anything about her sibling's guilt, and once again, her words had mirrored those of her sister. What was happening here? They thought each other guilty, and were so desperate to keep each other in the clear - was that why they were pointing the finger at Carter?

It certainly seemed that way. I cleared my throat.

'Harvey, it seems to me-'

'Can we just leave it alone, Payton? I have nothing more to say.'

Suddenly, like the rays of the sun as it moved from behind a cloud, I realised what had happened in this room while we were fooling about with locked doors upstairs.

I took a moment to think before speaking.

'Harvey, you may not have any more to say, but I do. And I think you should hear this! You don't think for one minute that Carter killed the girl, but I can see that you are scared for your sister. You really think that she had something to do with this, don't you? Well I certainly don't. I have said from the start that Maeve's murder was a premeditated affair - that our killer had set the girl up to implicate Carter in Charlotte's death all those years ago. And if that is the case, then Petra simply didn't have time for planning - she only met the girl on the morning of her death! No, our murderer had spent time with the girl - nurturing her, preparing her. Feeding her hatred of her father. Most of the household gave her the cold shoulder. In fact, there were only two people close enough to her-'

I stopped myself.

It can only have been one of the two of them!

Not the two sisters, but the two people who were close enough to the girl to bend her mind. Only two people in the house had any time for the girl. Of course! I had been told on numerous occasions that only two people had gained her confidence.

I went on, tentatively.

'We can rule out Petra, Harvey. And I think we both know that you have not murdered anybody. Oh! It's all so clear now!'

'What is, Payton?' squeaked Beryl, on the edge of her seat.

Alison Moore entered the room backwards, pushing her rump against the door, a large tray in her hands. I leapt to my feet in something of a panic.

Miss Moore studied our faces.

'Have I missed something?' she chimed. 'Budge those papers over for the tea tray!'

I leapt into action.

'Allow me to clear a space, Miss Moore!' I gathered up the Clarion and a small number of magazines and laid them in a neat pile at one end of the coffee table. Then I made for the door.

'Excuse me, ladies!'

Petra Blake collided with me in the doorway, a plate of buns in one hand.

'Payton! You can't run off like that!' Harvey bellowed

behind me. 'What is it? What is it you know?'

I budged on by.

'Please excuse me! I… I need a little air.'

Once in the hallway I took in my breath and steadied myself. My head was spinning a little. On the staircase, Constable Jacobs was heading downwards.

'Where is the inspector?'

'He's at top of the house, talking to Carter. Man's putting up a bit of a fight-'

'You must fetch him! I insist! Please alight and bring him to the library immediately! I have some news - tell him to leave Carter - I know who's behind all this!'

'Not sure he'll do that-'

'Just fetch him!'

Jacobs frowned, turned and made his way up the staircase with the heavy steps of a sullen child.

'Poste haste, Constable! Pip pip!'

I made my way into the library.

I needed somewhere quiet to think.

'Did you not want a cup of tea, Mr Edgar?'

At this polite enquiry I almost leapt out of my skin. Alison Moore came up behind me, a cup and saucer in hand.

'No thank you,' I replied swiftly.

'Well, I've brought you one all the same.'

I took the clattering cup and saucer that was held out and forced a smile. I found myself praying that the woman would leave, but instead she closed the library door behind her. I went to the desk, placed the steaming teacup on top, and sat. Miss Moore leaned against the door and watched me with narrowed eyes. A silence fell, and it wasn't a comfortable one.

And then, she issued that starchy smile.

'You've worked it all out, haven't you?'

I said nothing. But she was right.

'You know, you really shouldn't interfere so much, Mr Edgar. Everyone wants Carter to be our killer. Let's leave it at that.'

I sipped my tea, willing my hand steady. My adversary stepped over to the stepladder and perched on one of its steps.

'Turned out to be a strange holiday for you, hasn't it, Mr Edgar?'

'I have certainly had duller weekends,' I replied carefully.

'Going back to London as soon as the roads are cleared, are you?'

'Indeed.'

'Fair enough. No point in waiting around here as we are picked off one by one. Soon the only one of us left will be the mindless old brigadier up in his nest.'

I cleared my throat.

'Thank you for the beverage, Miss Moore. Now if you don't mind, I'd like a little peace and quiet.'

The secretary didn't budge an inch. It was as if I hadn't spoke.

'I've never liked this time of year, Christmas. There's something so…false about the whole thing, don't you think? People come together against their better judgement, to drink and to feast, pretending that all the stress and misery of the other three hundred and sixty three days in the year didn't matter.'

She fell silent, and I waited for more. It didn't come.

'All the same,' I said quietly. 'If I can be left alone-'

. 'No, I think I'll stay, Mr Edgar,' she replied firmly, and with a hint of menace. 'Perhaps I can help fill in any gaps you may have? Anything you haven't been unable to discover during your petty investigations?'

It was time for a little bravery. I lifted my chin.

'What I don't understand, Miss Moore, is why would anybody want Arnold Prosper dead.'

The secretary blinked, and then shrugged.

'Or poor old Mr Lloyd, come to that!' she replied dreamily. 'Perhaps we'll never know.'

'Arthur Lloyd was in the wrong place at the wrong time. A born servant, forever hovering with muted discretion. I have witnessed his stealth; the man was a silent shadow. It is clear that he came up from the pantry steps and witnessed Prosper's demise. He would have ran, of course, but not fast enough it seems. So the point remains - why Arnold Prosper?'

Miss Moore frowned.

'He wasn't a very nice man,' she said slowly.

'True, but he has been *not a very nice man* for decades, and nobody has seen fit to slit his throat thus far - so why now? He was a marvellous chef. And despite his bluster, I doubt that he meant any harm.'

The woman gave a snort that became a sharp cackle.

'Didn't mean any harm? Mr Edgar, the man was a bully! And a monster!'

'That is a little harsh!'

'Not harsh enough, Mr Edgar! You heard what he said about our dear General. He stood over the poor dead thing and laughed! Said he wanted to cook the beautiful bird. You heard him! It was clear he had done it. Just for a laugh!'

I hadn't expected to be talking about that damn dead bird again.

'Now, I really don't think-'

'Prosper always hated the bird, and I hated him for it. He killed the General for a laugh. And he got what was coming to him.'

The secretary was visibly shaking. I leaned forwards, the words coming from my mouth with barely a thought.

'Did you murder Arnold Prosper, Miss Moore?' I asked. She peered at me with sparkling eyes, and with what could have been a grudging respect. Her silence spoke volumes. When she did speak, it was with chilling coolness, and a wry smile.

'I'd never have guessed it would have been you, Mr Edgar.'

I had expected her to continue, but she was tight lipped.

'What would have been me?' I pressed.

She sighed. It was an exaggerated, child-like sigh.

'The next to die,' she said, simply.

Chapter IX
In which Payton Edgar makes some noise

For what seemed like an age we froze, the two of us fixed in position, not speaking, only staring at each other. Miss Moore, perched on the edge of the stepladder, was leaning forwards as if entranced by my company. She had on her face a look of guilty rapture. It was certainly not the kind of look one would expect a murderer to offer their prey.

Had I misheard?

I summoned up all the strength I could and, forcing myself not to take my eyes from the woman, continued slowly.

'So then, you've said why Prosper needed to die. What about poor Maeve Taylor? What did she do wrong?'

'Hummph! I don't know what you mean!' replied Miss Moore teasingly, playing a game.

Forcing an innocent smile, I set down my tea and edged forwards just a little. I was being very brave.

'You were close, you said so yourself. And yet you claimed that she didn't tell you her secrets. Well, I think that she did, and that you used them to your advantage.'

I could see the relief on Miss Moore's face as she nodded and began to reveal some truths.

'Maeve was a silly little girl. Dying Mum tells her of her true parentage, and off she goes with a yearning heart and butterflies in her brain, headed out on a fervent mission to find *Daddy*. She didn't realise how useful she was. But there was no death in my plan, not at first.'

'What's your problem with Carter?' I asked boldly.

'Gideon was ruining everything we had, Harvey and I. It was all about the two of us until he came along with his rotten stinking pipe and puppy dog eyes. He fooled Harvey into believing she was still in love with him. She wasn't. She only had time for the business and for me... before him. So one of us had to go.

'It was the girl who gave me the idea. She appeared from nowhere, and soon I was her confidante. Carter's secret love child! I couldn't have wished for better... ammunition.

'So why not just tell Harvey the truth, and have it done with?'

'Simply revealing Maeve's identify wouldn't have been enough to break them up. Harvey is blind when it comes to that man, and so forgiving. I knew she'd forgive him anything. Or almost anything. And I was right, wasn't I? When she found out that the girl was Gideon's, it took her a minute, but she forgave him. No, I knew that it would need something pretty solid to kill their union. And so I spun a tale – and rewrote some history!'

Daddy-dear was just a disappointment to poor Maeve. She was ready to believe me when I told her that all he wanted was Harvey, and that he had even drowned his daughter to keep her to himself. We had to avenge Charlotte, I told her, and she was the one to do it!

'She was so angry at him, it was easy. She put up a good performance, don't you think? A few details slipped to Harvey here and there, to sow the seed that there was a connection between her and the dead girl. Wearing Charlotte's clothes, playing her songs, all that. And then, to have Charlotte herself telling everyone that she was drowned at his hand was a stroke of genius on my part. Certainly livened up old Turpin's séance, didn't it? It was a gamble, but Harvey believed it - at first.'

'But why kill the girl?' I persisted.

'It still wasn't enough, Mr Edgar! I realised this after the seance. Words from the spirit world - not really proof of murder, is it? Nonsense, really. But, I thought to myself, if our lie had been true and Carter had indeed drowned his daughter, what would he do when accused? And the answer was obvious – silence the girl!

'And so I arranged to meet her that night, to talk about our next step in the plan.'

'Which was murder!'

'Well, yes, Mr Edgar, but she didn't know that. She never knew what hit her.'

'And then making it look like Carter did it, switching the stag figurines and all that. All very original.'

She clearly didn't like the dryness of my tone.

'It was a good plan, Mr Edgar, and was on its way to working.'

'So what went wrong?'

Miss Moore huffed.

'The General died, that's what went wrong.'

The words hung in the air for a horrible moment.

'Harvey knew he'd never harm the bird - never mind

murdering a young girl! It was ridiculous, but the death of the bird ruined everything.'

I searched for something to say.

'And so you offed Prosper – and again made it look like Carter.'

'Getting Prosper was revenge, pure and simple. Revenge for the death of the General. But yes. using Carter's knife was an added bonus.'

'Killing two birds with one stone,' I uttered, only realising my poor choice of phrase all too late. Miss Moore's expression darkened.

For a moment I sat dumbfounded. The death of the bird had reaped consequences - terrible consequences. Hold yourself, Payton, I told myself. Deep breath, in and out.

Miss Moore was still talking.

'I have discovered a wonderful thing, Mr Edgar. Murder is so, so easy! Maeve was out like a light, and the poetry of dressing it up like Charlotte's drowning was just beautiful. Getting Prosper and seeing him staked out on the kitchen surface like a bloody rabbit was one of the most satisfying things I have ever done. And Mr Lloyd – well – although I should perhaps regret that - it was the thrill of the chase, all the same. Murder is… *fun*. Why does nobody ever say so?'

'You killed a police officer!' I put in. She had the gall to look affronted.

'I found him searching through my things in my bedroom! What else is a girl to do?'

'Harvey will be very displeased when she finds out-'

'Harvey will never find out! And besides, I am the best secretary she's ever had. She treats me like family.'

'And you repay her by murdering or framing anyone who comes close to her? What sort of secretary are you?'

I caught a flash of madness in her eyes. I had touched a nerve.

'And what kind of restaurant critic are you? One who has never eaten a Chinese meal? One who hates beetroot? One who doesn't know the meaning of the world Deipnosophist?'

She saw my indignation and nodded wildly.

'I know everything that goes on in this house! You'd be amazed what you can hear listening behind doors, *Margaret!*'

And then she was up, more than matching my height, her look one of grave, almost comical severity. It sent a shiver of fear down my spine.

'Oh, dear, funny Mr Edgar. I'm terribly sorry that this has to happen to you.' This was said without the merest hint of regret.

The woman was quite, quite mad, and there was nothing for it but to flee. I stood quickly, and then with a swift step she reached up and knocked a sheathed sword from it's mount on the wall. She pulled away the dusty leather cover to reveal a surprisingly clean, gleaming blade.

Miss Moore and her sword stood between myself and the doorway, and I was trapped. It was all beyond ridiculous. Where were those idiot policemen? We were surely only seconds from the others in the house, and a call for help was all I needed.

I looked along the wall for another sword or any weapon I might use, but all I had to hand was an old mounted blunderbuss rusted with age. Across the room, however, I saw the only thing that could possibly save my bacon.

With the deftness of a young buck I shot across the library floor, immediately sensing Miss Moore's reaction as she leapt to attack. But I was too clever. She had, of course, expected me to make a bolt for the door. Instead I cut to my left, leaving her careering away from me. Her blade was heavy, and she dragged it a little.

The car horn was only loosely mounted on the wall, and easy to retrieve. I swung around to face my foe, brandishing the instrument as deftly as any shotgun, praying that the rubber bulb had not perished. I gave it a short, loud blast.

Pppparrrrp!

It was even louder than I could have hoped for. She jumped.

'Help!'

Ppppharrrrp!

'Help me!'

'Pppparrrrp!

'Help!'

Miss Moore made a step forwards as if to pounce, and was blasted back by the loud rasping of the horn as I repeated this pattern again and again.

'Pppparrrrp! Pppparrrp!'

The deafening honking horn was better than any firearm. My adversary stood bamboozled by the sheer ridiculousness of it, as I blasted away, my confidence growing stronger with every squeeze of the bulb.

Beryl was the first to arrive, sending the door crashing open.

'What's all this noise? Having a Jamboree?' she began, only to be pushed violently aside by the murderer as she dropped the blade and made a run for it. Poor Beryl bounced off of Miss Moore and into the wall. Behind her, the shadows of others approaching could be seen and I shouted out in my loudest bellow.

'Stop her! She killed them all!'

Standing and his constable stood like lemons as the offender pelted past them and out towards the back of the house, Instead of taking pursuit, they came at me with bewildered expressions. Beryl had composed herself and, seeing that the chase was on, plummeted after Miss Moore.

'What's going on, Edgar?' Standing griped.

'Get after her! That woman you just let get away is the reason you are here! Miss Moore has just confessed to murder – murder of young Maeve, of Prosper and the butler, not to mention poor Whitby! And you have just let her mosey on by. She's gone out the back, but you might head her off at the front if you hurry!'

It was Constable Jacobs who moved first, with Standing following reluctantly, hobbling as he went. We met Harvey and Petra Blake at the foot of the staircase.

'What is it, Payton?' Harvey asked softly.

'Miss Moore,' I replied hurriedly. 'She killed them all!'

'*Alison*?' I heard her breathe as I hurried to the front of the house after the others. 'But she said it was Petra!'

'She said it was you!' Petra exclaimed. 'She *knew* it was you!'

'A last ditch attempt to pin it all on Carter,' I called back. 'Your secretary is a most proficient liar! Come on!'

Suddenly we heard the roar of an engine and muffled shouts from outside.

'Look out, Sir!'

Once through the heavy front door I saw Jacobs, red faced and breathless, pointing down the driveway. Inspector Standing was shuffling through the snow with Beryl a few strides ahead. Suddenly there was a roar of an engine and Harvey Blake's gleaming red sports car shot out form the garage and pushed through the snow. The top was down, and Alison Moore was crouched over the wheel.

'She's off, Sir!' Jacobs called pointlessly to Standing. There was nothing anyone could do - the car picked up speed as it careered down the drive, heading towards the gatehouse. Unfortunately the huge iron gates were fixed open, and there was no doubt that our murderer would escape.

Suddenly, Mrs Turpin and the vicar come into view at the gatehouse, followed by Raymond. They watched as Miss Moore headed their way. For a fleeting second I thought Raymond would run out in a moment of madness and throw himself into the path of the car, but he stood fixed and useless on the spot.

I watched as Beryl, who had made impressive progress down the driveway, bent down, drew herself back and then threw something at the car with all her might. It looked like the dogs ball.

What happened next all happened very quickly, and very noisily.

It may have been the ball bouncing across the bonnet that caused a distraction, or the gamble Miss Moore had taken with the snow and ice. Certainly, she had not accounted for the gaggle of chickens that littered the gatehouse and the driveway. At first a couple of birds scattered and skidded, feathers flying, and then a number of the poultry bounced across the bonnet. Even from far back at the house I could hear the rising screams from the hens as they scattered clumsily around the car.

Whatever the cause, she lost control, and quickly. We all watched in horror as the convertible slid from the driveway in a cloud of feathers, skidded aside on the ice and struck the brickwork of the gates with a sickening crunch. The driver briefly joined the chickens in the air as she was flung from her seat, only to hit the ground heavily, and to slide across the ice, coming to a rest against the gatehouse fence.

Officer Jacobs was still running, but there was no need.

Poor Raymond Turpin looked down over the body of Alison Moore and began to wail.

Chapter X
In which Payton Edgar looks for fortune in the umbrella stand

Dear Margaret,
My husband refuses to travel. We live in central London, and I would love to take a fortnight's holiday in Wales or Scotland, or even a shorter stint on the continent. My husband says that there is enough to do where we live and that travel makes him ill, but I know it is also about saving money. How can I convince him to stray a little further afield?
Morag, Mayfair

Margaret replies; *holidays are all well and good, but what does one have to show for it after the event? Vague memories and an empty wallet. London is indeed a beautiful, darling city, and there are endless things to do in one's spare time. There is only one phrase worth citing in this case, Morag - there is no place like home.*

'I think,' Beryl began quietly, 'next Christmas, I shall spend it alone. Quite happily, deliciously, *quietly* alone.'

We were standing on the platform awaiting our train.

'A superb idea,' I replied.

She sighed dreamily. 'No death. No blood-drenched snow. No drama. Just me, my drinks cabinet and Father Christmas.'

'Sounds divine, my dear.'

I would have gone on, but Harvey Blake was approaching. She had on a thick dark green duffel, the collar upturned to meet her hair which was pulled up and clipped neatly at her crown. There was no evidence of the toil of recent days - in fact, she looked bright eyed and had a rather sanguine disposition. She said her goodbyes to Beryl, and then surprised me by cupping my hand in hers.

'I want to give you something, Payton. Call it an apology if you like, for the trying few days you've had.'

Trying few days!

'As well as a new chef, I shall be looking for a new secretary now, too. Let me find one for you while I am at it! You would benefit from an assistant, I guarantee you.'

Unless the secretary turns out to be an insane and blood-thirsty murderer, I thought to myself. I shook my head gently and retrieved my hand.

'I do like the idea,' I began, truthfully. 'And perhaps I will take your advice, but I would rather choose an assistant for myself. I have, you see, particular standards.'

If she was offended by my refusal she did not show it.

'Very well. I just feel I owe you something, after this… difficult time.'

'You have given me the key, and that's special enough.'

An office, right beside my favourite restaurant! No more sitting in cold, draughty old Thistle House and being hounded by the rumble of those formidable printers. Harvey was nodding.

'I will let you know when I'm in town. Perhaps I can catch you for lunch one day.'

'It's a date,' I replied firmly.

Our train was approaching. Harvey helped us in with our bags, and then caught my sleeve as I was about to board.

'And don't forget the advice of the spirits, Payton!'

'I beg your pardon?'

'Madame Turpin - she advised you to look in your umbrella stand, did she not? Fortune lies in the umbrella stand!'

There was nothing to do but to nod politely and pull myself up onto the carriage.

Fortune lies in the umbrella stand indeed!

These words must have been swimming around my subconscious as I hung my coat and hat by the door that evening. I was greeted by Lucille, almost as if I had been missed. Bending, I nudged my fingers into her fur and fussed over her until she leapt up abruptly and padded away.

I took my case and made for the bedroom with a curious warm, comforting feeling inside. It took me a moment to place it - I was happy to be home. My home is my castle. I adore my thick carpets, polished surfaces and gorgeous knick-knacks, and was blessed in many ways.

A lucky man.

The thought of luck and fortune gave me pause, and I set down my case again.

Look in the umbrella stand I had been told. *Fortune lies*

in the umbrella stand.

I found myself striding back across the room to my front door with some urgency and, as I approached the umbrella stand, my steps became hesitant and uncertain. Was it about to release untold treasures? Silly, I told myself, but sometimes – just sometimes – a silly prediction can be a correct one.

Fortune lies in the umbrella stand.

Gingerly I peered over the edge and looked within. Darkness.

I reached my hand slowly inside and felt around.

My heart sank.

It was entirely empty.

Epilogue

That evening I was reclining in my armchair with my leather slippers and a mug of warm milk when Grace Kemp returned home, laden with bags of shopping.

She asked if I had enjoyed a pleasant Christmas and, tired of mayhem and murder, I replied in the positive. It would have done me no good to mull over the drama of the holiday. Grace was in a fine mood, and chatted away happily.

'Caught some bargains today, by golly! Got some sundries for Elizabeth, too. And a little something for you.' She set her bags down and rummaged within. 'Now, I know that you've been feasting upon fresh game, fancy liquors and wondrous cheeses, but I bought you this.' She pulled out a tin and raised it proudly.

'Steamed pudding?' I gasped.

'Steamed pudding!' she replied.

I could have kissed her.

'Oh, and there's something else.' She trotted around to the mantlepiece, lifted up a folded piece of paper and held it out.

'A lady called Rosemary phoned while you were away. Actually, she called a number of times.'

My silence was received with raised eyebrows.

'I've jotted the dates and times and her number on this paper.'

'Rosemary?' I whispered fearfully. I felt a familiar, creeping dread rising from my gut.

'Your ex-wife!' said Grace, as if this was news. She was clearly thrilled by this turn of events, and was beaming from ear to ear. 'She wanted to know what you were up to, and we chatted a little. At first, I thought she was calling to wish you a happy Christmas, but she wasn't.'

'No. She wouldn't have been.'

'Message is - she wants you to call her *immediately* on that number there. It is urgent, apparently. She wouldn't say why.'

Grace lifted her bags and set off for her room, only to shoot a foxy grin over her slender shoulder in the doorway.

'Your ex-wife, Payton!' she trilled suggestively.

'My ex-wife.'

I lay back and inspected the ceiling.

Rosemary! As if things hadn't been bad enough. Christmas ruined by a deranged and bloodthirsty murderer, and now here comes Rosemary, crawling back into my life - just in time to spoil a brand new year.

I closed my eyes tight, crumpling the paper in my fist.

Rosemary! What had I done to deserve this?

Whatever it was she wanted, there was no doubt that it would be bad news.

Poor, poor Payton…

The End

Thanks…

I would like to thank Judith and Sally for their time and effort (and nitpicking!) when proofing this book. I would also like to thank Christopher for being forever supportive - and honest, when it's needed!

MJT Seal

24274045R00146

Printed in Great Britain
by Amazon